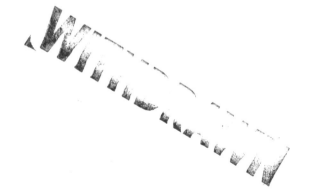

PREPARED FOR
RAGE

**Center Point
Large Print**

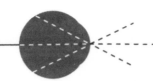

**This Large Print Book carries the
Seal of Approval of N.A.V.H.**

PREPARED FOR
RAGE

DANA STABENOW

CENTER POINT PUBLISHING
THORNDIKE, MAINE

This Center Point Large Print edition
is published in the year 2008 by arrangement with
St. Martin's Press.

The text of this Large Print edition is unabridged. In other
aspects, this book may vary from the original edition.
Printed in the United States of America.
Set in 16-point Times New Roman type.

ISBN: 978-1-60285-166-5

Library of Congress Cataloging-in-Publication Data

Stabenow, Dana.
    Prepared for rage / Dana Stabenow.--Center Point large print ed.
       p. cm.
    ISBN 978-1-60285-166-5 (lib. bdg. : alk. paper)
    1. Space Shuttle Program (U.S.)--Fiction. 2. Terrorism--Prevention--Fiction.
  3. Florida--Fiction. 4. United States. Coast Guard--Fiction. 5. International relations--Fiction.
  6. Large type books. I. Title.

PS3569.T1249P74 2008b
813'.54--dc22

2008000522

For
Captain Craig Barkley Lloyd,
who has twice now tolerated my presence under way
with unfailing patience and good humor

and for the crew of USCG (WHEC 724) *Munro*
EPAC Patrol Spring 2007:

Now,
for the information of all hands,
for service above and beyond the call of duty,
you are hereby awarded
the Most Meritorious Order of the Quill Pen

in recognition of the aid and assistance provided
in the setting, characterizations, and plotting of this
novel.

Thank you.

It looked as if a night of dark intent
Was coming, and not only a night, an age.
Someone had better be prepared for rage.
　　　　　—Robert Frost, "Once by the Pacific"

Semper Paratus.
　　　　　—Motto of the U.S. Coast Guard

PART I

The hum of either army stilly sounds,
That the fix'd sentinels almost receive
The secret whispers of each other's watch:
Fire answers fire, and through their paly flames
Each battle sees the other's umbered face:
Steed threatens steed, in high and boastful neighs
Piercing the night's dull ear; and from the tents
The armorers, accomplishing the knights,
With busy hammers closing rivets up,
Give dreadful note of preparation.
—WILLIAM SHAKESPEARE, *KING HENRY IV*, PART 2

PROLOGUE

PAKISTAN, 1994

She screamed, once, a single, helpless cry of agony, despair, and betrayed innocence.

Hearing it, all the strength drained out of his legs and he sagged to his knees between his captors. His forehead touched the ground before Faraj and Nasser managed to pull him upright again.

All the men of the tribe were there, massed outside the hut, their attention fixed on the doorway, little more than a hole knocked in the dried mud wall. A small oil lamp threw almost no light on the interior, hiding what was happening inside in indifferent shadows.

No one looked at him. No one even glanced in his direction. Their shoulders were hunched, their backs taut, their feet splayed on the ground as if they were about to step forward.

To get into line.

To take their turn.

Only the stern eye of the council kept them where they were. The four men inside would inflict all the justice Allah required.

For not the first time during the last seven hellish days did he regret his return. Even more bitterly did he regret his departure. He should have rejected the scholarship bestowed by a benevolent corporation that had led to his five years in the West. Had he stayed safely at home, free of the corruption of infidels and their indecent ways with women, he would not have fallen so easily into conversation with the wife of another man.

But that first naïve conversation had changed everything. He wondered again where she was, what had happened to her. He wondered if there was another hut somewhere, with another tribal council and another crowd of men standing around it, straining to hear the tear of clothing, the striking of flesh on flesh, the panting, the grunts, the groans. Or had she been killed, stoned to death by her own husband?

If Allah were merciful, she would have been beheaded.

As he should have been. Suddenly, without volition, he heard himself bellow, "Where is it written?"

The hands manacling his own loosened in surprise and he took advantage, tearing himself free, not to run, no, instead, just this once, to stand up strong in front of the men of his village and accuse them face to face of the evil that they did. "In what sura is it written that my sister should be punished for my crime? Why—"

Hashim Hassan, the youngest member of the council, took a step forward and backhanded Akil across the face. Hassan was a big man, broad across the shoulders, arms heavy with muscle from loading and unloading goods from the one ancient Ford pickup truck that was the sole asset of his freight business. Akil heard his cheekbone crack. Blood welled from his mouth and splattered down his shirtfront.

He and Hashim had been born into the same village not a month apart. They had gone to school together, studied the Koran together. They had flown hawks together from childhood, competing with others from as far away as Gujar Khan. He looked up at Hashim's hard and unyielding face. Where now was the blood brother, the companion of his childhood, the friend of his adolescence?

He spit out blood and cried, "Did not the Prophet himself say to the girl who had been raped, 'Go now, God has already pardoned you'?"

Hashim hit him again. This time he spit out a tooth. "I am guilty! I admitted it! I—"

The rest of the council looked annoyed and the eldest

snapped out a command. The third time Hashim hit him Akil lost consciousness, his last thought a fleeting relief that at least now he would not have to bear further witness to the shame that his own criminal carelessness had wrought upon the most beloved member of his family.

WHEN HE WOKE HE WAS FACEDOWN IN THE DIRT. HE couldn't see out of his left eye, and he couldn't breathe through his nose. For a moment he couldn't remember where he was, and then memory flooded back in a scalding rush.

Over the thrum of blood in his ears he thought he heard sobbing. He squinted around, and through blurred vision managed to distinguish a shape on the ground in front of the hut. He rose up on his elbows and dragged himself to it.

"Adara," he said, around a tongue that felt swollen in his mouth. He reached out a trembling hand to touch her shoulder.

She flinched away. She was naked but for her qameez, and it was torn to shreds. She had pulled one of the few remaining folds over her head, covering her face, hiding from her shame. She was curled into a fetal position but he could see that her legs were covered in blood, the rest of her body in bruises and rapidly crusting cuts. They had not just raped her, they had beaten her with their fists and kicked her with their boots.

He cringed from the sight of his sister's nakedness,

and of her wounds and all that those wounds meant, and steeled himself to speak. "Adara," he said again, and began to sob. He let his head fall forward, once, twice, a third time, again and again, beating his head against the dirt. A scream built in his throat and backed up until it could no longer be contained and he let it loose, a long, high howl of anguish that went on and on.

It was carried on the night wind to the circle of mud houses that formed the village not a thousand yards distant, but no one came to help them.

AKIL KNOCKED SOFTLY. THE DOOR CRACKED. AN EYE peered out. "Go away," a gruff voice said.

"Uncle," Akil said. "Please."

"Go away!" the voice said, more loudly this time. The door slammed in Akil's face.

Akil staggered back to Adara, clad now in his shirt and sitting on a rock by the side of the lane staring vacantly into space. At least she had stopped weeping. "I'm sorry, Adara," he said—how many times now? "He won't let us in."

Her breast rose and fell in a soundless sigh. "None of them will," she said, her voice the merest thread of sound. "Akil, you must end this."

"No!" he shouted. She flinched. "No," he said, more temperately. "No, Adara. We will find someone who will help us, give us food and shelter for a night, and then we will leave this place."

"And go where?" she said. "Our parents turned us

away. Three of our uncles, two of our cousins. There is nowhere left for us to go, Akil."

"I'll find a place," he said. "Trust me, Adara. I will find us a place to go, where you can be safe."

And he would have, he knew he would have, but when the third cousin refused to let him into her house and he returned to Adara, he found her hanging from the branch of a neem tree, strangled on a knot made from the sleeve of his own shirt.

1

NEW ORLEANS, SEPTEMBER 2005

"I feel like I'm in a third-world country," Parker said, breaking a silence that had endured the entire distance from the *Iwo Jima*, moored at the Riverwalk in downtown New Orleans.

"Haiti," Helms said. She looked around with the same expression of bewilderment she'd worn all day. "Where is everyone? There should be ambulances and helicopters and—and police cars." She looked back at the two officers, almost pleading. "It can't be only us. It can't be."

Everything in St. Bernard Parish was backwards, if not upside down. The cars were in the water. The boats were on the land. Enormous barges, stripped of their containers, were beached hundreds of feet from the nearest canal. Trailers had been forcibly separated from their tractors and were scattered haphazardly across drenched and flattened fields like so many giant Tonka toys. Electrical transmission towers lay on their sides, half-submerged in bayous much deeper and wider than they had been not twenty-four hours before. The houses, those that remained standing, were minus doors, windows, roofs.

The landscape was not improved by the almost total absence of life. Once they saw a woman peer out at them from behind a tree. It didn't make any of them feel better when she screamed, a high, thin, terrified sound, and went crashing headlong through the underbrush, getting as far away from them as fast as she could. Once they saw a dog, a pit bull, emaciated and hostile, who growled menacingly at them before it, too, ran off. Cal would have shot it if he'd thought to bring a gun.

He realized with a faint sense of shock that they might actually need one.

The dog had been savaging the body of a woman. In spite of the swelling and the decay after a week's worth of lying in the sun, it was obvious that she had not died in Katrina, but afterward, and that she might have found her death a merciful ending to what had come before. And like all the other bodies they had found that day, she was black.

Cal had never before been quite so conscious of the whiteness of his skin.

Parker got a poncho out of the back of their jeep— they had run out of body bags—and covered her, holding his breath so he wouldn't retch. He backed off and stood looking down at the olive green bundle for a moment. "Animals," he said.

"Americans," Helms said, in such disbelief it was almost a question.

Parker raised his head and looked at Cal. "I was stationed in D.C. in 2001. I thought I'd never see anything like that again." He shook his head. "I hoped I wouldn't. But this—this is—" Words failed him. Parker was in his forties, in the Coast Guard long enough to work his way up to chief warrant officer, a veteran of patrols in the Caribbean and the Eastern Pacific and the Bering, like Cal, a cutterman.

On 9/11 Cal had been in New York City, testifying at a UN hearing on international maritime regulations. He had been in a cab on the way to the United Nations building when the first plane had gone in. It had been a beautiful morning, he remembered, clear, cool, the streets of New York filled with parents taking their children to school, people headed to work. He'd reported to the scene as soon as news of what happened had penetrated his meeting, and worked three days and nights helping to dig people, mostly dead, out of the debris. He, too, had never wanted to see anything like that ever again.

"Where is everyone?" Helms said. A yeoman with much less time served, still in high school when the planes went into the towers and the Pentagon and that field in Pennsylvania, she had watched the response on television with the rest of her peers. There had been a massive response of fire and rescue personnel and equipment to that disaster. She looked around now, expecting a line of response vehicles, ambulances, fire trucks, heavy equipment to begin the process of recovery to roll up and disgorge the people who were supposed to be doing this kind of work, people who were trained in it. "I was just here to see New Orleans," she said numbly. "I wanted to hear some good music, eat some beignets, walk around the French Quarter." She looked at Cal again, imploringly. "Captain, where is everybody?"

He couldn't answer her.

They waited with the body. The bad news was that it was their twenty-first body that day. The good news was that the Disaster Mortuary Affairs team wouldn't be that far behind them, so they wouldn't have to wait long.

And they didn't, the pickup driven by the same two exhausted men whipsawing around the wreckage on what was left of the road and skidding to a halt a few feet from Cal's knees. This time they didn't even say hello, just went for the stretcher, stained with unmentionable substances from previous retrievals, muscled the body onto it and into the pickup, the back of which was getting crowded.

No one asked for the poncho back. The men didn't say good-bye. The three of them stood watching as the pickup careened around an overturned midnight blue Buick LeSabre with three of four tires missing and rattled off.

The sun was setting behind a gathering bank of low-lying clouds, leeching the light from the destroyed landscape and rendering everything suddenly more sinister. It began to drizzle, and a moment later the drizzle increased to a steady rain. If anything the sense of menace increased.

"Let's get back," Cal said.

The yeoman looked up the road. "There have to be other bodies," she said.

Cal knew how she felt, but he could feel the presence of many eyes trained on them, and again felt the acute lack of any kind of protection. "Tomorrow," he said.

But the next day the FEMA representative mercifully asked, "Who here knows about ships?" Cal put up his hand and found himself deputy director in charge of three cruise ships brought into New Orleans to provide temporary shelter for those left homeless by Katrina. He brought Parker and Helms with him, and the three of them gladly left the collection of bodies to other authorities.

He found himself reporting directly to the Coast Guard vice admiral, who was acting as the principal federal officer for Katrina response, and for perhaps the first time in his life didn't rue the fact that the old man was a friend of his father's. Between the Port Authority, the stevedores' union, and the ship's agent, all of whose offices were a shambles, it was a challenge just to maintain the ships' water reserves, which entailed finding sixty tanker trucks to deliver eight hundred tons of water per day per ship.

Finding them was one thing, keeping them was something else again. Across the six most affected parishes potable water was in short supply and tanker trucks capable of delivering it were in high demand. When he found one, it was all he could do to hang on to it before it was lost or stolen. One was hijacked right off the dock before it had even managed to offload its cargo, and when eventually the truck was found again the hijacker was apprehended in the act of selling said cargo for a dollar a gallon. He could have gotten five, he explained to the arresting officer, but he didn't want to price himself out of the market.

Initially Cal had no staff except for CWO Parker and YN1 Helms, which didn't help, and cell phones didn't work inside the skins of the ships so he couldn't even yell for any. Then by a rare stroke of luck he fell heir to what he decided ought to be designated the only national treasure walking around on two legs.

"Lieutenant Commander Mustafa Awad Azizi reporting for duty, sir," the national treasure said, snapping off a very smart salute and proffering his orders.

Cal read through them. Born in New Jersey. Academy graduate four years behind Cal. BS in civil engineering. A good mix of duty stations, including two years on patrol in the Bering Sea as a JG and two years at the yards in Seattle. He looked up, and said irritably, "At ease, Commander."

Azizi relaxed his stance. He was of medium height, with dark skin and dark hair that even with a regulation cut managed to look like the mane of a lion.

"New Jersey, huh?" Cal said.

"Yes, sir," Azizi said, "in spite of the fact that I look like Ali Baba and all the forty thieves put together, Trenton, New Jersey. My folks are a generation removed from Trinidad, and six generations before that the Tigris-Euphrates river valley."

Cal gave him a sharp look. Azizi smiled, which transformed his face, dominated by a long, broad nose with a distinct curl at the end, large flashing eyes, and a lot of teeth that looked to have received the assiduous and unstinting care of an attentive dentist from early on. "Yes, sir, Iraq."

"I didn't ask," Cal said mildly.

"No, sir," Azizi said. "I can't help my name or the way I look, but post–9/11 I've found it a good tactic to address it at once. Makes everyone relax."

"A pre-emptive strike," Cal said.

"Exactly, sir," Azizi said cordially.

Cal handed Azizi's orders back to the junior officer. "I could give a shit about your heritage, Azizi. Especially now. I'm one lone Coast Guard officer in the middle of one of the biggest messes this nation has ever had to dig itself out of. There are supplies pouring in and no way to get them out again to the people who need them. We've got a ton of first response people, fire fighters, EMS, doctors and nurses, and more on the way from every state in the union, and no place to put them to work because there is no electricity, which means no refrigeration and no air-conditioning. Hell, even the local EMS guys are sleeping in their ambulances."

He thought of his first week on scene. "And we've got bodies stacked up from here to Shreveport, and more of them every day, too, and damn few resources to deal with them. We can't bury them because the graveyards are all flooded, and even if they weren't we don't have any way to get them there."

"Yes, sir," Azizi said. "How many of us are there?"

"Well. I've got a chief warrant officer and a yeoman, although I don't know how long I'm going to hang on to either. The yeoman was on vacation in New Orleans when Katrina hit, and the CWO was changing planes from Atlanta to Dallas–Fort Worth en route to his next duty station when they closed Louis Armstrong Airport. But for the moment anyway, there's four."

Azizi looked at him for a moment. "I see."

Cal smiled. "And that, Commander, was the good news."

Azizi digested this in silence for a moment. "What's the bad news, sir?"

"I'm the boss."

Azizi looked delighted. "Really, sir? Well, then, let's get started."

It turned out that Azizi had an almost preternatural ability to hotwire anything on wheels; fork lifts, pickup trucks, even a motorized shopping cart liberated from a nearby supermarket. After a day of watching him in action Cal said, "So, you can hotwire anything, can you?"

Azizi shrugged, grinning.

"Does that mean you can un-hotwire anything, too?

Make them impossible to steal?"

Azizi considered. "Well, sir, like I told you. I'm from New Jersey."

Cal had no further trouble hanging on to the tanker trucks.

Azizi also proved to be a first-rate scrounger, which as anyone who has ever served on a battlefield will attest is a skill to be cherished. The food on the three cruise ships improved markedly almost from the day of Azizi's arrival, and CWO Parker, who liked his grub, was moved to say that Lieutenant Commander Azizi ought to be put up for a medal.

The four of them did not long remain the only Coasties on the scene but Cal was indisputably the one with the most stroke, including the direct line to the old man, which he tried not to over-exploit but which proved to be a significant asset. When the police parked their cruisers so that they blocked access to the docks where the ships were moored he had six of them towed so the water tankers could offload, and no one so much as blinked in his direction. Had to be a first in relations between an East Coast intellectual elitist in Coastie blue and a bunch of brawny down-home Louisiana cops, most of whom were living in their cruisers at the time and so had a right to be a little cranky.

They were probably hoping they'd get a room on one of the ships. Everyone wanted a room on the ships. Short of presidential visits, of which there were two, both unwelcome and both so far as he could see productive of nothing more than a massive logistical headache for the people on the ground (and after the first visit he wanted to fall to his knees and give thanks he didn't work for the Secret Service), Cal gave first priority to those Louisiana residents who had lost their homes. He held staterooms even for those who had been evacuated out of state and had to be repatriated. When he turned down his third flag request (this time a Navy admiral whose dog robbers threatened to write to Congress if he didn't let them overnight on board) he was summoned to Baton Rouge, from where the vice admiral was running relief operations for Katrina and Rita. A helo took Cal off the ship and set him down in the parking lot of the commandeered office building that was serving as HQ. He was escorted promptly to the vice admiral's office.

The vice admiral looked at him over the tops of half-glasses. "I hear you bounced Jim Levy off the *Aurora Princess.*"

Cal braced himself. "Yes, sir." He offered no explanation and no apology.

The vice admiral's face relaxed into a grin. "Never did like that asshole. How about a drink?"

They spent a genial half hour with rather more conversation about Cal's father and his slam-dunk re-election prospects than Cal would have liked. At one point the vice admiral gave him an overall assessing look and said, "You look older, Cal. And taller, somehow. You're not growing up on me now, are you?"

At the end of the audience the vice admiral shook his

hand, escorted him personally to the door, and congratulated him in a loud, penetrating voice on a job very well done within conspicuous earshot of some thirty loiterers. "Amazing what the U.S. Coast Guard can do to get the job done with no resources and no experience in disaster relief on this scale, isn't it, Cal?"

"Gives a whole new meaning to search and rescue, sir," Cal said, returning the handshake with interest, and then got the hell out of there.

The helo took him straight back to the *Aurora Princess*, still moored at the Riverfront, where a delegation from Princess Cruises swarmed around him on touchdown. The chief complaint seemed to be his continual unavailability to discuss the use to which their ship was being put. They had what they obviously considered was a brilliant solution to this problem. They wanted him to take occupancy of the owner's suite, which had the latest in state-of-the-art communications, the inference being that with him in residence there they could reach out and touch him whenever they wanted.

They managed to muscle him into the glass elevator leading to the suite—he had to admit to a certain curiosity to see it—but when they got there he took one look at the Jacuzzi, which could have slept five, and the bed, which could have slept ten, not to mention the phone with six lines mounted at the head of the bed, and made a polite but very firm refusal.

He was ushering them kindly but firmly down the gangway when a motorcade only slightly smaller than the president's pulled up. The driver got out and opened the rear door, and a tall man in his early sixties climbed out. His hair was the white gold some blond men were gifted with as they age, he had a smile whose teeth could be seen to flash all the way from the deck of the ship, and he was dressed in a three-piece gray pin-striped suit that anyone but a blind man could see had been lovingly cut to display his broad shoulders, his still-slim waist, and his long, muscular legs.

The cruise ship people, momentarily dazzled by this vision, stopped short. One of them said, "Hey, isn't that Senator Schuyler?"

Another one looked from the senator to Cal and back again. "You're that Schuyler?"

Cal was spared an answer when the senator caught sight of him and waved. His long legs ate up the distance between the car and the bottom of the gangway. The cruise ship people forgot Cal and trotted down to meet him, hands out. The senator, never one to neglect an opportunity to gladhand a potential campaign contributor, shook hands, slapped backs, and all in all seemed to be delighted with his new best friends. There was a reason he kept getting re-elected. There were, in fact, many.

Cal was essaying a soft-footed retreat until his father looked up and raised his voice. "Cal! Come on down here!"

Cal, caught, reversed course and stumped grimly down the gangway.

His father embraced him, beaming. "I see you've all

met my son, Cal. That's Captain Cal Schuyler to all of us peons, of course." There was a dutiful laugh. The senator, now looking suitably grave, said, "Cal and the Coast Guard are doing a heck of a job down here. I venture to say they're the only federal agency that is being of any help at all. I don't know where these poor folks would be without them." He shook his head. "Tragic, just tragic some of the stories I've been hearing. Washington has really fallen down on the job. There will have to be an investigation, of course." The senator, not currently a member of the majority party in Congress, tried not to look overjoyed at the prospect. He wasn't entirely successful.

He turned to his son and only child. "Cal, these good folks tell me there's an empty room on board with my name on it. You mind showing me up there?"

There wasn't a whole hell of a lot he could do at that point, so he said baldly, "Sure, Dad," and led his father and his father's entourage to the owner's suite.

"What are you doing here, Dad?" he said when they had a moment alone.

His father raised an eyebrow. "Why, I'm serving my tax-paying constituents, son, by getting a firsthand look at what's going on down here. You should see the newspapers, they're saying Louisiana might as well be Bangladesh for all the federal help they're getting."

"That's true enough," Cal said.

"Billy tells me you're doing a hell of a job," the senator said. "How did you get here, anyway? I thought you were in Alameda, bossing cutters around."

"I was. The vice admiral asked me to fly in ahead of him, give him a good picture of what was going on, what was needed. Then he asked me to stay on for a bit. I've got a good second in Alameda, so . . ." Cal shrugged. "How long are you staying?"

"Just the night, I'm afraid, I've got a fund-raiser in Amherst day after tomorrow."

They ate in the owner's suite that night, the senator's aides staving off starvation with a deli spread they'd brought with them from D.C. Cal invited and then ordered Azizi to join them. "Azizi," the senator said meditatively, ladling out an assortment of pâtés. He handed Azizi a basket of crusty bread. "Where's your family from, Commander?"

Azizi trotted out his American by way of Trinidad and Iraq family history. If the senator noticed that the litany was a little rote, he didn't mention it. "I see you wear a wedding ring, Commander," he said instead. "Tell me about her."

A bleak look crossed Azizi's face. "She's dead, sir."

The senator looked concerned. "I'm sorry for your loss, son," he said, and with his usual effortless social charm led the table talk away from any dangerous personal topics to the latest Hollywood date movie, inevitably starring Cal's mother as a glamorous grandmother determined to see her estranged daughter and granddaughter reunited and wed, not necessarily in that order.

They were lucky Azizi came from New Jersey and not Massachusetts, Cal thought, or the talk would have been all about the senator's reelection campaign.

Later, when guests and staff had left them alone for a few minutes, it was. "Dad," Cal said, trying to stave it off, "you know I have no interest in politics."

"I'm not saying you have to run for office, Cal, but you've got your twenty in. Isn't it time you moved to shore for good? I could use you on my staff. It's no secret that my relationship with the armed services isn't the best. I could use a liaison who speaks the language." He paused. "And we haven't been able to spend a lot of time together, not since you graduated from the Academy. Not since you joined up, really."

Or ever, Cal thought, and braced himself. His father had first played the patriot card and then the father-son card. He waited for it. Here it came—

"And although she'll never say it, your mother misses you, Cal. She was saying to me only the other day she couldn't remember the last time she'd seen you for more than a flying visit."

There it was, the mom card. Although Cal's mother had never allowed him to call her anything but "Mother," and the moment he'd entered high school she'd insisted on "Vera" henceforward.

"She sends you her love," the senator said. "She wanted me to remind you that we're going to the Cape Cod house for Christmas this year."

Maybe Vera was mellowing. If she was playing grandmothers nowadays, maybe she'd finally come to terms with having a grown son. "Maybe I can make it this year."

"And," the senator added fatally, "she told me to tell you she's inviting the Whitneys to join us." His father winked. "Including that cute little Bella. You could do a lot worse, Cal."

Every hair on the back of Cal's nape stood to attention. "I can't promise for sure I'll be there, Dad," he said, and tried to turn it into a joke. "You know I don't have any graven-in-stone plans beyond my next ship."

His father blinked at him benignly. "Well now, Billy's not sure you've got anywhere to go in the service but ashore. After Alameda you're headed for a 378, the biggest cutter in the Coast Guard fleet. Your tour will be, what, two years? There really isn't any place left for you to go in the Coast Guard after that, not at sea, not if you want promotion."

"Then I'll get an icebreaker," Cal said.

"Now, Cal, there's only three of those, and you know only two of them work." The senator winked again.

Cal felt his chin push out. "Then I'll put my name in for one of the new Deepwater ships."

"Billy tells me those ships have captains four or five years out."

"The vice admiral tells you a hell of a lot, doesn't he?" It was his first sign of temper, and a warning sign for both of them. He gulped down the rest of his coffee and got to his feet. "I'm dragging, Dad, I've got to turn in."

"I'll see you tomorrow before I leave," the senator said, bloody but unbowed. The senator always knew when to back off.

"I'll try," Cal said from the door, "but I've got an early morning and a full day." It wasn't a lie. His days in New Orleans ran from 0600 to 2200.

He pretended deafness to any last comments he might or might not have heard, and retired to the four-bed stateroom he was sharing with Azizi and a couple of civil engineers from Boise who had shown up out of the blue one day looking for somewhere to volunteer their services. He was the first one in that evening, and he commandeered the only comfortable chair and got out his cross-stitch, which was admirable at soothing the savage breast. The current project was the Alki Point Lighthouse with the Seattle Space Needle in the background and a seagull on outspread wings against the blue water in the foreground. He'd just finished the browns and greens of the rocky point in the midground when Azizi came in, who examined Cal's cross-stitch with a critical eye. Azizi had just gotten out his knitting when the two civil engineers staggered in from a day spent surveying the levees.

The civil engineers exchanged speaking glances. "If you were ever on a three-month EPAC patrol waiting on a go fast that never came, you'd learn how to cross-stitch, too," Cal told them. There was enough of an edge to his voice that the civil engineers decided that in this case discretion was the better part of valor and retired without comment.

The next morning, to avoid a prolonged farewell Cal timed his arrival at the head of the gangway to coincide with his father's departure. The senator waved from the limousine, and Cal threw him a bone by way of a snappy salute. The senator beamed, was tucked tenderly into the limo, and the long black car moved off in stately fashion. Cal heaved a sigh of relief and got back to work.

He was back at the head of the gangway that afternoon when another batch of what he had come to think of as his refugees left the ship to return to their lives ashore. They had boarded the ship with all they owned in a plastic garbage bag and a thousand-mile stare, and they were leaving with a look of life and returned hope. It was amazing what clean sheets, three squares, a night's sleep in a secure area, and above all air-conditioning could do for your outlook.

He turned from the gangway and found Azizi watching him. "Something up, Azizi?"

Azizi hesitated. "Permission to speak freely, Captain. And without prejudice."

Cal shrugged. "Go for it." He even managed a grin. "What happens on the *Aurora Princess* stays on the *Aurora Princess*."

Azizi squared up in a stance that wasn't quite belligerent. "I'd heard about you, sir."

It wasn't what Cal had been expecting, and it wasn't welcome, either. "Lieutenant Commander, I—"

Risking a slap down, Azizi ignored him. "You're quite the golden boy of the U.S. Coast Guard. Callan T. Schuyler, child of privilege, old money from Boston, a three-hundred-year American pedigree that includes three signers of the Declaration of Independence, one Civil War general, a Roughrider, and a Navy nurse who was killed by a Japanese kamikaze off Okinawa in World War II. Got the Academy appointment and after graduation all the plum jobs because his dad's a U.S. senator. Got all the ladies because his mom was the most beautiful actress of her day and he got her looks." He stopped, waiting to see how his boss would take such plain speaking.

Cal, resigned, made a come-on motion with his hand. At some point in every duty station this conversation or one like it had to be endured. He'd learned fast that getting mad only exacerbated any preconceptions people had, and to suffer through and move on.

Azizi took a deep breath. "Smart, nobody denies that, but the general consensus is too lazy to try very hard. And why should you? It's not like you had to work for anything, it was all dropped right into your lap."

He paused again. Cal was frowning a little, but he didn't say anything.

"Your crews love you, especially the women, although in spite of all the rumors you've never been accused of dipping your pen in the company ink. Word in the fleet is that your COs, even if they do wish you'd be a little more enthusiastic, rate your job performance as consistently good. One even called you brilliant after that incident on the Maritime Boundary Line in the Bering Sea—" Azizi stopped obediently when Cal raised a hand, and then resumed."—and you got an award for the volunteer work you put in at the World

Trade Center after 9/11. Although you don't like to talk about either, and I hear tell you've had to be reminded to wear the ribbons."

There was a brief silence. "You know a lot about me," Cal said finally, "for a guy I met less than a week ago."

Azizi shrugged. "You're one of those people who get talked about, sir. Have I offended you?"

Cal gave a tired laugh and pulled his cap off to run his hand through his hair. "Like none of that's ever been said before, to my face or behind my back. Tell me something I don't know, Commander."

Azizi looked over Cal's shoulder at the stream of people heading down the gangway; men, women, children, all of them moving with a new sense of purpose in spite of the months and years of rebuilding their city, their community, their homes that lay in front of them. There were infants in arms, toddlers, kids from grade school to high school, parents, grandparents. Some of them had been through the nightmare in the convention center, some had lucked out and survived the deluge after the levees broke in their homes and later been evacuated. Most of them were black, and much had already been made in the national and international press of America's neglect of its Southern minority population in the destructive wakes of Katrina and Rita.

Azizi was as dark-skinned as half of the people going down the gangway, which, Cal thought, might have been why they were having this conversation.

"They call me Taffy, sir," Azizi said. "Mustafa's a little too much for most Western tongues to get around, and I've never liked Ziz, which is what I get stuck with when I don't tell people I've already got a nickname I can live with."

"Taffy," Cal said, trying it out.

"That's right, sir. Taffy."

After a moment Cal held out his hand. "Hello, Taffy."

"Hello, sir." Their hands met in a firm grip, quickly released before either man could be accused of overt sentiment.

Taffy consulted his clipboard. "One of the water tankers threw a rod this morning. I've got a line on a mechanic but in the meantime I've got a rumor of a couple tankers over in Alabama. I'll need the helo to get the drivers there, and we'll need drivers we can trust—have you ever driven a tanker truck, sir? No? Well, it's fairly easy, once you master the gears and figure out just how high your ass is in the air, you shouldn't have any trouble . . ."

2

"So this is a new one, Patrick?"

"It's a new name, sir."

"But the same old faces?"

"Certainly some of them, sir. Lights, please?"

The lights dimmed in the anonymous conference room. Patrick Chisum, special agent newly in charge of the CIA's Joint Terrorism Task Force, tapped a button on his notebook and the PowerPoint program began, a series of head shots interspersed with graphic pictures of bomb scenes, maps, dates, and casualty figures.

"They are calling themselves Abdullah."

"Just Abdullah?" His boss, Harold Kallendorf, sounded a little disappointed. "No Lord High Everything Allah? No Holy Judges, Juries, and Executioners of the Great Satan and All Who Sail in Him? No Fuck You and the Horse You Rode In On Jihad?" He sighed in what everyone hoped was mock disapproval. "Just suck the romance right out of the world, why don't you, Patrick."

There were dutiful chuckles from around the table, as in this group of government officials from the security departments of the FBI, the NSA, Immigration, Customs, the Border Patrol, the Army, Navy, Air Force, Marines, and Coast Guard, none held a higher rank than the new director. A dutiful chuckle in response to the ranking man's sallies, no matter how lame, was de rigueur.

"Just Abdullah, sir," Patrick said, having waited patiently until he had regained everyone's attention. He hadn't chuckled, either. He didn't do chuckle. "It means 'servant of God.' The group came first to our attention with the bus bomb in Baghdad at Christmas."

"Remind me of the damages."

"Thirteen dead, over fifty injured, including bystanders."

"Any Americans?"

"No, sir, Iraqis."

"Well, that's a mercy, anyway."

Next to him Khalid stirred. "Yes, sir," Patrick said quickly, and clicked to the next slide before Khalid broke into rash speech. The screen displayed a large graph that resembled a genealogical tree, with head shots next to each name where they were available. Most of the photos were blurry, and most of the names were aliases. Patrick thought it was a perfect illustration of how much they didn't know about Abdullah, which was why he'd included it.

There was a moment of silence while Patrick let them work their way through the chart. "We believe that the bin Laden organization funded the group initially with a grant of two hundred thousand dollars, at the instigation of al-Zarqawi. We believe that al Qaeda remains the main source of their money, although we believe that they encourage all of their cells to raise money independently, from whatever local Muslim population they happen to be in at the time."

He called up the next slide. "Zarqawi's cell is for the most part made up of fellow Jordanians. One of the very few exceptions is a man we know only as Isa, and we believe Isa is the head of Abdullah."

"Is that short for Isaiah or something?"

"No, sir, we believe it is the Arabic name for Jesus."

Kallendorf looked at him. "You are fucking kidding me."

"No, sir," Patrick said. "Jesus was a prophet for Islam. There is also a suspicion among our analysts that the name was adopted to play on the evangelical Christian belief of the Second Coming."

Kallendorf digested this. "So by adopting the name, this Isa is saying he's the second coming of Christ?"

"With the prophesied worldwide death and destruction attendant on that, er, coming, we think so, yes, sir."

Kallendorf leaned back in his chair. "Guy's got balls, I'll say that for him. And maybe even a sense of humor. Jesus." He shook his head, became aware of what he'd said, and laughed. The half of those present who got the joke laughed, too.

"It also means that he has some education, we believe some of it possibly in the West," Omar Khalid said, speaking for the first time. He was of medium height, with dark hair and eyes. Arabian-born and a naturalized American citizen, Khalid was one of the few agents the CIA had who were fluent in Arabic and Farsi. Recruited out of grad school where he'd been majoring in Islamic studies, he'd spent fourteen years in the field in the Middle East, shadowing, eavesdropping on, and infiltrating mainstream and splinter terrorist groups from Beirut to Libya. When at last his cover was blown, his masters in Langley had pulled him out of the field one step ahead of his executioners and parked him behind a desk. He had predicted 9/11, or something very like it, and had been laughed at for his pains. Afterward, he had been thoroughly investigated, just to be sure he himself hadn't been part of the conspiracy. He bore it all philosophically, because like most immigrants whose families had sacrificed a great deal in pursuit of the American dream, he was a true believer in truth, justice, and the American way. Lately, however, Patrick had noticed that Khalid had begun to show signs of restlessness, even of anger. It's hard to be a prophet in one's own time and to have one's prophecies at first ridiculed and then suspect.

Kallendorf shrugged, his massive shoulders throwing menacing shadows against the screen. "Most of the guys on the planes had degrees in engineering. That nowadays the terrorists are fielding intellectual ideologues is not news, gentlemen."

"No, sir," Patrick said, and squeezed Khalid's arm before he spoke again. The slide show became a series of more blurry photographs of groups of men in jellabas and kaffiyehs, succeeded by a series of more head shots with the numbers across the bottom cropped off. "We believe Isa was the only non-Jordanian in Zarqawi's cell. We believe he may be Irani, or possibly

Yemeni, although some sources have him Indian-born, which"—Patrick allowed himself a small, disbelieving smile—"we believe is reaching. We believe him to be in his late thirties or early forties."

"We believe a hell of a lot," Kallendorf said. "Do we know anything?"

"We are still gathering information, sir."

"Which, freely translated, means we don't know shit."

Patrick refused to be rushed. "I'd rather not assume too much in advance of hard data, sir. Our original intelligence on Zarqawi was wrong. Osama bin Laden and al-Zarqawi hate each other, and that hatred only increases as time goes on. Bin Laden wants to kill Americans. Zarqawi is killing mostly Shiites. Bin Laden's mother is a Shiite."

He nodded at Khalid, who leapt to life like a yappy poodle kept too long on a leash. "If Isa isn't Jordanian, it may explain why he has decided to strike out on his own. We're closing in on Zarqawi. When he's gone, we believe this Isa has no chance of being named to take his place as the leader of the Iraqi insurgency. There is an Egyptian, a protégé of Ayman al-Zawahiri, who we believe will be named as the next leader of al Qaeda in Iraq. Al-Zawahiri is bin Laden's right-hand man, and any protégé of his is certain to be seen as more trustworthy than a protégé of Zarqawi's."

"Wait a minute, wasn't Zawahiri the guy who ran the op that killed all those tourists in Luxor in 1997? I thought the Russians had him locked up."

"They detained him for six months in 1996," Khalid said. "He was carrying four different passports under four different names from four different countries. None of the countries would own him, so the Russians cut him loose on the Azerbaijani border. Where we lost him." It probably came out a little harsher than Khalid meant it, but it was only the truth, after all.

"Ah." Kallendorf stroked his chin. He'd had a beard when he had been named director. Patrick thought he must be missing it. "So you think this Isa blew up a bus in Baghdad, killing—"

"Thirteen," Khalid said.

"—and wounding—"

"Fifty," Khalid said, adding helpfully, "including bystanders, some of whom staggered off home before help arrived. So we don't have a hard number on wounded."

"—and this is Isa's, what, his calling card? His debutante ball? His curtsey to the queen?"

"We believe Isa did it to demonstrate his independence, yes, sir, his determination to distinguish himself from his master."

"It also signals Zarqawi's determination to hand off operations to Isa when the time comes," Patrick said. "No matter what al Qaeda thinks about it."

"'Watch me, Dad, see what I can do'?"

"Essentially, sir, yes. From both men."

"Lights." The lights came up and Kallendorf swiveled around to face them. "This a one-off, or are we looking forward to more love letters from this asshole?"

Patrick and Khalid exchanged a look. "We believe the bus bombing was Isa testing his wings, sir," Patrick said.

"And what the fuck does that mean when it's at home?"

"He was flying solo," Khalid said. "Seeing if he could operate on his own."

"Maybe even a test," Patrick said. "To prove to Zarqawi he was worthy."

Kallendorf got to his feet, moving with the ponderous authority of sheer physical size that reminded them all of the linebacker he used to be. Deliberately, Patrick thought. Kallendorf's was a carefully cultivated presence that had intimidated employees, superiors, and congressmen alike for twenty years, culminating in the top job at a federal agency less inured to the mood swings in the White House than everyone would like to think. New to the job, he wasn't new to the Beltway.

But he wasn't a career bureaucrat, either, and he did not lack either intelligence or humor. He achieved his full six feet nine inches and said with deliberation, measuring and weighing each word as it was produced, "Gentlemen, I'm the FNG around here and I know it. You all think I'm just some candy-ass with enough money to buy myself the job the last guy screwed up, and I know that, too. I've shot my mouth off some in front of Schuyler's oversight committee down on the Hill, you've heard about it on *O'Reilly* and watched it on YouTube, and my guess is right about now you're wondering how to contain any damage I might do to your revered institution."

Kallendorf meditated for a moment. "Yeah," he said finally. "Might as well go for broke." He raised his head, a look in his eyes that legend had it had disintegrated more than one defensive line in the three Super Bowls Kallendorf had started in. "It's not the damage I might do to your institution that you ought to be worried about, gentlemen, it's the damage this institution can do to the nation, and the world. The CIA's been making bad calls since they tried to blow up Castro with an exploding cigar. If I had my druthers, I'd take all the money we're pouring into our Middle Eastern antiterrorism efforts and write a check to the Mossad, with one set of instructions: Go get 'em, tiger. Then I'd go before every television camera from ABC, NBC, CBS, CNN, BBC, and Al Jazeera and tell them what I'd done."

He looked around the table, looking as if he were savoring the moment. Most of them were veterans who'd seen their share of congressional hearings and so maintained their poker faces, but he appeared to be satisfied. "I'd bet my left nut that it'd take all of two seconds before terrorist cells'd be folding like cheap card tables all over the world, because I guarantee you that our enemies are way more scared of the Mossad than they are of the CIA, the FBI, the NSC, and all the rest of you yahoos who opened the door into Iraq II combined."

Patrick had worked for the CIA for too long to blink

at this trenchant assessment. "Understood, sir."

"I doubt it," Kallendorf said. "I want intel, gentlemen, I want a lot of it, I want it yesterday, and I don't care how you get it."

"Yes, sir."

There wasn't much to be said after that. Patrick exchanged meaningless pleasantries with the rest of the men and women as they filed out the door. Some of them looked a little shell-shocked. Others looked angry. Patrick looked at his watch, and estimated that the first outraged phone calls would hit his desk possibly before he got back to it.

Speaking of which, Khalid could barely contain himself until the door closed behind the last of them. "Jesus fucking Christ." He pulled out his cell phone and flipped it open.

"Don't do it," Patrick said. When Khalid, unheeding, started punching numbers, Patrick reached over and closed Khalid's phone. "Don't do it, Omar."

Khalid looked indignant. "Why the hell not? You heard him. This guy's got no experience, he's a hack, he admitted it right here in this room. He's going to have all the gears jammed in six months, probably less."

Still staring at the door, Patrick said slowly, "A lot of reasons, not least of which is in trying to screw over Kallendorf, you'll screw yourself worse. This guy isn't a fool."

Khalid wasn't ready to give up. "Senator Schuyler will listen to us. He's always been a friend to the agency. Maybe he can help us get somebody in here with a clue about operations."

Not without sympathy, Chisum said, "Kallendorf was handpicked for the job by the president of the United States, Khalid. You want to go up against the White House? Especially this White House? They'll crucify you. Hell, what's worse, they'll leak your wife's name and your kids' schools. Besides." He stacked his notes together. "You won't be telling Schuyler anything he doesn't already know."

Khalid folded his cell phone and pocketed it, but he wasn't convinced. "You remember the Church hearings, Patrick."

"Not personally, no," Patrick said mildly. "I'm not that old."

Unheeding, Khalid said, "You know what they did to the agency. You know what kind of damage this administration can do in the two years it's got left. Kallendorf's the end result of that Iraq witch hunt on Capitol Hill. They're still looking for somebody to hang for Gulf War II, the president knew he wasn't going to get anyone with a paper trail through the confirmation hearings and so he used the job to pay off a campaign debt instead. I mean, hey, I can see his reasoning, if Congress is never going to allow you a competent director, might as well use the position to pay off someone who helped get you elected." He reached for the phone again.

"Don't do it, Khalid," Chisum repeated.

"Why the hell not?" Khalid said again, in understandable frustration. "What the hell have we got to lose?"

"Most of all . . ." He turned and looked at Khalid and said soberly, "Most of all because Kallendorf's not wrong."

3

They met for the last time in a cramped, dark room in a tumbledown house at the edge of a dusty village well off the beaten track, miles outside of Baghdad and as secure from surveillance as one could reasonably be and still be in Iraq. He looked around at the men left to him. They looked back, fearful but trusting. They had been together a long time, and they believed in him.

And if they didn't believe in him, they had believed in Zarqawi, and Zarqawi had chosen him to be second in command. Zarqawi's legend lingered on.

How many times could the Americans have killed him? In Mosul, in Ramadi, time and again in Kurdistan? He knew now—everyone knew, that was the wonderful thing about the Western media—that the American military had forwarded plans for attacking the Khurmal camp at least three times, and that each time Bush the Unbeliever had been so busy plotting his invasion of Iraq that the attacks had been brushed aside.

Each time they had hesitated, and each time he had eluded them. But now, now Akil had seen the proof with his own eyes. He might have been able to ignore this report as just another rumor, but this time the news was not only on CNN and the BBC but on Al Jazeera as well.

On a summer evening in Iraq, Zarqawi, his wife, and his eighteen-month-old daughter were killed by two bombs dropped from American jets. Photographs of his body, including close-ups of the all-too-familiar features of his face, even distorted in the rictus of a horrible death, were too clear to be disbelieved.

"Today, Zarqawi has been terminated," Nouri al-Maliki, the thrice-cursed Iraqi puppet, said from his American-built stage. "Every time a Zarqawi appears we will kill him. We will continue confronting whoever follows his path. It is an open war between us."

An open war, and a holy war. In truth, jihad. "How did they find the safe house?"

Karim lowered his voice. "It is said that the Americans had been tracking him for some time."

"Yes, yes," Akil said impatiently, "but this we all knew. They almost had him half a dozen times this year alone. But the safe house, Karim, how did they know of the safe house?"

The rest of the men had squatted just far enough away so that they might be out of earshot. Or might not. Karim satisfied himself with an eloquent look.

And how else, Akil thought, surveying the room over

46

Karim's shoulder, allowing his eyes to sort through their faces. How else but an informant? But which one? Saad, whose Saudi ties he had always suspected? Jumah, who alone among the Jordanians in the cell had been very angry over the planned chemical attack in Amman?

"Who will lead us now, Akil?"

Karim's voice brought Akil back from his speculations. He raised his palms with a shrug. "Allah will dispose."

Karim was not to be so diverted. "It should be you, Akil. You walked beside him for the last seven years. You were his first recruit after he was released from prison."

"I am not Jordanian, Karim."

"It should not matter. You were with him when he made bay'ah to bin Laden, both times you swore allegiance side by side."

"But they thought we were killing the wrong people, Karim. They said so, time and again."

"You were killing the enemy!"

Faces turned at Karim's raised voice. "Gently," Akil said, "gently, my friend. Allah shall dispose of me as he sees fit."

"God helps those who help themselves," Karim said tartly.

Akil regarded him with a steady eye. "And where is that written, Karim? I am not familiar with the verse."

Karim ducked his head. "Ay, Akil, you catch me out." He looked up, a smile tugging at the corners of his mouth. "I heard it on an American television program."

In spite of his grief, Akil felt his lips twitch in response.

The next day Akil gave orders for the cell to disperse. "Stay on the move," he told them. "Travel no more than two together. Rest no more than one night in a single place. Work toward the Syrian border. Trust no one. No one," he repeated firmly. "Our leader was betrayed. Who knows who else has been betrayed? Check your email as often as you can." He raised an admonitory finger. "Never from the same computer twice." There were nods all around. They were well drilled in security protocol. Still, he knew there would be lapses. People grew tired, or lazy, and careless. It didn't matter, now, but he was expected to say it, so he did. "You will hear from me soon." They were expecting to hear that, too. "Inshallah."

"Inshallah," they echoed, and by ones and twos, dispersed.

He and Karim set out on foot, with the clothes on their backs and a thick wad of American dollars. Any border, no matter how well guarded, was susceptible to bribes. This was especially true of the Syrian border. They were stopped many times, and each time either their identity papers passed muster or the cash smoothed their passage.

They spoke but little, both concentrating on escape. There had been much opportunity in Iraq, their way in opened by the invasion and occupation. The country they left behind was in shambles, and the invader, bent on crusade, was on the verge of being utterly routed instead.

He had had a part in that, Akil thought, and not a small one. He smiled to himself.

It was a long way from Pakistan, and not only in distance.

After Adara's death he had wandered across Pakistan, his only goal getting as far away from his tiny village as possible. Eventually he settled in Hayatabad. With his fluency in English it was easy for him to get a job answering the 800 number for an international banking firm. He rented a room from a Hindu family who, while they shunned the Muslim socially, were only marginally solvent and were more than happy to cash his rent checks. He made no friends, although at work he was appreciated for his willingness to trade shifts with anyone wanting a day off to celebrate a birthday or a wedding or a high holy day.

For years he did not pray, and when after years of turning his shoulder to God he began praying again, he did not go to the mosque. Never again would he tolerate intercession, interpretation, guidance. His appeals were simple and direct, from him to God. He prayed for strength. He prayed for wisdom.

He prayed for vengeance.

The years passed. God did not answer his prayers.

He did not hate God, though. He hated the mullahs who held his people by the throat. Even more did he hate the Western powers who supported them. After his years in America, he understood the rationale behind it, that the pursuit of capitalism required a stable base. That stable base was provided by a strong leader, whose absolute authority was made possible by allowing the mullahs and the imams free rein to enlighten the faithful as to the will of Allah and the laws of the Koran. They would not foment rebellion if left alone to practice—and enforce—Islam as they saw fit. Akil had never dreamed of questioning the source of that dual and complementary authority. Truthfully, he had never really paid much attention to it.

Clearly not as much as his parents had. The memory of the closed door of what had been until that moment his home still burned redly in his mind.

Adara had been his only sibling, a bright-eyed, mischievous child grown into a beautiful woman, the light of their family's life. And now she was gone, and he would never see or speak to his parents again. He had, essentially, orphaned himself that night.

In the lonely years that followed, he had time to reflect on the forces that had worked such havoc on his life. He read a great deal—histories, the Koran, newsmagazines—finding nothing adequate in any of them to explain why he was where he was now. He did, however, believe that he had achieved a better understanding of why the world was where it was. That understanding did nothing to alleviate his anger.

Quite the contrary.

They had burned witches once for sleeping with the devil. It was easy to see America as the devil in bed with his own nation, made even easier by the memory of Adara's body hanging from the neem tree. That memory was the last thing he saw before he went to sleep at night, and the last thing he dreamed before he woke again the next morning. It never varied. In a way, he was glad of it. The memory and the dream nourished his anger, kept it alive.

One day in the summer of 1999, he met a man. The man was not in his first youth, with slightly stooped shoulders and a hard round belly, although his stubby-fingered hands were strong and calloused. He had dark eyes, a long strong nose, and a wide upper lip edged with a thick black mustache, a description that could have fit almost any man in the Middle East, but unlike them, once seen this man was not forgotten. His bright eyes snapped with interest, his speech was rough but decisive and ultimately spellbinding, and his whole attitude was one of purpose and resolution.

The first time Akil met him was at a coffeehouse near where he worked. The man who occupied the desk next to his introduced them.

"Ah, Akil," the man said, examining the young man with those bright eyes. "A good name. It means 'intelligent,' and 'thoughtful,' " he told the others around the table.

There was a bobbing of heads. In another group there might have been some fun poked at Akil, but no one felt they had the right to take liberties with the sober young man, especially without invitation from their host, of whom they were all slightly in awe.

They would become more so.

"And where do you come from, Akil?" the man said.
Akil told him, and then had to explain where in Pakistan it was. Briefly, because even now, five years later, awareness of his exile brought him pain.

The older man's eyes were steady on his face. "And now you live in the big city. What do you do here?"

He was grateful that the subject had been changed. It was only later that he realized the man had seen his distress and had changed it for him deliberately.

The man's name, he said when asked, was Ahmad, Ahmad al-Nazal. He was Jordanian, and when asked he said with a self-deprecating smile that he did many things, none of them really well. For a time he had been a journalist. A few years after that he had gone into video rentals, which explained his near total recall of every movie made since *Ben-Hur* (Ahmad adored Hugh Griffith). Later, he said, he had worked in a computer store, where he had acquired enough skill to introduce Akil to the Internet. It was from Ahmad that Akil learned of the wonders of email, the ease of anonymous communication, and its incredibly infinite reach. Akil was astonished at how much Ahmad knew about online banking, including things that were at this time only possibilities spoken of in executive meetings. Ahmad predicted that soon everyone with a bank account would be able to pay bills without money ever changing hands. Sums of money would be moved from one account to another from one country to another with a pass code and a keystroke. One's banker would never know one's

face, a distinct advantage, Ahmad said, in certain pro-
fessions.

Ahmad was also a student of history, with his own
theories as to the causes of the many global conflicts
current the world over. Akil's thought had not gone
beyond the local, what he could see, what he had experienced. Ahmad took a more global viewpoint, quoted
Clausewitz and Sun Tzu, and lectured Akil and a small
but ever more devoted group of acolytes on the ability
of guerilla warriors to attack not only the enemy's
strength but, and what Ahmad said was even more
important, the enemy's morale.

There was some politely but inadequately concealed
disbelief at this assertion. Ahmad saw it. "No," he said,
"I assure you," and hastened to give examples dating
from the Scythians attacking Darius to the American
war of independence. "A guerilla army has certain significant advantages over a regular standing army," he
said. "It's smaller, for one thing, which makes it not
only more mobile but easier to conceal, and infinitely
easier for its soldiers if escape is necessary. It strikes
not on command but when it wills, at dawn, in the
middle of a week, on a high holy day, keeping the
enemy in a constant state of apprehension over where
the next strike will be."

They digested this in silence. Akil, looking around,
saw no skepticism. They were all young men, unmarried, some religious, some not. And indeed Ahmad
spoke very little of religion.

"A guerilla army," Ahmad said, "targets the enemy

not on its flank but at its heart. A school bus. A government building. A hotel."

"You mean civilian targets," Akil said.

Ahmad shrugged. "A guerilla army has one more attractive facet. It is made up of people who volunteered because they support the same cause. True believers, if you will."

"Freedom fighters," someone suggested.

Ahmad nodded equably, but Akil, watching closely, saw his eyes glitter. With excitement, perhaps. Or was it triumph? How long would conversation have gone before Ahmad himself had introduced the phrase "freedom fighters"? "There are many names. Rebels. Partisans."

Terrorists, Akil thought. At least so far as Western propaganda was concerned.

"Soldiers of God," one excitable young man said.

The others looked startled. Ahmad smiled again but made a shushing movement with his hands, as the excitable young man's words had reached tables other than their own. "Regular armies fight because they are doing their two years of national service," he said, in a lower voice, "or they have been called up in a time of war. Often a war they have little interest in fighting." He smiled and raised an eyebrow. "Like in *Platoon*," he said.

They laughed, and the conversation shifted so smoothly from talk of real war to talk of war movies that no one but Akil noticed.

Over the next few months there were many other conversations on many other topics in coffeehouses around the city. Occasionally Ahmad would invite a favored few to a simple meal in his apartment.

In October the man at the desk next to Akil's came back from lunch pale and sweating.

"What is it?" Akil said.

"They are arresting Arab militants all over the country."

"And so?" Akil said. "You aren't a militant. You have nothing to fear."

"Ahmad is one of them."

It was a purge of dissidents by the government, under pressure from the West. The dissidents were imprisoned briefly and then expelled from Pakistan.

Ahmad invited a select few to his apartment to say good-bye while he packed. "Come," he said, "no long faces. It could have been much worse."

"Where will you go?" one of them said.

Ahmad closed his valise and straightened. "I was thinking . . ."

He turned to look at them. "I was thinking I would go to Afghanistan." There was a moment of breathless silence. "You go to join the Taliban," Akil said.

Ahmad lifted his shoulders. "Perhaps." He paused with uncharacteristic hesitation. "I did wonder . . ."

"What?" Akil said.

Ahmad smiled at him, at the circle of intent, watching faces. "I did wonder if you might like to come with me."

Akil knew then that God had been listening to his prayers after all.

· · ·

A WEEK LATER, HALFWAY TO THE BORDER, THEY HEARD that al Qaeda had released a video of Ayman al-Zawahiri, who called Zarqawi "a soldier, a hero, an imam, and the prince of martyrs."

Karim snorted. "And it only took them sixteen days after he died to admit it."

A week after that bin Laden himself released an audio recording, which Akil and Karim heard in a café in Haditha whose television was tuned to Al Jazeera. "Our Islamic nation was surprised to find its knight, the lion of jihad, the man of determination and will, Zarqawi Musab al-Zarqawi, killed in a shameful American raid. We pray to God to bless him and accept him among the martyrs as he had hoped for."

Karim raised an eyebrow at Akil. "What do you think?"

"A very poor-quality recording," Akil said, and drained his cup.

They heard the broadcast of bin Laden's second audio tape in Abu Kamal, barely but safely over the border into Syria. "Our brothers, the mujahedeen in the al Qaeda organization, have chosen their dear brother Zarqawi Hamza al-Muhajer as their leader to succeed the amir Zarqawi Musab al-Zarqawi. I advise him to focus his fighting on the Americans and everyone who supports them and allies himself with them in their war on the people of Islam and Iraq."

Karim stared at Akil. "An Egyptian?"

"So it would seem," Akil said.

"You are not surprised," Karim said, almost an accusation.

Akil glanced at him, amused. "Zarqawi was as a father to me, and bin Laden hated Zarqawi. He didn't like Jordanians much, either, he thinks you are all spies for Amman. And never forget that his mother is a Shiite."

Karim brooded all the way to Damascus, where Akil replenished their funds and sent emails to the cell members directing them to contact their new leader. He ignored any replies by the simple process of discontinuing that account.

They spent two nights at the Four Seasons; a risk, Akil admitted, but Zarqawi had left the Swiss account in a very healthy state, and what was fate for, if not to be tempted? He was sure the Prophet would have understood. They outfitted themselves in a Banana Republic a block down the street, Karim looking very smart and very Western in his new clothes, and young enough to think of his appearance as something other than camouflage.

They ate a sumptuous meal in an Indian restaurant in a quiet neighborhood, and found a late-night café where the waiter didn't hurry them over their coffee. Karim watched the girls walking by in giggling groups. Akil watched the omnipresent television hung from the ceiling in one corner, this one tuned to CNN. An earthquake in the Far East, more bombings in the Middle East, a plane crash in South America. Tony Blair on his way out due to his slavish allegiance to

George Bush's Iraqi agenda. A space shuttle landing at Cape Canaveral after a successful mission to the International Space Station, and then someone from NASA came on to talk about the retiring of the space shuttle in 2010, and the missions scheduled between now and then.

In business news the world's stock exchanges were climbing to new highs, well into recovery from the burst tech bubble a few years back. Construction of new homes was also at a new high. Rupert Murdoch was buying more newspapers and media conglomerates. There was a brief spot on Al Jazeera and how it had become the voice of record to Muslims everywhere. An American media company was being simultaneously lauded and chastised for carrying Al Jazeera on its basic programming. It seemed even the Pentagon was watching Al Jazeera nowadays. Pity it wasn't the White House.

Karim spoke to him twice before he heard him. "I'm sorry, Karim," he said, turning. "What did you say?"

"You have not told me where we are going," Karim said, a little diffidently. One learned not to question in Zarqawi's organization, one learned to obey. "Or when. Or what we do next."

Akil forced a smile. "All in good time, Karim."

Karim looked at him, worried. Isa seemed very preoccupied and remained so all the way back to the hotel.

It wasn't until they got to the airport and Akil gave him his ticket that Karim realized their destination was not the same. "Isa!" he said in consternation. "I want to go with you! I follow you! I look to you!"

"Gently," Akil said, embracing the younger man and kissing him on both cheeks, for indeed he was fond of Karim. They had fought side by side since the invasion of Iraq, in Mosul, in Baghdad, in Fallujah. He trusted Karim, he really did, or he did as much as he was willing to trust anyone. Zarqawi had taught him well in that respect. It was a wrench to sever his last tie from his old master, and Karim's skill really was unequalled at building and setting IEDs, but Akil's plans had no place for him and he held to his purpose. "Where I must go, you cannot follow."

Karim had tears in his eyes. "But where do you go?"

"First to Paris," Akil said, pointing at the next gate, where the agents were preparing to call the flight. "And then, who knows? Bush the Unbeliever says that it is better to fight us on our ground than for the Americans to fight us on theirs. I am beginning to believe he is right, Karim."

He kissed Karim on both cheeks again and stepped back. "Go with God, little brother." He even smiled a little. "Go, now. They are calling your flight."

He watched as Karim dragged his feet down the jetway, and he waited while the airplane backed away from the concourse. He waited while it made its ponderous way down the taxiway, he waited until it turned onto the runway, and he waited until he saw it lift off, rising swiftly into the air.

He waited until it was out of sight before turning and walking past the gate that was boarding passengers for

Paris in favor of another farther down the concourse, whose agent was just announcing preboarding for its flight to Barcelona.

In Barcelona he checked into a quiet hotel a block off Las Ramblas. The next day he spent wandering through the city, guidebook in hand, dutifully admiring buildings by Gaudi. He tried to take a photo of La Pedrera, only to discover that his battery had died. He clicked his tongue, received a sympathetic glance from an American man, and put the camera away with a sigh.

"There are lots of camera shops on Las Ramblas," the American said.

Akil gave a rueful nod. "I should have checked it before I left home."

The American drifted closer. "Where's home?"

"India. Mumbai. And you? American?"

The other man made a face. "Is it that obvious?"

Akil laughed. "I'm afraid so. Are you here on business?"

"I'm on leave. My ship is in Naples. I'd heard about the Maritime Museum. When I got my leave I flew over to have a look."

"Navy?"

"Coast Guard."

Akil's smile vanished. "U.S. Coast Guard?"

"Yes, really," the other said, laughing a little. "Is that so awful?"

"No, of course not," Akil said, forcing himself to relax, by an act of will putting the smile back on his face. He cast a covert look around. They were not being observed so far as he could tell, and he knew he had not been followed to Barcelona. He had not spoken of his next plans to anyone. He looked at the other man, tall, slender, with coloring much like his own. Here was an opportunity it would be foolish not to embrace. He decided to pretend to a little knowledge. "You rescue people at sea who are in trouble?"

"Among other things. You?"

"I write computer software," Akil said, with a dismissive shrug. "Not quite as exciting."

"Necessary, though," the other man said. "You should see our communications room on board ship. Looks like Mission Control at NASA during a shuttle launch."

Akil bowed his head, accepting the implied compliment gracefully.

"Adam Bayzani," the other man said.

"Arjan Singh," Akil said. They shook hands. "What's at the Maritime Museum that is so interesting that you'd spend your leave in Barcelona?"

"I don't know, haven't been there yet."

What was at the Maritime Museum, among many other things, was a full-size replica of a galleon that fought at the Battle of Lepanto, the last sea battle to employ galleons. Bayzani was good company, and if his covert sideways glances were a little languishing it was nothing Akil couldn't deal with. They dined together that evening at one of Barcelona's many waterfront restaurants, during which Bayzani made a delicate but perfectly recognizable overture. Akil's rebuff was hesitant enough to leave room for Bayzani to hope. A prize was all the more valued if it was hard-won. They exchanged email addresses, shook hands, and parted.

The next morning, his carefully casual wanderings brought him to a shop specializing in electronics from cell phones to laptops, where he asked to see the proprietor. A short, squat man whose butt and thighs were so massive they waddled independently of the rest of him, he listened to Akil's needs with eyebrows like black caterpillars politely raised over a swarthy, sweating moon face. "Of course," he said. "The battery is of no moment. The other, a few hours, no more. Over here, if you please, señor." He took Akil's photo, and repeated, "A matter of a few hours only, señor. Be pleased to return this evening after seven." And that evening Akil returned to the shop to pick up his camera, along with a set of identification papers in the name of Dandin Gandhi.

He had already checked out of his hotel. He went directly to the station and boarded an overnight train for Bilbao, where he boarded a plane for Paris de Gaulle. In Paris he took the Metro to Gare du Nord and a train for Amsterdam. From Amsterdam, he took a train to Germany.

Nowhere was his identity questioned. Truth to tell, except when he boarded a plane, his papers were almost never checked. The European Union was very accommodating to travelers.

4

She'd been named to the astronaut program five years before. She'd lived, worked, hoped, prayed for the day when she would be named to a shuttle crew.

In another four years, the shuttle program would end. The space shuttle would be retired, and NASA would move on to the next new thing. The next new thing was sounding a lot like the old new thing that scientists had been advocating for years, the return of the big dumb rocket, reminiscent of the days of the *Saturn V.* Preferably a big dumb unmanned rocket.

Atlantis was already scheduled to be cannibalized for parts for *Discovery* and *Endeavour.* The astronaut corps could hear the clock ticking down on the time left. There was already covert talk of what they were going to do after.

After, Kenai might open a vein and climb into a nice warm tub.

Today, she'd been named to a shuttle crew.

It was, however, nothing like she had imagined it would be. She had imagined joy unconfined, trumpets sounding, bells pealing, the exploding of champagne corks. She had imagined calling her parents and hearing their pride, and their fear. She had imagined the envy of her peers in the astronaut corps.

She hadn't imagined the spare, dry voice of Joel

Minster, director of flight operations, informing them that there would be a sixth member of their crew, not an astronaut. What, in their more charitable moments, the astronauts referred to as a part-timer. Joy unconfined was checked, to be replaced by a stunned silence when they found out who it was.

"Please tell me you're kidding, Joel," Kenai said at last, with as much control as she could muster up on the spot.

Joel, known to some as the Great Conciliator and to others as the Great Suck-up, spoke her thought out loud. "I don't know what you're complaining about, Kenai. You've got your first mission. Doesn't happen to everyone."

Won't happen to a lot of them, was the thought in everyone's mind. And picking public fights with the man who might one day be in charge of assigning her to a precious second wasn't the smartest thing she could do, so this time she bit her tongue and kept her mouth shut.

Joel tucked his clipboard beneath an arm, gave a general nod, and left.

The door had barely closed behind him when the trash talk ensued.

"I don't know about you but this is just what I want on orbit, some dipshit rich kid fucking around on board." Bill White, an ex-Navy test pilot flying his second mission as pilot, was furious.

"We're launching the replacement for the Hubble, we're launching a communications satellite and an orbital observatory, we're conducting—how many experiments is this mission up to now?—and on top of all that we've got to babysit some spoiled brat?" This not-quite-shouted comment from Mike Williams, a mission specialist with a postdoc in astronomy and astrophysics from the University of California who divided time into parsecs and as a result was usually the most patient and laid-back of astronauts. Today he waved long, lanky arms in emphasis, accidentally knocking the back of one hand against a table edge. He swore, which shocked them all into momentary silence, and sucked his bloody knuckles.

Into that silence stepped Laurel Freeman, a physicist from Stanford. She was almost sputtering with rage, but then Eratosthenes was her baby and as payload commander she took as a personal insult anything that affected its timely and successful deployment. Her father had been a stevedore on the Long Beach docks and in times of stress it showed up in her vocabulary. She was short and burly with a square face beneath a mop of untidy brown curls and it wasn't much of a stretch to imagine her offloading containers herself.

When Laurel paused for breath the mission commander stood up. "All right," Rick Robertson said. His voice was low and even, which had the natural effect of making them all shut up so they could hear him. "This is what's been handed to us. It sucks. Are any of you ready to give up your seat in protest?"

None of them were. There wasn't one of them who wouldn't have volunteered to be ballast on this mission or any other. Rick knew it. They all knew it. Rick was a test pilot from Texas Tech by way of the Air Force. This was his third shuttle flight and his second as commander. At five feet seven inches, he held himself with such parade-ground erectness that he seemed six feet tall. He looked at Kenai and said in his slow drawl, "Anything to add, Kenai?"

He'd deliberately mispronounced her name again, and it worked to defuse the situation. "It's KEE-nigh, not Kenya." She paused long enough for the delay to be felt. "Sir."

There was a very small laugh, but Rick gave her a brief, approving smile.

"Who's this guy again?" Bill said, his flush subsiding.

Rick consulted the bio Joel had handed him. "Well, at least he isn't a prince."

"The shuttle program already has its quota of princes," Mike said with feeling.

"Also U.S. senators," Laurel said, still steaming. "And U.S. representatives."

Heavily, Rick said, "He is a sheik, however."

"Jesus, Mary, and Joseph," Bill said. "And what lame-ass experiment is he bringing along?"

"Way-ull," Rick said, drawing out the word in the best Chuck Yeager imitation so dear to all aviators, "he ain't got no lame-ass experiment. We are deploying his satellite."

"The ARABSAT-8A?" Kenai said. "He's a Saudi?"

"No, Qatari," Rick said. "His family has a controlling interest in a media conglomerate." He paused, and then, with obvious reluctance and not a little apprehension, said, "A media conglomerate which owns, among many other things, Al Jazeera."

There was a moment of charged silence. Media coverage was a de facto part of any shuttle mission, but that didn't mean that any of them regarded the press as anything but the bane of their collective existence. They'd all been burned by the incautious remark in front of the wrong reporter, and they'd all learned to keep a discreet distance, especially lately, when astronaut adultery and boozing on the job, not to mention sabotage, were making more headlines than successful missions. The news that they would be spending seven days cooped up in the small confines of a shuttle on orbit with an owner of one of the largest and most influential international television networks in the world was news they did not welcome. In fact, "Oh, fuck me," Laurel said, and slammed out of the room. Mike wasn't far behind her and his language was even more colorful.

Bill looked at Rick. "Well, that went over well."

"They'll be all right," Kenai said loyally, and spoiled it by saying, almost pleadingly, "Is he going to be broadcasting on orbit?"

"Ya think?" Rick said.

They sat in gloomy silence for a moment. "The sun's about over the yardarm," Bill said.

Rick looked at the clock on the wall. "It's five o'clock somewhere," he said, and looked at Kenai. "Join us?"

"Building 99?"

Rick shook his head. "Too touristy. I know a place."

THEY GATHERED AROUND A TABLE IN A SMALL, DARK drinking establishment where the varnished wooden bar had a brass foot rail and the booths were upholstered in real leather. The bartender knew Rick by name, and the two people sitting at opposite ends of the bar looked up briefly and incuriously and then got back to the more serious business at hand. Bill had scotch, no ice, Kenai had a beer, and everyone had a good laugh, including the bartender, when Rick ordered a cranberry cosmopolitan. "I like the color of it," Rick said, refusing to be shamed into a more manly drink. "It looks like the sky over the folks' ranch at sunset."

They drank while reading their part-timer's bio. "He's studied communications and aviation, it says."

"Where?"

Bill tapped the bio. "It says here."

"Where here?"

Bill shrugged and handed Kenai the folder. "Doesn't name any schools. Doesn't say if he soloed. Doesn't say if he stuck it out anywhere long enough to pick up a degree. Looks like a kid with ADD whose daddy has too much money."

The bio was only a page long, and even that had been padded. " 'Hobbies include skiing, scuba diving, and polo'?" Kenai tossed the bio on the table. It slid into a puddle of beer, and the paper quickly absorbed it, leaving a big brown stain. "Oh yeah. This is gonna be fun."

The two men were veterans of military aviation programs and both had seen action in the Gulf. Kenai wasn't military but she had spent the last five years in rigorous training, including flying in the backseats of T-38s, training in vacuum chambers and sea survival, and she'd been CAPCOM on the last shuttle flight. They'd all stood up under severe stress and performed, and performed well. Rick, Mike, Kenai, Bill, and Laurel had worked together, played together, partied together, and on occasion, mourned the loss of a comrade together. They knew each other and they trusted each other not to screw the pooch in an emergency situation, of which there had to be six or eight on offer every second of any mission.

Now they were being asked to accommodate a stranger, an unknown, unschooled, untrained, 330 miles up, for over two point one million miles, for seven days, one hour, six minutes, and sixteen seconds, with nothing between them and vacuum but a thin metal shell. It was an awfully long time, during which one error could put all their names on the Astronaut Memorial at the KSC Visitor Center. It was not one of the honors to which Kenai, a type A competitor like any other astronaut, had ever aspired.

"This is basically your NASA sales incentive," Bill said. "We'll give you a seat on the shuttle if you hire us to launch your satellite."

"Pretty much," Rick said. It wasn't anything that

hadn't been done before, but no one liked it, least of all the astronauts. It burned mission specialists in particular, because the line to get into space was already long enough, and to have someone unqualified, inexperienced, a joyrider for crissake, jump in ahead of them was almost unbearable. A few couldn't bear it and quit. Everyone else stuck it out but none of them were happy about it.

And it was a mission commander's nightmare. "We'll run him through shuttle emergency escape procedures, how to eat, sleep, use the toilet." Rick fixed them with a beady eye. "But mostly we make it very, very clear that he doesn't touch anything. If he can be trained to take a shit without his ass touching the seat, do it."

They finished their drinks and went home, not as light of heart as a newly named Prime Crew ought to have been.

THE NEXT WEEK KENAI AND BILL WERE SCHEDULED FOR one of the unending meet-and-greets that astronauts were assigned to around the country, to show the NASA flag to the various services and contractors that designed, built, maintained, and manned the infrastructure that made shuttle operations possible, and to remind them of the real men and women flying the craft and operating the equipment the contractors built. They strapped into a T-38, Bill on the stick, Kenai in the backseat, and took off for Miami and the U.S. Coast Guard base there.

The Coast Guard was a substantial presence offshore during shuttle launches, deflecting clueless sailors, gaping rubberneckers, and on occasion even alligator poachers from taking their boats in too close to the Cape during countdown and launch. Rick's first launch had been put on hold at T minus thirty when a charter boat skipper in a thirty-five-foot Carolina Classic pretended to have lost power and was drifting ashore with the current, all the better for his four drunken clients to snap photos of themselves in front of the shuttle standing white and gleaming against the gantry. At eight hundred dollars a day each they were probably expecting something other than being boarded by a Zodiac full of irritated Coasties, their skipper arrested and their boat commandeered, but that was what they got, and the shuttle raised ship after only a sixty-minute delay, which had to be some kind of record. Rick told them that the astronauts on that mission had been of one mind when informed of the reason for the hold: to limber up the big gun on the foredeck of the cutter and blow the offending boat out of the water.

Today they landed in Miami and were picked up by a starstruck chief petty officer who couldn't take his eyes off Kenai, who had to remind him more than once that he was veering over the line into oncoming traffic. It was only after Bill offered to drive that the CPO managed to focus on the road. When they got to District 7 headquarters they discovered that the CO had mustered the entire workforce in the parking lot to greet them, many of whom wanted their pictures taken with the astronauts. Bill said a few words, Kenai said a few more, and many, many photographs were taken, after which ordeal Kenai's new love slave hustled them out to the *Munro*, a high-endurance cutter 378 feet long that would head up offshore security during their launch.

The *Munro* also had its entire crew on parade and the helo, a Dolphin HH-65, rolled out for their inspection. The executive officer, a stunner who looked like Naveen Andrews, welcomed them with a smile and a firm handshake and introduced them to the *Munro*'s captain, whose handshake was equally firm and who invited them to join him for lunch after their tour of his ship. Kenai and Bill repeated their thank yous and were happy to accept, after which the captain commanded his crew to fall out and go to their duty stations. He vanished up a ladder and the XO, one Lieutenant Commander Mustafa Azizi, proceeded to run Bill and Kenai's butts off over *Munro* from bow prop to aft steering and all points above, below, and in between, including a stop in the Combat Information Center, or Combat for short, a cool, dark room the width of the ship's beam filled with banks of computers and monitors. It was located amidships, two decks down from the main deck. "This is where everyone comes when it's rough or hot," said OSC Cutburth, a tall, laconic man with a shaved head, batwing ears, and a grin part saint and part Satan. The operations specialist chief radiated a quiet pride in his domain and in his crew. They were the only members of the crew who didn't have tans.

"If the engine room is the heart of *Munro*, Combat is the brains. OS2 Carrey." A thin, dark young man wearing Buddy Holly glasses whose hair stood up in agitated tufts came out from behind a console to shake their hands, beaming. "It's an honor," he said about seven times.

"And communications. OS3 Pachuco." A short, plump woman with raven hair bundled carelessly at the back of her head and an Aztec face Hernán Cortés would have recognized gave them a shy smile. "And detection and identification of all surface and air contacts. OS2 Riley." Another thin, dark young man with equally bad hair, this time with John Lennon glasses, raised a hand in a vague wave without lifting his eyes from the screen in front of him, his hands busy at a keyboard. The chief let the silence stretch out, until Riley raised his head, made eye contact, and gave them a curt nod. He looked sullen, as if he might be a little impatient with all this astronaut nonsense. Kenai's heart warmed to him.

"Forgive him," the chief said dryly, "he's better with bytes than he is with people."

"We all are," came a swift response from someone else, and the chief grinned. "True enough. At any rate, this is where we maintain Maritime Domain Awareness, keeping watch for yahoos, trespassers, and strays during your launch."

Kenai thought of Rick's last mission and said with emphasis, "Thank you."

"Over here, we track and control the helo." A young black man whose outsize shoulders and biceps made up for his lack of height went from dead serious to a megawatt grin so bright it made them both blink. "OS3 Griffin."

"What does OS stand for?" Kenai said.

"Operations specialist," Cutburth said. "OSC stands for operations specialist chief."

"And the ones, twos, and threes?"

"How high up you are in the pecking order. You go to school, you pass your tests, you break in at OS3, and move up."

"And you call each other by your job titles. Is that a Coastie thing?"

He nodded. "People change all the time, rotating in and out of duty stations, on and off ships. Job titles don't." He waved a hand at his domain, very much master of all he surveyed. "In Combat we coordinate search and rescue operations. We collect and disseminate intel." Nods all around. "And of course, in a worst-case scenario, we fight the ship."

"We get to shoot the big gun," his number two, an OS1 Cortez, said. She was a slim blonde with an impish expression and a crackling personality. In spite of the diamond on her left hand Bill gravitated toward her the way a compass needle does to true north and for a few moments there Kenai was afraid she might have to walk home. "What's the big gun?" she said.

Mention of a firearm, especially a big one, naturally brought back Bill's attention. Chief Cutburth whistled up GMC Colvin, the gunner's mate chief, a compact man who looked made entirely of muscle, with an air of authority either natural or cultivated—probably a bit of both, Kenai decided—that made everyone stand straighter in his presence.

Chief Colvin gave them a tour of the 76mm gun on the gun deck, forward of the boat deck and two decks below the bridge. The casings on the ammunition were three feet long and weighed anywhere from thirty-six to fifty-six pounds. It could fire four different kinds of ammunition up to eighty rounds a minute, and had a range of about six miles.

"Hell, you could take us out if you wanted to," Bill said, impressed.

"Please don't," Kenai said.

Chief Colvin's face broke into what Kenai was sure was a rare smile. "I'd love to show it off for you," he said regretfully, laying a hand on the 76mm's housing, "but it's impossible in port," and on that mournful note they were escorted to the hangar deck, where the aviation detachment—two aviators, a gunner, a swimmer, and a mechanic—was mustered.

"Helos," Bill said loud enough to be heard, with a grimace exaggerated enough to be seen by everyone on the flight deck.

Kenai gave an elaborate shudder. "They're sort of the bumblebees of the aviation world, aren't they? Amazing they ever get off the deck."

"And this, this is what we're relying on to haul our asses out of the drink if we go splash," Bill said, squinting at the helo with a gloomy expression. "Definitely a product of low-bid design."

The junior aviator, one Lieutenant Noyes, grinned and said sympathetically, "Fixed-wing types, I take it? Don't be nervous, girls, we'll recover said asses, and we won't need a mile of runway to do it."

Everyone laughed and relaxed, and Bill and Kenai got a hands-on demonstration when the AvDet did a turbo wash of the rotors, followed by a brief stop to admire the artwork on the inside of the door to the av shack. Kenai's favorite was the coastal outline of Mexico with the signatures of the AvDet from a 2000 EPAC patrol and the caption "No drug busts, no migrants, no real SAR, no reason to be here, 57 days!" Bill's favorite, naturally, was the upside-down helo with the caption "Will fly for beer!"

They were reacquired eventually by the XO and led forward, emerging on the boat deck. The XO helpfully pointed out a valve fixture protruding at head height from the bottom of the boat davit, labeled in hand-drawn letters "the Darwin sorter," which he said had sampled the DNA of a goodly number of the crew. They negotiated this hazard successfully, followed by two more sets of stairs, which he took at a hustle, and they perforce followed him at the same pace. "I'll take zero gee anytime," Kenai said to Bill. She hadn't meant the XO to hear her but like all good command cadre officers he had a highly developed sense of selective hearing and he paused to give her a sunny smile. He wasn't even out of breath.

On the deck just below the bridge the XO knocked at a door, behind which Captain Schuyler was waiting with drinks and sandwiches. Barely registering his presence on her peripheral vision, Kenai fell on them like a starving dog.

Once the twin threats of famine and dehydration had been staved off, Kenai noticed the sitting room was furnished with bronze leather furniture, cherry bookshelves that looked as if they had been built to spec, the latest model iPod docked in a stereo speaker system, and a luxurious carpet that looked fresh off a Persian loom and brought forward in time two thousand years.

She looked back at the skipper, whom she found regarding her with a considering blue gaze that reminded her of Robert Redford in *Butch Cassidy and the Sundance Kid*. "Cal Schuyler," he said, holding out a hand. "You remember, the captain? I would have said something before but I didn't want to get in between you and the food."

Bill choked over his soda and Kenai, well into her second sandwich, laughed out loud. Schuyler's gaze remained steady on her face for a long moment.

He had, he told them, taken command of the *Munro* just that August. "Our home port is actually Kodiak, Alaska. We should be doing an ALPAT—Alaska patrol—in the Bering right about now."

Surprised, Bill said, "What are you doing in Miami?"

Kenai was doing her best to look invisible but Schuyler wouldn't let her get away with it. "It's her fault." When she squirmed and Bill still looked blank,

Schuyler said, "She's related to Douglas Munro."

"Munro?" Bill said. The light dawned. "Oh. I didn't make the connection. Munro like the ship?"

"Exactly like the ship," the XO said. "Douglas Munro saved a bunch of Marines off Guadalcanal. He's the only Coastie to win the Medal of Honor."

"That's what the banner is above the lookout station," Kenai said. The captain nodded.

"Oh yeah," Bill said. "The blue banner with the white stars?"

The captain nodded. "Just like the Medal of Honor. Normally, we task a 210—that's a two-hundred-ten-foot cutter—to bulldog offshore security during a shuttle launch. This time"—he smiled at Kenai, and she caught the glint of mischief in his eyes—"this time the powers that be decided that since we had a relative of the only Coastie ever to win a Medal of Honor flying on the space shuttle, the least we could do was bring the ship named for him around to do the honors."

Munro was a week away from their first patrol during their Miami hiatus, doing drug interdiction and migrant interdiction in the Caribbean. "And any SAR case that crops up, of course, plus safety boardings and inspections."

"We'll do three months on patrol," the XO said, "and then three months in port. If everyone's schedule holds together, we should be on our last inport in Miami when you're getting ready to launch."

"What happens when we go up?" Kenai said.

"We'll be retasked," the captain said, and nodded at

78

the young mess cook standing silently next to the door with hands folded and expression anxious. "All right, Roberts, we're done." She came forward and cleared away the food and brought them coffee in large porcelain mugs embossed with the *Munro*'s seal, and offered cream and sugar around.

"Thanks, Roberts, that'll be all," Schuyler said.

She blushed and cast a covert glance at the astronauts. Kenai, replete with food and disinclined to move, said with real heroism, "Would you like the skipper to take your picture with us?" She got a hand under Bill's elbow and heaved the both of them to their feet, and the young seaman produced the camera that had been burning a hole in her pocket since they'd arrived. They posed and smiled, the camera flashed, the young seaman went on her way rejoicing, and the captain closed the door firmly behind her before anyone else on his crew could sidle inside. "We'll be retasked," he repeated, "as command for offshore security during your launch. We'll be on station as soon as they move your vehicle to the pad, and we'll be there until you're in orbit, coordinating security and, if necessary, SAR efforts."

He didn't pretty things up, did Captain Schuyler. "Let's hope it won't be necessary," Kenai said dryly, and he surprised her with a wide, dazzling grin that put interesting creases at the corners of his eyes and mouth. His eyes were very blue. Sailor's eyes. She thought he might be blond, but like every other male crew member she'd seen he'd shaved his head almost down to the scalp in preparation for sea showers on patrol and it was hard to tell. Come to think of it, he didn't look anything at all like Robert Redford. Robert Redford was a troll by comparison. "That'd be my plan, ma'am."

He escorted them out. At the head of the stairs leading to the boat deck, Kenai's love slave came up the gangway. He looked up, saw her, and hurtled himself up the boat deck with reckless abandon.

The shout came in unison from both XO and captain: "Look *out!*"

It wasn't in time. The CPO smacked into the Darwin sorter at a velocity that put Kenai forcibly in mind of a crash test dummy hitting a windshield. He went down, hard.

"OOD!" the captain shouted, and a moment later an inquiring face peeped around the hangar. "Pipe the corpsman to lay to the starboardside boat deck!"

The CPO had pulled himself to a sitting position by the time everyone reached him. Blood was flowing freely from his forehead where a knot the size of a golf ball was already rising to attention. The corpsman, a tall man with gentle hands and a grave bedside manner belied by eyes brimming with laughter, assisted him to his feet and took him off to sick bay.

"I'll get you another driver," Captain Schuyler said. At the gangway Schuyler touched Kenai briefly on the elbow. She let Bill go down ahead of her.

"You staying in town tonight?" Schuyler said.

"We are," she said, refusing to let her smile show past her eyes.

There was an answering smile in his own. "Seven o'clock? I know a place where they brew the beer out back and the steak comes to the table still mooing."

"Sure," she said, "but I can't stay out late, early flight home tomorrow."

He stepped back and gestured at the gangway. As she passed he said in a low voice meant only for her ears, "Not a problem."

HE PRESENTED HIMSELF PROMPTLY AT SEVEN P.M. AT HER hotel room door, dressed in deck shoes and a blue polo shirt tucked neatly into tan chinos. She was dressed equally casually, hot pink tank top, white slacks, and strappy little sandals that revealed nail polish to match the tank top. "Pretty in pink," he said.

She smiled. "Thanks."

He looked past her. "How's the room?"

"Palatial. See for yourself."

He displayed a bottle. "A drink before we go out?"

"Veuve Clicquot? I like your taste in drinks."

He nodded at the balcony, visible through the sliding glass doors. "Have a seat. I'll bring them out."

It was a beautiful evening, nothing left of the sun but a band of color that matched her tank top on the horizon, stars appearing overhead, the air on the balcony soft on the skin. The pop of the cork sounded behind her. Kenai pulled the chairs to the edge of the balcony and sat down in one and crossed her feet on the railing, Biscayne Bay, the Miami skyline, and the Atlantic in front of her. "Is it Callan?" she said when

81

he brought the glasses, gently fizzing.

"Cal," he said, raising his glass to hers. "From Callan. Family name. My father's side of the family is very big with the passing on of family names. Where's the Kenai come from?"

"The Kenai River. It's in Alaska."

"Sure, where all the big salmon go home to die."

"I was raised on it."

"Your dad a fisherman?"

She shook her head. "A pilot."

"Sure, how you learned to fly. Brothers, sisters?"

"Nope. You?"

"No. You know what they say about only children."

"Overachievers R Us."

He laughed. "When did you decide you wanted to be an astronaut?"

"What, you haven't read the press release?" She drank champagne, dry, a shivering along the tongue, delicious. "Again, I applaud your taste in wine." She looked at him, broad shoulders, strong throat, firm chin, mouth hovering always on the edge of a smile, eyes so blue. She put down her glass and knotted a hand in the front of his shirt and pulled. Irresistibly he leaned forward until their lips were almost touching. "Close your eyes," she said, her voice the merest breath of sound.

Obediently, he closed them. She rescued his forgotten glass, which was about to tip out of his hand, and set it on the table next to hers. She turned back to see his eyes still closed, and noticed that his breath was coming a little faster. She rubbed her face lightly against his, nose, lips, cheeks, a long extended nuzzle that branded him with her scent, a faint, flowery perfume, a hint of Tide, and a growing muskiness that spoke of her own arousal. He shifted to ease the sudden tightness of his chinos. "Be still," she said, and kissed him, a long, warm, wet, sensuous invitation, and nipped his lip as she drew away.

His eyes opened, dazed, and she said, her voice husky with laughter and desire, "In just fourteen hours from now, I'll be on a plane heading north and west. I don't have time to dance."

She watched as his eyes focused and narrowed. His hand came up and traced the neckline of her top, lingering at the exposed cleft of her breasts. A wave of heat started there and flooded south, loosening her thighs. His hand slipped between them, to press his palm firmly against her.

"Oh," she said, breathlessly, and let her hand slide down over his and press. He lunged out of his chair and tossed her up into his arms. Once inside, he let her slip down the front of his body until her cleft rested against his erection.

"Oh," she said again, and made an involuntary movement, lifting her hips to invite and encourage. Her head fell back. "Oh," she said, this time drawing out the word on a note of discovery and desire. It was like being struck by lightning. They began to tear at each other's clothes, fumbling in their haste, stopping only to snatch a kiss or a caress, their urgency overriding the desire to linger over every piece of newly exposed skin. She wasn't wearing a bra and he descended on the nipples beneath the hot pink tank top that had so tantalized him with lips and teeth. He had never felt so ravenous for the taste of a woman. She cried out once and he stopped, afraid he'd hurt her. "No," she said, her voice hardly recognizable, "harder."

She'd never felt so hot, she could hardly breathe for it. She couldn't speak, she couldn't see, she could only feel. He fell to his knees and opened her up like a ripe, sweet melon, feasting greedily, and she came in a powerful, rolling wave that robbed her legs of the little strength she had left. He swore softly and caught her, easing her down, kneeing her legs apart and coming between them, frantic with the need to get inside her. "Jesus," he said, sounding as astonished as she felt, almost trembling with need, and thrust into her.

"Oh!" she said, her head going back, her legs coming up around his waist.

He tried to slow down, to take his time, to wait for her, and he might have been able to, if she hadn't latched on to his ass with both hands and said between her teeth, "Harder."

IN THE END THEY ORDERED UP ROOM SERVICE. SHE CAME out of the bathroom, knotting the robe at her waist as he was signing the check. The door closed behind the bellman, who she was glad to note was too well trained to gawk. NASA no longer expected its astronauts to be as whitewashed as the original Seven, but there was a long line of them waiting for shuttle assignments and the Madonna was always going to be preferred over the whore.

The room was in fact palatial, with a bed the size of a trampoline and the balcony overlooking Biscayne Bay that was only slightly smaller. "The hotel must be running a special, or it's empty," she said. "I don't ever remember NASA paying for a room like this." She raised an eyebrow in his direction.

The fizz had gone out of the bottle he'd brought and he'd ordered up another with their meal. He popped the cork and poured. "I confess, I made a call after you left the ship, and had your room, uh, upgraded."

She grinned, approving of his light manner. She didn't know what had just happened but she knew she didn't want to talk about it. "I'll say."

"You're not angry?"

She laughed and accepted the glass he held out to her. The clock on the nightstand read eight o'clock and she and Bill were scheduled for departure at nine the next morning. "One glass more after this one," she said, "two maximum is my limit for tonight."

They raised their glasses to each other and sipped. "So, Kenai," he said as they settled back into their chairs on the balcony.

He was evidently as determined to keep things light as she was, and she approved, but the muscles in her thighs felt pleasantly sore and she smiled to herself. "I was born in Seldovia on Kachemak Bay, went to high school in Homer across the bay, went to college—first time—at the University of Alaska–Anchorage. BA in English."

"English?"

"English."

"Sorry," he said, "kinda expecting, I don't know, astrophysics."

"Try electrical engineering," she said. "The doctorate, anyway. That was later, at the University of Washington."

"Yeah," he said, "and the master's?"

"Also electrical engineering, also U-Dub. You?"

"I have not achieved the rarified air of the doctorate," he said, and she accepted his bow of mock humility with a queenly nod, spoiling it with an infectious giggle that would have had him on his knees if he hadn't caught himself. Whoa there, fella, he thought. "Just a couple of lowly masters," he said, "one in organizational administration and the other in strategic studies."

"Where?"

He grinned. "Harvard and the Naval War College."

She thought of the sheikling her mission had just inherited and said ruefully, "Wanna go for a ride?"

"What?"

She shrugged and drank champagne. "Probably no harm in telling you, it'll be all over the news soon enough."

He heard her out, and at the end of it said, "Hard on the rest of the astronauts waiting to be assigned to their own missions."

She was surprised at his instant comprehension, and grateful. "Exactly."

"And," he added, continuing to follow her thoughts with an accuracy that made her distinctly uneasy, "I hate taking on new crew the day I'm supposed to leave the dock. Taking on an untrained, unknown crewman on a space shuttle mission seems to me to be a thousand times more dangerous. Short of an actual sinking, there isn't a hell of a lot an inexperienced crewman can do to *Munro*. But to *Endeavour*?"

She nodded. "Yes," she said, serious, "very dangerous. You should hear the stories the other crews tell about getting stuck with a part-timer." She sipped champagne. Again, excellent, dry and crisp. She looked at him with approval. "Worst story I ever heard. His experiment broke, he had a gold medal case of space sickness, and he couldn't defecate. Seven days on orbit, this guy's constipated, puking nonstop, and his entire reason for being on board has just gone away. The CDR said he thought he was going to have to put the guy on a suicide watch."

Cal laughed before he could stop himself. "Sorry," he said.

She chuckled. "No, it's okay. It is funny and they made it home in one piece." Her smile faded. "But the last thing we need on orbit is no faith in a crewmate. One of these days one of these part-timers is going to elbow the wrong switch and the mission's going to go balls up."

"I see they're retiring the space shuttle," he said.

"Not before I get my turn," she said, and he laughed again. "How'd you get to be captain of one of the biggest ships in the Coast Guard fleet?"

"Grew up in Massachusetts, where we spent the summers in Cape Cod in a house with its own boat dock that was never without a boat. Can't remember sailing for the first time, but it was probably before I could read." He smiled, reminiscent. His mother loved sailing, too. Aside from the fact that his father was (a) loaded, (b) Beacon Hill aristocracy, and (c) on his way to becoming a U.S. senator for the first time, that he owned his own sailboat was probably why she had married him. It was the one uncontested point of reference between mother and child. He shook his head and smiled at the woman next to him, admiring the sight of toned muscle beneath smooth skin as her bathrobe slid from her shoulder, revealing the curve of one breast. She saw him watching, and didn't pull her robe closed. "Any day I get a ride on a boat is a good day for me," he said. "It's all I ever wanted."

She nodded, understanding without question. "All I ever wanted to do was fly."

The sun had faded completely into the west. The glow of lights from the Miami skyline was subsumed by a star-covered sky. There were faint sounds of traffic from the street below. "Married?" he said, much more idly than he felt.

"Wouldn't be here if I was."

Her answer was firm and she met his eyes straight on. She meant it. He nodded. "Understood. Me, either.

Ever really listen to those vows?"

" 'For richer or poorer, in sickness and in health'?"

" 'Forsaking all others, so long as you both shall live'?"

They shivered in unison. "Very scary," he said. "Nope, I'm a practicing coward. Never had the guts."

"I heard that," she said. "And, you know, the job."

"And the job," he said. He put down his glass and reached out to brush her hair out of her eyes. It was short and silky, and her eyes were big and brown with laugh lines gathering at the corners. He slipped one hand behind her head and pulled her into a kiss while the other untied her robe and slipped inside to explore.

She pulled back and said a little breathlessly, "Possibly we should go back inside."

His eyes were very blue, their pupils a little enlarged, the corners crinkling as he answered her smile with his own. "Possibly we should."

They were in less of a hurry this time—they even made it to the bed—and the result was even more satisfactory.

The next morning he said, trying not to invest the question with anything more than a casual interest, "You get down to Florida a lot?"

She said, trying not to look as pleased as she felt, "You get to Houston much?"

"There are ways," he said.

"Yes," she said, "there are."

5

In spite of Patrick's best efforts, it hadn't taken long before Khalid's version of Kallendorf's all! new! and improved! plan for agency operations was setting off ring tones and melting down blogs all over Washington. Well, nothing Patrick could do about that, or about the fact that three months later Khalid was exiled to the U.S. Embassy in Tajikistan.

Patrick had spent the year since collating and culling information on terrorist activities foreign and domestic, real, planned, anticipated, and suspected, trying to match events to perpetrators, and failing signally. He wasn't dismayed, or even disappointed. Such was the nature of intel on prospective guerilla warfare actions that too much of it was gleaned after the fact. The forces arrayed against al Qaeda and all its offspring were oftentimes too slow to recognize a threat. When at last it was recognized, action was all too often stifled in a welter of interagency and international rivalries and protocols, not to mention the occasional ripe diplomatic snafu.

He spent as much time as he could justify collecting data on Isa. Something about the shadowy figure—the ballsy name, perhaps? the Baghdad bombing, which had been the very model of the modern urban terrorist attack?—had captured his imagination. He was determined to gain on this man, and he would spare no energy, no agency resource until he had his hand on Isa's shoulder.

His wife had divorced him two years before. They'd been unable to have children, and he'd signed over the house so he didn't even have a lawn to mow. It had been pretty bloodless, all things considered, a marriage contracted in the fumes of a college lust that faded soon after graduation, leaving behind a civility that over time chilled into indifference. He was grateful that she'd had the courage to make the break, and they were both relieved when it was over. She had already remarried, relieving him of any guilt or anxiety over how she was getting along. There was nothing to distract him from the job at hand. Truth to tell, he'd always been more interested in it than in his marriage.

One day, when he'd assimilated as much information as he could hold, he told his assistant that he wasn't in and closed the door on her disapproving but unsurprised face. With movements that had become ritual, he sat, carefully unbuttoning the jacket of his three-piece bespoke suit, swiveled his desk chair to face the window, propped his feet up on the windowsill, folded his hands over the incipient potbelly that didn't worry him as much as the hairline which appeared to be in full retreat from his forehead, both aging him beyond his forty-two years, and regarded the well-polished toes of his black wingtips with a contemplative frown.

Patrick Chisum was that complete anathema to incoming administrations everywhere, a bureaucrat, one of those bland, behind-the-scenes figures, the nameless, faceless legion of laborers that kept the wheels of governance creaking along in spite of all the posturing on Pennsylvania Avenue and the Hill. He had a very fair idea of his own value, and it didn't take long for every new administration that swept into Washington promising to reduce spending beginning with the federal payroll to learn that Patrick Chisum and his knowledgeable brethren were all that kept the nation one step ahead of chaos.

He wasn't worried about Kallendorf's legendary line-clearing abilities. Patrick had been recruited into the agency right out of Yale, the ink still wet on his advanced degree in Islamic studies, and over the last twenty years he'd worked his way steadily up the ranks until he achieved his goal, the Middle East desk, specializing in terrorist groups beginning with Osama bin Laden, whose chief characteristic so far as Patrick was concerned was that, like the Hydra, each time one group was destroyed and its members captured or killed, another two groups sprang up in its place. It took unending patience, a sharp appetite for detail, and a wealth of experience to disentangle the various Islamic terrorism groups and separate them out as targets for observation and either arrest or elimination. Without vanity, Patrick knew that he was essential to that effort. The posturing of appointed rentapols who served solely at the pleasure of the president was far less important than the job at hand.

But Kallendorf was right in one respect. American

intelligence agencies had degenerated into an international joke. There were too many of them; CIA, FBI, DIA, NSA, the individual intel-gathering agencies of the Army, Navy, and Air Force, and the list went on and on, all getting in each other's way, stepping on each other's toes, fighting battles over turf instead of fighting the enemy, refusing to share intelligence or alert one another to ongoing operations. Collectively, they had failed utterly to predict the fall of the Berlin Wall, which caught the first Bush administration totally unprepared to deal with the disintegration of the USSR and the sudden independence of Warsaw Pact states. They had ignored their own agents' warnings of terrorist activity within American borders prior to 9/11, the FBI being most grievously at fault here. But his own agency was far from guiltless, having signed off on the WMD in Iraq, and later on Saddam's links with al Qaeda.

Their wholesale failure to anticipate the rise of the sectarian insurgency in Iraq and the return of the Taliban in Afghanistan, the consequences of which played out on every television in America at six P.M. and ten P.M. each night, had led to a disgust for the ruling party that the American electorate had made manifest in the last election. Everyone but the man in the White House seemed to know that it was only a matter of time before the United States suffered its own regime change.

If Patrick wanted to take it personally, those failures and others had led almost directly to the swearing in of

Harold Kallendorf as director of the Central Intelligence Agency. He had been given an unusually united mandate from both Congress and White House to shake up the institution, fire the deadwood, and streamline and update the intelligence-gathering process, with the desired end result an improvement in product accuracy and an increase in the speed of its delivery. Hence, the review in the briefing room in January.

But that wasn't what had him frowning at his wingtips. Kallendorf's idea of reaching out to an agency not their own wasn't necessarily a bad one. Especially when an old friend was at the other end of the line.

He'd just returned from Guantánamo Bay, where he had observed the interrogation of a young Jordanian named Karim Talib. He'd been picked up in a sweep of Fallujah six months ago, and the gators at Gitmo had finally broken him the week before. One of them, an old friend of Patrick's well aware of his new obsession, had called Patrick and said that he might like to hear this in person. Bob's tip-offs were usually pretty solid, so Patrick had hopped a C-12 out of Andrews and been present on the other side of the glass when Bob, a not unintimidating figure, leaned over the young Muslim man whom he must have outweighed by a hundred pounds and purred, "Now. What was it you were telling us yesterday, Karim?" When Karim said nothing Bob let the purr drop to a menacing growl. "Now, Karim, you don't want me to have to jog your memory, do you?" He smiled at Karim, lips pulled back to reveal a set of canines that looked ready and able to rip into raw meat.

Karim didn't look as if he had any intention of resisting, but his teeth were chattering so loudly that he could hardly get the words out.

"You worked for Isa," Bob said.

Behind the glass, Patrick stiffened.

"Y-y-y-yes," Karim said.

"From when to when?" Bob said.

"F-f-f-from 2003 until you k-k-killed Zarqawi."

"Three years. You must know him pretty well."

A spark of defiance gleamed in the young man's eyes. "Y-y-you'll never catch him."

"I'm sure you're right," Bob said cordially, and pulled up a chair. He gave Karim's knee a comforting pat. "I want you to tell me all about your time with him, Karim. Everything, every tiny little detail you can remember." He smiled at Karim again and Karim flinched back. "Take your time. I've got all day."

"I-I-I already t-t-told you everything I know."

"I don't think so," Bob said cheerfully, and gave Karim's knee another encouraging pat. "Start talking."

"W-w-what do I get if I do?"

Patrick had to admire the little terrorist. Terrified as he was, he was still trying to bargain.

Bob shrugged and worked his head. His neck cracked with a loud pop and Karim jumped so hard it moved his chair a couple of inches across the floor. "What do you get?" He smiled again at Karim.

"Maybe I let you live to see the dawn."

Karim, who evidently got most of his courage from putting together bombs to be detonated far from his person, started talking. A lot of it Patrick already knew, such as Isa's predilection for and proficiency at Internet banking and communications. The particulars of Isa's dispersal of Zarqawi's cell after Zarqawi's death were news. Isa dispensing with the services of a group of men he and Zarqawi had trained from terrorist infancy seemed wasteful. Why cut loose your experienced personnel, when you had so much time invested in them?

Answer, Patrick thought, because one of them betrayed your boss. You don't know which one, all you know is it wasn't you, so better to cut them all loose. Even wimpy little Karim.

Karim, now weeping over his own betrayal, knew more than he would say about the bombing in Baghdad and nothing at all about Isa's current whereabouts. He drew a heartrending picture of his and Isa's farewell in the Damascus airport. "I didn't know where to go," he said, sniveling. "I didn't know what to do. So I went back."

Patrick shook his head. Embarrassing.

The speaker was quiet for a moment, but for Karim's sniffling. "Almost the last thing he said to me," Karim said wearily, "was a quote from your president Bush."

"Oh?" Bob said, bored. "What was that?"

"He said that Bush said that it was better to fight us on our ground than for the Americans to fight us on theirs."

"Oh, yeah?" Bob said.

Irritated at Bob's apparent lack of interest, the little terrorist said with a snap, "And then he said that he thought Bush was right."

Shortly thereafter Bob joined Patrick over a cup of coffee before Patrick headed north again. "What do you think?"

"Is he gay?" Patrick said. "He sounds like he's in love with Isa."

"Something we'd thought of, too, he talks like Isa jilted him in Damascus," Bob said. "He didn't write, he didn't call, it's all one long moan." He cocked an eye at Patrick. "Anything you can use?"

"It's all grist for the mill, Bob," Patrick said thoughtfully. "He was in on that bus bombing in Baghdad."

"Ya think?" Bob said. "I'm going to sweat the little weasel until he tells me exactly how he designed and built that bomb, every nut, every bolt, every wire. I want to know where he got the parts, what the original target was, who picked it, who changed the target and why, and who gave the order for execution. When I have a confession, signed, witnessed, notarized, recorded on tape and on video, then at least, even if they won't let us hang him, he won't be exercising that talent on the streets of anyone's town ever again."

Patrick's driver poked his head in the door. "Time to go, Mr. Chisum."

Patrick drained his mug. "I appreciate the call, Bob, thanks."

"Thanks for the newspapers and the magazines and

the smokes," Bob said. "See you next time."

No, Patrick thought now, it didn't hurt to ask a friend for help. His mind made up, he dropped his feet and swiveled back to his desk. He dialed twice before remembering to get his secretary to turn the phone back on, and then he had to redial because he got the country code wrong and wound up talking to a Josie Ryan in Limerick. They had a delightful conversation about the menu for the family dinner she was serving to her husband, Gerry, two daughters, and three sons (a fourth had moved to Alaska, probably partially due to the amount of grandchildren now in evidence). She inquired after Patrick's plans for the holiday, clucked her tongue over his having none, and extended an invitation. He declined with sincere regret and redialed. There was a brief silence, the double rings of the European telephone, and a click. "Knightsbridge Institute."

"Patrick Chisum for Hugh Rincon."

"One moment, please."

It was more like five before he was rescued from Muzak hell. No one ever played Yo-Yo Ma on hold. "Patrick?"

"Hello, Hugh. How are you?"

"Fine. What's it been, two wars?"

"More like three," Patrick said, "but who's counting. How's London? How's Sara?"

"Both good."

"She still stuck at the IMO?"

Hugh sighed. "Yeah, for a second tour."

"The people who make those assignments could be changing."

"So we saw," Hugh said, and left it at that.

Patrick respected the reticence. Hugh Rincon was ex-agency, married to an XO in the U.S. Coast Guard. They'd been involved in a lively adventure involving North Korean terrorists in the North Pacific a few years back, and the fallout had included Hugh's resignation from the agency and Sara's exile to the International Maritime Organization. Rumor had it she'd lipped off to the president himself, in the Oval Office no less, but Patrick doubted a career officer would put her future in such jeopardy and took the rumor with a large grain of salt.

Hugh had followed her to London, where he had signed on with the Knightsbridge Institute, an extremely well-funded global think tank which produced ruthlessly researched papers on subjects ranging from China's embrace of the free market to the military preparedness of Dakar to the economic impact on Central and South America of the legalization of drugs in America. The Institute was known for having the best resources available on every possible global topic whether it be speculation or reality. Patrick faced up to the fact that this was going to cost him. "I've got the Middle East desk, Hugh."

"What happened to Harvey Moskowitz?"

"Retired last year."

"His idea?"

"No."

"Figures. If you're going to screw up, first thing you have to do is get rid of anyone who might have a clue." A pause. "I was an Asia desk man myself, Patrick."

"I know, but you've moved onward and upward. I need your help on a little project."

There was a smile in Hugh's voice when he replied. "I don't think the U.S. government can afford me."

"If we can afford the Mossad, we can afford you."

"What?"

"It's a long story. Let me run my topic by you first," Patrick said. "I'm tracking a terrorist calling himself Isa."

"Head of Abdullah," Hugh said immediately, and Patrick could hear keys clicking in the background, "formerly of the Zarqawi group, believed to have formed his own group after Zarqawi's death, responsible for the bus bombing in Baghdad in, what was it, December oh-five. That Isa?"

"That's the one."

"Never heard of him."

It surprised a laugh out of Patrick. "Very funny." He sobered. "This guy isn't done, Hugh. I've got all kinds of rumors filtering in through the usual sources and a few unusual ones." Patrick told Hugh about Karim. "I think Isa's recruiting and I think he's got plans. Just one time I'd like to get the jump on one of these bastards."

"Yeah, I heard about just missing al-Zawahiri. Bad luck." That blown operation had been all over the front pages for weeks now. "You think you got another mole at Langley?"

"That, or bin Laden's intel is better than ours."

Which wouldn't be hard, both of them thought and Rincon charitably didn't say. "What do you need, Patrick?"

"Anything you've got on him. Anything you can get on him until he's either dead or my beck-and-call boy in Gitmo."

"All right. I'll put together a package and send it over. Along with a rate schedule."

"Yeah, yeah."

"Payable upon delivery, Patrick. You sure the new man will go for that?"

Patrick thought back to Kallendorf's first briefing. "The new man will go for anything that gets results."

AFGHANISTAN, DECEMBER 2006

"Never doubt that they are looking for him, master. It is only a matter of time. They will find him, and they will interrogate him, and he will tell them everything he knows about us."

"Do you tell me that he will betray us? Has Isa ever proved himself disloyal, in all his years of service?"

Ansar covered his slip smoothly. "Not of his own will, master, certainly. But it is well known by those who know that no man can long bear torture without offering everything he has to make it stop."

"He could lie."

"He could." Ansar let his response lie there without elaboration. It needed none, and he knew it.

The old man meditated on this intelligence, so long that the rest of them wondered if he'd fallen asleep.

At last he stirred. A frail hand came up to comb his beard. "Is there tea?"

There was a brief hiatus in the discussion while hot mint tea in thick glasses was brought on a silver tray carried by a thin boy with curious eyes. He served the old man first, and set the tray on the rug in the middle of the circle of men. He retreated to the door and loitered there, hoping to remain. He was frustrated in this when he intercepted a dismissive scowl, and slunk out.

The wooden door closed with not quite a slam, raising a rectangular puff of dust from the mud brick walls surrounding it. The dust caught in the single ray of thin winter sunshine streaming in through the window and hung motionless in the still air. The old man coughed, and sipped his tea. It brought color to his pale, drawn cheeks. "Zarqawi trusted him."

They exchanged glances. "He did," one of them said, "but, and forgive me, master, as we all know, Zarqawi Musab al-Zarqawi was ruled more by his instincts than by his intellect. It is entirely possible that he was . . . deceived."

"Still, Ansar, in how many years, did Isa ever fail him?"

"Then who betrayed Zarqawi?" the first speaker said bluntly.

"You think it was Isa?"

"I do," Ansar said firmly. He may have had doubts but this was about power. There was no room for uncertainties in this argument. The old man was in poor health. After the first attacks that had toppled the government, after the American forces' attention had been redirected to Iraq, he had never been in any real danger of apprehension, but a life lived on the run, even with the resources the old man had, was wearing on the individual. And on his organization.

The old man meditated over his tea, the veins in his hands standing out beneath the soft folds of crepe skin. His thin body looked lost in the folds of his robes. "How did they find out about the bus bombing in Baghdad?"

They exchanged glances. "He told them, master."

"After, yes." The old man sipped his tea. "Of course, it is natural to wish to take credit for a blow dealt on behalf of the one true God. Allahu akbar."

"Allahu akbar," came in a soft murmur in reply.

"But someone told them of the attack before it happened. They were waiting for him. They nearly caught him. The bus was a target of opportunity, not the intended one. And even then, I don't think he would have told, had credit not been given wrongly to al-Zawahiri."

There was silence. Into it the old man said, his voice a gentle thread of sound, "It was the last time they have gotten close to him." He sipped tea. "I notice also that we have not heard from him directly since Zarqawi died. Is this not so?"

Uncertain glances were exchanged.

"Almost six months," the old man said.

There was a murmur of agreement. Ansar said boldly, "All the more reason to find him, master. I say this not out of distrust or a wish to punish, only to discover information. If he is planning an attack, we should know of it."

The old man shifted on his pillows. Courteously, Ansar leaned over and put a hand to his elbow to help him, and received equally courteous thanks.

When the old man spoke again his voice was thready but perfectly audible. "I have a wish to see Isa again, to speak with him, to take counsel of him."

Ansar could say only, "Yes, master."

"And if he should somehow have become convinced that I would no longer greet him as brother, that my arms are no longer open to embrace him . . ." The old man let his voice trail away.

Ansar leaned in to catch the fading words, and for the first time since they had entered the room, the old man's eyes opened. He looked at Ansar with a cold, clear, steady gaze that entirely belied the air of frailty that clung to him.

"And, Ansar," he said, that bare thread of sound somehow infused with a sudden menace, "if I thought that Isa had been betrayed to the infidel, I would spare no effort to discover the traitor in our midst."

In spite of the chill mountain air that penetrated the room, Ansar found himself sweating. There was only one answer. "Yes, master."

The old man nodded once and gave a dismissive wave. "Leave me."

They filed out, their robes sweeping the dirt floor of the house as they went. Outside, the pale December sunshine filtered down through the steep sides of the valley, an inconsequential and transient warmth. It was a tiny village, the houses built around a spring-fed pool. Above the village was a long, man-made cave that had once been home to a Buddhist shrine, the figures and paintings long since destroyed by the mullahs. The road that led to the village was wide enough for a motorcycle and no more. The road, the houses, the sparse vegetation, the rocky outcroppings of tor and crag, all were covered with a thick layer of snow, the top of which had frozen into a hard crust of ice. From the direction of the spring they heard the chop of an ax. A woman covered in black from head to toe came out with a tray of feed, and hens gathered round her skirts, clucking. There was no other sound.

"How long has he been here?" Ansar said.

"Two months," Bilal said.

Ansar shivered.

"Ansar," Bilal said.

"What?"

"Does he truly think Isa was betrayed to the West? And that one of us betrayed him?"

Ansar, his equilibrium restored by the cold bite of the winter air, said, "He is old. The old have fancies."

Bilal noticed that Ansar took care to keep his voice down so the rest of them could not hear, and lowered his own voice accordingly. "But he is right. They were waiting for Isa in Baghdad. He barely escaped."

"But he did escape," Ansar said.

"You sound as if you wished he hadn't."

Ansar shrugged. "It is true, I don't trust him. He is not one of us. He was educated in the West. And someone betrayed our brother Zarqawi to the infidels."

"You think it was Isa?"

"I think Isa is not the first person to be seduced by his own ambition." Ansar's eyes strayed to the tiny cottage from which they had just emerged. "And he won't be the last."

Bilal looked troubled, and Ansar slapped him on the back. "Come! Let us return before the light is gone, and we are lost and fit only for food for the wolves."

"And Isa?"

"I will send word." Ansar gave an elaborate shrug. "What Isa does when he receives it is another matter."

"What happens if he does not come?"

"The old man can send word." Ansar's smile was thin and humorless. "What he does when Isa does not respond is another matter."

A WEEK LATER IN AN INTERNET CAFÉ IN ISLAMABAD, A message duly went out. A month later, when there was still no response, this was reported to the old man.

He sighed and covered his eyes. After a moment he dropped his hand. "Find him," he said. "Find him and bring him to me."

6

If 9/11 had taught them anything it was that the simplest plan was the best plan. A small cell, independent, autonomous, well-funded. A clearly defined target. A strong leader to give the cell a focus, and to help them keep it. And most important, a clearly stated expectation of results, which Akil had found to be most motivational. Not a threat of what would happen if there were no results, no, no, nothing so crude, but the implication was there, and he made sure it was frequently reinforced.

Money was the least of his worries, a huge relief, but over the past twelve months since Zarqawi's death and his departure from Iraq, he had taken the precaution of emptying out the account in Bern in small increments and placing them into a series of other accounts in various banks in different Western nations. He had learned a great deal answering the phone for the bank in Hayatabad all those years ago, Zarqawi had filled in the blanks he hadn't been able to fill in for himself, and he put it all to good use now.

The result was a tidy sum of working capital resting anonymously in three different bank accounts, one in the Grand Caymans, one in Hong Kong, and the third in the original bank in Bern, naturally under a different name. Sooner or later, al Qaeda would come looking for that money, and he wanted to be certain it would be well out of their reach.

Sooner or later, they would come looking for him, too, and they wouldn't stop until they found him.

Or until he returned to them, trailing clouds of glory, his own man, master of his own wildly successful organization, and owing fealty to none. He smiled at the thought.

He opened two more accounts, one in New York and another in Miami, with the minimum balance necessary to avoid fees. One of the things he despised most about capitalism was the rapacious capacity of Western banking institutions to bleed their customers dry in fees. Did not the Koran say that which you give that it may increase your wealth has no increase in Allah, but that which you give in charity shall have manifold increase?

But then so much of Western culture was haraam. It amused him to use their own unclean practices to bring them down, and this was where his time in the West informed his actions. He'd chosen the American banks on the basis of the quality and efficiency of their web sites, and set up an automatic bill pay plan to deposit monthly amounts from one to another that approximated a credit card payment and a car payment, respectively. Nothing was more sure to draw unwanted attention than sums of money sitting idle, thereby accruing no income to their hosts.

All this took time, since haste in withdrawals and deposits was another flag for official attention, but he was in no hurry. He got a job drawing blueprints for the new Düsseldorf airport extension and worked himself seamlessly into the local expatriate Muslim community, forging friendships with young Muslim men of promise.

Identifying likely recruits was never difficult, especially since the West had seeded the ground so well for the introduction of Muslim extremism. Everything about their various societies, their creeping secularism, their capitalistic greed, their abominably unfettered women, and above all their support for the state of Israel and their acquiescence to the subsequent subjection of Palestine, affronted the very ideals of Islam, firing the imams to denunciations and calls for action that fell on ready ears. The resulting harvest of disaffected young men was thick on the ground in every Western nation and ripe for the picking.

Germany was no different. As in France, England, and Austria, Muslims, imported for cheap labor, had taken up residency and settled in to produce a second generation that by features, coloring, and dress alone were guaranteed to grow up isolated, alienated, and angry about it. In Düsseldorf there was a small, provincial colony of them, and within this colony Akil looked to replenish the cell of Abdullah.

One man, Rashid Guhl, seemed at first very promising, bright, inarticulate, and a rapt follower of the local imam who preached a carefully obscure jihad against the Far Enemy every Friday from the local mosque. Isa cultivated Rashid's friendship over some months, and then Rashid repaid him by falling suddenly in love with the daughter of the owner of an appliance store. Isa knew better than to try to talk him out of it, instead attending the wedding to wish Rashid and his new bride the very best of luck, but afterward he allowed himself to withdraw gradually from Rashid's new life. There was nothing more debilitating to a sense of mission than family entanglements.

Instead he concentrated on Yussuf al-Dagma and Yaqub Sadiq, Yussuf another engineer in his own firm, and Yaqub Yussuf's best friend from childhood, now a traffic engineer in Düsseldorf. Both were of Lebanese descent, with parents who had immigrated in search of relief from the constant conflict with Israel. Both were single. Both spoke English, albeit with the hideous British accent of their primary schoolteacher, and both held dual citizenship in Germany and Lebanon. Neither was quite as religious as Rashid, who was now beating his Western-born wife into wearing the hijab, and Yaqub was something of a ladies' man and a little erratic. They both regarded themselves as strangers in a strange land, though, and Akil played on that sense of exile. It was not to be expected that these men, softened by a birth and an upbringing in a Western culture that at least pretended to tolerance, would be of that same burning, single-minded drive and that matchless experience and ability as his original men, veterans of the streets of Gaza and Beirut. He did not dare show his face in either place, however, not yet, and so had to make do with the clay at hand.

The three of them took to meeting over coffee after work and talking long into the night, the core of a group of young men with shared feelings of dislocation from their homelands, of not fitting into their new worlds whether they'd been born into them or not, and of revulsion of Western mores from the consumption of alcohol to the length of women's skirts to Western, particularly American, imperialism. To them, the invasion of Iraq was a crusade, nothing less, the first wave of the attempt to subjugate and then obliterate Islam from the world.

Some of the hotheads in the group began speaking outwardly of taking direct action, of targeting local unbelievers for retribution. "The Jews," someone said, and someone else laughed and said, "Are there any Jews left in Germany?" Akil said nothing to encourage them, but neither did he say anything to discourage them, maintaining a silence in which the others read what they wished to read. Incidents of broken windows and assaults soon followed, with a great deal of boastful swaggering after the fact. When no repercussions were forthcoming, a Muslim woman who was seen talking to a German shopkeeper was beaten on the street, and a Protestant church with a woman priest was vandalized.

Akil used the resulting hubbub to suggest that he, Yussuf, and Yaqub begin to meet elsewhere. They agreed. Another man, Basil ben Hasn, overheard and volunteered to join them. Yussuf and Yaqub made him welcome and Akil concealed his displeasure. He didn't like Basil. The young man listened too much and spoke too little, making it difficult to see into his heart. And he was from Jordan, a nation notorious for collaborating with the United States. Bin Laden was not altogether wrong in his distrust of them, they had betrayed too many fighters to the West, some of whom Akil had known personally, and some of whom were now rotting in Guantánamo Bay.

And one of whom had very probably betrayed his master.

If he was wary of enemy action, he was far more alert to the possibility of action by his so-called friends. So, instead of moving their meeting to his living room and giving his fixed location away to anyone who might be interested enough to follow them, they moved to another coffeehouse at the edge of the neighborhood. It was far enough away from the first one to separate themselves from the first establishment's patrons, but close enough that when a week later the riot began they heard the noise from five streets away and ran to investigate.

It was a scene of chaos, drifts of tear gas making their eyes water, men shouting, women screaming, police with riot shields striking at everyone within reach of their clubs. With a faint shock Akil realized that their intent was to contain the inhabitants of the coffee shop where he had first begun to meet with his recruits. The line of officers tightened, one bloody Muslim head at a time. When someone fell, they were dragged away and tossed into the back of a police van.

One of the victims was Rashid's new wife, her veil twisted in a tumble of long black hair, her face bruised and bloody. Akil wondered what she was doing out so late, and resolutely banished the memories of Adara the sight brought to mind.

The police line re-formed and stepped slowly but inexorably forward. "But why are they attacking the coffee shop?" Yussuf said.

There were other policemen there, too, Akil realized belatedly, not in uniform but unmistakable nonetheless. Americans, many Americans in cheap suits and bright ties, and Interpol, he thought, or at least representatives of some European security force.

It was time to call in reinforcements. Akil found a discarded bottle and threw it as hard as he could.

The bottle hit the back of one of the helmets, hard enough to cause the policeman wearing it to stumble to his knees. The line broke and turned to see where the new attack was coming from. By this time the gathering crowd behind Akil and his friends were screaming and shouting insults, and they took to his example with enthusiasm. A rain of objects, including rocks, cobblestones, bottles, and cans, hammered down on hastily raised riot shields. The rain increased to a hail, and by the time the hail became a storm the police line had regrouped and begun to advance at a well-disciplined trot.

"Come on!" Akil said, and led his three companions on an agile, serpentine dance through the crowd. At the corner he said, "Split up! Yussuf and Yaqub that way!

Basil, with me!" He didn't wait to see if they obeyed; he grabbed Basil's arm and sprinted down an alley, around another corner, and up a street. Basil had shrugged free of his grip and was a pace ahead of Akil. He saw that the boy was laughing.

"This way!" Akil said.

"But that's back to the riot!"

"I know a different way! Follow me!"

At the top of the street the noise of the riot, which had been decreasing, began to increase again. There were the sounds of metal crunching as cars were overturned, the glass of storefronts shattering, the shouts of men, the screams of women and the cries of children, the orders of police commanders bellowed in the vain hope they would be heard above the cacophony.

Akil turned toward it and increased his pace so that he pulled ahead. This time there was no hesitation; Basil's feet thudded behind him. At the corner at the top of a little hill Akil stopped without warning, turned to his right, and stuck out a foot. Basil tripped over it and as he fell forward Akil grabbed the back of his jacket and the seat of his pants and assisted his headlong hurtle into the crowd running up the hill. It parted to let him sprawl on the pavement at the feet of advancing policemen with riot shields and clubs.

In one smooth movement Akil continued his turn and reversed course, gaining on the leading edge of the fleeing, screaming crowd until he was able to duck down an alley, another, a third, emerging finally blocks away. He smoothed his hair, steadied his breathing, and walked at a sedate pace back to his one-room flat.

He got out his small, shabby suitcase and began to fill it with slow and deliberate movements. There was time. Yussuf and Yaqub would take extra care in returning. If they returned at all, if they chose to follow him.

They would. After all, he had, and they were as he had been once, young, callow, untried, searching for something to give their lives purpose and meaning, a way to leave something behind, a path that would take them to glory. Any and all of the above. His mind filled with memories of another leave-taking, years ago and half a world away, the day he had followed Zarqawi into Afghanistan.

There had been no hesitation on his part, no second thoughts that October in 1999. He left his job and all his belongings, save a few things in a small pack, without so much as a backward glance.

They found a house in Kabul, and Zarqawi began immediately to recruit expatriate Jordanians living in Afghanistan to plan and execute a series of terrorist attacks in Jordan. He kept an attentive Akil at his elbow, watching, learning, in the beginning fitted for no task more arduous than fetching tea from the café down the street. Jordan had to be taught not to hold the United States so dear, Zarqawi explained, and the attacks would serve to get and keep their attention.

The following year Zarqawi was given the task of overseeing an al Qaeda camp near Herat. When they arrived, he handed Akil over to the training master with instructions that Akil be taught the full curriculum. "Play no favorites here," the training master was told, and the training master took to this instruction with a zealous and unrelenting enthusiasm.

At the end of that formative year, Akil could route an anonymous email, drive a D6 Caterpillar tractor, and field strip an AK-47, reassemble it, and shoot and hit a moving target. He could create a web site, outrun a platoon of recruits, and send a suicide bomber out on his mission with words stirring enough that the young man—and sometimes the young woman—believed absolutely that paradise was waiting on the other side of their trigger finger. He could hijack a bus, a train, an airplane. He could kidnap an uncooperative Pakistani city official right out of his Peshawar office in broad daylight. He could negotiate terms for his release, and he could kill him if such terms were not forthcoming, or even unsatisfactory.

Yes, he could kill. Of all the skills he learned that year in the camp near Herat, it was his most difficult and ultimately his proudest achievement.

His first was a Reuters journalist traveling in an area still controlled by the Taliban, with whom Zarqawi had very close ties. The journalist had been filing uncomfortably accurate stories about the Taliban's renascent activities that were appearing in newspapers all over the world. Alerted to his presence, Zarqawi declared that here was an obvious agent of the Central Intelligence Agency and sent Akil and six trained veterans after him with his blessing.

It was almost absurdly easy, a simple roadblock that stopped the jeep and extracted the driver and the translator. Both, aware of the reality of life in Afghanistan at that time, were white and shaking. Akil filmed the journalist bound and gagged in front of a two-day-old issue of the *Independent News Pakistan* and sent the driver off with it, trembling with relief.

The journalist, a middle-aged white man thick through the waist and addicted to Marlboro cigarettes, was Canadian, spoke English and French, and was at first philosophical at his capture. No ideologue, his view of the world and its leaders was sanguine and cynical and very amusing, and Akil quite enjoyed his company while they waited for the negotiations to play out. Ransom was demanded, and refused. A deadline passed. When Akil, properly masked, shot the translator on camera, in front of the journalist, the journalist was shocked and disbelieving. Conversation ceased. Akil regretted the necessity, not least because conversation ceased afterward.

When the second deadline passed and Akil had the journalist dragged before the camera, squat and malevolent on its tripod, under the impetus of sudden inspiration he borrowed a dagger from one of the other men, a sharp curve of silver, the hilt set with semiprecious stones. He turned the camera on, and walked toward the journalist, forced to his knees with his arms twisted behind his back. The journalist swore and began to struggle. One of the men holding him laughed.

Akil could sense their excitement. He went around behind the journalist, knotted a fist in his hair to pull his head back, and looked into the camera lens. "In praise of Allah!"

"Allah!" "Inshallah!" "Allah!" "Death to the infidel! Death to America! Free Palestine!"

"Motherfucker," the journalist said, his voice a growl of hatred, staring up at Akil through narrowed eyes, his teeth bared. "Do it if you're going to and stop preening for the fucking camera."

Akil brought the knife down and in one clean stroke cut the man's throat open from ear to ear. The gush of blood was immediate and immense, turning the hand that held the knife red, flooding the front of the journalist's body and splashing the men holding his arms. The weight of the body tore the wound open further and left Akil holding it up by the journalist's spine. He tossed the body from him and it thumped soddenly to the floor.

Again, he looked straight into the camera's lens. He raised the bloody blade in the bloody hand. "Alhamdulillah!"

The men's cries rose around him. "Alhamdulillah!" "Alhamdulillah!" "Alhamdulillah!"

It was the beginning.

There was a soft knock at the door, and the memory faded for the reality of the flat in Düsseldorf. When he opened the door, he found Yussuf and Yaqub standing there.

"Basil?" Yaqub said.

He shook his head gravely. "They caught up with us. Basil told me he would distract them, and for me to run."

He made mint tea and they toasted the bravery and self-sacrifice of their missing comrade. Yussuf was fervent in a prayer for those who had been hurt and arrested. Yaqub was quieter and a little hesitant, regarding Akil with wide, troubled eyes.

Akil took no outward notice. It was their first taste of action. There had to be reaction of some sort. He smiled to himself. It was a law of physics.

When their glasses were empty Akil began again to pack. They watched him in silence until Yussuf said tentatively, "You are leaving us?"

"It has become too dangerous for me to stay," Akil said. He sorted through a selection of shirts and tucked them neatly into his case.

"Where will you go?" Yussuf said.

"Somewhere else," Akil said.

"But where?" Yaqub said.

"And to do what?" Yussuf said, the one Akil had always thought the superior in intellect.

"To continue my work," Akil said. He sorted through the papers in his desk. None in a name anyone would recognize, so he left them. He pulled out the German passport in the name of Dandin Gandhi he had bought in Barcelona and deliberately ripped it apart, piling the resulting fragments in a large bowl. He lit a match and the three of them watched his photograph melt and reduce to charred ash.

"Your work against the infidel," Yussuf said. "For the greater glory of Islam."

"Yes," Akil said.

Yussuf nodded at Yaqub. "We wish it to be our work as well," Yussuf said. "We will go with you."

Yaqub looked at once thrilled and frightened, but he didn't contradict his friend.

Akil closed his suitcase and stood it next to the door. He shrugged into his jacket and stood for a moment, looking around the room, checking to see if he'd missed anything. No.

He looked at the young men. "You understand that if you set out on this path there is no turning back."

Yussuf met his eyes steadily, without flinching. Yaqub was breathing a little faster than normal, his color high. He shifted from one foot to the other, once starting at a sound from the street.

Akil always felt bound by honor to give them more than Zarqawi had given him. His face was serious, his voice grave. Their eyes widened and they glanced at each other before looking back at him. "You will leave behind family, friends, everything you have ever known. You will be hunted by policemen of every nation, always on the move, often hungry, always tired, never again knowing a night's peace, and at the end only death."

"But a glorious death," Yussuf said quickly.

"Glorious indeed," Akil said. The rest came by rote. He had said it so many times he was hard put to it to infuse the words with any conviction. "We will either convert the infidel to the true faith, make them our slaves, and have sole dominion over the earth, or we will put them all to death. If we ourselves die in this endeavor, Allah will take us as his own, and we will be most richly rewarded in the afterlife."

"Seventy-two virgins for each of us," Yaqub said, and nudged his friend.

Akil pretended not to hear this. As useful for recruiting suicide bombers as it might be, he himself doubted the seventy-two virgins. "But all this you have had from the imam, and you are men of faith, so I need not repeat it to you here. My concern is what happens between now and then. It is not an easy task, what you wish to do."

"We will follow you," Yussuf said immediately.

"Today? Now? Are you this moment prepared to walk behind me out this door and never look back?"

"We are," they said in chorus. Yussuf walked to the door and opened it for Akil.

He didn't look back, but their footsteps echoed in his ears.

7

THE CARIBBEAN, JULY 2007

Munro was ten weeks out of Miami, trolling for go fasts before they headed back to port, when they spotted their first northbound freighter of the patrol. "Has she seen us yet, XO?"

The XO had binoculars glued to his eyes, feet spread

to keep his balance in the slow swell rocking the ship. "I don't think so, Captain. Oh. Yeah." A long sigh. "Now they have."

"Damn it." Cal looked over his shoulder. "Launch both boats."

The coxswains, Garon and Myers, had been standing at his heels, waiting for the word. Their boarding teams had long since dressed out and were standing by the two small boats. "Aye, sir," they said in unison, and vanished down the ladder, probably afraid he'd scrub the boarding. Any day they didn't get their hands on a small boat was a bad day for them.

Although none of the crew relished the thought of taking migrants aboard. Most of them had probably been seasick by now and it was more than likely that the sanitation facilities were nonexistent. The last time they'd had to take on migrants the ship had stunk for a week afterward. He stifled a sigh. "Try to raise her again, Ops."

"Aye, Captain." Behind him Cal heard Lieutenant Terrell, the operations officer, key the mike for the marine radio. "Unidentified motor vessel, this is the USCG cutter *Munro*. Heave to, heave to, I say again, heave to, heave to."

Silence on the radio. They weren't responding. Cal heard the whine of the winch on the davit and went out on the starboard bridge wing. The hull of the orange rigid inflatable had barely touched the water before Garon started the engine and the wake boiled up behind the stern. The crew released shackles fore and aft, the sea painter was away, and Garon gunned the engine and the small boat pulled away from the *Munro*'s hull in a wide arc, wake a white froth in a blue sea.

Cal went back inside the bridge and met the eyes of the XO coming in from the port wing. A quick nod told him the portside boat was safely away.

He squinted at the sky, a calm blue with a few cumulus clouds on the horizon, reflected in the glassy surface of the sea. At least they wouldn't have weather to contend with.

He returned to the bridge. Taffy was looking through his binoculars. Cal picked up his own and went to stand next to him. "How many?"

"Can't tell yet. There's about half a dozen people on deck. They say they're fishing but they've got no gear in the water or showing on deck."

Cal adjusted his binoculars and zeroed in on the tattered flag fluttering off the freighter's stern. A crew member had bent it on just moments before. "Haitian."

"Yeah."

"So they say."

"Yeah."

Over his shoulder Cal said, "Where are we, BMC?"

"Forty-two miles south of Providenciales Island, Captain," Bosun's Mate Chief Guilmartin said promptly, without looking down at the radar. "About a hundred and fifty miles north of Haiti."

Cal exchanged a brief glance with the XO. They had yet to take a migrant on board and already the crew was figuring out how long it would take to get them back to their country of origin and, more important, off *Munro*. Cal didn't blame them. Freighters smuggling migrants were all about the transportation and not at all about the hygiene.

Taffy muffled a curse.

"What?" Cal raised his glasses again.

When first sighted, the eighty-foot freighter had had maybe half a dozen people on deck, but when the white-hulled cutter with the orange stripe angling back down the hull bore down on them people began pouring up on deck. Like all coastal freighters encountered during Caribbean patrols, it was hard to see how this one kept her gunnels above water. She was wooden, her hull flaking paint and riddled with worm, her exhaust so black and her wake so uncertain Cal couldn't see how she'd made it out of whatever harbor she'd sailed from, let alone managed to get twenty miles off Miami Beach.

And now her hold was emptying itself onto her deck, where the sudden weight topside created a dangerously unstable condition on a ship that was already a hazard to navigation.

Inevitably, she began to roll, a little roll at first and then, very quickly, a lot, so that she was shipping water over the sides. They could hear the screams of the frightened passengers on the cutter's bridge. Cal bypassed Ops for the marine radio. "Unknown freighter, unknown freighter, this is the cutter *Munro*. Stop your people from packing the deck, you're going to capsize."

There was no discernable result and Cal went on the pipe and repeated the message, his voice booming out across the water.

"She must be taking on water," the XO said.

"Boat in that bad of shape, probably got the pumps running all the time. Probably shut them down to go all ahead full when they spotted us." To Terrell he said, "Tell the boats to keep their distance until things quiet down over there, they can't do any good if they get swamped by a bunch of panicked migrants."

Terrell gave the order. The two small boats veered off to idle on either side of the freighter. Seeing this, the people on the freighter began to shout and wave with one arm, flailing for something to hold on to with the other as the freighter's wallows increased in angle and velocity. The crowd on deck continued to increase as more people clawed their way up from below.

They were close enough now that Cal could hear the shouts and screams. Again, inevitably, a man fell overboard, screaming, followed by a second, then a little girl. Three people jumped in after her, and then a rain of bodies overboard, too many to count.

The freighter rolled heavily to port and swamped the deck. The rushing water swept half the remaining people topside overboard. Relieved of their weight, the dilapidated little freighter swung even more rapidly to starboard, probably further impelled by water rolling back and forth belowdecks, as textbook a display of the free surface effect that Cal, watching helplessly half a mile off their starboard beam, had ever seen. She rolled again and this time she kept going, all the way over, water swamping the gunnel, lines, buckets, boat hooks sliding down to the gunnel and over the side, the house disappearing beneath the waves, until at last she was keel up, there to display a soft-looking hull playing host to an entire biosphere of seaweed.

And people everywhere in the water, screaming and splashing frantically and grabbing for each other. The few who could swim struck out away from the sinking ship and began to tread water. Some of them were already being picked up by the small boats, who had moved in and were tossing PFDs to the people in the water.

"Son of a bitch," Cal said. "Dead slow ahead. Pipe Doc and all EMTs and stretcher bearers on deck now."

"Dead slow ahead, aye."

"Doc's already on deck, sir."

"Every free hand on deck as well."

"Already there, sir."

"XO, get down there and direct traffic. Ops, call the beach and bring them up to speed. And call the mess deck and tell the senior chief that we've got what looks like about two hundred extra for lunch."

"Two hundred extra for lunch, aye, sir."

AT THE END OF THE DAY IT WAS 214, ALTHOUGH THE DEAD weren't dining and many among the living were already victims of malnutrition and as yet incapable of ingesting solid food. Some, including many of the women, showed unmistakable signs of torture and abuse. Almost all of them were suffering from exposure and severe dehydration. Nine of them had drowned, including the little girl who had been third into the water.

BM2 Hendricks, the bosun's mate who had been the boarding team leader on *Mun 2*, offered up this information still in his PFD and LE belt, his helmet under his left arm, speaking in a consciously dry, factual voice that was wavering just this side of cracking. His hair was a reddish sheen over his scalp, his eyes were normally a bright blue, and he had pale skin reddened by constant exposure to sun and wind. He was twenty-three. Today, he looked a shell-shocked twelve. It was moments like these that made Cal feel his age.

"I couldn't let the boats get too close, sir," Hendricks said miserably. "There were so many of them, grabbing anything they could hold on to. They would have swamped us."

"You did right," Cal said. They were in the captain's quarters. On the bridge everyone would have been listening and Cal wanted to give Hendricks breathing space.

"We threw them PFDs but of course they didn't know how to put them on and they were too panicked to get into them in the water anyway. Most of them kept their heads enough to hold on until we got to them, but some of them just . . ."

"Matt." Cal had to repeat his name to get his attention. "Matt, listen to me. I want you to grab a shower and some clean clothes. I want you to tell the rest of the boat crews and boarding teams to do the same, and then I want you to take them down to the galley and tell the senior chief that the captain says to fry you all a steak."

An expression of revulsion crossed Hendricks's face. "I couldn't eat, sir, I don't think any of us could after today."

"It wasn't a suggestion," Cal said, and reached for the phone. "I'm calling Senior Chief myself."

The bosun's mate hesitated.

"That's an order, BM2," Cal said again, letting his command voice kick in. The BM went into an instinctive brace. "I'll be down on the mess deck myself in half an hour, and I expect both crews there. Understood?"

Hendricks, looking steadier on his feet, said, "Understood, aye, Captain," and left the cabin. Cal called the chief in charge of the mess and spoke sharply enough that even that temperamental gentleman knew enough to say smartly, "Yes, sir," and no more. New York steaks weren't normally on the standard issue Coast Guard menu, but now and then Cal liked to put his father's money to work for Coastie morale. He was sure the senator would approve of this use of Cal's patrimony, and in any case he wasn't about to ask him.

A few moments later there was a knock at the door. "Yeah."

The executive officer poked his head in. "All clear?"

Cal waved him in. "Close the door and have a seat."

Taffy doffed his cap and sat across the desk from Cal.

"We lost another one. A young woman. According to Baby Doc, she'd been beaten and raped repeatedly, as in recently."

"How recently?"

"Last night. This morning. Since they left port, Baby Doc doesn't know. She's very young. And pretty." He grimaced, and ran a tired hand through his hair. "Well. She was."

"Somebody on the boat," Cal said. It wasn't a question.

"Baby Doc says more than one. Marks on her wrists and ankles where they—"

Cal held up one hand. "Got the picture." He made a conscious effort to relax his jaw. "We should have let the fuckers drown."

"They didn't all rape her, Captain."

"They all know who did, though."

"Most likely someone in the crew. Or all of them. They'd regard it as part of the price of passage." Taffy shrugged. "We've got them segregated from the migrants. Well. We've separated the ones with passports from the ones without. There are only six with passports."

"Find any weapons?"

The XO shook his head. "Passengers say they had them. Probably the first thing that went over the side when they spotted us. They know the penalties for getting caught with automatic weapons on the high seas."

Cal nodded. Piracy carried hefty penalties in the United States, including serious federal time.

"Do you want me to start an investigation?" Taffy said without enthusiasm.

"No point," Cal said. "She won't be the only victim. We've got enough on our hands without conducting a criminal investigation that would likely turn into half a dozen separate cases before we're done. We'll be at the dock tomorrow. Leave it to the authorities onshore." Cal looked up. "You've got them under supervision?"

"Our guests have more military police standing watch over them than Baghdad."

"Everyone's been fed?"

"Senior had the FSs cook up a mess of rice and beans."

"Good." Cal brooded for a moment. "I'm declaring the derelict a hazard to navigation. Do you concur?"

"If I concurred any more I'd be genuflecting."

"Destroy it."

"That'll make the gunnies happy. Nothing Chief Colvin likes more than to get in a little target practice." The XO rose to his feet and picked up his cap. "Anything else, sir?"

"No. Wait, what'd we do with the bodies?"

"Emptied out the reefer and stacked them to the ceiling." Cal grimaced. The XO pretended not to see. "Senior Chief says best speed for port or it's ice cream for breakfast, lunch, and dinner."

"Thanks, XO."

He lapsed into a brooding silence.

"Something bothering you, sir?"

Cal shrugged, playing with his pen. "Nothing. Well.

It's something, but it's not something we can do anything about."

"Sir?"

Cal jerked his head in the general direction of the freighter. "How many more got through while we were picking people out of the water? Two? Five? A dozen? How many of these banana boats beached themselves on a Florida beach and their cargo walked ashore?"

"We can't stop them all," the XO said.

"We can't stop hardly any of them," Cal said. "We're spending billions, trillions in Iraq and Afghanistan to bomb the shit out of people who never had a pot to piss in, let alone enough money to buy a one-way ticket on one of these floating coffins. And here we sit, our finger stuck in a dike that is leaking like a sieve in a hundred other places. We can't stop them all. We can't contain them all. God knows we can't make their own countries more attractive so they'll want to stay home."

The XO considered this. "Today was a good day, sir," he said, a hint of a question in his words. "At least most of them are alive to make a run for the border another day."

"Agreed," Cal said. "I just worry about who else is coming into the country on all the boats we're missing. Be pretty damn easy for some bin Laden wannabe to bribe the right skipper, waltz off the ship somewhere north of Palm Beach, and hitch a ride north so he could light off his backpack nuke in the middle of Dupont Circle."

"I'd like to see bin Laden wading ashore at Palm Beach," the XO said meditatively. "All those little old ladies with blue hair and lime green polyester pantsuits would beat him to death with their Gucci bags before his feet were dry."

Cal laughed, as he had been meant to. "Point taken. Anything else?"

Taffy hesitated. "You up for a little crew confabulation?"

"I don't even know what the hell that means, but it's got to be better than people drowning on my watch." The words came out a little harder than he'd meant and he winced. "Sorry, Taff. Talk to me."

"OS2 Riley."

Cal groaned. "Not again."

"Afraid so. And this time it's someone on the ship."

Cal groaned again. "Who?"

"ET3 Reese. He says it was consensual, she says it wasn't."

Cal swore. "Where?"

"Miami. Last inport. Neither of them live there, don't have family there, are pretty much at loose ends when they go ashore. A bunch of the crew rented rooms in a motel. It started out men with men and women with women."

"And it didn't end up that way. Man, his wife is going to kill him this time."

They both considered that eventuality with pleasure. "What I don't get is how such an undernourished, snot-nosed little twerp gets all the girls," Taffy said.

"Does he still have money troubles?"

"Big ones. Too much house, too much car, too many toys. Not to mention the wife and the two kids, ages one and three."

"How did we hear about this?" Cal said.

"She came to see me."

"In Miami? And she's just getting around to tell us about it now?"

"She told her mother, and her mother told her not to tell. Yeah, I know, but I get the feeling Reese comes from a family that's just barely getting by. I think she's sending money home. She needs the job."

Cal rubbed both hands over his head. His hair was long enough again to be mussed. He wondered if he should call Papa Doc for an appointment for a haircut, and decided it was too close to returning to port. In port, hair was a good thing. Gave Kenai something to hold on to. "What made her come forward now?"

"She says he's coming on to her again."

"Now? Underway?" Cal felt a slow burn.

"I get the feeling"—the XO was notorious for starting sentences this way, and Cal had learned that more often than not Taffy's feelings were right on the money—"that liquor was involved in the onshore incident, although she says no. If that is the case, her judgment was impaired. When she sobered up and realized what she'd done, she was horrified."

"He wasn't."

"No, sir, he wasn't. The way she tells it, he's looking to continue the, er, relationship on patrol."

"What does he say?"

"Denies everything except the first incident. Which he says was consensual."

"I am tired of this punk screwing around on my ship," Cal said. "Get rid of him for me, XO."

"I'll break out the keelhaul, sir," Taffy said cheerfully. "Just say the word."

"I wish." Cal brooded. "Okay, call shore and have the investigators meet us at the dock. In the meantime, ask Reese if she can last another ten days on the same ship as that asshole."

"And him?"

Cal fixed Taffy with a fierce eye. "Tell him he might like to keep out of the captain's way until then. I don't suppose I could restrict him to quarters?"

"Alas, sir," Taffy said, getting to his feet, "he is by law innocent until proven guilty."

"You're the only guy I know who can use 'alas' in a sentence without sounding like a pansy."

Taffy grinned. "Why, thank you, Captain," he said, and fluttered his eyelashes.

Cal turned serious. "However it turns out, XO, I've had about enough of this selfish, self-involved little brat. Time for the Coast Guard to make his services available elsewhere."

"Understood, sir. He's a presenter at some kind of workshop somewhere when we get in. Always assuming the investigators are done with him by the time he's supposed to leave. So at least you won't have to suffer his presence in port, or not for the short term.

Afterward, perhaps I can, uh, divert his return to the ship. We'll see."

The door closed behind the XO.

Cal, inexplicably, felt better. On a ship with 150 mixed-gender crew members, situations like this were inevitable, although on taking command of *Munro* he had worked tirelessly to ensure they wouldn't happen with any frequency, if at all. Well, he had failed, but dealing with the fallout from something like this was a lot easier on the psyche than fishing dead bodies out of the water.

He went down to the mess deck to make sure his boarding team members were eating right.

8

WASHINGTON, D.C., AUGUST 2007

"Damn it!"

Chisum rarely swore, and then only mildly, but it was enough to make his personal assistant raise her eyebrows. "Bad news?"

He looked up from the report and said with feeling, "Sometimes probable cause really gets in the way."

"Yes, it does, and I thought that was why the previous administration did away with it in these cases. Also habeas corpus and—"

"Thank you, Melanie, that will be all."

"Certainly, sir." Melanie swept out, and he couldn't

help it, he had to watch. Women nowadays had forgotten how to walk, or maybe they just didn't care, striding along like they were in a race, all trace of what had once been an inviting softness to a man's hand long since worked ruthlessly off at the gym and leaving something perilously close to the stringy haunch of a greyhound behind.

Melanie was a throwback. A pocket Venus of a blonde in her midthirties, she wore heels and pencil skirts topped by a variety of soft sweaters in even softer colors, and every day he sent up a prayer of thanks to whoever had assigned her to him when Birdy had left. A forty-year veteran with an institutional memory that went back to the agency's roots in the OSS, Birdy was irreplaceable, but even Birdy was subject to the march of time. When she retired in October, Melanie had replaced her, and Patrick had suffered so instant and overwhelming an attraction that he had hidden it behind a curt, distant manner.

Even if every fiber of his being urged him to throw her down on his desk each time she walked in his door. "Whoa there, down, boy," he said beneath his breath. She was too good at what she did to treat with anything less than respect, so he locked his fantasies into a steel vault with a fail-safe lock and doggedly returned to the report.

Isa or someone bearing a striking resemblance to him had been spotted in Auckland, of all places. The source reported he had it on good authority that Isa was recruiting from among the Maoris for the purposes of launching a terrorist attack from down under.

Which was about as reliable as any humint his agents were fielding nowadays, he thought glumly. Everyone was hedging their bets, scarred from too many years of being slapped down for intelligence the previous administration either disbelieved or suppressed in pursuit of their almighty crusade. Except they didn't call it a crusade. They'd learned that much.

There were times when he thought he ought to finally register to vote.

There were others when he looked at the people in office and the ones running to replace them, and was overwhelmed by a sense of hopelessness and impending doom.

Still, he could not afford to overlook any lead, and while the hard intel was grinding to a temporary halt the rumor mill was hitting high gear. Along with the sighting in York, he had reports of additional sightings in London, Darfur (from a recently evacuated aid worker who did some freelance work for the agency on the side, and whose product had never been all that reliable), Baghdad (at the site of an IED resulting in three killed and which he knew was nonsense because Isa would never have been so careless as to flaunt himself at the scene of one of his own attacks), Toronto (which frightened him; he'd sent a rocket back to the agent who had submitted it, requesting an immediate re-interview and a more thorough canvas of other possible witnesses), Bern (which he almost believed, given how well funded the al Qaeda cells were and how scrupulously they looked after their money), Moscow, and the list went on and on. Isa had been sighted fifty-three times in the last six months, three times in three different cities on three different continents on the same day.

Boeing was good, but they weren't that good.

The phone rang. "The director on line one," Melanie said, sounding fluttery. Patrick had noticed most women did around Kallendorf. Guy looked like a bull elephant and had about as much finesse but he had to beat the women off with a stick. Chisum smoothed back his thinning hairline, sucked in his potbelly, and picked up the phone. "Chisum here."

"I have your report in front of me," Kallendorf said without preamble. "Anything to add?"

Chisum thought swiftly, and then decided there was no margin for defense. It was what it was. "No, sir."

"When did we last talk about this Isa?"

By now he knew that the director remembered exactly when Chisum had briefed him on the terrorist, the day, the hour, probably down to the color of Chisum's tie. "At the annual JTTF briefing, sir."

"That's almost a year ago, Patrick. What have you done for me lately?"

"It's not like he's posting his schedule on the Internet, sir."

"No, it's not," Kallendorf agreed, a little too easily. "Maybe he's retired."

Patrick found himself on his feet without knowing how he got there. He forced himself to speak calmly.

"Fanatical terrorists don't retire, sir. Usually they are killed. Rarely they are captured. They don't retire."

"Then he's been killed or captured. I think it's time to reallocate some of our intelligence-gathering capabilities to more worthy targets. Convince me otherwise."

Chisum took a deep breath. "Sir, Isa was Zarqawi's right-hand man and his closest confidant. He is widely believed to have pioneered Zarqawi's use of the Internet for banking, communications, and recruiting. I can definitely place him in Düsseldorf in June."

"Sez who?"

"I—acquired the information through a third party," Chisum said carefully.

"You trust this source?"

"Absolutely, sir."

Kallendorf grunted. "Which means we paid for it. I don't like buying intelligence, Patrick."

"I don't think anyone's going to give it to us for love, sir," Chisum said before he could stop himself.

There was a moment of silence, followed by a booming laugh. "What was Isa doing in Düsseldorf?" Kallendorf said, still chuckling.

"Recruiting," Chisum said baldly.

"Identify anyone?"

"Two, before Isa made our informant."

"Made him, did he? What'd he do to him?"

"Started a riot, and then threw him into the advancing line of riot police."

"No shit. Guy's got style, gotta give him that."

Chisum said nothing.

"Our snitch must have survived," Kallendorf said.

"Must have," Chisum said dryly. He sat back down. "According to him, the two recruits were young Muslim men, both German-born of immigrant Lebanese parents, both with degrees in engineering."

"What the hell is it with al Qaeda and engineering degrees? You'd think they wouldn't let you into the gang without one."

Chisum shrugged. "It's probably a lot like anything else. It's not what you know, it's who."

"What did they say about Isa?"

"Everyone we spoke to described Isa as a quiet man who socialized primarily in the coffeehouses with men his own age or younger."

"He gay?"

"Hasn't been any rumor of that so far. His boss says he was a reliable and competent if undistinguished employee."

"No proselytizing in the workplace, eh?"

"No, sir."

"We got any idea of what he's planning?"

"We know he's been bouncing money from bank accounts in Switzerland to all over Europe, both the Americas, and the Caribbean. I think Hong Kong, too, although the Chinese are even cagier than the Swiss about giving up information."

"Okay, mostly Western banks, then probably a Western target."

"Considering that, and considering also that we

know Isa went to school in the West, and that both of his German recruits are fluent in English, yes, sir."

"So either us or the Brits."

"Yes."

"You talked to them?"

"MI5? Frequently."

"Talk to 'em some more. Any line on these recruits?"

"Yussuf al-Dagma and Yaqub Sadiq. They vanished from Düsseldorf the same day Isa did. We talked to their families, their friends, their coworkers. Only Yussuf al-Dagma's family had met Isa, who was at that time using the name Dandin Gandhi."

"Gandhi," Kallendorf said. "First Jesus, and now Gandhi. This guy got a martyr complex or what?"

"Yes, sir. Their description matches the few eyewitness descriptions we have."

"They were cooperative?"

"I'm told they are very worried about their son. The family has become pretty acculturated, and reasonably secular. They said that al-Dagma has been obsessing over Israel and Iraq, and that two years ago he started going to the mosque. We talked to the local imam, who was very cagey, but our people on the ground say he's been doing a little inciting to riot on the side."

"What was this riot about?"

"Nothing to do with the imam, not this time. Someone tipped off the local cops that there was a terrorist cell meeting regularly at a coffee shop frequented by young Muslim men. The informant who was trying to get close to Isa, once he was up and moving around again, did a little investigating and found out that Yaqub Sadiq had been sleeping with a married woman, also Muslim. As I'm sure you know, that's a beheading offense under Islamic law. The agent thinks the husband made an anonymous call."

" 'Hello, 911? This guy is banging my wife, so come on down and arrest all these bin Ladenites hanging out at the local Starbucks where my wife's lover buys his cappuccino'?"

"Uh, essentially, yes, sir."

"And they bought that?"

"I don't believe he mentioned his wife's lover, sir," Patrick said in a wooden voice. "We are at present speculating as to the exact occurrence of events."

"Holy shit," the director said, unheeding. "The Germans must hire their cops from the lowest common denominator up."

"Yes, sir," Patrick said. He was determined to cling to his point, no matter how difficult Kallendorf made it. "This could be good news for us, however."

"What, that German cops are simpletons?"

"No, sir. If Sadiq joined Isa's group as a means of escaping the consequences of sleeping with someone else's wife, it means that he may not be a true believer, he may just have wanted to get out of Dodge. If that's so, and if I can find him, we may have a way in."

"Any luck with that?"

"We canvassed the airport and the train stations with photos of the two. Nothing yet. They must have driven out of town, flown out of somewhere else. We're working with Interpol on that, but . . ." Chisum shrugged. "It was six months ago, and most airport rentacops can't remember who they screened in the last five minutes. And Isa never leaves much of a trail. He's patient, and he's cunning. I've got head shots of the recruits and I've distributed them to the heads of security in every American, Canadian, and Mexican airport, FBI, Interpol, and of course agency-wide. We're looking. It's only a matter of time before we find them."

"And when we find them, we find Isa?"

Chisum battled with temptation, and won. "That's not a given, sir. He communicates almost exclusively by email, at least after the initial recruitment. If he continues operating the way he operated in Baghdad, he will recruit them, work out a plan for them, and then he'll cut them loose except for email contact." He diverted from a lifelong self-imposed tact and discretion for a moment to say bitterly, "Son of a bitch won't even use a cell phone."

"I don't blame him," Kallendorf said, "have you looked at the sigint center lately? You could lock yourself into a safe with four-foot-thick walls and drop the safe into a thousand feet of water and they could still hear you whisper sweet nothings into that cute little blond secretary's ears. What's her name? Melissa?"

"Melanie."

"Melanie, that's right. Always smells so good. Love that in a woman." Silence. "Will he stop at two recruits?"

"No, sir. The average al Qaeda cell isn't large, but it's usually around ten or twelve people."

"Looking for more of the same?"

"Yes, sir. Young disaffected Muslim men, middle or even upper middle class, well-educated, often unemployed but not always. The preference is for unmarried but it's not a requirement. Most of them are pretty homely, too, which I think is deliberate."

"Can't get a girl, so give them a bomb instead?"

"Freud would be proud of you, sir."

Fortunately for Patrick, Kallendorf didn't hear that last remark. "And this Isa is the only al Qaeda contact the others will meet."

"Yes, sir."

"Cut off the head, the snake dies."

"With al Qaeda it's more like a hydra than a snake, sir."

"Huh. Hydra. Good one. I'll have to remember that. Yeah. All right, Patrick, carry on. But I want some hard data on this asshole soonest, and I want his ass in the bag sooner than that." Click.

Chisum replaced the receiver carefully back in its cradle.

The door opened and he looked up. "Everything all right with the director?" Melanie said.

"Everything's just fine," Chisum said.

"Anything you need to run up to his office, you just ask."

"Thank you, Melanie," he said.

"I was just going down the hall for some coffee," she

said. "Would you like some, Mr. Chisum?"

"I would, thank you, Melanie."

"Be right back, then." She smiled and closed the door gently behind her.

It might have been the first time he wished he'd gone for the director's job. It wouldn't be the last.

9

"Why me?" Kenai said. It was more of a demand than a question, but at least then no one could accuse her of whining. "Why not Bill, or Mike?"

"Thanks a bunch, there, Kenai," Mike said.

"He's a Muslim, Rick," Kenai said, keeping her eyes on their commander. He was the one who had to be convinced. "He's not going to like having a woman for a babysitter. Think of how it'll play back home, a woman, an inferior instructing him. They'll see it on television every night, and he'll know it. He's not going to like it."

Her voice ended on something perilously close to a plea. Rick, leaning against a desk, his arms folded, frowned at the floor and said nothing. The rest of the Carnivore Crew watched and waited. There was no effort, individually or together, to take her part. She couldn't find it in her heart to blame them. None of them wanted to be the babysitter, either.

"It's your first time on orbit, too," Joel said in a tone that brooked no argument. "You'll know what to keep him away from."

"How about we keep him away from the shuttle altogether?" Laurel said brightly.

Joel pretended he hadn't heard her. He consulted the omnipresent clipboard. "I think that's all for today. Press conference on Monday, don't forget, clean flight suits all around."

The door closed behind him. "Nice try, Nanook," Laurel said.

"But no cigar," Mike Williams said.

Kenai gave a half-hearted shrug. "Worth the effort. I thought maybe when he didn't show for the Vomit Comet training in March . . ." Her voice trailed off, and she shook her head.

Rick looked up. "Somebody's got to wet-nurse him, Kenai. Sorry you drew the short straw."

There was an almost imperceptible relaxation of tension around the room. That was that. "Okay," Kenai said, dismissing the sheik for more important matters, "you've all got the updates on the robot arm modifications? Good. It'll add about twenty minutes to each deployment, a small price to pay for the increase in sensitivity. She's handling like something out of Robert Heinlein now anyway."

"Unless you're the one EVA, holding on to five thousand pounds of satellite with your fingertips," Mike pointed out.

"Bitch, bitch, bitch," Bill said. "You'd kill anyone

who tried to take the job away from you, Gator."

Bill had a predilection for nicknames, and he'd called Kenai Nanook from the first day he met her, since she was from Alaska and "nanook" was the local word for polar bear. Mike was from Florida and he had a long, wide, flat nose that naturally led to Bill calling him Alligator. When the secretaries over at admin got to hear of it, they were the Carnivore Crew from that day forward. After that, the deluge. Now Laurel from California was Condor, Rick from Washington State was Killer Whale, Killer for short, and Bill from Minnesota was Wolverine, partly because he was from Minnesota but mostly because he was a huge X-Men fan. It didn't hurt that he looked a little like Hugh Jackman, only black.

A week later, the sheik in question arrived for an introductory visit. He looked like Disney's Aladdin, only older and more arrogant, and from the first he proved to be labor intensive. Kenai was right, he wasn't happy with a woman as his partner, and he said so. Joel, to his credit, ignored his hints that someone of the sheik's stature in the Islamic community and his family connections and their immense wealth and political profile and blah blah blah really ought to be taken in tow by the mission's commander. The director of flight operations nipped that suggestion in the bud immediately.

Joel was probably afraid of what Rick would do to him if he did, for good reason. Rick did not suffer fools gladly, and people who inflicted fools upon him had been known to rue the day, if not resign on the spot.

The sheik had various other concerns, usually delivered to Kenai in an imperious voice as he looked down his very long nose. For one thing, he had seen photos of previous crews in space and he'd noticed that often the crew was wearing shorts. He trusted Kenai would not be orbiting the earth half-naked.

Kenai exchanged a glance with Laurel, who happened to be loitering within earshot. "I'm sorry, sir, I just assumed . . ."

"Assumed what?" the sheik said loftily.

"That you had been briefed." She did her best to look as if she were reluctant to be the one to bring him the bad news. "This mission . . ."

His brow puckered. "Yes?"

"Well, sir, this mission will be accomplished totally in the nude."

If Laurel hadn't burst out laughing he might have taken this horror straight to Joel, but as it was he didn't speak directly to Kenai for three days, which at least proved he wasn't entirely stupid.

But it was yet another unwanted distraction in the now only eleven months leading up to launch. Kenai gritted her teeth and tried to be more accessible to the royal pain in the ass. She grudged the valuable chunks of time he ate up, but it was better for her to intercept any further problems before they got to the commander.

And let's face it, Bill was right, she would have killed anyone who tried to take the job from her. There was nothing, no irritation she would not suffer to pass that magic mile marker of fifty miles up that would turn her silver astronaut pin to gold and make her a bona fide astronaut.

Flight was all she had ever wanted, from the moment she was four when her father had lifted her into his lap, put her hands on the stick of his Cessna 172, and performed a simple right bank. She'd agitated for a shot at the right seat from the time she was eight, but her father wouldn't let her try until her feet reached the pedals without assistance.

She had almost a hundred hours in dual before she had her license, which she got the day she turned sixteen, a full six months before she bothered to get her driver's license. She only got around to getting her driver's license because she got tired of waiting on rides to the airport.

She graduated from high school a year early and seven years later was out the other side of a BA in English—she'd always liked to read, and she'd noticed that the ability to write simple declarative sentences was a serious asset in the world of aviation, especially when dealing with the FAA—and an MS in electrical engineering. By the time she was a sophomore in college she was qualified to fly commercial and put herself through school flying Twin Otters and then Beechcraft 1900 for Era Aviation between Homer and Anchorage on weekends. Upon graduation she went to work for Boeing in systems design. Shortly thereafter she was test-flying jets right off the drafting table, in between times taking her doctorate, also in electrical engineering. Her doctoral thesis was an overview of the evolution of electrical systems during the design and operation of the space shuttle, and ended with the proposal of a radical new design for the next generation of manned space flight vehicles that was energy efficient without reducing power. It was well written and relatively easy even for a layman to understand. It was what got her the job offer from NASA.

The goal had always been to fly in space. With no apology and no regrets, she figured she'd read too much Heinlein at an impressionable age and never recovered. It wasn't that they didn't know better now, no Venusian dragons or three-legged Martians, but the knowledge did not quench her thirst to go see with her own eyes.

It was an all-consuming passion, one that had cost her two good men and many more friends. She didn't regret the loss. The lovers and the friends wanted too much of her time, time taken away from the left seat. Cal wasn't the only man she'd ever been with who understood that, but he was the only one who was, so far, willing to accept it as part of the price of her companionship.

It was also the *Challenger.* It wasn't something she talked about a lot because the few times she had she'd received some very odd looks. It wasn't that she wanted to ride a rocket and have it explode beneath her. She didn't suffer from a death wish, she had every intention of living to be as old as she possibly could and then tack on another twenty-five years to read all the books she'd missed when she'd been focused on technical manuals. It was that the *Challenger* had left shoes to fill, and her feet itched to step into them.

Her father had been all for her applying to the astronaut program. Her mother, a stay-at-home mom, had never quite forgiven her for embracing such a dangerous occupation, especially since she was an only child, but she loved Kenai and supported her nevertheless. She had no family distractions, and after her two abortive attempts at romance no relationship distractions, either.

Sometimes she worried a little that she was turning into a drone. But mostly she was excited and challenged by her profession, a siren song that lured her, enticed her, charmed her, enslaved her. Call it the call to adventure. *The Power of Myth* had been assigned reading in her modern lit class. She'd liked it well enough, but one thing she had never understood, either in the text or in any of the subsequent novels they read and applied it to, and that was the hero's refusal of the call. She could not conceive of a day when adventure called and she wasn't the first to step up to answer.

Although the month Sheik Jilal al-Hussein spent with the Carnivore Crew did test her resolve. He seemed to take space travel as his birthright, a privilege that required no reciprocal sweat equity. He was by turns dismissive, contemptuous, and downright rude, and always and ever arrogant. He questioned everything, from the shuttle emergency escape procedures to how to work the toilet, which, to be fair, was a procedure that tested them all. He demanded a list of the food items that went into their on-orbit menu, searching the ingredients for pork products, and he looked mutinous at the news that he would have to hang his sleep sack mere feet away from two female infidels, neither of whom were his wives.

The less said about his delayed ride on the Vomit Comet, the better. He refused to go on a second, for which the test director of the Reduced Gravity Program sent the Carnivore Crew his profound thanks.

"The Reduced Gravity Program?" Cal said, grinning.

"NASA-speak for riding simulated weightlessness maneuvers in the KC-135."

"At which the sheik did not perform well?"

"At which the sheik outpuked Barfin' Jake Garn. We were all kinda hoping he'd make himself too sick to ride. If he's that seasick on orbit, it's going to be seriously uncomfortable for all of us, even Rick, who's been up twice and never been sick."

Cal understood. In rough weather on *Munro*, all it took was the smell of one seasick crewman to infect his entire berthing area. "Who picked this guy anyway?" Cal said.

"We're launching his company's satellite." Kenai's voice was muffled, speaking as she was from a prone position on the sand. Cal was anointing her back with sunscreen, paying deliberate attention to every square inch of exposed flesh. Every now and then she let out an appreciative groan.

Munro was at the dock in Miami under Taffy's watchful eye. They had both managed to wedge a free weekend into their schedules, and Cal's father had a friend whose brother-in-law knew someone who owned a luxury condo on South Padre Island who was more than happy to loan it to the senator's son for a weekend. Probably there was a legislative trade-off involved but that was his father's business and the less Cal knew about it the better. At any rate it was the end of the month, almost the end of the season, and the beach was almost deserted.

Kenai had temporarily handed the sheik off to Wolverine, who accepted the assignment with suspicious enthusiasm. Bill was a superb pilot, probably the best one in their class of astronauts—even the other pilots said so—and Kenai had a feeling that the sheik was on for his training ride in the backseat of a T-38. She hoped for Bill's sake it didn't prove as stressful as the Vomit Comet. "When's your next patrol?"

"We're scheduled to leave November fourth. Probably be a week or two after that."

"Sounds like a shuttle launch."

He laughed. "It's a forty-year-old ship. Lots of moving parts that weren't necessarily designed to work together. I've got a good engineer officer this time around, and he's determined we're not leaving the dock until all systems are go."

"Good for him."

"And then of course the crew has to get their grocery shopping done."

"You don't feed them?"

"We feed them, and we feed them pretty well, but three months is a long time. Comfort food gets you through it."

She raised her head. "What's your comfort food?"

He ran a suggestive fingertip down her spine. "Hmm, well—"

This time she laughed, and tucked her face back into her arm. "Given my absence," she said, her voice muffled.

"Good tortillas. Corn, not flour. I don't know where he gets them, but Senior orders in these huge green flour tortillas and makes wraps out of them."

"You don't like wraps?"

"I don't like green tortillas."

"Eyew. I don't blame you."

"I make chips out of the ones I buy. As long as the tomatoes and the cilantro last I make salsa to go with them. Guac if we have avocadoes."

"You go down to the galley?"

"I've got my own. Didn't I show you?"

She'd only been on *Munro* once, the first time they'd met. By mutual agreement, after that they had met away from both of their worksites. They'd met at her house in Houston, where the astronaut corps had press avoidance down to a fine art, and at his rented penthouse suite in Miami, where the security was as expensive and thorough as his trust fund could make it. He had agreed to borrow his father's Lear for a trip to Alaska after his next patrol and her first deorbital burn, but she had yet to tell her parents she was dating someone again and Cal had yet to bring anyone home. From the outside this might have seemed a little paranoid, but they were both people who valued their privacy. They were also the both of them a little spooked to find someone who fit this well this late in the game, and there was an unspoken agreement not to hex it by inviting anyone else in. They were both grimly aware that the first paparazzi who scored a photo of Senator David Tecumseh Schuyler's fair-haired boy snuggling up to NASA payload specialist Kenai Munro would be set for life.

"What's the mission for this patrol?" she said.

Unseen by her, he made a face. "The usual. Intercepting drug smugglers."

"What happened to that boatload of migrants you picked up on your way in?"

"Repatriated. Immediately. We dropped them at the dock at Port-au-Prince."

"Harsh, after what they went through to get to America."

"At least they lived. They can try again."

She raised her head. "You sound like you're sorry you caught them."

He shrugged and capped the bottle of sunblock. "It's my job. It's what I get paid for. If I don't like it, I can get another."

Her brown eyes were steady on his face. "And if it weren't?"

He stretched out on the towel. "Then, hell yes, let

'em in. They spent their life savings on passage to America, looking for a better life. Nothing our ancestors didn't do, it's why we're here. Those folks on that freighter, they suffered for the chance, bled for it." He thought of the little girl falling overboard when the freighter started to roll. "Some of them died for it. Who the hell am I to bar the door? Who knows what that kind of single-minded drive and determination and willingness to sacrifice would bring to the United States?" He took a swig from his beer. "My father's successor could have been on that boat. We'll never know now."

She put her head back down. "You should run for office."

He swiveled his head to meet her mischievous look. "Hah hah, very funny. Okay, you got me."

She shrugged. "It's the only way to change things."

He pointed a finger at her. "Boats, remember? Why I got into the Coast Guard in the first place? Boats, not Capitol Hill. Suits and ties and three-martini lunches. Always looking for more money to run." He shuddered. "Don't ever say that again. Don't even think it. Never gonna happen. Not until after my first lobotomy, anyway."

"So," she said. "Drugs."

"Drugs," he said. "Immigrant mitigation and search and rescue, too, of course, but mostly we're on the drugs. It's not like we ever catch enough of them to make a difference, but I've got to hand it to us, we're right in there pitching."

"I'm whelmed by your enthusiasm."

Her tone was a nice balance of curiosity and criticism and generated no offense. He capped the bottle and lay down next to her. "It's such a waste of the nation's resources, Kenai. I've got a new support officer and we're running down the budget and Suppo tells me if I don't spend at least a million dollars on fuel every patrol, *Munro*'s not working hard enough. And that's just fuel, and we aren't even paying for that."

"Who is?"

"JIATF. Joint Interagency Task Force. Made up of all the three-letter agencies and then some. They work out of Key West. They're the ones who put the C-130s and the P-2s in the air and find the go fasts—or don't find them—and send us the intel. And we go get 'em. Or sometimes we do. Most times we don't. It's a big ocean."

She was silent for a moment. "I would think it would be, I don't know, kinda soul-destroying to be constantly not finding what you're trained to go look for."

He gave a short, unamused laugh. "You could call it that." He sighed. "It's the job, though."

"It's not what I think of when I think of Coasties," she said. "I think of you going to get my father when he wrecked his Cessna. I think of you saving my high school buddy Ole Johanssen when his crab boat went down off Slime Banks. I think of Katrina. The Coasties were the only government agency who had it together after Katrina."

"True." He was aware that his voice had warmed. He had told her a little about his part in Katrina. "I mean, don't get me wrong, it was truly awful, but I felt like we were really making a difference down there. Felt good."

"And this doesn't?"

He shrugged. "The Coast Guard has always intercepted contraband off the nation's coasts, Kenai. We have since before the nation was barely a twinkle in Washington's eye. Hell, up in your own state, Roaring Mike Healy's *Bear* was a revenue cutter."

"Why does this seem different to you, then?"

He took a long swallow of beer, thinking. "It's not my business, I know that. I don't make policy, I don't pass legislation, I'm just the cop on the beat, swinging my billy club. But it's such a waste of resources. If someone wants to stuff powder up their nose or shove a needle in their arm, it's stupid but it's their business."

"So you'd decriminalize drugs?"

He thought back to the patrol, to the only time they'd come close to accomplishing what it was that all the might and resources of the United States of America, the greatest nation ever to exist on planet Earth, had sent him to the Caribbean to do.

They had been making what Cal described to Kenai as a gentle and inoffensive course south-southwest when Ops picked up the binoculars and found what appeared to be a small skiff adrift off their port beam. Ops tried to raise them on the radio and got no response. He called Cal to the bridge. Cal, relieved to be taken away from the massive quantity of email in his in-box, responded promptly and examined the boat through the binoculars. It rocked in the swell, its cockpit deserted.

"Let's lower a boat and go take a look," Cal said, which was perfectly within their authority. The disappearance of the boat's crew, always assuming they weren't sacked out below sleeping off the previous day's consumption of alcohol, always a possibility this close to Miami, had to be investigated. The skiff, unmanned and adrift, was a hazard to navigation.

They'd been about to launch the helo. "Do we continue the launch, Captain?" Terrell said from flight ops.

Cal hesitated, but only for a moment. "Launch the small boat first."

"Aye, Captain."

A boarding team was assembled, BM2 Morelli's legendary dimples clearly visible from the bridge wing two decks up when he straddled the coxswain's seat. "Load, lower, and launch," Cal said into the radio. The boat deck captain shouted, "Boat moving!" The winch on the davit whined, the small boat settled into the water with barely a splash, fore and aft shackles and sea painter were released, Morelli goosed the engines, and they were off.

Cal watched them go, not without envy. He remembered those first halcyon days after he qualified in LE. He had always been first in line for any boarding party. The worst thing about moving up in rank was that you left all the fun jobs behind.

"We never get to play with the big toys anymore," a voice said at his elbow, echoing his thoughts, and he turned to see his XO staring after the small boat with an exaggeratedly mournful gaze. He laughed dutifully, and they both went back inside to monitor the radio traffic. "Anything yet?" he said to Ops.

Terrell shook his head. Next to him, Velasquez, the ET3 who doubled as one of their translators, spoke into the mike in Spanish, hailing the drifting boat. He waited. They all waited. No response.

Cal looked around and noticed that the bridge, already crowded with the flight ops crew, had become even more so in the few moments he'd been out on the wing. BMC Gilmartin was behind the nav table, pretending to instruct BM3 Stamm on the finer points of charting the next waypoint. HCO Harris was there, pretending she hadn't signed off on Suppo qualifying as helo control officer the day before. Suppo, a chunky chief warrant officer with merry eyes, pushed his glasses up his nose and raised an eyebrow at Cal, who repressed an answering smile, mostly because Harris was watching. EMO Olson was on the port wing, watching the small boat approach the skiff through binoculars, ET1 Jones behind the nav eval station, so they were more than covered if any of the electronics pooped out.

Taffy looked at him. They didn't have to say it out loud. The gang's all here, and then some. It had been a long patrol with very little action, and nobody wanted to miss out.

160

They all wore looks of suppressed excitement. He himself hated this part. Each second seemed to tick by more slowly than the last, and he had to rigorously suppress an active imagination that pictured hostiles on the skiff erupting from belowdecks and opening fire on his boarding team.

He knew that due to rigorous and continuous training his crew was ready for almost anything they might encounter. He knew that in thirty-five years of intercepting narcotics shipments in the eastern Pacific and the Caribbean only once, one time, had a uniformed member of the U.S. Coast Guard had a weapon pulled on him. He knew that in that instance the Coastie had been able to talk the asshole down without drawing his own weapon. He knew that the smugglers were very well aware of what would happen to them if they were caught with automatic weapons on the open sea. He knew that they also had a very lively appreciation of the penalty for injuring or killing an American citizen, and that they were well aware—none better—how effective the helo on *Munro*'s flight deck was at stopping go fasts from, well, going fast. Or, for that matter, going. On occasion, when the smugglers saw one of them coming, they stopped their boat and literally put their hands in the air. Once one of *Munro*'s small boats had reached the scene of a go fast disabled by the helo's .50-caliber to find the go fast's crew lined up on the deck, all of them with their bags packed and ready to transfer to the cutter.

None of this mattered. Cal still sweated out the time

between the approach of the small boat and the boarding team leader's first report.

"*Munro*, Mark 1, ops normal."

"Mark 1, *Munro*, ops normal, aye," Ops said into the mike.

Cal raised his binoculars. The small boat had closed to within a mile of the skiff and was making a big, slow circle. They all jumped when the radio erupted into life. "*Munro*, Mark 1, we see four new Yamaha 200s on the stern of the vessel!"

Before Ops could reply, through the binoculars Cal could see three men appear suddenly in the well of the vessel. A wake boiled up from its stern.

"Holy shit," someone said.

"Set go fast red!"

"Go fast red, aye, Captain!" Behind him he heard BM3 Stamm pipe, "Now, set go fast red, set go fast red!"

"Set flight quarters!"

"Now, set flight condition one!" Stamm's voice echoed over the ship so immediately on the heels of the order that Cal knew Stamm had been anticipating it. "Close all doors and hatches! Remove all hats topside! The smoking lamp is out!"

"*Munro*, Mun 1, ops normal!"

"Mun 1, *Munro*, ops normal, aye." Cal watched long enough to see the small boat settle into pursuit of the go fast and then went out on the bridge wing in time to see the aviators head aft at a run toward the hangar deck. Back inside the bridge had become crowded with deck officers, phone talkers, ETs, and HCOs, and loud with radio chatter between the officer of the deck, the helo communications officer, the landing signals officer, and Combat. At one point the noise level got so high the XO raised his voice and said, "Okay, everyone, take it down a notch."

Cal couldn't blame them. Part of their mission was to act as sentry between the wholesale drug smugglers in Central and South America and their retail market in the United States. Insofar as *Munro*'s very presence was a deterrent, well and good, but going a whole patrol without even the smell of a bust was disheartening to even the most motivated, best-trained crew. Everyone was excited at the prospect of a chase.

The closed-circuit television screen showed the helo on the flight deck, its rotors accelerating into a blur. A voice sounded over the speaker. "Hangman, this is Tin Star, we're ready for the numbers."

Suppo's voice was quick and sure as he went down the list: wind speed and direction, altimeter, the pitch and roll of the ship. The aviator, a lieutenant commander who had driven ships for two years before going to flight school and who consequently had a better idea than most aviators of what was going on on the bridge at that moment, read the numbers back and requested a takeoff to port. Suppo looked at Cal. "Permission to conduct flight ops, Captain?"

Cal nodded.

Suppo keyed the mike. "LSO, HCO, helo is cleared for takeoff to port, take all signals from the LSO, green deck."

"Green deck, aye," the conn officer said.

"Green deck!" the phone talker said, and switched the hangar lights to green.

"HCO, LSO, green deck." Cal recognized Chief Colvin's voice on the speaker. On the screen he watched the chief make a counterclockwise circle with his right arm and point to port. The pitch of the rotor blades increased and the helo lifted off, put its nose on the small boat, and shot down the length of the ship with neatness and dispatch, fifty feet off the deck.

"Get us up on turbines," Cal said.

The OOD, a newly minted ensign named Schrader, relayed the order to the engine room, which order was repeated back at the usual full-volume engine room bawl. A moment later main gas turbine one kicked in with its distinctive whine and *Munro* began to move over the water like she had a purpose.

"All ahead flank," Schrader said.

"All ahead flank, aye," the helm answered, and then she said, "Wait a minute."

"What's the problem, Roberts?" Schrader said.

"The rudder, sir," she said, a little uncertainly. She looked up at the rudder indicator and with more decision said, "It's stuck."

"Stuck?"

"Yes, sir, stuck, at five degrees port." In sudden indignation she said, "We're in the middle of chasing a go fast and they're throwing a drill at us, too?" She looked at Cal accusingly.

"This isn't a drill," Cal said. He exchanged a look

with the XO, and had to admire the way both of them refrained from screaming with frustration. "All stop, and pipe the EO to the bridge."

"All stop, aye."

"EO, lay to the bridge, Lieutenant Raybonn, lay to the bridge immediately."

Almost before the words had stopped echoing around the ship the EO stepped onto the bridge. The XO explained the situation tersely. The EO, a tall man with neat features and a calm expression, listened without comment and retired immediately to aft steering, where they heard later MK1 Bensley and EM1 Ryals were already wrestling with the rudder.

For the next few minutes, *Munro* went around in a very big, very slow circle. Everyone on the bridge waited for word from the helo. They sent an ops normal message and weren't due for another for fifteen minutes, but the boats hadn't been that far away, they should have made contact by now. Cal imagined *Mun 1* getting farther and farther away from home and the go fast getting farther and farther ahead of the small boat.

"OOD, MK1."

"MK1, OOD," Schrader said into his radio.

"OOD, we've manually brought the rudder amidships."

They all looked at the rudder indicator.

"MK1, OOD, rudder amidships, aye." Schrader lowered the radio and said, "Rudder amidships, Captain."

"All right," Cal said. At least now, with twin screws, they could steer the ship.

Ops was on the radio to *Mun 1*. "They still have the go fast in sight, Captain."

"Good to know." Cal's phone rang. It was the EO. He listened and hung up. "It was a dust bunny," he announced.

There was a brief silence, unusual in the middle of launching the helo. "I beg your pardon, Captain?" the XO finally said.

"A dust bunny," Cal said. "That's what jammed the steering linkage at five degrees port."

No one believed him, but he was the captain so no one said so, until the EO reappeared on the bridge with the dust bunny in question, a tiny scrap of fabric, oil-soaked and well-chewed, on display in the palm of his hand. "We figure someone was mopping oil out of the steering linkage with a rag and left this behind."

"Of course at the most inopportune possible time," the XO said tartly.

From the expression on the EO's face, a normally very unflappable man, Cal rather thought the XO was right.

They spent the rest of the day chasing the go fast.

"He would not stop for anything," he said to Kenai.

"I thought you could shoot out the engines."

"We could," Cal said, "if, a, the .50-caliber on the helo hadn't jammed, and b, we didn't have a problem fueling the helo when she came back to gas up."

"Yeah, gas is kinda important," Kenai, the veteran pilot, said. "What happened?"

"We thought at first something was wrong with the fueling system, but it turned out during the last refit the helo manufacturer had installed a new fuel coupling without telling anyone and without updating the specs. You know at a gas station when your car is full the handle clicks off?"

"Yeah?"

"That was what was happening when we tried to fuel the helo. It took us a week to figure out what the hell was going on."

"So you didn't fly for a week?"

"Oh no, we flew, the engineers figured out a way around it."

"Must have been frustrating."

"Yeah, well. Been nice to have caught ourselves a live one." He sighed. "We aren't seeing a lot of action this side of the isthmus since we got the smugglers here pretty much bottled up."

"Bottled up where?"

"There are three natural chokepoints in the Caribbean. Mona Passage between Puerto Rico and the Dominican Republic, Windward Passage between Haiti and Cuba, and the Yucatán Channel between Cuba and Mexico. If they're coming north, they are most likely coming through one of those. We know it, they know we know it, and they've gotten a lot cagier because of it."

"So what can you do?"

"Chase them," Cal said. "Chase them until they run out of gas. Chase them until they break down. Chase them until we catch up with them. Box them in with another cutter."

"What did you do this time?"

"Well, we caught up with him. We fired a stitch of warning shots from the machine gun across the bow to make them slow down. They never do, but we try. Then the goddamn .50-caliber jams, so they can't take out the engines."

"So they got away?"

"The aviators told me they flew so low over the go fast that the go-fast guys stood a pole up in the middle of the boat so they couldn't get close enough to drop a net, which they know we do sometimes so we can snarl their prop."

"Clever," Kenai said.

"Yeah, they've had a lot of experience running from us," Cal said. "Anyway, we chase him all day. Eventually, we've got two Coast Guard cutters, our helo, two Customs jets, and a Jamaican Navy patrol boat all engaged in pursuit of this yo-yo, and guess what?"

"What?"

"He got away."

"You're kidding."

"I wish."

"I didn't know Jamaica even had a navy," she said. "How much did that cost the nation?"

"It's better you should not know. The only upside is when last sighted he was headed south, which means he didn't get his drugs to market."

"They will eventually, though."

"They will," Cal said. "Or somebody else will. We're intercepting more drugs here and in EPAC every year, and you know what that means?"

"What?"

"It means we are responsible for driving up the price of drugs in the U.S. Supply and demand."

"You'd rather be in the Bering?" she said. "Twelve-foot swells, forty-knot winds, and ice forming on the bow?"

"In the Bering we'd be doing a boarding every other day, if not every day. Plus in the Bering there is always the possibility of a search and rescue. Out here . . ." His voice trailed off.

"You don't feel that the Coast Guard's efforts are being utilized to their fullest potential?" she said, a smile in her voice.

"I think we're pissing away any relevancy we had as a service," he said.

"Ah. I was trying to be diplomatic about it."

"I noticed."

"I like the dust bunny part of the story best," she said.

"You like a three-hundred-seventy-eight-foot cutter being put on hold in the middle of an operation?" he said a little dryly.

"Well," she said apologetically, "yeah. It has such a ring of . . ." She thought for a moment. "Inevitability, I guess. It's the little things that will screw you, every time. A tile falling off the shuttle. A morning temperature low enough to freeze an O-ring."

He so didn't want to go there. At least his cutter still

floated when it got into trouble. Space shuttles exploded. "*Munro*'s almost forty years old, with a bunch of systems some of which are older than that, none of which were necessarily designed to work together. And let's face it, it's not like the Coast Guard ever gets first pick of the tech. A lot of our systems fall off the backs of trucks headed for the Navy. Sometimes I think it's a miracle we get off the dock."

"There's a story," she said, "so far as I know actually true. Gus Grissom was being interviewed on the radio one night, and when the host asked him how he felt waiting for launch on top of a Mercury rocket, he said, 'How would you feel sitting on top of a million different parts, all of which were manufactured by the lowest bidder?' "

Cal laughed. "Yikes."

"Yeah, and that was back when all astronauts were de facto heroes and NASA could do no wrong." She stretched.

"Grissom was one of the guys who died in the capsule fire, right?"

"Yeah. Grissom, White, and Chaffee."

"You ever wonder if . . ." He hesitated.

"Every day," she said. "Every time I strap myself in. I'd still kill anyone who tried to take the job away from me." She smiled. "Just like you."

He thought of the go fast getting away, in spite of the massive amount of American manpower and assets arrayed against it. "Yeah," he said, a little wearily. "Just like me."

"Part of your problem is you're tired."

"And you aren't?"

"Time for me to be tired when we're wheels down."

"So long as you aren't arrested for homicide before you lift off."

She laughed. After a moment, she said, "Not loving the drug war, are you, Cal?"

"Not so much, no. If I had my druthers, I'd treat all drugs like alcohol, legalize them and tax the hell out of them and earmark the proceeds to underwrite the cost of marching every sixth grader in the nation through a detox center. 'There, you little twit, right there, see that guy sweating and shaking and screaming that the big snake's gonna get him? That's what'll happen to you if you use drugs.' After that, it's up to them and their parents."

He closed his eyes against the bright sun. "And I could get to work on stuff that matters. Like making sure your sweet ass gets itself safely in the air."

She raised her head from her arms again to smile at him. "You think my ass is sweet, do you?"

"Roll over here and I'll show you how sweet. Oh, never mind." He drained his beer, picked her up, and carried her into the bungalow.

10

The target was the very symbol of America's power and prestige. Its destruction would be a blow at the heart of everything they held dear, their capitalistic egotism, their imperialistic arrogance, their technological superiority.

Nothing and nowhere is safe from me, from us, he thought. That was the message he wished to send. It was the only message that had a chance of bringing the West to its knees, and that was what he wanted, a supplicant knocking at his door and begging to know how to make him go away.

The deaths would be minimal by comparison to 9/11, to the bombings in London and Madrid and Iraq, but there were names among them that would give pause to both East and West. If his time with Zarqawi had taught him anything, it was that no matter how many bodies were given up for cannon fodder, there were always more bodies to take their place. No, it was time to try something different, something spectacular, something that would burn indelibly into the hearts and minds of the enemy, something that would strike at their pride, at the very heart of who and what they believed themselves to be.

Further, the destruction of the cargo would throw down his gauntlet before his former masters in

Afghanistan, a defiant gesture of independence. He meant them to know that he would not be intimidated or brought to heel, and from that moment on they would know it. After this, they would have to treat him as an equal member. After this, his counsel would be valued.

Better, he would be feared. And with that fear would come respect. Isa and Abdullah would rank equally with bin Laden and al Qaeda. He would no longer follow, he would lead.

Yussuf and Yaqub had done well, recruiting from the Muslim communities in York and Leeds. He looked them over again. Most in their late teens, three in their early twenties, only one of them married, most of them with ordinary looks, and two actively unattractive. Again according to instruction, Yussuf and Yaqub had also selected as much as possible for surface ethnicity, dark skin, features tending more toward the African than the Arabic. Two of them were doctors. Four of them were engineers, which meant they had been trained to have a healthy respect for the laws of physics, and were conversant with the properties of electricity and the principles of elementary chemical reaction. Unafraid of complicated machinery, they were sons of Martha, they could make things work. He smiled at his comparison of these warriors of Allah to the Christian progeny of the sister of Mary, but only to himself.

They had been told as he had told Yussuf and Yaqub that this attack would be a second 9/11, only this time a simultaneous series of attacks on multiple targets in the West Coast of the United States: the airports of Seattle, San Francisco, and Los Angeles. They were so inexperienced that they didn't even ask how they were intended to get past American security, notoriously tight since 9/11, but Akil told them anyway. Years had passed, the Americans had been lulled into a false sense of security by thinking that terrorist activity had been moved to the battlegrounds of Iraq and Afghanistan, it was time again to test their homeland defenses, over which he was confident they would pre-vail, to the greater glory of Allah.

Very little of this was true, of course. It was not time yet for any of them, not even Yussuf and Yaqub, to know their true target. Security must rest only with him until the last possible moment. He had told Yussuf and Yaqub to select educated recruits wherever possible, because in his experience the more education, the more effective the recruit, and the more long-lived, which meant a better return on the training investment.

"I know," he said in closing. "It sounds a little non-specific, and at the same time a little . . . grandiose." He smiled. "But 'a man's reach should exceed his grasp, or what's a heaven for?' "

"The Prophet is wise," Yaqub said, and Yussuf nodded.

Akil refrained from pointing out that the words were from Browning, not Mohammed. If Allah was going to hand him a convincing quotation straight out of English 111, he was ready to accept it as a gift to further his argument. For one thing, it meant his time in America had not been entirely wasted.

Not that they needed convincing. Yussuf and Yaqub, coming ahead of him to York, had done well. The recruits were eager to volunteer their help, and their ideas came thick and fast. Most of them were improbable at best and fantastical at worst, and entirely unnecessary. For this job, all he needed were warm bodies with guns and two or three with a working knowledge of ordnance, which he could teach them himself.

He didn't tell them that, either.

Still, he knew better than to quash their enthusiasm, restricting himself to murmured comments that guided and instructed, never exhorted or dictated. At one point he said, "It is very important that events be synchronized in any operation." They agreed to that. Later he said, "Reconnaissance of the target we select is essential." Still later he said, "And of course we will need people familiar with the necessary materials. There will be training. We will be told where and when, and of course our travel will be arranged."

He was always careful to speak in the first person plural, and they responded, including him in their deliberations, deferring to his experience, following his extremely discreet and diplomatic lead.

He had selected York to recruit for the newest cell because he appreciated history, and York had one of burning Jews alive. The north of England had a growing Muslim community as well as a high rate of unemployment, fertile ground for the creation of a disaffected minority ripe for insurrection.

He had also chosen York as a good place to hide from his masters in the East as well as from the powers in the West, at least temporarily. He had never operated in England before this. Further, he well knew the al Qaeda leadership would not approve of his real target. Al Qaeda was interested in body count, not in counting coup. The infidel set too much store by life and not enough on the hereafter. To deprive them of what they held most dear, and to take it from as many as possible at the same time, was the mantra of the Islamic insurrection. Only when the West tired of being constantly under attack, so the thinking of his erstwhile masters went, only when Isa and his like had taken enough of those most precious lives would the enemy be defeated and Palestine be free once more.

He monitored a few select chat rooms and blogs on the Internet, and he knew the word had gone out to find him and bring him back into the fold, whether he was willing to come or not. They would find him, sooner or later, he understood that. But not yet, please Allah, not yet, not until he completed what he had set out to do. When he went back, it would be on his own terms, not as a supplicant, or worse, a prisoner. The humiliation of the prospect drove him to work even harder to hide his efforts from their sight.

He still controlled a great deal of their money, and they would want results for an investment of that size. They had left him alone after Zarqawi's death, partly because he was an undeniably effective operator, as he had showed these with the Baghdad bombing. They had been waiting, though, watching, hoping that if they gave him enough rope he would hang himself with it.

The image again called Adara to his mind, the slack sway of her body from the branch of the neem tree, the white knot of his shirt beneath her jaw, her eyes wide and dull in the moonlight. He accepted the memory, held it closely to him, embracing, accepting, owning the pain.

So often lately in the doing he forgot why. It was good to remember.

That evening he attended the first of several meetings with the young men carefully selected in advance by Yussuf and Yaqub, who had been in York for five months vetting prospective members. For this one meeting they were in the back room of a neighborhood community center, the door closed against the sound of the teen dance being held concurrently in the gymnasium. It was an inspired move on Yaqub's part, as most of their recruits weren't much older than the teenagers at the dance. Also very probably an opportunistic one, as Akil had observed Yaqub's dalliance with some of the more attractive young women. He did wonder occasionally if Yaqub's dedication to the cause might be a bit challenged by his hormones, but it wasn't a problem that hadn't come up before. He smiled to himself. So to speak.

Yaqub had set up the room in advance of the meeting, and Akil could see how much the businesslike setting impressed them. The dry-erase boards on easels, the tables in a sober line facing the boards, the pull-down screen mounted on the wall, the computer with its PowerPoint presentation, and the slide show that went off without a hitch, giving a brief history of the birth and flowering of the jihad, its heroes, its villains, and its future goals. It was very professionally done, designed with just the right proportion of sentimentality to ideological fanaticism, and ending with a long close-up of a smiling Osama bin Laden looking strong and confident, his gaze fixed a little over their left shoulder, at a future which held the promise of an inexorable spreading of the word of Islam across the globe. Akil might be breaking away from al Qaeda to form an independent faction of his own, but he knew better than anyone how useful the image was in recruitment. The West's pursuit of bin Laden after 9/11 had elevated him to a holy figure, revered as none other by right thinkers of Islam. At this point it didn't matter if he were ever caught or if he died in one of his refuges in the Hindu Kush. The legend would live on.

When the lights came up Akil deleted the presentation and cleaned the dry-erase boards with solvent, after which he turned and with a grave look searched the ten faces, one at a time, for boredom or, worse, ridicule. He found neither. They sat erect in their plastic bucket chairs, eyes alert, hands folded almost in an attitude of prayer.

Normally, training ran in three stages: basic indoctrination into Islamic law and guerilla warfare; training in explosives, assassination, and heavy weapons; and then instruction in surveillance, counter-surveillance, forgery, and suicide attacks. This could take as long as a year and sometimes longer than that. Akil himself had trained for almost thirteen months.

There wasn't time enough for the full course with this group, however, the schedule was far too tight. It was the one thing he didn't like about this operation. He had never liked keeping to someone else's timetable. It caused haste, and haste caused carelessness. He hadn't lived this long by being careless.

In this case, though, he reminded himself, the end result would be well worth the inconvenience. It was another reason for the size of the cell, and for the group training. He was breaking his most stringent security protocols, and he knew it, risking all their lives and his own freedom. Still, it could not be helped, and if they were successful the reward would be great.

His two lieutenants answered questions, Akil dropping in an occasional low-voiced comment when Yussuf or Yaqub got off track. The recruits were too awed to speak to him. Most of them couldn't even look at him. Good. Awe inspired unquestioning obedience in the faithful.

They met over a month, never in the same place and never on the same day of the week, and once, again upon Akil's instruction, changing locations at the last moment, more as an exercise in tradecraft than because he thought they were being watched. At the end of their last meeting, he gave them the same speech he had given Yussuf and Yaqub before sending them ahead of him to England, almost word for word. "You understand, once you set out on this path, there will be no turning back. You must leave behind family, friends, everything you have ever known. You will be hunted by policemen of every nation, always on the move, often hungry, always tired, never again knowing a night's peace, and at the end only death."

"But a glorious death," Yussuf said immediately, as he had on that day in Düsseldorf.

Akil nodded his head once, gravely. "I cannot tell you what will happen in the end. We will either convert the infidel to the true faith, make them our slaves, and have sole dominion over the earth, or we will put them all to the sword."

They looked back at him, attentive, alert, perhaps breathing a little faster, but with no timidity or faint-heartedness or second thoughts on display. Yes, Yussuf and Yaqub had chosen well. "If we ourselves die in the execution of this sacred task, Allah will take us as his own, and we will be most richly rewarded in the after-life."

"Seventy-two virgins for each of us," Yaqub said, exactly as he had said it in Düsseldorf.

"But you are men of faith, you know what will come to you, so I need not repeat it to you here. My concern is what happens between now and then. It is not an easy task, what you have chosen to do."

"We will follow you," Yussuf said, predictably.

"Today?" Akil said to the men sitting in front of him.

"Now? Are you this moment prepared to walk behind me out this door and never look back?"

They were on their feet cheering with one voice when he was finished. That the cheer was led by Yussuf and Yaqub was not noticed.

He smiled, then, patting the air with his hands. "Your joy in being about good work is music to my ears, but quietly, please, brothers, quietly." They subsided, eyes brilliant with excitement.

"You leave tonight," he told them.

"Where are we going?"

It was a natural enough question, and he saw no reason not to answer it. "You will be traveling separately, some on different planes, and I urge you not to congregate in the air or at either airport, and certainly not as you are going through customs and immigration. Yussuf has your identity papers and your airline tickets. You were each of you told to bring a suitcase large enough to be checked. Did you?" Eager nods all around. "Your destination is Vancouver, British Columbia."

"Canada." "Canada!" "Canada?"

"You will be met." There were some old contacts Akil trusted because they worked exclusively for money. "Yaqub will give you the details. You will travel by various means from Vancouver to a small training camp. There, you will learn to use small arms. The four best with the small arms will train on larger weapons." He didn't specify, and by now they knew enough not to ask. "You will also learn how to hide in plain sight, either on the move or in place, in a community such as your own here in York."

"When will we see you again, master?" Yussuf said.

"Soon," Akil said soothingly. He was keeping the timetable as vague as possible. When he gave the call, they would move into immediate action. He would withhold the target and the means of taking it out until they were on the last leg of their journey. "After your training, which should take all of your time for the next two months, you will be instructed to either return to Vancouver or go on to Calgary, Edmonton, or Winnipeg, there to hide in plain sight until you hear from me."

They digested this in silence, their awe momentarily suspended in lieu of the practical considerations involved. There were a few more questions. One of the older men had his elbows on his knees, his hands folded in front of him, his head bent over them as if he were praying. "What is it, brother?"

"My wife is pregnant."

"You are to be congratulated," Akil said courteously. "May it be a son."

The engineer raised his head, his face troubled. "I have a family, friends, a good job."

"Are you having second thoughts, brother?" Akil said softly. "There is no shame in that. The movement is not for everyone. Allah needs as many of the faithful in this world as he does in the next." A statement bin Laden would have refuted with vigor, but Akil wanted only true believers in this cell. The right touch of ideological fanaticism required so much less hand-holding down the road.

"Oh no!" The engineer was clearly shocked at the suggestion. "I see no other way," he said, more moderately, after Yaqub frowned at him and gave the door a significant look. This evening they were in a room off the main hall of a railroad workers' union headquarters, the walls oak-beamed and plastered. "Our people are being dishonored, oppressed, tortured, slaughtered by the tens, the hundreds of thousands. These people voted in this government, they support it. That makes them directly responsible for its actions, and we must hold them accountable for those actions. And then there is Palestine. No," he said. "There is no going back."

It now sounded as if Akil were in need of being convinced, which was what he had intended. He contented himself with saying mildly, "Then what troubles you?"

"I worry that after I have gone to paradise my family will suffer, my friends, my community." The engineer raised a troubled face. "It doesn't seem fair."

"Never fear, my son." Akil placed his hands on the man's shoulders and looked earnestly into his eyes. "We will do our best by them. They shall not want. And they will live in the knowledge that their husband, their father, their friend died a hero. Died for them. Died for Allah."

The engineer's face cleared. "Then I am ready to do my duty, to serve my people and my faith."

"Inshallah," Akil said. They embraced, and the

others stood in a circle around them, their faces lit with a glow of righteousness and camaraderie.

Really, he had become very good at this.

THE NEXT DAY HE TOOK THE TRAIN TO LONDON. ALL around him the English sat, oblivious to their imminent danger and unconscious of their apostasy, every second person chattering about nothing into a cell phone, others buried in the sports sections of their newspapers, when any but a fool could see the head-lines. Another car bomb and thirty more dead in Iraq. An American Army helicopter downed by a resurgent Taliban in Afghanistan. In London Dhiren Barot sen-tenced to forty years in prison. Israel launching mis-siles into Gaza.

Madness. Madness, all of it. And his part in it mad-dest of all.

In London he checked into an anonymous hotel and spent the afternoon in pilgrimage, first in three rides on the tube, on the Circle Line from Liverpool Street to Aldgate, on the Circle Line again from Edgware Road to Paddington, and on the Piccadilly Line from King's Cross St. Pancras to Russell Square. From the station at Russell Square he walked and took a series of buses to Tavistock Square, where he stood in silence for ten minutes, communing with the spirits of the departed. It had been another simple plan, well executed. He only hoped his next plan was as blessed.

A pity they'd all been caught, but then there were always casualties in war, and they didn't know enough beyond their own operation to cause him any harm.

The next day he flew to Lanzarote. Adam Bayzani met him at the luggage carousel. He'd already rented a car, and a hotel room. Over cocktails, Akil played with the swizzle stick in his mai tai, loaded with chunks of pineapple, melon, and maraschino cherries, and met Bayzani's warm gaze only infrequently. Over dinner he was hesitant, curious, shy, and, in the end, willing. He allowed Bayzani to lure him out onto the beach. The sky was filled with stars, and a waxing moon rose swiftly to bathe the ocean with a benign silver glow. It was all very romantic.

When they got back to the room Akil insisted the lights be turned out before he allowed Bayzani to undress him. In bed he was timid, letting the other man take the lead, teach him how to kiss, how to touch. Bayzani was in no hurry, experienced enough to be patient, allowing the anticipation to build, certain the payoff would be all the sweeter for the wait.

He was right, it would have been, and he didn't know any better until Akil rolled over to pin him down, his hands caught beneath him, a hard knee pressing his legs apart. "Oh," he said, suddenly breathless, heart pounding. The pupil was changing places with the master. Bayzani was willing to have it so and then Akil, as a continuation of the same smooth motion, shoved the five-inch plastic swizzle stick he had palmed at the bar all the way into Bayzani's left ear. It required little force, running in all the way to the little knob at the tip.

Bayzani's breath caught on a thin scream. Akil even had time to push the stick in and out a few times before Bayzani's body bucked once, twice, three times, legs thrashing, writhing, straining, shuddering in a cruel parody of sexual pleasure. He was young and fit and once he almost had Akil off, but by then it was too late.

He went limp. All the life sighed out of him in one long, ragged, rattling exhalation. He voided his bladder and bowels. Akil, lighting a lamp so he could see, watched Bayzani's pupils become fixed and dilated.

Adam Bayzani no longer lived there.

Akil was pleased. The swizzle stick had been an impulse, an improvisation. He was always looking for new, undetectable ways to kill with weapons that wouldn't set off a metal detector. He hadn't known the stick would work that well, guessing that at most it would reduce Bayzani to a drooling vegetable, which might have suited his purposes even better, so long as Bayzani lost the power of speech and cognitive thought. No, too chancy. Bayzani's death was preferable.

He looked down at the staring eyes almost with affection, pressed his cheek briefly against one growing rapidly colder, and unwrapped himself from the body. He stood upright and pulled out the swizzle stick. It cleaned itself upon extraction. There was almost no blood or brains on it or on the pillow beneath Bayzani's head. He put it carefully in his shirt pocket, where he might have put it after using it to clean his teeth, and straightened the bedclothes. He pulled them to the corpse's chin, and stood in thought looking down at Bayzani with a meditative expression, as Bayzani's urine dried on his thighs.

Bayzani had rented the car and the hotel room. The restaurant where they'd had dinner was on the other side of the island from the hotel, and they had done nothing to attract anyone's attention. No, there was nothing to connect him to the body in the bed. When the maid came in in the morning it would look as though Bayzani had died in his sleep. There might not be an autopsy on this island where the authorities preferred no news stories about unusual deaths among the tourists, their main source of income, but if there was and the true means of death was discovered, by then Akil would be far away.

He showered and dressed. Bayzani's uniform fit him very well, a little tight around the waist, but that was all. He switched the tags on their two bags and pocketed Bayzani's passport, identification, and airline ticket. He waited quietly until four in the morning, not even turning on the television, before slipping from the room, placing the Do Not Disturb sign on the doorknob as he closed the door behind him.

There was no one in the hallway. He left by a back door. On the beach, he sat in the sand to watch the sun come up, a beautiful smear of red, orange, and gold across a tropical sky, eclipsing the moon. At eight he went in search of coffee, and at eleven he was back at the airport, boarding a flight for Dublin, and there, one for Heathrow, and finally, for Turkey.

· · ·

IN ISTANBUL HE CHECKED INTO THE RENAISSANCE POLAT Hotel as Adam Bayzani. It was a tall glass wedge of a building on the edge of the Sea of Marmara. The Strait of Bosphorus was just up the Sahil Caddesi, which naturally put him in mind of Byron, and indeed, Istanbul did walk in beauty like the night, especially at night. The conference didn't begin until Wednesday, so he had two days to explore the city, which he did as much as possible on foot. Anyone observing would have thought him just another tourist there to take in the sights, and for these two days he almost felt like one.

The souks were wonderful, a crowded concatenation of life, rude and smelly and noisy and dirty, merchants shouting out their wares, children scuffling in alleys, women walking about freely and scandalously without the hijab. He thought for a wistful moment of how much Adara would have enjoyed herself here. He could have bought her those gold-leaf earrings from the dark-skinned jeweler who with that nose had to be Jewish, a handful of dates from the cart pushed by a young man in a ragged tunic and a too-big fez that kept falling over his eyes, a tiny cup of thick coffee from a stand where a cloud of flies swarmed over a spill of sugar. There were stalls of silk and copper pots and spices. A mule was being shod next door to a one-room dentist's office where a patient sat in mute misery with his head back and his mouth filled with tools, and in the next stall an old man made rivets for a bucket out of tiny triangles of tin as a crowd watched with the marveling eyes of those to whom manual labor was a foreign concept. Many of them were Americans.

That evening he lay awake thinking about Turkey. They were trying so hard to push their way into the European Union. He wondered if they would succeed. He wondered if they had read through the EU constitution and knew that if they adhered to the letter of it, it would make them a target in the eyes of many Muslims. They already had enough trouble with the Iraqi Kurds on their border, and he wondered why they were courting more. He let his mind play with the idea of Istanbul as a possible future target. They could use a warning.

The next morning he rose early, showered and shaved, and dressed very carefully in the blue uniform that he had had cleaned and pressed on arrival. His registration packet, including the agenda, had been waiting for him when he checked in, and he looked over it as he rode the elevator down. On the seventh floor it stopped and a woman, a blond American in the same uniform, stepped inside. She was a commander.

This was a meeting of an international organization with member nations numbering in the hundreds and individual representatives in the thousands. It was a piece of extraordinary bad luck that the first person he would bump into would be one of Bayzani's fellow officers, and in such close quarters that contact would be unavoidable. From the wealth of information he had been able to elicit over the series of emails he had exchanged with Bayzani throughout their ripening courtship, he had learned that the U.S. Coast Guard was a relatively small government agency, with a quickly rotating duty roster. Sooner or later, everyone in the Coast Guard worked with everyone else. Would this officer have known Adam Bayzani? Served with him at a duty station or on a ship?

He must be bold, there was no alternative. Because any American man would have in this situation, he said, "Adam Bayzani, District Seventeen, law enforcement."

"Juneau?" she said, and he breathed easier.

He didn't know, but felt it safe to nod.

"Sara Lange, IMO," she said, extending her hand. Her grip was cool and firm. "I'm from Alaska, originally. Born and raised."

In spite of all his training, all the years spent pretending to be what he wasn't, he stiffened. She noticed, and he summoned up a practiced smile. "Just assigned," he said. "I don't know the place all that well yet."

"You will," she said. "You'll see a lot of action."

"So I hear." Determined to direct the conversation into safer channels, he gestured at the agenda. "Are you a presenter?"

She nodded. "Piracy and armed robbery against ships."

"Really." Again she surprised him. He wouldn't expect a topic like that to be placed in the hands of a female. But then Western females were notorious for interfering in and pretending to an expertise in subjects that should be left strictly to men. When Islam triumphed, as triumph it would, women would be put back firmly in their right and proper place. "Quite the topic. What led you to it?"

"Oh," she said, it seemed to him a little too casually, "it was the most interesting of what was on offer. When were you transferred to Juneau?"

They reached the lobby and the door opened, and he was spared the necessity of answering. He smiled. "See you in there."

She abandoned her curiosity with a pleasant nod and preceded him out of the elevator. He exited behind her, and while he was culturally disinclined to ogle women he was still a man, and he couldn't help but admire the view as she walked away, trim and supple in her neat blue uniform, blond hair confined to a simple chignon at the nape of her neck.

The eighty-second session of the IMO's Maritime Safety Committee began on Wednesday, the twenty-eighth of November, featuring panels on topics ranging from new ship construction standards to communications in search and rescue to dangerous goods, solid cargoes, and containers, among many others. He attended several, taking care to remain always in the background, avoiding any attention, striking up no conversations beyond a pleasant greeting or a casual comment on content. Although he was greatly tempted he did not attend Sara Lange's panel on piracy, thinking that the less familiar any one attendee became with his face the better. He didn't want to give her any opportunities to trip him up over his alleged duty station, either. He'd never been to Alaska.

He made his contact as scheduled, on Friday, the last day of the conference, when most of the attendees had tired of sitting in a convention center listening to mid-level bureaucrats from a dozen different nations drone on about ship stability, load lines, and fishing vessel safety. Akil spotted him during an already depopulated flag state implementation panel that morning, and by the aids to navigation panel at three that afternoon many of the rest of the attendees had wandered off to sample the delights of the Hagia Sophia, Topkapi Palace, and the Grand Bazaar. They made eye contact as the meeting ended, nodded pleasantly, and left separately.

Four hours later Akil let himself into a room in a nondescript businessman's hotel in a homogenous suburb of the city. He set up the coffee service for two, pulled the one chair into a position in front of the television, and used the remote to channel surf. He found a *Baywatch* marathon, propped his feet on the bed, and settled in.

He came out of a doze and looked at the time. One A.M. His contact was late. He used the bathroom and made coffee in the pot provided by the hotel. It was lukewarm and tasted of mildewed cardboard. He paced to the window, which had a third-floor view of the parking lot. A taxi came. He drank the second cup of coffee, equally dreadful, and waited. No knock at the door. Another taxi disgorged a load of drunken salesmen and giggling women, who trooped inside a room. Shortly thereafter loud music was heard. Still no knock.

At three A.M. it finally came. He padded over to open the door and the man slipped inside, dressed now in casual shirt and slacks, eyes strained behind round, wire-rimmed glasses. He opened his mouth as if to speak and Akil said, "Softly. We don't want to wake the neighbors." He went to the bathroom and turned on the water in the sink. He motioned the man to stand close to him near the television, which was still on, a low susurration of background noise, it and the water enough to mask their conversation if anyone was listening. "What kept you?"

"I met someone who knew me. He was with a group and they wanted to go to dinner." He grimaced. "I couldn't get out of it." He hesitated, looking at Akil. "I thought you would prefer to wait, rather than have me call."

Akil nodded. "You were correct." He sat in the chair and motioned the man to sit on the foot of the bed. He hitched the chair forward until their knees touched and leaned forward, speaking in English. The other man listened intently, asking only the occasional question.

When Akil was done he sat back, watching.

The other man had folded his arms across his chest and was frowning at Pamela Sue Anderson running down the beach. "Is something wrong? Do you dislike the plan?"

The other man looked up. "No, I—" He caught

Akil's glance and stopped the word in mid-utterance. "It is ambitious, but the target is worthy of any effort. The impact of its destruction will be a humiliating blow from which the Americans will not soon recover."

Akil noted the use of "the Americans." Disassociation in a traitor was usual and expected. Still, no reason not to test him. He said in a neutral tone, "There are those who would say it does not leave enough bodies on the ground."

The other was too intelligent to be drawn. "What do you say?"

Akil allowed his lip to curl. "I have believed for a long time now that our strategy has been flawed. Bodies are easily buried and soon forgotten. The psychological impact of the destruction of a national icon will be much more lasting."

Tentatively, the other man said, "And 9/11? That had no lasting impact?"

Akil shrugged. "It led eventually to the greatest recruiting tool we have ever had, the invasion of Iraq. But do you see the West withdrawing? Do you see other countries insisting on that withdrawal? I do not."

The other took a deep breath and let it out slowly, elbows clasped on his knees, hands knotted in front of him.

"But still you are troubled," Akil said. "Do you find the plan ill-conceived?"

The other man feared Akil and the question enough to give it serious thought. "No," he said. "It is simple, it takes advantage of common practices and occurrences in the region, and of existing personnel and equipment in the area. Properly executed, nothing will look out of the ordinary until the very last moment, and by then it will be too late."

"What, then?"

He hesitated. "I am only one man, one of a crew of many men. And women. If somehow they managed to stop me, if I fail, the responsibility will be mine."

Akil smiled. "You will not fail."

The man looked at him, wanting more.

"And Allah will reward you in paradise."

He looked less than convinced. Ah, a realist.

"It is good that you worry," Akil said, rising to his feet. The other man rose as well. "Not to worry would be a sin of pride, of overconfidence. If you fear that you will fail, you will work that much harder to succeed."

Akil walked him to the door. The other man paused. "Yes?" Akil said, making him ask for it.

"When am I to be paid? I wouldn't ask, but I have debts, and a family—"

"I understand," Akil said soothingly, hiding his contempt. "Check your account. You will see that half the payment was deposited today, as we agreed. The other half the day after."

"And no one will know? No one will know it was me?"

"No one," Akil said, with such certainty that the other was appeased, at least until he was out of Akil's reassuring presence.

"Will I see you again before the day?"

"You will not," Akil said gently, allowing a moment for that fact to sink in. When the other man left this room he would be truly alone, until the day. Akil smiled. "But check your email. I will write. You will not be entirely abandoned, brother."

The other man looked alarmed. "Everyone's email is filtered through intelligence. It may be seen by eyes other than my own."

"Almost certainly," Akil said. "I will be discreet. But when I write, you will know it is me."

They embraced and kissed, embraced again, and Akil felt the other man's shoulders shudder. "Be brave, brother. You will not fail me." He allowed his voice to rise just a little, as if he were taking an oath. As if he were prophesying. "We will triumph. Our brothers and sisters, our mothers and fathers, our families and our friends will look on what we have done and be proud, and in the end, Islam and the will of God will triumph over the West."

He shook the man's shoulders once, gently.

"Inshallah."

"COAST GUARD," THE IMMIGRATION AGENT SAID IN acknowledgment and approval at JFK.

"Semper Paratus," Akil said.

The agent smiled.

This identity was the best so far. Everyone loved the Coast Guard.

"Where have you been?"

"Turkey. Istanbul." As if the agent couldn't see that from the visa on the passport.

She was heavy and black, a middle-aged woman in a well-fitting and well-cared-for uniform, her badge and her shoes both shiny. Her expression was friendly and her voice a pleasant surprise, a low contralto. So many Americans found it necessary to shout, as if to make sure no one overlooked their presence. "Business or pleasure?"

The question was rote and the agent's interest appeared casual so he allowed himself a small joke. "In Istanbul? Always pleasure," he said. "But business got me there. A conference. IMO."

"IMO?"

"International Maritime Organization. The Coast Guard is the U.S.'s representative to the IMO."

"Ah." The agent handed back his passport and sketched a salute. He smiled and returned it with a crisp, military gesture.

He maintained that military posture all the way through the airport. Taking a series of cabs and trains, doubling back once just in case, because he was always more aware of the shape of his features and of the color of his skin in the United States, he ended at Grand Central Station, where he went into the men's room a Coast Guard officer and came out a civilian dressed in Dockers and a Gap T-shirt under a sports jacket, no tie, and deck shoes, no socks. The uniform, stripped of any identifying marks and stuffed into a plastic bag, was dropped in an alley, where, if the lurking shadows at the end of it were any indication, it would be on sale on Canal Street within the hour.

He stayed the night in a Holiday Inn in Manhattan, in the middle of a convention of high school women's soccer teams, not one of whom slept that night. Neither did he, and he was less polite than he might have been to the bank clerk the next morning when he showed his Luther King identification for the last time. The lock box contained two passports, one Canadian, one Costa Rican, and a tattered black-and-white photograph. He took all three and returned the empty box to the attendant. He'd had this lock box for long enough. He'd wait a few months and then close the account via email, leaving nothing behind that might lead even the most able bloodhound to sniff out a trail to him.

At the Fifth Avenue branch of his Bahamian bank, he transferred funds to two already existing accounts, one in Florida and one in Haiti. He ate a late breakfast at the Carnegie Deli—he was not at all reluctant to admit that one of the things the Americans did better than anyone, along with beds and showers, was breakfast—and walked down Seventh Avenue to a cybercafé, where he paid for an hour's time on a computer with Internet access. He created a Yahoo! email account—he had used Hotmail in Istanbul and Earthlink in York, he liked to spread his Internet presence around—and sent a dozen messages. There were two immediate replies, one from Yussuf. All members of the cell, traveling separately as ordered, had arrived safely at the camp. Yussuf reported no undue interest in any of them or in the camp.

He had expected nothing less but it was still good to know. Leaving the café he took a bus to Ground Zero to pay his respects. The hole in the ground was filled with heavy equipment moving mounds of dirt. There were barriers shielding some of the work from view. He'd read somewhere that the construction workers had found more remains recently. Good for another headline, he supposed, and therefore useful in continuing to make the existence of their enemies felt.

He blended easily into the crowds of people, many with tear-stained faces, moving slowly past the wall of photographs, reading the epitaphs of the victims pictured there.

He had other faces in his mind, of course, faces that were not represented here. Not victims, never victims. Soldiers, they were. Soldiers in a glorious army, an army of virtue and right, or so his leader would say. He smiled a little, intercepted an incredulous look, and remade his expression into something appropriately mournful.

Afterward he did some shopping, enough to fill the carry-on suitcase he also bought, because nowadays people who traveled without luggage were automatically suspect, especially in America, and that evening paid a scalper $750 for a seventh-row center seat to *Jersey Boys*, which he enjoyed immensely.

The next morning he took the AirTrain to Newark International, where he boarded a flight for Chicago, where he changed airlines and flew to Seattle, where he changed airlines again and flew to Mexico City.

From Mexico City he flew to Port-au-Prince.

11

WASHINGTON, D.C., DECEMBER 2007

The phone rang. It was Hugh Rincon. "Isa's in the U.S."

Patrick straightened in his chair so fast he propelled himself away from his desk and bounced off the windowsill. "How do you know?"

"He was spotted by an immigration agent in JFK."

"He was spotted by Immigration in JFK?" Chisum said, his voice rising. "And I'm hearing about this from you instead of our own people, why?"

"You came to me," Rincon said, and left it at that. To his credit he didn't sound one bit smug.

"Wait a minute, you said they spotted him. They didn't grab him up?"

"The agent told her supervisor she thought this guy was worth a look. The supervisor disagreed."

Patrick digested this. At last he said, without much hope, "Did they at least follow him? Find out where he was headed?"

Rincon's silence was answer enough.

Chisum rubbed a hand over a suddenly aching head. "Anything else?"

"He entered the country under the name of Adam Bayzani. He was wearing a U.S. Coast Guard officer's uniform. The agent asked him where he'd been and he said Istanbul for a conference." Rincon took a deep breath. "There is more. Patrick, Sara just got back from an IMO conference on marine safety in Istanbul. You're not going to believe this, but she thinks she rode down in the elevator with this guy."

"What?"

Rincon repeated himself.

Patrick's first instinct was to scoff. Outside of Dickens this much coincidence was highly suspect. On second thought, he knew enough about Sara Lange to know that she was nobody's fool. Neither was Hugh Rincon. "All right," he said cautiously. "How'd he feel to her?"

"Bent," Rincon said bluntly. "The first information Coasties exchange after names is duty stations. She said this Bayzani said he was posted to District Seventeen, and then when she said she was from Alaska he shut down completely. For the rest of the conference whenever she saw him he was going in the opposite direction at flank speed. Her words."

"She make contact again?"

"She tried. She left a message on his voice mail to join her for drinks the last day. She never heard back from him. The whole thing felt wrong to her, so she told me about it when she got back, and then she checked the Coast Guard personnel list."

"And?"

"And there was an Adam Bayzani, all right."

"Was?"

"Was. She emailed him, and when he didn't email back, she emailed his CO."

"And?"

"And Adam Bayzani was in fact a commander, and he was in fact assigned to District Seventeen. The problem is, he's dead."

Chisum sat up straight. "When?"

"His body was found the week before the IMO conference started in Istanbul."

"Murdered?" Chisum said, sure of it.

"No. Died in his sleep, according to the police report."

"When and where?"

"Lanzarote."

"Where's that?"

"Canary Islands."

"What the hell was he doing in the Canary Islands?"

"Working on his tan. Lanzarote's a vacation destination for Europeans."

"He was on leave?"

"Yes. His boss said he was stopping off for a week in advance of the IMO conference."

"He alone?"

"He rented his car alone and he checked into his hotel alone."

"But?"

"But his boss said that Bayzani acted like he would be meeting someone."

"He say who?"

"No. His boss said he seemed happy lately. Evidently a pretty morose guy at the best of times. No girlfriends, kept his private life private, nobody he worked with had ever been to his apartment. His boss thought he might be gay."

"Really." Patrick digested this in silence for a moment. "Was there an autopsy?"

"No."

"Why not?"

"When a tourist dies, the local authorities get the body out of there as fast as they can. Tourism is pretty much their living. Anyway, I'm not sure they even have an ME."

"Can we ask for an autopsy?"

"The body is on its way home to his family in Los Angeles."

"All right, I know people in L.A.," Chisum said, cradling the phone between his shoulder and his ear so he could access the directory on his computer to look up names of helpful colleagues in L.A. "Any footprints on Bayzani's service record?"

"None that I can find, outside of his heritage. His family is fourth-generation American. He does have a Jordanian great-grandfather. His grandfather served in the Eighty-second Airborne during World War II. His mother was a Navy nurse in Vietnam. He was a Coast Guard Academy grad himself. They're all as American as apple pie, no red flags anywhere."

"Crap."

"Now for the good news."

Patrick perked up. "There's good news? Did the son of a bitch finally get on a phone?"

"Not that good, but almost. He had to have a passport to get into the country, and passports have to have photos."

"We've finally got a photo?" Patrick said, disbelieving. "A current photo?"

"Okay, don't start hyperventilating, it's doctored, our resident geek tells me some kind of computer overlay program where they alter the original photo to resemble the current holder without looking like it's been got at by a kindergartner with a crayon. There is a general ethnic similarity between Isa and Bayzani, probably one of the reasons Isa picked him, and the photograph's a little blurry, but it's the best we've had so far."

"You're sure it's him? This isn't an 'all Islamic terrorists look alike to me' kind of thing?"

"As sure as I can be," Rincon said, not taking offense. "As I don't have to tell you, the photos we've got of him aren't good, but I was pretty sure from the get-go this was the same guy." He hesitated. "Patrick."

"What?"

Rincon spoke, sounding as if he were choosing his words very carefully. "There was an—incident involving maritime shipping two years ago."

"I know," Patrick said. He'd looked up the case file after he'd called Hugh for help on Isa.

"Yeah, I know you do, and I know you know that I'd

like to stay out of jail for violating state secrets. Kind of a personal quirk. The only point I'm making is, I think attacks by air are pretty much over. I think the terrorism community is moving on to attacks on maritime targets, in particular busy ports."

"We've been talking about that ourselves."

"Not enough," Rincon said tersely. "Not nearly enough, Patrick."

"Forward me what you've got," Patrick said.

"Will do." Rincon hung up.

Melanie brought him the fax from Hugh just as Chisum was sitting back from issuing an all-agencies alert as to Isa's probable presence inside U.S. borders. The phone began ringing as he spread the pages across his desk. "Get that, will you, Melanie, thanks. And I'm not in for the rest of the afternoon."

"Yes, Mr. Chisum." She was curious but too well-trained to ask, and he watched her walk out the door with his usual attentive wistfulness. He shook his head and pulled out his Isa file to compare the photographs. The ones in Iraq were group shots, taken from a distance. Everyone was burnoosed and bearded. Isa's head was circled, and in another print blown up. The quality of the print was atrocious, and what resemblance there was between it and the clean-shaven, smiling face in the passport photo was minimal at best. The group photo was more about personality than likeness. He was standing a pace in the rear behind Zarqawi, looking solemn, even a little studious, his hands folded, his lean figure a study in stillness.

The two photos Rincon had been working from were only marginally better. One was a black-and-white head shot taken with a long lens, picking Isa's face out of a crowded Baghdad street. He was seated at an outdoor café, drinking something from a tiny cup, facing someone with his back to the camera. Isa's face was seen over the second man's shoulder, looking straight into the camera lens. The resolution was grainy and his expression couldn't be made out, but there Patrick nevertheless got a clear impression of vigilance, as if Isa were always alive to his surroundings, might even be somehow aware that his photograph was being taken at that very moment.

The third photograph was another group shot, this time a posed shot of a Zarqawi grip-and-grin with bin Laden. The accompanying caption read "Peshawar, Pakistan?" Neither man looked overcome by joy at the encounter, but by the date on the photo, this was right after the hotel bombings in Jordan, and at that time no one in Arab leadership, legitimate government or terrorist, was pleased with Zarqawi.

And once again, at Zarqawi's shoulder, stood Isa.

He compared the two faces first to Bayzani's service file photo, and then to the doctored passport photo. He'd have the photos looked at by their own geeks down in tech services, but he was sure in his own mind that Rincon was right. It was Isa.

And that meant Isa was indeed in the United States.

He read the account of the immigration agent who had cleared Isa for entry. No useful knowledge to be gained there, except that Isa appeared to be at least superficially well versed in Coast Guard lingo. He made a note to inquire into Bayzani's past movements with care and attention. If he'd been spending time spilling his guts to Isa about his job, Patrick wanted it all down, chapter and verse.

While he had been perusing the file he was aware of the phone ringing nonstop outside his door, Melanie's voice a soothing counterpoint. At precisely sixty minutes and one second her tap was at the door. At his response she came in, set down a large stack of pink telephone slips, and departed again.

He thumbed through the slips. Mostly panicky demands for more information. Since he didn't have any, he shoved them to one side and assumed the position, feet crossed on the windowsill, hands folded on his stomach, frown aimed at the horizon.

No way to catch up to Isa until he surfaced again. Isa was a very cautious man. So far as Patrick could tell he never spoke on the phone, he never emailed twice from the same address, and he never flew directly to a destination, always employing multiple segments on multiple airlines, never booking them all at once, spreading his purchases around on Orbitz, Travelocity, and the airline web sites. No, Isa didn't make mistakes often, and truly, in these two instances, Istanbul and New York, he had erred more on the side of bad luck than bad judgment. Better to be lucky than good, as the old saying went. American immigration agents by and large were trained to look more at documentation than they were at faces and behavior.

Political correctness was all very well, but at what cost to the nation's security? The men on the planes had been recruited from upper-middle-class Saudi families, well educated and for the most part well off. Therefore American security forces manning American borders ought to be looking hard at upper-middle-class, well-educated, well-off men of the Islamic faith of every nationality. Never mind that there were millions of Muslims who did not subscribe to the notion that killing was the way to revenge, redemption, and paradise. Nobody ever hijacked an El Al jet and that was because El Al knew all there was to know about profiling and then some.

We could take lessons, Chisum thought now, and we should. As he had told Khalid nearly two years before, Kallendorf wasn't all wrong.

But Isa's first real piece of bad luck had come in Istanbul. He had learned enough, probably from Bayzani, to know that he'd have to have a duty station on offer when asked. Alaska would have seemed sufficiently remote to be safe. What were the odds, he would think, that he'd find himself riding an elevator with a Coast Guard officer born in Alaska?

Turns out, pretty good odds if he'd had anything but a superficial knowledge of the U.S. Coast Guard, who maintained a very large presence in Alaska, a state with 36,000 miles of coastline if you included all the islands, peninsulas, and archipelagoes.

That was not the real question, however.

The real question was, what was Isa doing at an IMO conference on marine safety in the first place?

There were two possible answers to that question.

One, he was there to learn what measures the international maritime community was putting in place to ensure the safety of vessels and crews working the high seas, for the purpose of confounding those measures and launching an attack against pick a target.

Two, and the answer Chisum considered far more probable, Isa was there to meet someone. Someone already inside the maritime community. Someone with a solid working knowledge of the shipping industry.

Or, or perhaps including, a working knowledge of ports. Western ports. Busy ports. Vulnerable ports.

But then, they were all vulnerable. Less than three percent of containers coming into U.S. ports were examined for contraband. Anybody could tuck anything inside of a container, stick it on a Horizon Lines ship, and feel pretty secure that it would never be spotted.

On the other side of his door he could hear the phone still ringing, though less frequently than before, and Melanie's voice still desolate at her inability to oblige any of the callers. She was really very good. She came in with another sheaf of phone messages. He looked at the clock. "Hey, it's after five. Go on home, Melanie."

"I can stay, Mr. Chisum. You could use the help."

"You have to have something better to do than babysit me, Melanie."

She smiled. She had a dimple in her right cheek. Her

skin was like ivory. He recognized the triteness of the observation at about the same time he realized he'd been staring. He could feel the color creep up over his face, and he said gruffly, "I appreciate it, Melanie, thank you."

And again he watched her walk out of his office. Rumor had it that she'd been seen outside the office in company with Kallendorf. He hoped it wasn't true, and not just because it would mean the director had a spy too close to Patrick for comfort. He liked Melanie. He liked her a lot. She had thus far proved not only decorative but capable and efficient as well. True, he also liked the thought of her naked and stretched out on a bed, but he tried not to dwell on that. It was always a mistake to dip your pen in the company ink. Particularly this company.

He swiveled back to his computer and got online. The IMO's web site displayed an impressively far-reaching organization, with at a rough count over 170 member nations, including ones like Bolivia, Switzerland, and Mongolia, which so far as he could recall without looking at an atlas were landlocked. The U.S. Coast Guard was the United States' representative at the IMO. He wondered who other nations sent. Be worth finding out. He made a note.

Then there were the government and non-government organizations affiliated with the IMO, some of which might prove productive of investigation, like the Arab Federation of Shipping, the Organization of Arab Petroleum Exporting Countries, the International

Association of Ports and Harbors. This last looked interesting so he pulled it up, and found links to countries with links to various of their ports. He clicked on Ireland in memory of Josie Ryan and on the Shannon page somewhat to his dismay found all the information he could wish for about the port, including maximum vessel dimensions and a scale map showing seven separate ship-berthing facilities.

He sampled some of the other port pages, and while some web sites were better than others they were all very informative.

He swiveled back to the window and reassumed the position.

On ports at least there was all the information Isa could wish for on the Internet if he were planning an attack against one. He would have no need to attend a conference on maritime safety to learn more.

No, he would attend a conference on marine safety to meet someone there. Patrick was now certain of it. Someone who had either information he needed, or expertise. Or both.

But Patrick wasn't going to catch him to ask him, at least not today. Maybe tomorrow, or the day after that, but that was then. He'd put everyone on the alert. All he could do now, maddening as it was, was sit back and wait for Isa to be spotted.

Maybe, he thought, just maybe he was looking at this from the wrong direction. Isa was in the wind. Someone might stumble across his path again, but the odds weren't in their favor. They'd been incredibly lucky in the two contacts they'd had, both by conscientious, practicing professionals, but it was fatal to depend on lightning striking that way a third time.

And besides, Patrick was tired of being a step and a half behind this guy. It was time to do a little backtracking, find out what made the guy tick so they'd have some idea of what he might do next, and where.

Chisum turned back to his desk and picked up the phone. This time he got the nation code right and Hugh Rincon's voice mail came on. He realized that it was after ten o'clock in London. "This is Patrick Chisum again. Who else attended that conference in Istanbul? I want a breakdown by names, professional organizations, and nationalities."

He hung up and frowned at the clock on his desk. The minute hand swept inexorably around, counting down the seconds, the minutes, the hours.

Like he needed reminding.

12

HAITI, DECEMBER 2007

It took him a pitifully short time to find what he was looking for in Haiti, which cost him in U.S. dollars the equivalent of a used car, which he found even more pitiful. While he was conducting his business he stayed in a modest room at a resort hotel, renting a girl for the weekend so as to maintain his cover as a car salesman on holiday. She was a straightforward businesswoman, with a refreshing lack of curiosity even that first night when he gently refused her sexual services and insisted she sleep in the second bed. "Arm candy only, then," she said, as if it wasn't an unusual request, and didn't offer a discount. Time paid for was time paid for. On a professional basis, he had to respect that. She insisted on half up front. He respected that, too.

After he concluded his business, he maintained his cover by spending the weekend at the hotel lounging poolside with his paid companion, taking an hour off to find a cybercafé and check in. Yussuf and Yaqub were in Canada, one in Toronto and the other in Vancouver. They reported all cell members accounted for and settling in to their various temporary lives.

On Monday morning he paid the girl the other half of her fee and checked out of the hotel. He took a cab to the airport, a flight to Mexico City, a second to Cartagena, and a third to Miami. It took two days for him to arrive at his destination, but he had never lacked for patience.

In Miami, he took an airport shuttle into town to one of the big box hotels on Miami Beach, took a bus back to the airport, and picked up a nondescript sedan reserved in the name of Daoud Sadat. He drove south to an anonymous suburb bisected by a major arterial lined with big box stores, did a little shopping at Target, and then consulted a street map purchased at a gas station. He turned right out of the Target parking lot, turned left at the next light, drove down a series of quiet side streets, and parked in front of a shabby, ranch-style home on a large lot festooned with palm trees and a prowling bougainvillea barely restrained by a chain-link fence. The house two doors down had had its trim renewed, and across the street someone had just replanted their yard, brave in poinsettia plants and new grass, but the neighborhood had the air of fighting a hopeless battle, as if a wrecking ball and upscale condominium high-rises were just one developer with a vision and a city councilman in his pocket away.

His knock was answered by a young woman with a grave face. "Yes?"

"Daoud Sadat. I believe I am expected."

She nodded. "You are. Please come in, Mr. Sadat." She reached for his suitcase.

He waved her off. "Thank you. I'll carry it."

"It's no bother." Her eyes were anxious.

"For me, either." He gave her a reassuring smile, and was rewarded by one in return. The change it made in her face was extraordinary, lighting her eyes, lending color to her skin, dimples to her cheeks. Her teeth were white and even.

She looked, he thought with a faint sense of shock, like Adara.

"Please follow me," she said.

She led him through the house to the kitchen, a large room at the back with appliances of varying ages against the walls, the center of the room dominated by a large wooden trestle table with benches on both sides and a captain's chair at either end. "Mama, this is Mr. Sadat."

The kitchen may have been as shabby as the exterior of the house but it was scrupulously clean. The woman at the stove was her daughter again in face and form, with twenty years and twenty pounds added on. Her dark hair was knotted at the back of her head, her dress was buttoned firmly to her throat and wrists with a hem that brushed her ankles. She wiped her hands on the dish towel knotted around her waist and bowed her head in his direction. "Mr. Sadat. I am Mrs. Mansour. This is my daughter, Zahirah."

He nodded to both of them. "Daoud Sadat. I wrote about a room?"

"Of course. I will show you. Peel the eggplants, Zahirah."

"Yes, Mama."

Mrs. Mansour led him to a room past the kitchen. It was clean and pleasant enough, containing a full-sized bed with a firm mattress plentifully supplied with pillows, a small writing table with a straight chair in one corner, in another an easy chair facing a television, and its own bathroom. "There is no tub, only a shower," Mrs. Mansour said.

"It is no matter," Akil said.

"I'm sorry that there is no telephone, Mr. Sadat, but I have the number of the telephone company. The connection is here." She pointed at the box low on the wall. "All you have to do is call them and have it hooked up. It may take a few days." She straightened.

"And as you can see, your room has its own entrance," she said, opening the door. It had a window curtained only in white nylon sheers, but the encroaching bougainvillea obscured the neighbor's house. He looked outside. A cement walkway led to the front of the house. "You can be as private as you wish here, Mr. Sadat."

He shut the door and smiled at her. "I can see that, Mrs. Mansour, thank you."

"The breakfast things will be on the table in the morning: cereal, rolls, fruit, coffee. I rise very early to go to work."

"Ah. Where do you work?"

"At a dry cleaner's. My daughter, also, will be gone very early, so you will have the house to yourself."

He smiled. "I will be at work early, too."

"You already have a job?"

"I do," he said gravely. "I am a software engineer."

She nodded. "For Lockheed, probably."

"Yes," he said, raising his eyebrows in well-simulated surprise.

She took it as an implied rebuke for curiosity into his affairs and apologized. "It's just that their headquarters are so near, I assumed—"

He patted the air. "It is no matter, Mrs. Mansour, I quite understand. Your daughter works as well?"

"My daughter goes to university," Mrs. Mansour said.

"You must be very proud."

"It is why we moved here. It has been . . . difficult,

but it was her father's dearest wish."

He steered her off further confidences by inquiring as to how she would like the rent, suggesting cash since he had not had time to open an account in a local bank. He paid for a full month in advance, including the deposit, over her protests, and escorted her to the door.

He barely had time to unpack the meager belongings in his suitcase when a soft knock sounded. He opened it to find Zahirah standing behind it with an armful of fresh towels and two bars of Ivory soap still in their wrappers. "For your bathroom," she said.

She hung the towels and the washcloths and unwrapped the soaps, putting one in the dish next to the sink and one in the dish in the shower. "Dinner is at eight, Mr. Sadat," she said. "Is there anything else you need?"

"Nothing, I thank you."

Her eyes went past him to his open suitcase. "But—I thought my mother said you were a software engineer."

"I am."

"You have no computer?"

He did not. He would never be so imprudent. He carried a flash drive in his left-hand pocket at all times. It was an indulgence, to carry that much information around with him, but it was necessary, and it was small enough to be easily disposed of at need. The information on it, mostly names and contact information, was encrypted and he backed it up to an online server in a name he never used for anything else.

But she was still wondering about his lack of computer, so he said, "I left it at work."

"Oh." She was doubtful but accepting. "Most engineers bring their work home with them." She met his eyes and a delicate flush stained her cheeks. "I'm sorry, Mr. Sadat. It's none of my business."

He smiled to show no offense taken, and changed the subject. "You and your mother don't wear the hijab."

A wary expression crossed her face. "The hijab is traditional, not religious."

"You and your mother are reform, then?"

This time her answer had teeth in it. "There is nothing in the Koran that advocates the hijab."

He surprised them both by laughing.

"What's so funny?" she said, still hostile, and a little bewildered.

The laughter had felt good. It had been a long time since he had laughed out loud. He sighed. "You sounded like my sister," he said simply.

"Oh," she said. She sensed his sorrow, and her hostility drained away. "My father—"

"Yes, I know, your mother told me," he said.

Again she was surprised. "She did?"

"That he wished for you to go to school. It is easy from that to understand the rest. Thank you for the towels and the soap. I will see you at dinner."

"Oh," she repeated. "Of course. Until dinner, then."

The door closed softly behind her and he stood where he was, listening to her footsteps go down the hall.

13

The messages were waiting for her when she got back to the hotel. She called the instant she got to her room and was greeted with, "Where the hell have you been?"

"Touring the topless towers of Ilium for *Smithsonian* magazine," she said.

"What? Are you all right?" Hugh Rincon did not consider poetry necessary, and Elizabethan poetry even less so.

"Girl's gotta earn a living," Arlene Harte said.

"Whatever. Call me back from a pay phone?"

"All right."

She found a coffee shop whose owner was willing to accept an exorbitant amount of money for the privilege of loaning out his telephone, a massive black instrument that looked as if it had been used by George Raft to call in a hit on Humphrey Bogart. It even had a dial, and its cord was straight.

It was at least in the owner's office, and the owner's office had a door that closed. She negotiated her way through the intricacies of Turkish long-distance and a short time later had a surprisingly clear connection to London. "What's up?"

"I need you to go to the Renaissance Polat Hotel and find someone with a good memory who remembers an International Maritime Organization conference held there a couple of weeks ago."

The desk had a tattered phone book on it and she was already puzzling her way through the Turkish Yellow Pages. "Okay, got it. What do you need?"

"Someone masquerading as an officer in the U.S. Coast Guard attended the conference, I think to contact someone else who was attending legitimately."

" 'Someone'?"

"The someone is what I want you to find out. The guy masquerading as the Coastie was Isa."

She drew in a breath and blew it out again. She knew who Isa was. She'd been doing a story on Petra in Jordan when the Baghdad bomb had gone off. "Are we sure he's gone? I've always enjoyed being in one piece."

"Oh yeah, we're sure," Hugh said grimly, "because we're pretty sure he's in the U.S."

Arlene felt the hair rise on the back of her neck. "Holy crap."

"Yeah. Anyway, I FedExed a package with photos to your hotel this morning."

"What exactly do you want to know?"

"If anyone remembers Isa, who was traveling under the name of Adam Bayzani. Commander Adam Bayzani. Find out if he was seen with anyone else. If he was, find out if anyone overheard any part of that conversation."

"You know you're dreaming, of course," she said. "This is Isa we're talking about, the practically invisible terrorist."

"I know," Hugh said gloomily. "Realistically, best-case scenario is you find his maid, who says he was such a nice young man, every morning he left a generous tip on his pillow. This guy won't even pick up a phone, he does everything anonymously via email with multiple addresses he never uses more than once. After we took out his boss, I'm guessing he won't even use satellite phones anymore. But he was at that conference, I'm sure of it. It lasted three days. Someone has to have seen him doing something." In spite of himself his voice rose. "Somewhere!"

She said nothing and Hugh got himself back under control. "Anything, Arlene, any scrap of information you can dig up is more than we've got now."

"Who am I working for, Hugh?" she said slowly. "This is starting to sound personal."

"It is personal," he said. "Sara was at the conference. He rode down in the elevator with her the first morning."

"Jesus Christ."

"She was in uniform, Arlene, and they introduced themselves. And as I'm sure you recall, Isa doesn't suffer a witness to live."

"I remember," Arlene said soberly.

"But for the record, you're working for us, or at least it'll be our name on the check."

"But?"

"But our friends across the pond are footing the bill."

"So, you're saying I can pile on the expenses."

"Anything, any scrap of information, Arlene," he said again, not responding to the joke. "Solid gold."

· · ·

ARLENE HARTE, MIDFIFTIES, COMFORTABLY PLUMP, determinedly blond, and relentlessly single though far from celibate, had reported from the various fronts of global wars for the Associated Press for long enough to earn a recognizable byline, a syndicated column, and an occasional spot on *Washington Week in Review.* Gunfire, however, had palled after thirty years, though travel had not, and there followed a comfortable retirement, the most part of which she spent freelancing articles for the *Smithsonian, National Geographic Traveler,* and *Travel+Leisure.*

The rest of her time was spent working freelance as a spy for her country, ferreting out information that opposition organizations and nations would much rather not be unearthed. Hugh Rincon had recruited her when he'd been on the Asian desk at the CIA. When he had resigned, she followed him to the Knightsbridge Institute, where the governmental oversight of company activities was significantly less, the pay was pleasurably more, and the job was, to say the least, eclectic. Arlene was invaluable to them. Her cover as a freelance writer, especially with her CV, got her in many a door that would be closed to anyone else, and her unthreatening appearance coupled with a ferocious intellect, an almost preternatural capacity for assimilating the details of global current affairs, and a gift for sniffing out people who liked to talk did the rest. It didn't hurt that she could write, her reports a model of clarity and a gold mine of intelligence. As soon as the intel in them cooled off they were commandeered by the instructors to show the new guys how to get the job done.

The Knightsbridge Institute, in fact, had just given her another raise, her sinful second in eighteen months, and when she finished the Troy story she had planned to head for Elizabeth Arden in New York.

Regretfully, she decided that Liz would have to wait a few days.

The Renaissance Polat was an abstract thrust of aggressively modern glass that looked more than usually phallic, as was the invariable manner of the glass-and-steel structures of nations clawing their way to first-world status. She went inside, consulted the directory, and saw an international nursing conference was currently being held in the public rooms. She found the bathroom, and from a capacious shoulder bag extracted a navy blue blazer with brass buttons, neatly folded and stowed in a gallon-size Ziploc freezer bag. She shook it out and pulled it on over her white T-shirt and chinos, and surveyed herself in the mirror. She fished around in the bag again and produced a pair of reading glasses with clear rainbow frames, which she perched on the end of her nose, over which her green eyes looked out inquiringly. She gave a satisfied nod, closed her bag, and walked out with a stride that somehow managed to hint at orthopedic oxfords worn on long nights on the kidney ward.

The conference was being held in half a dozen rooms with concurrently running programming. It was coming up on the hour. She selected a panel at random, "Shaping Healthy Behaviors," and went in. The speaker was a young woman with a bright red face and a stutter, and most of the audience looked as if it was just about to stop being polite and head for the door, but they weren't Arlene's concern.

At the back of the room stood a woman in the universal uniform of the hotel employee, a maroon vest over a white shirt with a black bowtie, black slacks, and comfortable black shoes. She stood next to a table holding a large stainless steel carafe, cups, pitchers of water, glasses, and trays of sugar cookies, most of which remained. It didn't speak well for the hotel baker.

Arlene busied herself pouring a cup of coffee, which to her surprise was the real thing, dark and aromatic. She sweetened it and poured in a healthy dollop of cream and by then the panel had wound down and the crowd, most of them women of varying ages, shapes, sizes, and nationalities but all of them looking relieved, streamed out of the room. She loitered until the last of them had departed, and smiled conspiratorially at the server.

She didn't smile back, a bad sign, but Arlene didn't give up easily. She sipped her coffee, closed her eyes in exaggerated ecstasy, opened them, and smiled again. This time there was a lightening of the woman's expression.

Encouraged, Arlene nodded at the podium and cast her eyes upward. This time the woman definitely smiled. Arlene grinned in response and shrugged. "At least it's a free trip to Turkey."

"You are a nurse, too?" The woman's English was heavily accented but easily understandable.

"I am," Arlene said mendaciously.

The woman hesitated. Arlene looked sympathetic and encouraging.

"Do you do the—" The woman gestured toward her back.

"Back injuries? Well, it isn't my specialty, but . . ."

Five minutes later they were ensconced in a dingy little break room over some very nice homemade lamb sandwiches in pita bread, and the woman, whose name was Nawal, was relating the problems she'd been having with lower back pain. Arlene listened attentively, and was even able to offer a few practical suggestions (there were few topics on which an experienced reporter could not offer an educated opinion), and by then of course they were boon companions.

Other hotel employees appeared and were introduced, and shortly thereafter Arlene was running an impromptu clinic, dispensing advice on a variety of ailments in her role as visiting nurse clinician. When an opportune moment presented itself she made a laughing observation on conventions and the typical convention-goer being a cross between the bread and butter and the bane of hotel staff everywhere, and they were fairly launched. It took only a few more judiciously innocuous comments to nudge the conversation into the right path, and a few more exclamations of disbelief and a rueful headshake or two to keep it going until someone caught sight of their watch and there was a general exodus.

Arlene ate lunch in the break room for the next two days. "It's so seldom at these things we get to meet real people," she said to excuse her presence, and they seemed to accept her as just another mad American.

The last day, she took a fond farewell of Nawal and went back to her hotel to pack. She alerted the front desk as to her departure and arranged for an early checkout the following morning.

She went to bed early, woke early, and took a taxi to the airport. After she checked in for her flight she called Hugh Rincon to report in. "There was a rumor in the hotel about the young officer in the Coast Guard uniform."

"How many Coasties were there?"

"They said only the two, Sara and Bayzani. Both American, you'll note."

He was looking at the list of attendees to the IMO conference. There had, in fact, been five Coasties present. If the hotel employees were identifying them by their uniforms, and if the Coasties had not dressed in their uniforms, then it was no wonder they missed them. He resolved to contact the other three, and made a note. This obsessive-compulsive propensity to tie up loose ends was one of the things that made him such a good investigator. "But?"

"But, number one, he didn't tip, which proves he wasn't American. Number two, he spent his last night in the hotel somewhere else. He just walked out the evening before and they never saw him again. He didn't even check his voice mail."

"He stiff them?"

"No. The room was paid for in advance, by credit card."

"You get the account number?"

"Yes, but you and I both know it won't do any good. Isa's way too crafty for that."

"What about his passport?"

"He collected it on his way out. He said he was going out to eat, and he'd return it to the desk when he came back."

"Was he carrying a bag?"

"He had a daypack over his shoulder, enough maybe for a change of clothes, according to the front desk clerk."

"He left everything else behind?"

"He did."

"Where's his stuff?"

She smiled into the phone. "In the hotel's lost and found. Or it was."

Hugh said sharply, "Was?"

She gave the anonymous little roll-on suitcase reposing at her feet a fond look. "I've got it now."

"I want you here on the next available plane," Hugh said.

"I'm calling from the airport. I land at Heathrow at three P.M. British Airways."

"I'll pick you up."

"I never doubted it," Arlene said. "Okay, see you then."

His voice caught her just as she was going to hang up. "If he wasn't American, did anyone have an idea as to where he was from?"

"They thought he might be Afghani. One of the front desk clerks who thought he detected an accent. I wouldn't bet the farm on that, though, he was the only one who felt that strongly."

"So, not Middle Eastern, but definitely Asian," Hugh said thoughtfully. "I was pretty sure he wasn't Jordanian, no matter what Chisum's people were telling us. But one of the Stans? How the hell did he get that high up in al Qaeda?"

"I'm guessing that was a rhetorical question," Arlene said dryly. "Something else, Hugh."

Her tone, sober and maybe even a little frightened, brought him up alert. "What?"

"I reached out to a couple of contacts I have here and there, and—"

"Here and where?"

"Here, in Istanbul. There, in Damascus, and in Peshawar."

"And?" Hugh said with foreboding.

"And I went to see my friend in Istanbul."

Her friend in Istanbul, Hari Assoun, lived in a third-floor flat in a crowded block that reminded Arlene of neighborhoods in Naples, or Brooklyn. Laundry hung above the street in lines strung between the buildings, kids played soccer between parked cars, and tables spilled out into the street from cafés on every corner.

Hari, a tall man with thinning hair, a slight stoop, and a remembered strength in his large and now very spare frame, had been happy to see her, and not only because there might be a fee in it from her. Arlene had the knack of turning informants into friends. Sometimes it could be a hindrance, sometimes a danger, but sometimes, as with Hari, it could be a gift. He bustled around a kitchen the size of a postage stamp to brew her some of the Turkish coffee he knew she loved, and putting out a plate of nougat, which she loathed but which she ate without complaint and lied about the taste afterward.

They discussed her family ("Arlene, my dear, you got to get married. Who cares for you elsewise in your old age?"), his family ("My wife, she is with someone else now, but she will be back, I know this thing in my heart."), and world affairs ("Is this president of yours mad, Arlene? Is he blind and deaf? What is America thinking with this invasion, this war? We Turks know all about war, Arlene, we have Iraqi Kurds sitting across our border from Turkish Kurds, waiting to join hands and make their own country, and then what? Chaos! Anarchy! Apocalypse!").

After two cups of coffee, when Arlene could hear the blood sizzling nicely in her veins from the caffeine, she got to the point. Hari at first was obdurate. "No, Arlene, much as I want to help you always, this man I will not discuss." She coaxed and pleaded, and did not make the mistake of offering more money.

Hari was for hire, not for purchase.

After some grumbling followed by dire warnings ("This is dangerous, my very dear Arlene. You could get hurt. I could get hurt. Your future husband could get hurt!") Hari allowed as how, yes, he did still come in the way of the odd bit of information, and yes, perhaps, on very rare occasions there might be a whisper of Isa.

"And what is the whisper, my very dear Hari?" Arlene said, giving him a soulful glance.

He made a face. "They are looking for him."

"Everyone's looking for Isa, Hari," she said patiently. "Who in particular this time?"

Hari met her eyes and said very soberly, "Al Qaeda is looking for him, Arlene, and, my very dear friend, you do not want to be caught in the crossfire when they find him."

She said now to Hugh, "You remember Hari Assoun?"

"The old Republican Guard guy, who split Iraq when Saddam invaded Kuwait? Sure. He ran a dead drop for al Qaeda in Istanbul, didn't he?"

"He was never a true believer, he just needed the cash. I offered him more and he came over."

"Okay. And?"

"He tells me that the al Qaeda organization is very quietly putting the word out for Isa to phone home."

The skin crawled on his scalp and Hugh could actually feel the hair on his head standing straight up. "Hari says that Isa is operating independently of al Qaeda?"

"It is certainly one possible inference," Arlene said very carefully indeed. "Before you ask, it's more than a rumor. I confirmed it with friends in Baghdad and in Peshawar. Isa's on his own."

"Son of a bitch," Hugh said.

"SON OF A BITCH," PATRICK CHISUM SAID WHEN HUGH called him to bring him up to date. "We got ourselves a rogue terrorist?"

"I've done some asking around of my own since I talked to Arlene. It's not common knowledge, not yet, but one of my own sources says that the al Qaeda network has put out what amounts to an APB on Isa. The word went out almost a year ago—"

"A year ago! Jesus Christ!"

"They're keeping it very quiet."

"They sure as hell are! Hugh, what the hell is going on?"

"They don't trust him. Bin Laden hated Zarqawi, and Isa was Zarqawi's right-hand man. Bin Laden himself wants to see Isa, as in yesterday. At first it was very much within their own network, but when he didn't surface they started to panic and asked everyone, whether they were good at keeping their mouths shut or not. Finally the word trickled down to our source. It is becoming more generally known, though. If Arlene tracked it down, there are undoubtedly four or five reporters on the same story hot on her trail."

"Jesus Christ, Hugh," Patrick said again. "I can't even begin to imagine what this might mean. A rogue terrorist? What is that, isn't that like an oxymoron or something?"

"I think it's redundant," Hugh said.

Patrick didn't hear him. "What, al Qaeda isn't radical enough, isn't murderous enough for Isa, blowing up the towers, the Pentagon, and the Capitol with flying bombs wasn't enough? He has to form his own organization so he can think up something even better?"

"Or worse," Hugh said.

"Definitely worse," Patrick said. "All right, thanks for the heads-up. I'm going to talk to some of our people now. Let me know if you find anything in the suitcase, okay?"

"Okay. It doesn't look promising, though, I'm sorry to say."

"Jesus Christ, Hugh," Patrick said. "It's bad enough dealing with bin Laden's bunch, but at least we've got a dim idea of what to expect. This guy—"

He couldn't finish the sentence, and hung up.

PART II

Our cruel and unrelenting enemy leaves us only the choice of brave resistance, or the most abject submission. We have, therefore, to resolve to conquer or die.

—GEORGE WASHINGTON, TO THE CONTINENTAL ARMY ON AUGUST 27, 1776

14

HOUSTON, JUNE 2008

Lately, Kenai woke up, went straight to her computer, and logged on to the National Weather Service, set for local conditions at Cape Canaveral. It only forecast ten days out but she couldn't help obsessing. Weather delays were the bane of shuttle launches, and July was a month into hurricane season. There was nothing either she or Mission Control could do about the weather, of course, but checking the forecast gave her the illusion of control. Knowing is always better than not knowing.

She'd formed the habit of going in to work early, because the Arabian Knight (when the secretaries over at admin found out he was royalty he'd had a new nickname before lunch, although the astronauts had several, much less complimentary ones) had taken to appearing promptly at eight A.M. each morning, ready to tolerate, if not with good humor then at least with equanimity, whatever indignities his infidel babysitter would inflict on him that day. She had begun to feel a faint hope that he might not, after all, kill them all on orbit.

That morning he came to her with a request that, on the face of it, seemed innocuous. He would be doing daily television broadcasts from the shuttle, which would be launching on the day of the full moon. They'd be on orbit for eight days, which meant the moon would be visible toward the end of the mission. He wanted to observe the new moon during one of the broadcasts, which would naturally enough go out over the family network and appear on virtually every television screen in the Islamic world from Morocco to Indonesia.

She took this first to Rick and then to Joel. Neither had a problem with it. "Anything that keeps him out of our hair," Rick said. So the request had been approved, and no one thought much more about it until two days later when they were going over the on-orbit schedule, revised now to accommodate the Arabian Knight's broadcasts, and Laurel said, "Wait a minute, isn't the moon a big deal in the Islamic religion?"

No one on the Carnivore Crew knew. Joel was summoned, and he scurried away in search of the nearest imam, who when found allowed as how, yes, the moon was a big deal in the Islamic religion. Joel came scurrying back and Rick Robertson sat his royal pain in the ass down and went over the script for his lunar broadcasts word by word.

The Arabian Knight was upset. "It's not even Ramadan!"

"I don't care," Rick said later. "Nobody's issuing a call to prayer from one of my missions."

He glared at Kenai, who thought of protesting that it wasn't her fault, and settled instead for a wooden "Yes, sir."

The sooner they launched, the better.

Cal laughed when she told him. "Who knew dating an astronaut would be this entertaining?"

"Always glad to provide the light relief," Kenai said, yawning, and reached up to turn out the light. She tucked the receiver between her ear and the pillow and snuggled in.

"Am I going to see you again before you light the candle?"

She smiled to herself. Cal was coming along in astronautspeak. "I don't know. Probably not."

"We still on for going away when you get back?"

Her mind was filled with nothing but the mission, but she was willing to play along with the notion of a future after orbit. "How's your schedule looking?"

"We'll be headed to dry dock in Alameda by the time you get back. Refit and repairs and then back to Kodiak."

"Are you going north with her?"

"Yeah, for another year."

"And then where?"

"Don't know yet."

"What's on your dream sheet?"

He smiled to himself. Kenai was coming along in Coastiespeak. "Not much, yet. I can't decide if I want another boat."

"You went to the Academy, right? So you've got your twenty in?"

"Yeah."

"Do you want a shore job?" She couldn't decide if she liked the idea of him more available to her or not. Assigned to a ship, he would be gone on patrol half the time. It seemed to be working well for them so far. If it ain't broke, don't fix it.

"I don't know. I don't like doing the same thing over and over again, I know that much."

"So, not another 378."

"I don't think so. And no guarantee I'd get one anyway, in fact probably exactly the opposite. There are more people waiting for the captain's chair on a cutter than there are waiting for a seat on a shuttle."

"Mmm. Where are you that you could call me, anyway?"

"Can't say. BSF. Brief stop for fuel."

"And you're low on fuel why?"

"Chasing go fasts."

"Catch any?"

"Not yet," he said grimly. "At this point we're all looking forward to the shuttle launch as the highlight of the patrol."

Six months. He had never stayed so long in one place before, not since he was a child in Pakistan. At first it made him uneasy. He'd kept his head down, reporting in to work every day without fail, keeping close to home in the evenings. His plan was already in place, his team was recruited and ready to move at a word from him, he had arranged their transportation. There was nothing now to do but wait. Waiting was good. His enemies might hope that he was dead, and the more time passed without word or deed from him, the more they would believe it.

He'd seen on Irhabi's blog that Ansar was still looking for him. Which meant that the old man was still looking for him, because Ansar would be happy never to see Akil again, happy to step into the power vacuum left by Zarqawi's death. Akil had given some thought to the possibility that Ansar had been the one who had betrayed Zarqawi's location to the Americans, before dismissing the notion. Ansar simply hadn't the courage it took to betray a friend. Neither had he the intelligence to plan it.

What he did have was the ambition to exploit the results.

Akil didn't trust any of them. He had trusted Zarqawi because Zarqawi had stood by him, in spite of his not being Jordanian, in spite of his pioneering of the Internet, in spite of his refusal to lip sync his way through prayers with the rest of them. He'd never lied to Zarqawi. He could barely tell the difference between Sunni and Shia, and he didn't care if the whole world bowed toward Mecca. He hated the West for reasons of his own, and he would do everything in his power to bring it down. He'd proved it over and over again to Zarqawi, with the result that Zarqawi had trusted him completely, going so far as to make him his second in command, a signal honor in al Qaeda for the not Saudi- or Jordanian-born.

He did not contact Ansar, or the old man, or anyone from the organization. He had let all previous email addresses lapse, so he could say with perfect truth that he had received no message recalling him to Afghanistan. When his mission succeeded, they would know where he was, or at least where he had been. Even the old man would be forced to judge his precious money well spent.

So far as he could tell, the American authorities remained ignorant of his activities. He had seen nothing, in the *Miami Herald* he read every morning or on the television in his room or on Internet news web sites, that led him to believe that they even knew he was in the country. So far his cell was holding together, maintaining an admirable silence. Yussuf and Yaqub had done a good job of recruiting.

There was a soft knock at the door. "Mr. Sadat? Dinner is ready."

"I'll be right there," he said, and shut down his computer. He'd bought it to satisfy the curiosity of his land-

238

lady's daughter. He only rarely used it to access anything more alarming than a Hotmail account registered to an Isaac Rabin, which he used to subscribe to online versions of *The New York Times*, *The Wall Street Journal*, and the *Atlantic Monthly*. Isaac Rabin belonged to Slate.com and iTunes, too, through which he downloaded news programs from NPR to his iPod. He'd also found a *Baywatch* fan podcast he listened to while taking ever-longer walks that were beginning to infringe on the edges of the Everglades.

Somewhat to his own surprise, he liked Miami. It was a vibrant city, filled with color and light and just the right amount of civil corruption, or at least enough to make him feel right at home. Everything was available here, for a price, including anonymity.

He left his room and went down the hall to the dining room to find Zahirah and Mrs. Mansour already seated. "I'm sorry to keep you waiting," he said, pulling out what had become his chair and sitting down.

"You work too hard, Mr. Sadat," Mrs. Mansour said in scolding tones, and passed the pile of bread rounds, still hot to the touch. The tagine was spicy, and he tore the naan into shreds and mopped his plate clean.

He sat back and Mrs. Mansour beamed at him. "I like to see a young man enjoy his food."

"I would be very hard to please indeed if I did not enjoy the food set before me at this table," he said.

Zahirah smiled at him, and again he was struck at how

much she reminded him of Adara. "Are you ready?"

He drove the three of them to a nearby theater complex where they each bought their own tickets to a Will Ferrell comedy and went inside sedately to find seats. Halfway through the film he whispered, "Will you excuse me?" and slipped out.

There was a coffee shop next door with an online computer free of charge to customers. He bought a latte with a shot of butterscotch syrup and waited tranquilly for the Goth gentleman with the black eye shadow and the multiple piercings to finish his purchase of a studded dog collar from an Internet store called Radiance Bound.

Online, he accessed a remote server, ran through a number of fairly simple algorithms, another much more complicated one, and sent out several emails.

He had mail waiting for him at a server in Canada. The cell was proceeding as ordered, slipping into Haiti one at a time, some through Mexico, some through Canada, a few even through Miami. They had no idea he was in Miami, of course.

He knew a real temptation to join them, to be in at the kill, for once to be an eyewitness to all his work and worry, to see a plan of his very own come to fruition with his own eyes.

It was impossible, of course it was. The chances of detection were high, the chances of survival very low. He had further work to do elsewhere. He could not waste the years of expertise he had accumulated for vanity's sake.

Still, he thought wistfully, it might almost be worth the risk.

Yussuf had reported in with his usual diffidence. Yaqub had written with his usual effusiveness, repeating that his life had had no meaning until Isa came into it. Akil distrusted such fulsomeness, but Yaqub had thus far proved trustworthy. If Yaqub survived the operation—extremely unlikely, in Akil's opinion—a more permanent place might be found for him. His would be a growing organization, after all.

A tentative hand touched his shoulder. "Mr. Sadat, what are you doing?"

He turned his head and saw Zahirah standing behind him, an expression of confusion on her pretty face.

WASHINGTON, D.C.

The familiar tapping of slender heels preceded the equally familiar tap at his door. "Mr. Chisum?" Melanie's artfully tousled blond head came into view. "Mr. Labi on line one. He says it's urgent."

After Omar Khalid was exiled to Tajikistan, Ahmed Labi was one of the few remaining agents fluent in Farsi and Arabic they had managed to keep in D.C., as opposed to the wholesale shipment of anyone with even a passing knowledge of any Middle Eastern language directly to Baghdad. Ahmed also had a working knowledge of Urdu, useful in Pakistan. "Ahmed, this is Patrick. What's up?"

Ahmed's voice was tense. "I've got something. I

think you should come down here."

"On my way." Patrick hung up, put on his suit jacket, straightened his tie, and shot out his cuffs. He marched out into the outer office. "Melanie, you really must start using the intercom to let me know when I have a call."

She said, perfectly calmly, "But I find out so much more when I can hear even a part of your conversations, sir."

His mouth opened, and closed again.

She held her serious expression for as long as she could, before it dissolved in a loud, joyous belly laugh. He stared, transfixed, as her creamy skin flushed; the line of her throat revealed when her head fell back, those lovely breasts outlined by the clinging blue of her sweater set. For a woman getting on forty, she had a lovely figure. He wondered how it would hold up divested of angora wool.

He pulled himself together. Company ink, he reminded himself firmly, and marched out into the corridor with the spine of a soldier on parade. He'd reprimand her later. Not anything permanent, heavens no, just a verbal warning, a hint toward the desirability of discretion in the workplace.

Oh, how he hoped she wasn't sleeping with Kallendorf.

Two floors down he was sitting across from Ahmed, examining a sheaf of papers, printouts of emails and web searches. "They just popped up two days ago," he said, sounding almost as dazed as he looked. "It was like magic. One of the geeks was trying out a new search algorithm, looking for names and pseudonyms of people on the list. We totally lucked out."

Patrick couldn't believe his eyes. "You're sure this is Yaqub Sadiq?"

In answer Ahmed tossed a photo across the desk. "We tracked his IP address to an apartment in Toronto. That's a photo we took of him on the street outside. And you're gonna love this."

He tossed another photograph to Patrick, and grinned. "That's his German passport photo."

Patrick still couldn't believe it. "He actually used his own name?"

Ahmed sobered. "If what you've learned is true, if Isa is operating independently of bin Laden, then he has to be recruiting from outside the organization. Al Qaeda has a pretty discriminatory recruitment process. Fanatics get in. Dummies don't. If it's like you said, Isa doesn't have that discretionary process to draw on anymore."

Patrick still couldn't believe it. "Which means he's hiring morons?"

Ahmed grinned, white teeth gleaming beneath a flourishing black mustache. "Let us say rather that young Yaqub Sadiq is very probably not the sharpest tack in the box." He stood up, cramming a wad of paper into his jacket pocket. "Wanna go for a ride?"

15

Until now, his decision to join with Isa had seemed the single most romantic action of his life, a joyous response to a call to adventure. He cast off the shackles of home and family with a light heart—an added benefit was an escape from the increasing suspicions of Janan's husband—and followed where Isa led, first to England where he had thoroughly enjoyed seeking out and recruiting the young men who now looked to him and Yussuf like prophets, then to the camp in British Columbia where he had found the training much less amusing, and now to Toronto, where, using the identity papers their forger had prepared, he had found a job as a barrista in a Starbucks and rented a room in a boarding house.

After a month he had moved in with Brittany, the blond night baker who provided the coffee shop's pastries. She was starry-eyed in love with him, and he with her, too, of course, that went without saying. He was particularly in love with her working nights, as it left her side of the bed free for a rotating cast of young women picked up across the espresso bar, attracted to his dark and (he fancied) dangerous good looks. He played fair, he told them firmly that his heart belonged to Brittany, but he did not discourage them from trying to change his mind.

He'd never suffered from a lack of feminine attention, even in the more strict Muslim community of Düsseldorf in which he was raised. In England his eyes had been opened to the possibilities for casual sex in Western culture, but in Toronto he felt as if he'd discovered a gold mine.

No, he'd never been more content, and he was grateful from the bottom of his heart to Isa for plucking him out of a world where the consequences for sex absent marriage could place one's life in literal peril. He was mindful of the debt he owed; he checked his email religiously, following Isa's diversionary instructions to the letter. He'd written them down, strictly against orders, but they were so complicated he was afraid he would forget them, and he'd taped the scrap of paper to the bottom of a drawer in Brittany's jewelry box where, amid a tumble of rhinestones and sterling silver, it would surely never be found.

Six months later he felt increasingly at home in the West, and it was a rude shock when he checked his email one evening and found the command to move on waiting for him. He went online and bought the ticket to Mexico City, and made reservations for the second flight, but the adventure seemed to have leeched out of his relationship with Isa. When Brittany came home the next morning, fragrant with yeast and sweat, and launched herself at him with her usual lusty joy, he made love to her with a single-minded ferocity that at first surprised her and then subsumed her. "Wow," she said after she caught her breath. "Where'd that come from?"

"I love you," he said, raising his head. "Let's get married."

She looked surprised and pleased. She was also a little puzzled. "Why now?"

He bent his head to kiss her. "I can't wait any longer."

"I didn't know we'd been waiting," she said.

He made love to her again without answering, and that afternoon they dressed and drove to Niagara and were married. It was a nondenominational service and therefore unrecognized in his religion, but he was nevertheless enchanted with the whole notion of Brittany forsaking all others but him so long as they both should live. They drove home and celebrated in bed, and she was late for work that night.

Naked, he got up and went to Brittany's computer and logged on to the Internet from home, something else Isa had strictly forbidden. He checked his email. Nothing more from Isa, but a message from Yussuf, a discreet reminder to bring currency, as all of their transactions after they bought their airplane tickets would be in cash.

On impulse he emailed Yussuf back (also forbidden) to the same email address (again, forbidden). Suppose they didn't go?

He had a reply less than an hour later. Four words. *He will kill you.*

"He won't find me," he said out loud. Isa was brilliant, no question, but by his own orders Yaqub had assumed the alias on his forged papers, papers ordered and bought by himself and Yussuf. Isa had never seen them. He had deposited the modest (almost meager, he had thought at the time) stipend Isa had doled out before they parted into a credit union, and sank without a trace into Toronto's millions. Again by Isa's orders, they communicated only by email, and that sporadically and from continually changing email addresses and computers. No phone numbers to trace to a physical location, no paper trail in a name Isa would know, a different IP address for each email. His identity appeared to be bulletproof. So long as he didn't draw attention to himself, he could live here indefinitely. As of today, he was even a married man. Children would undoubtedly follow. He smiled to himself. And as he was now married to a Canadian, Canadian citizenship would surely be that much easier to acquire.

A second email followed almost immediately, and his smile faded. *He will kill us.*

He felt a cold finger run down his spine.

Would Isa kill Yussuf for Yaqub's defection?

He thought of Isa then, a tall man with neat habits and a perpetually stern expression that made him appear much older than he was, livened only occasionally by a charming smile that Yaqub privately thought Isa should make a lot more use of.

Isa's sense of purpose was unmistakable and persuasive, almost hypnotically so. His loyalty to Islam was on the face of it without question, although Yaqub did wonder now and then if Isa wasn't a little less fanatical than your average Islamic freedom fighter.

He did not, however, doubt Isa's single-minded determination to accomplish his goals. He decided, regretfully, that Isa would kill Yussuf, thinking that where one was tainted by betrayal, both would be. Isa didn't like witnesses. Yaqub remembered very well how Isa had dealt with Basil back in Düsseldorf.

Yaqub and Yussuf had separated after they left Isa and Basil in the flight from the mob. In his panic he had taken a wrong turn and chance had found him on their heels. He would never forget the speed and strength the older man had shown in tripping Basil and throwing him in front of the mob. Yaqub himself had gone into an instinctive retreat, backpedaling around a corner and fleeing down a convenient alley. He had never told Yussuf what he had seen, but his awe at the display of murderous efficiency was what had tipped the balance in him following Yussuf into service with Isa.

It never occurred to him to wonder, then or after, why Basil had been disposed of in such ruthless fashion.

At present he was focused firmly on the matter at hand. If he had no doubt of Isa's reaction, the question then became, was Yussuf friend enough that Yaqub would sacrifice his newfound sense of contentment to save Yussuf's life?

He was still arguing with himself as he walked into the airport the following Monday morning. They always flew on Monday mornings, Isa's dictum holding that they were less likely to stand out in the crush of back-to-work business travelers. He had checked in online from his home computer—he gave a wistful thought to Brittany waking alone in their bed that afternoon, warm and sleepy and reaching for him—and checked his one bag. This also according to Isa, that people who checked bags were less an item of interest to the ponderous and so easily circumvented security roadblock the Far Enemy had thrown up against incoming travelers.

He smiled at the woman behind the counter and handed her his boarding pass. She was twice his age but that didn't stop him from running an admiring gaze over her. She scanned the bar code and returned a rather stiff smile before fastening a tag to his bag and putting it on the conveyor belt. She stapled the claim check to his boarding pass and handed it back. "Thank you," he said warmly, but she was unresponsive. Evidently not a morning person. He turned away, not seeing the man behind the counter who plucked his bag from the belt before it disappeared.

As he reached the line snaking out of the security checkpoint, someone tapped his shoulder. "Mr. Maysara?"

He turned to see a nondescript man in a tired three-piece suit smiling at him. "Yes?" he said, unalarmed. Perhaps he had left his passport behind.

"May I ask you please to follow me?"

Afterward he wondered why he had. The mild-mannered man in the unremarkable suit with the receding hairline and the belly going slightly to paunch had seemed so inoffensive, so little a threat. There was, too, something in the way he turned immediately after making his request, not once looking over his shoulder, as if he had never a doubt of Yaqub following him when he asked him to.

Whatever the reason, Yaqub followed him. It was done so quietly that barely a head in the crowd turned to watch them go through a gray door whose outline was almost indistinguishable from the gray wall that surrounded it. It led into a small gray room with another door. The man opened it and motioned Yaqub inside with a hand he then used to stifle a yawn.

"What's this about?" Yaqub said, finally asking the question, but he stepped obediently through the door.

A hand covered his mouth and he saw a confusing blur of motion from several unidentified people. There was a sharp sting in the side of his neck. He felt hands around his ankles, he was suddenly horizontal and in motion, and he plummeted down, down, down into a deep, dark well, absent sight and sound and sense.

HOUSTON

"Do you think it was deliberate?"

"What?" Kenai said. "Oh. Do you mean was the Arabian Knight planning to incite an international religious riot from the International Space Station?" She paused to consider. "I don't think so. But then I don't know him very well."

"None of us do," Rick said. "It's a problem."

They were still worried about the remarks the Arabian Knight might make when he broadcast from the shuttle. None of them spoke Arabic. "Then he speaks in English only," Kenai said. "One of us stands by the on-air switch and flips it if he shifts into Arabic."

Joel consulted the ever-present clipboard, a ruse because there was no way he could have anything on it pertaining to this discussion. Wisely, he said nothing.

Rick looked at Kenai. "You say you don't think he meant any harm. Why not?"

Kenai shrugged. "Like I said, I don't know him very well, but he just doesn't have the smell of fanatic to me. He's an arrogant, self-righteous little prick with delusions of grandeur, but I don't think he'd ever put himself in danger. He likes the high life way too much, and while he's really looking forward to being on orbit, he's looking forward even more to coming back and bragging about being a bona fide astronaut. What a shuttle ride means most to the Arabian Knight is an upgrade in arm candy, from Paris Hilton to, I don't know, Princess Stephanie."

"That's an upgrade?" Laurel said.

"Whatever." Kenai was impatient, wanting to get back to work, and not a little incredulous that this was still even a topic for conversation.

Rick frowned down at his feet. "All right," he said, ignoring Laurel's muttered comment. "But, Kenai, I want you to demand to see in advance whatever remarks he is preparing to read. Make sure there's nothing even remotely incendiary in them."

"I thought you already looked at them."

"I did. Now I want you to look at them. Try to time it to be as close to just before we go up as possible."

Kenai nodded. She had no time for this nonsense, none of them did, but she knew better than to argue. "Wilco."

Rick nodded, a quick decisive gesture. "All right." He looked at Joel. "Anything else?" The set of his mouth indicated that there probably shouldn't be.

Joel shook his head.

"Good. Let's get back to work." Rick straightened up and walked out of the room.

Mike stood up. "Well," he said.

Kenai interrupted him with one hand held up, palm out.

The door opened and Rick stuck his head back in. "I'll take a look at the Arabian Knight's scripts again, too, Kenai."

"You bet," Kenai said.

"Just in case," Rick said.

"You bet," Kenai said again.

Rick nodded and withdrew.

With a sigh, Bill said, "Why he's commander, I guess."

Laurel looked at Joel. "Just how bad do we need to launch this frickin' satellite, anyway?"

Only she didn't say frickin'.

252

"He woke up on the C-12," Patrick told Kallendorf on the phone. "He shouted a bunch of questions, in the worst English accent you've ever heard, and in German. We didn't answer him."

Kallendorf was impatient. "You didn't feed him, you didn't water him, you let him pee and shit where he sat. SOP, Patrick, I get it. What's he saying?"

"It's only been a day and a half, sir. We haven't even gotten him to admit to his own name yet. We have to be patient."

"Patient, my ass!" Kallendorf said.

The bellow was clearly audible all the way across the room. Bob and Mary pretended not to hear. Ahmed, clearly enjoying himself, made a fist and pretended to jerk off, rolling his eyes and letting his tongue loll out of his mouth.

"Isa's got a timetable, Patrick, which means our clock is ticking, too. You make that little son of a bitch squeal like Ned Beatty in *Deliverance* or you tell him I'll be down there myself to bite his nuts off with my teeth!"

Kallendorf slammed the phone down. His ears ringing slightly, Patrick replaced the receiver and heaved a relieved sigh. It could have been a lot worse.

Ahmed grinned at him. Bob, a short, hairless man with bulging biceps, looked at the ceiling. Mary, even shorter and thin almost to the point of emaciation, looked at the floor.

Robert Shadura was an ex-Ranger who had seen action under fire from Panama to Beirut to Afghanistan. When he had to retire, he'd settled in New York and done consulting work with an international security agency that specialized in the return of kidnapped American businessmen, which subsidized his basement flat on the Upper West Side. He entertained no leftover angst from any of the wars he had fought in, had no drinking habit, no family, and his only sin was a lust for Harley hogs, three of which were parked in a rented garage off Canal Street and one of which was an antique, a 1912 8XE V-Twin Legend, lovingly restored, that was worth over a hundred grand. He wouldn't have taken a million for it.

He was also a gifted actor. In the South Side Players, the amateur theatrical group to which he belonged, he was famous for his portrayal of Macbeth in the Scots play, and he doubled as choreographer for all the fight scenes in all the plays the South Side Players produced. He looked thirty-five, was actually fifty-two, and dated an unending series of beautiful actresses. All such relationships ended amicably, and one so blessed had been known to say in an awed, grateful voice, "I never met a man with such control!"

On occasion, at the behest of his country, Bob left the Harleys and the actresses behind for short periods of time when he allowed himself to be called back into service as an interrogator, a skill he had perfected in Iraq.

"Before we were so rudely interrupted," Patrick said. "You were saying?"

Bob, one of those admirable underlings with no interest, prurient or otherwise, in the doings of his superiors, resumed his narrative without so much as a blink. "He says he was going to Mexico on vacation. He says he never heard of Isa. He says he's a German national, he is innocent of any wrongdoing, and he demands to see his consul."

"How does he explain the forged Canadian passport in the name of Baghel Maysara?"

"He doesn't."

"He doesn't yet," Mary said, her voice as wispy as her appearance.

Mary Maria Santangelo weighed about a quarter of what Bob did, who was at least twice her age, and the closest she'd ever come to the armed services was an ROTC troop drilling on the Harvard quad when her date walked her home to her dorm on the Radcliffe campus. She looked like Dante Gabriel Rossetti's Persephone stepped down from the frame, only rather less well-nourished. A massive quantity of black hair was bundled back in a ponytail so heavy it looked as if it should bend her slender neck backwards from the sheer weight of it all.

Mary was a history major, with a doctorate in Middle Eastern studies. She had an eidetic memory and to the distinct disapprobation of his superiors Ahmed had made Mary free of the CIA files on terrorism. With her training in history she was able to digest massive quantities of data to place people into a proper context and events into a proper chronology. The result was an eerie ability to pull the one tiny nugget of information necessary to nudge an interrogatee over the edge from intransigence to cooperation. There were times when it seemed she could read people's minds. She'd been called a witch, and more than one detainee had made the sign to warn off evil in her presence.

She and Bob had two things in common: an unparalleled ability to elicit information from unwilling witnesses, and a long list of lovers.

Make that three. They both liked women.

Mary was also an intuitive chameleon, with the ability to become whatever the detainee wanted at the moment of his greatest need.

They worked extremely well together, bringing in results where other gator teams threw up their hands and walked away. When Ahmed had asked Patrick who he wanted for gators, Patrick's answer had been instantaneous. "Bob and Mary."

Ahmed had looked and felt doubtful. "They can be a little volatile."

"They can be spontaneously combustible," Patrick had said. "But we want results fast, and we want lethal information, right?

Intel that produced the death of a known terrorist. "Yes," Ahmed said, "we want lethal information."

"Bob and Mary are the best interrogators in the business. They trained half the people in Task Force 145. They'll get it done."

"You want him to get the full treatment?"

"Everything," Patrick said. "I want this guy scared. I want him thinking Abu Ghraib's still in business, and that he's got a front-row cell reserved just for him. I want him thinking we're sending him to Egypt or Romania for questioning if he doesn't talk to us in Gitmo. I want him scared shitless, Ahmed."

Looking at them now, Patrick saw nothing inherently terrifying in either Bob or Mary. Well, between the biceps and the tattoos, he might have been afraid of Bob if he'd bumped into him outside a biker bar. Mary, an ethereal waif with large, dark, tip-tilted eyes that looked always on the verge of tears, not to mention bony hips that looked always on the verge of slipping out of her inevitable low-rider jeans, didn't look strong enough to swat a fly, let alone scare the shit out of a hardened terrorist.

But they were the best. "We don't have a lot of time, folks," he said.

Bob and Mary exchanged an expressionless look. "How did you pick him up?"

"Idiot used his own name on an email. One of our guys was running a new program on a random e-comm search. I'd just sent out the BOTLF on our friend here, and his pal Yussuf, and their boss Isa. The guy inputs the names and runs the search, which—okay, this is as much as I understand. This program has the ability to search for hot-button words on the Internet, words like 'bin Laden' and 'al Qaeda' and—"

" 'Isa,' " Ahmed said.

"Yes, and 'Isa,' and this program can also trace them back to their originating server. Always supposing they aren't smart enough to route it through a couple of other servers to mess up the data trail."

"And he wasn't smart enough."

"He's been keeping his head down for six months. I think the serenity of his existence might have led him to believe that he was invisible."

"Ah," Bob said, "one of those." He smiled at Mary. "Ladies first?"

She looked at Patrick. "You want us to jack him up?"

Patrick shook his head. "There's nothing more worthless than information received through torture."

"Drugs, then?"

"I'm not crazy about drugs, either, you never know if you're going to get good intel or a regression to the time his father spanked him for picking on the girl next door."

"What, then?" Mary said.

"We've got people asking questions in Toronto, and we've got some intel from Germany. It all says Yaqub Sadiq likes women. No," he said, correcting himself. "Sadiq loves women. We think one of the reasons he may have joined up with Isa is that he'd been screwing somebody's wife and the husband found out. You can get killed for that if you're Islamic."

Mary's brow puckered, which was a pity, because it

was a broad, alabaster brow. "What was his name? The husband's?"

Patrick called up the file on his Blackberry. "Rashid Nurzai."

Something that might have been a smile crossed her face and was gone. "Is Nurzai Afghani?"

"I don't know." Patrick hadn't seen any need to check. "The file doesn't say." Beneath her considering gaze, he felt the need to redeem himself. "Sadiq was born in Germany. Of Lebanese immigrants."

She nodded once, a crisp gesture that seemed somehow out of character. But, Patrick realized for the first time, she could have tailored her appearance deliberately to lull a detainee into a sense of false security. "Follow my lead," she told Bob.

She didn't wait for permission or agreement, she left the room. Patrick got up and walked to the pane of one-way glass set into the wall, and felt Bob and Ahmed come to stand behind him.

Sadiq was handcuffed to a metal chair in an otherwise bare room. A pool of urine under the chair gleamed wetly in the room's one bright ceiling light. "Those the same clothes he was wearing when we nabbed him?" Patrick said.

"When we took him into custody, you mean?" Ahmed said austerely, and spoiled the effect by grinning. "Yeah."

"He must smell pretty ripe by now."

"Yeah," Bob said laconically. "Probably time to let him clean up. After a while they stop smelling themselves, so it's less of an incentive to talk. Better to clean him up and let him shit and smell himself again; more motivation."

"What's taking her so long?" Patrick said, the urgency he felt gnawing at him like a sharp set of teeth. Even more so now, he had the awful feeling of a clock ticking down in the background. The longer Akil stayed out of sight, the more afraid Patrick was of what he would do when he eventually regained the spotlight. Maybe it was a condition of being a spy but more than any other single thing Patrick Chisum hated and feared not knowing what was going on. When you had no knowledge of the horrors in store there was no way to stop them or, worst case, prepare for them. Ignorance was not bliss. Innocent people, hundreds of them, thousands, could die if he remained ignorant of Isa's plans. "Oh," he said, relieved, "here she is."

The door opened a crack. Mary peeped inside. She waited until Sadiq's head came up to see who was there. "Oh," she said, her voice a nice blend of nerves and compassion. "Oh, you look just awful." She slipped inside, took a quick look into the hall, and shut the door with exaggerated stealth. "You poor thing. I brought you some water."

She carried a glass of water in both hands like a supplicant. "Is she tiptoeing?" Ahmed said in a faint voice.

Bob said proudly, "She is in fact tiptoeing."

Mary held the glass to Sadiq's mouth, one comforting hand on his shoulder. He drank greedily, some of the water spilling down his neck. Mary made a distressed sound and used the tail of her shirt to dry him off, not forgetting to give Sadiq a flash of midriff.

"Oh, please," Ahmed said with dismay. "A honey trap? You cannot believe for one moment that that's going to work."

The corner of Bob's mouth quirked up. Patrick said nothing. He'd chosen his people, the best at what they did. Now all he could do was step back and let them go to work. Still, he was taut and tense as a violin string, vibrating at the lightest touch, the balls of his feet digging into the floor. Come on, he said silently, come on.

Inside the interrogation room, in the middle of mopping up Sadiq, Mary pretended to hear something in the hallway. "Oh, no! I have to go!" She bent down to look earnestly into Sadiq's eyes. "I'm so sorry about all this, Mr. Sadiq. They're so mean to you men, and it seems to go on forever. I'll get back when I can, I promise." She gave his shoulder another consoling pat and tiptoed out.

"My cue," Bob said, and left the room.

Barely had the door to the interrogation room closed behind Mary when Bob kicked it open again, his head pushed forward aggressively, his eyes full of contempt. He walked over to Sadiq and without preamble balled one hand into a fist and hit Sadiq in the face, hard enough to knock his chair over. The chair with Sadiq still handcuffed to it slid across the floor until Sadiq's head hit the wall with a thump clearly audible to the two men on the other side of the glass.

Bob walked across the room and kicked him in the

ribs. He looked down at Sadiq and smiled.

Sadiq groaned and coughed up blood and phlegm. There might also have been a tooth, but from behind the mirror Patrick couldn't tell for sure.

"Plenty more where that came from, friend," Bob said to Sadiq. "Where's Isa?"

Sadiq groaned again and tried to curl into a fetal position.

Bob shrugged. "Okay by me. I can keep this up all night." It was ten A.M. but part of the disorientation process was to divorce the detainee from real time. "No one will stop me. You're here until I say you can go." He leaned down and said into Sadiq's ear, "And I can do anything I want to." He straightened and reached for his belt buckle.

Sadiq's eyes went wide and his body bowed, heaving and struggling so violently the chair scraped a foot across the floor, his wrists straining against the handcuffs.

Bob laughed. His hand went to his fly.

"Jesus," Ahmed said.

Talk, you little fucker, Patrick thought.

The door to the room opened and Mary, looking frightened but determined, poked her head inside. "Mr. Crenshaw?"

Bob snarled. "What the fuck do you want?"

Her voice trembling, Mary said faintly, "I'm sorry, but Mr. Casawba wants a word."

Bob stormed past her into the hallway, refastening his belt and shoving her into the wall with a loud thud as he passed. The door slammed shut behind him.

"Oh," she said in a hurt voice. She pulled away from the wall, hand to her injured shoulder, and crept across the room. "Oh, what did he do to you?"

"Please," Sadiq said, coughing again. "Please help me."

Mary looked on the verge of tears. "I don't know what I can do." She blinked rapidly and said with brave determination, "Let's get you back up." With much heaving and struggling, she managed to right Sadiq and his chair. More ineffectual dabbing with her shirttail at the blood on his mouth, pretty concern over the lost tooth, and all the while Sadiq was saying in desperation, "Please, I don't know anything, I don't know why I'm here, please help me, please, get me out of here!"

Mary did cry then, actual tears, Patrick could see them distinctly, sliding down her cheeks. She was one of those women who looked good in tears, too, her nose didn't run and her eyes didn't redden. She knelt at Sadiq's side, the end of the heavy tail of black hair almost touching the floor, and held one of his hands below the handcuff, patting it ineffectually. "I can't do anything," she said, swallowing a sob. "I'm just a clerk. Bob—" She shuddered and cast a hunted look over her shoulder. "He's the lead interrogator here. He can do anything." She looked back at Sadiq. "Anything," she repeated, her lower lip trembling.

Sadiq swallowed hard, his horrified gaze fixed on Mary's haunted face.

Even to Patrick, this seemed the essence of melodrama, overkill in a major key, any self-respecting detainee would laugh Mary out of the room. Surely Sadiq would see this, would catch on to what they were doing, would reject their attempts with the contempt they deserved.

But Yaqub Sadiq was a novice terrorist, barely a year out of his middle-class cradle. Ahmed was right, Isa was operating outside al Qaeda and thus had no access to the culling process of the organization's usual thorough and ruthless recruiting practices. He'd been reduced to finding his own people, which, Patrick suddenly realized, must mean that he was in a hurry. Why?

He looked through the glass at the handcuffed man, hovered over by the waif with the ponytail. This was not the usual experienced, hard-shelled detainee. Yaqub Sadiq had been abducted and drugged and had woken up handcuffed to a chair in an anonymous room with no idea of where he was or what day it was. His captors had not identified themselves but Sadiq had to know they were American and Isa's sworn enemies. If not American, then they were at the very least American allies and at the very worst contract interrogators in friendly states with no constitutional guarantees of due process and no qualms about torture. They'd withheld food and water until his stomach was one big growl and his tongue was swollen in his mouth, and they'd refused him access to a toilet so that he was forced to sit in his own piss and shit.

From the intel gleaned in Germany Patrick had seen

photos of Rashid Nurzai, a very fierce-looking gentleman who looked ready to compete in the shot put in the next Olympics. He was surprised that Nurzai had only made an anonymous call, if he had. From that photograph Patrick would have expected Nurzai to take more direct action in a matter involving his wife. Patrick would have run from that himself.

The intel still coming in from ongoing interrogations in Toronto confirmed that initial impression. Sadiq's new wife, in a tearful accounting of their life together, stressed his loving nature. So did all the other women with whom he'd had significant encounters over the past six months. His boss spoke highly of him at work, his neighbors praised his friendliness and willingness to pitch in on communal chores. A few of them were a little snide about the parade of women in and out of the apartment and it would have been only a matter of time before his wife got to hear of it, but on the whole a good report was given by most of the people who knew him. They were certainly to a man and a woman shocked to hear that he was a terrorist-in-waiting.

But not a career terrorist. He'd never been arrested before, never been interrogated before. An amateur, in fact, with the barest veneer of tradecraft and no detectable inclination toward fanaticism. Patrick frowned through the glass at Sadiq, now sobbing with his face buried in Mary's breast, a Mary who winked at them over Sadiq's head. Next to him, Bob chuckled. "This isn't going to take much longer."

Patrick was inclined to agree with him. Sadiq was an

amateur, a terrorist of opportunity even, joining Isa as a way out of personal difficulties at home, with a natural inclination toward women curbed by a Muslim upbringing, and then sprung on an unsuspecting Western world. He was just settling into his new lifestyle when they had kidnapped him.

On the other hand, he had been apprehended at Pearson International, waiting to board a flight to Mexico City. No one among his Toronto acquaintances, including his wife, had been aware of his travel plans. This argued either dedication to duty or fear of Isa. Probably the latter.

"Come on," he said, out loud this time, "come on, you little bastard, give it up."

"Relax, Patrick—"

"Don't tell me to relax," he snapped. "That little fucker's the only lead we've got to a man who is responsible for the deaths of hundreds if not thousands of people all over the goddamn Asian continent! A terrorist who is now walking around the United States like it's his own backyard! How many Americans stirring half-and-half into their morning coffee or taking the bus to work or running their kids to school right now, right this minute somewhere in Dallas or Atlanta or San Francisco, how many is this little prick's boss planning on killing? Don't tell me to relax, Ahmed. I'll relax when that monster is dead on the ground in front of me and not before."

Surprised, Ahmed maintained a prudent silence. Patrick Chisum, the king of calm, was not known for outbursts of any kind. For a moment there, he had sounded a little bit like Harold Kallendorf.

Meanwhile, Mary was mopping the tears from Sadiq's face, and holding her scrap of lacy handkerchief—where on earth had she come up with that?—so he could blow his nose. "I wish I could help you," she said, her breath catching. "But I can't, I just can't."

She pushed him back in his chair and looked up earnestly into his face. "He'll hurt me," she said, her voice breaking. She squeezed out another tear. Her head drooped. "He's done it before. He can do anything. Anything." Her voice broke again on the word.

She looked up at Sadiq and shook his shoulder. "Tell him what he wants to know," she said urgently. "Tell him!"

"I don't know anything!" Sadiq said, his voice panicked.

She sat back on her heels. "Then I don't know what to say to you," she said sadly. "Unless . . ."

"Unless what?" When she didn't say anything, Sadiq said, bending forward as far as the cuffs would let him, "Tell me! Unless what?"

"There may be another way." She bit her lip. "I probably shouldn't tell you this, but . . ."

"What? Tell me what? Please, please help me!"

Mary looked over her shoulder at the closed door. "Is it true you're from Germany?"

"Yes, yes, I'm a German national! I want to contact my embassy!"

Mary looked uncertain. "I think they already have."

Sadiq looked confused. "What?"

"It's why Bob is so angry," she said, eyes huge wells of sympathy. "He might have to let you go before . . ." She made a vague, all-encompassing gesture, and they shuddered in unison. "You'd be sent back to . . . is it Düsseldorf? There's a man there, a Rashid Somebody?"

Sadiq froze, like a deer in the headlights. "Rashid Nurzai?"

"Yes!" Mary said excitedly. "That's him! He's vouched for you, says the government can release you into his custody to wait for the investigation. At least you'll be home. You'll be protected by the laws of your own nation." She sat back on her heels. "You can tell Bob you know that your embassy is looking for you. You can demand repatriation." She beamed at him. "He can't touch you once you're on your way home, and you're on your way home from the moment your embassy knows you're being detained."

He stared at her for a moment. Patrick held his breath. "Come on," he said, "come on, talk. Talk!"

Bob slammed back into the interrogation room— Patrick hadn't even noticed he had left the observation room—and snarled, yes, an actual baring of teeth, followed by the utterance of a loud, menacing growl that sounded like nothing so much as an infuriated and very hungry tiger. Sadiq actually cowered.

Mary leapt to her feet. "I—I was just—"

"Get out," Bob said.

Mary cast a scared glance at Sadiq and scurried out, giving Bob a wide berth.

Bob started toward Sadiq and Sadiq started to tremble. "Please—" he said, stammering. "Please, don't, I'll—"

"Shut the fuck up," Bob said, disgusted. "Jesus, if there's one thing I can't abide it's a sniveler. You're going home, asswipe." He unlocked the handcuffs and hauled Sadiq to his feet.

"Wait—" Sadiq said.

"What, you want to stay? You've had such a good time you want more? What are you, some kind of sicko?"

"No! I mean, wait! I mean—" Sadiq's feet scrabbled for purchase on the cement floor.

But Bob had him firmly in tow. "I can't see what a self-respecting freedom fighter like Isa saw in you anyway. What a waste of space. Still, there's someone back home who'll vouch for you, so you must be worth something to someone."

"Wait!"

"Oooh, nice little rent boy likes it rough, is that it?" Bob said, and gave Sadiq a shake, hard enough to rattle his teeth. He got him nose to nose and said, his voice a deep purr, "I'd love to have the schooling of you, pretty boy. Too bad."

He got Sadiq to the door and Sadiq, by a superhuman effort, managed to get his feet flat against the wall on either side of it. "Wait!" he said, almost screaming the words. "I'll talk! I'll tell you anything you want to know! Don't send me home! Please don't send me home! He'll kill me! He'll kill me!"

. . .

THE INTERROGATION HAD TAKEN LESS THAN TWO HOURS.
Sadiq was even now babbling every detail, from his
first meeting with Isa at the coffeehouse to packing his
bag yesterday morning, into the interested microphones of three recording devices and two even more
interested agents.

"How the hell did you know that would break him?"
Patrick said. He and Ahmed were waiting for transportation to the Gitmo airfield.

Mary smiled. "Nurzai is an Afghan name. Afghans
treat adultery as a capital crime, and the longer and
more painful the death of those found guilty, the better.
It was a calculated risk."

"But not that much of a risk," Bob said, looking very
relaxed. "He's not what I'd call a pro."

"No kidding," Patrick said. "Well done."

"Wait until we see what we get," Ahmed said.

"You're very cautious."

"Sadiq's a weak vessel," Ahmed said. "If I were Isa,
I wouldn't have told him anything worth knowing."

If it wasn't anything Patrick in all his urgency to find
and stop Isa wanted to hear, he knew deep down that it
was true.

HUGH RINCON ECHOED AHMED'S WORDS WHEN PATRICK,
back in his office the next morning, called to fill him
in. "It's one of the reasons you haven't been able to
catch the bastard," Hugh said. "He's one of the few terrorists capable of keeping his own counsel. He really

understands need to know. He lives by it. He survives by it."

"Yeah, well, anything, any detail we get from Sadiq, is more than we have now. Did you get anything off the bag Isa left at the hotel?"

"Negative. It was all Bayzani's stuff. Got some hairs, so you'll have a decent DNA sample when you need to ID the body."

"I like your optimism."

"He's in a hurry and he's making mistakes," Hugh said. "He's made two big juicy ones in the past year. All we have to do is catch him making his third."

16

MIAMI

Zahirah wasn't especially pretty, but she had an air of dignity that sat quaintly on her young shoulders and she was by no means unintelligent. He liked to think that she was what Adara would have become, if Adara had lived.

She smiled at him across the dinner table. He smiled back. Mrs. Mansour pretended not to notice, handing round the bread and olives in a businesslike fashion. They served themselves heaping spoons of rice and lamb stew and began to eat.

He was a little preoccupied this evening. Yussuf had emailed from Mexico City, and had reported all his cell members present and accounted for.

Yaqub had yet to make contact.

He was at present a day late. Yussuf had written to one of Akil's email drops, saying that he had not heard from him, either. In one way, Akil was pleased that the two young men had not broken protocol by contacting each other. They'd grown up together, were childhood friends. As a matter of natural human reaction he would have thought one of them would have broken the rules at least once, in spite of the strict injunctions against it he had laid on them. In the alien worlds to which they had been exiled, they could have been expected, even forgiven for having reached out for contact with the one familiar face left to them.

Irritatingly, this had not proved the case.

So Yussuf claimed.

Akil wasn't entirely certain he believed Yussuf, but absent a face-to-face confrontation he couldn't be sure. The Internet had certainly proved an excellent administrative tool, but like every other tool, it had its drawbacks.

He himself was leaving for Mexico City the next day.

"You are very quiet this evening, Mr. Sadat," Zahirah said.

He looked up to see her eyes twinkling in an otherwise solemn face. They had long since become Zahirah and Daoud in private. He doubted very much that they were putting anything over on her mother, but he went along with the subterfuge, refusing to admit to himself that he was enjoying it as much as she was.

They had grown inexplicably but undeniably closer over the past six months. Things had reached a head when she'd caught him checking his email when he should have been watching the movie with her and her mother. She'd accepted his explanation of finding the movie a bore but not wishing to spoil their enjoyment of the evening. They had agreed to tell her mother nothing, and this small deception had led to others. Before long, they were arranging expeditions of their own. They were all innocent enough, an art exhibit, a visit to a museum, a lecture at her university, but the fact that her mother knew nothing about them and did not accompany them as chaperone told its own tale.

At first he told himself it was only to distract her, but it wasn't long before he had to acknowledge the truth.

He'd never had a girlfriend before.

In spite of the judgment of his village council, in spite of the punishment inflicted on Adara for his supposed crime, he had never slept with Husn.

Husn kept house for the UNICEF representative in their small market town. As the only English speaker in the village, upon his return home he had been designated the local UNICEF contact. He and Husn had met for the first time at the Gilberts' home.

Looking back, it hadn't seemed that momentous an occasion, the event that would change all their lives so radically. Mrs. Gilbert had been teaching Husn English, and letting her spend an hour of each workday reading through the Englishwoman's collection of Mills & Boon romance novels, which increased her comprehension, if not her vocabulary. "Is love in the West really like this?" she had asked him shyly, holding out one of the books.

"I don't know," he had said, feathering the pages. "All I did was study. All I wanted was to complete my degree and get back home again."

"Were there female students at your college?"

"Yes, many, in some classes more than half."

"Do they wear the hijab?"

"No."

She was entranced by the thought of a country where she could walk down the street with the sun on her face. More questions followed. He started to bring in his textbooks, history and political science and even algebra. She devoured them all, and pelted him with questions that taxed his learning to the utmost.

He would have been lying if he had said he hadn't been attracted to her. Of course he was. She was beautiful, with dark-lashed eyes, luminous skin, and a skein of silken black hair with intriguing bronze highlights, the mere presence of which was in itself exciting because he was unaccustomed to seeing anyone other than his mother and his sister without the hijab. He had avoided contact with the women in his classes in Boston, shocked at their free ways and even more so by the display of skin. His four years had been spent buried in his books, and he had been in such a hurry to get home he hadn't even waited for the graduation exercises, arranging for his diploma to be mailed to him and flying out the evening of his last examination.

He never learned if Husn had been attracted to him. He had always been careful never to so much as touch her hand. When he gave her a book, he held it out by one corner, and she took it by the opposite corner, standing far enough apart so that their arms had to stretch to reach. Conversation took place always in the kitchen or the sitting room, with him on one side of it and her on the other. Mrs. Gilbert, who had not taken well to the Muslim life, and who had made no secret of her contempt for the way the women in it were treated, seemed to believe she was conniving at a romance and took advantage of every opportunity to leave them alone.

Of course they had been caught, if caught was the right word. The cook had walked in one day when Husn was reading something out loud in English. The cook must have gone straight to her husband, who had in turn gone to Husn's husband.

And a week later they had come for him, and for Adara.

He looked across at Zahirah. Her father had wanted her to be raised a good Muslim woman, but he had wanted her to be more than that. She was educated, independent, bare of head and face. She would wither and die in a place like his village. She would be stoned to death in a day in a place like Afghanistan.

She gave him a questioning look. He returned a slight, unrevealing smile and bent again over his plate.

Later that evening there was a soft knock at his door. He hesitated before getting up to answer it, fully intending to plead tiredness as an excuse not to admit her.

But it wasn't Zahirah, it was her mother.

"Mrs. Mansour," he said, startled.

"Mr. Sadat," she said. She looked grave. "May I speak with you?"

"Of course." He stood aside to let her in.

She came in and stood, her hands folded primly in front of her, and waited until he closed the door. "Forgive me for being so blunt, Mr. Sadat, but it has not escaped my notice that you and my daughter have become very close."

So much for subterfuge. He bent his head in wary acknowledgment, and perhaps a little in apology, too.

She took a deep breath. She looked nervous but determined. "I am very sorry, but I am afraid I must ask you to leave this house. You must never return, and you must promise me that you will never seek out my daughter again."

There was a moment of strained silence. "I see," he said at last.

"I'm glad," she said. "I'm sorry if it gives you pain to hear it, Mr. Sadat, but you will not do for my daughter."

He couldn't resist saying, "You're saving her for a rich man?"

Her eyes flashed. "Indeed, sir, I am not. If Allah wills it and a rich man captures her fancy, so be it. It is foolish beyond permission not to imagine that in this world enough money commands an easier life. But she will choose, and my Zahirah does not hanker after riches. She wants the companionship of a like mind, a partner in life. And that you will never be."

Again, he couldn't resist. "And why not?"

"For one thing, you are far too old for her. I will not have Zahirah living out her life caring for an elderly husband, as I did."

She stopped. He prodded her on. "And?"

"And." She gave him a narrow-eyed look. "I don't know why you are here in the United States, Mr. Sadat, or what your purpose is."

He stiffened in shock.

"I only know that you are not who you say you are."

"I—"

She raised a hand. "I don't care to know. You have resided under my roof for six months with a false name and a false identity. You are not Egyptian, Mr. Sadat, and may I say I find your taking of that good man's name in very poor taste. You appear to have had no friends in the area before you arrived, and you appear to have made none during your stay. Your supervisor— did you think when I saw you growing closer to my daughter that I would not inquire?—your supervisor says that while your work is satisfactory you seem merely to be waiting. Waiting for what, Mr. Sadat?"

He opened his mouth, and nothing came out.

She gave a grim nod. "Yes. Well. We Muslims here in the United States of America have had quite enough of that sort of thing. Your kind have generated a constant threat to any of our race and religion who reside here. We don't need you stirring up more trouble."

Again he was able to say nothing.

"I cannot prove anything against you beyond my suspicions, Mr. Sadat," she said, "and it is undoubtedly very unfair of me, but nevertheless I want you gone from my house and my daughter's company by tomorrow morning. Am I understood?"

His mouth a hard line, he said, his voice clipped, "You are."

"Good. Then I have no further need to be here."

She went to the door, waited for him to open it, and swept out. A small part of him was able to admire her style while the rest of him clanged the alarm, even as he moved to pull his case out of the closet and begin packing. What had given him away? How had he betrayed himself to Mrs. Mansour? How could she know he wasn't Egyptian?

He brought himself up short. Would she give him away? Was she even now calling the authorities?

He wasted nearly five minutes thinking about this. No, he decided. If she was going to betray him, she would not have confronted him. She had no proof to offer the authorities anyway, she had said so herself.

He was leaving tomorrow morning, on a ticket purchased with a credit card account that no longer existed. He had planned to come back after he saw the cell off on their mission. Now he would go somewhere else.

Sternly repressing the thought of Zahirah, he filled the small bag with a haphazard collection of clothes, the selection unimportant as it was only to lend him credibility with TSA and would be abandoned upon arrival at his destination.

He finished quickly and cast a glance about the room. His newly opened eyes saw how at home he had become here, that insidious feeling fostering the collection of various knickknacks. The stuffed bear Zahirah had won the day they attended the carnival. The small bookcase filled with books. The poster of the Everglades, bought at the shop the day they had taken the tour. He shook his head, tossed his computer on top of the clothes—there was nothing incriminating on it but it would look odd if he left it behind—and zipped the case closed.

He let himself out the side door and stepped softly down the sidewalk to where an elderly beige Ford four-door sedan was parked. He put the case in the trunk and slid behind the wheel. The engine started without fuss and he pulled away from the curb, willing himself not to look in the rearview mirror.

He parked in the garage at Miami International in the deepest, darkest corner he could find, and killed the engine.

From the backseat came a whisper of sound and he whirled instinctively, throwing his body over the gearshift and thudding into the passenger seat. He launched himself into the backseat in a continuation of the same movement and came down with all the force of a sledgehammer.

"Daoud!" she said, the barest breath of sound left to

her after he slammed into her chest, his hands around her throat and squeezing.

"Zahirah!" he said, astonished.

She choked, pulling feebly at his hands, and he loosened them. He sat up and drew a shaky hand through his hair. He tried to collect his scattered thoughts, to regain some semblance of his customary equilibrium. "What are you doing here?" he said, and marveled to hear his voice shake over the words.

She bent over, wheezing as she tried to catch her breath. He couldn't help himself, he patted her back soothingly. "It's all right," he said, "it's all right now. I'm sorry, I didn't know it was you."

She looked up, her breath still coming fast, her eyes frightened. "Why did you attack me like that?"

"I didn't know it was you," he said again, very gently. "I'm sorry. Zahirah, what are you doing here?"

She blushed. He could barely see it in the dim light of the garage. She looked down, and her voice dropped to a whisper. "I—was coming to talk to you. My mother was there before me. I heard what she said to you. When she said you had to leave tomorrow, I knew somehow you would leave tonight. I went out and hid in the back of your car." She waited, head bent, for him to say something. When he didn't she looked up again. "Oh, Daoud, how could she have been so cruel?"

His mind had been racing while she spoke, the thoughts chasing each other like rats in a cage.

"Daoud?" she said timidly. "I want to be with you, and I know you feel the same way." When he didn't respond, only stared at her with a stone face, she said, "Please, Daoud, won't you say something?"

At last his expression broke. A smile of a sort spread across his face. She looked relieved. "That's better," she said with a trace of her old spirit. "For a minute I thought you weren't happy to see me."

"I am always happy to see you, Zahirah," he said.

She blushed again, her love making her deaf to the mournful note in his voice. "I am happy to hear it."

He felt his hands slide of their own accord around her waist. His head bent to hers, and she raised her face eagerly to meet his lips in their first kiss. Her lips were warm and wide and smooth, and he thought that in another life he might have been able to lose himself in them forever.

He deepened it, pulling her to him so that her breasts pressed into his chest. The soft curves were so warm and full against him, he'd never felt anything like it. He stretched out backwards so that she lay full length against him and her legs naturally fell to either side, so that the feminine heat of her was pressed full against the erection that had suddenly and inexplicably manifested itself.

"Oh!" she said, raising her head to stare down at him.

He pulled her back down into another kiss. He didn't want to talk.

She was as virgin as he was. There was a breathless bit of fumbling with unfamiliar fastenings and undergarments, a matter of deciding what went where, but they managed. He was trembling with the need to be inside her but he forced himself to wait, to play with her gently until she was slippery with desire. She stiffened at the sharp pain of his entry and he summoned up all his willpower to hold himself still, letting her become accustomed to him before he began moving again. When he did he moved very slowly, in and out, going as deeply as he could on the downstroke, pulling out almost all the way, continuing so until he felt her hands on his back pulling him down. He began to move faster, and she pushed up to meet him, gasping, eyes staring blindly up. When her climax came she squeezed around him, milking him, sucking on him, and his own end came with a shout he muffled in the musty fabric of the seat next to her head.

"Oh," she said some moments later. "Oh, Daoud. I didn't know it could be like that."

He raised his head and slid his hands to her throat, his thumbs caressing the hollow beneath her chin. He was still inside her, his wetness and her own such a warm haven. She kissed him, with a tenderness that brought tears to his eyes. "I didn't, either," he said.

Her neck—such a slender, fragile stem—broke easily when he twisted it. The cracking vertebrae sounded like distant gunfire.

17

Back in port, Cal turned everyone loose, which since they were only temporarily homeported in Miami didn't mean much. They all knew working the shuttle launch was more of a PR mission than it was a real job, and crew was bailing right, left, and center. D7 was keeping *Munro* in bravo-24 status, available for recall and sailing within twenty-four hours in the event of urgent tasking, but when the "Liberty, liberty, liberty!" call went out over the pipe most of the crew scattered to cheap motels and holed up for three days, leaving a skeleton crew just large enough to respond to an emergency behind. Cal hoped they managed to stay out of trouble when they started checking out the bars. He remembered some pretty wild times as an ensign in Miami, assigned to a 110 off the Everglades. Lots of opportunity for a Coastie to get into trouble if he or she wasn't careful, but these were grown men and women and it was pretty much up to them. The XO cautioned them against sailing into stupidland and turned them loose.

It was a great honor to work security during a shuttle launch, no doubt, but the crew was homesick, discouraged that people had died during their last patrol and they had been unable to save them, and that they hadn't responded to any SARS or made any drug busts on this one. "I guess all the smugglers have up and moved ops to EPAC," the XO said, inspecting the map of the Caribbean Cal had duct-taped over the map of Alaska in the wardroom. He looked around and smiled. "Damn, we're good."

"Yeah," Cal said, without enthusiasm. "How many left on board as of liberty this morning?"

"Forty-four."

"Okay."

"You taking off?"

Cal thought about Kenai in Houston. "I don't know yet. Probably not."

"When do we leave?"

"Three days."

"The thirtieth? Why so early? Won't take us a day to get up there."

"Oh, uh, let me think. Because we're *Munro*, short for Douglas Munro? The only Coastie recipient of the Medal of Honor, in whose honor you will recall we are named? Related to Kenai Munro, a member of this particular shuttle crew?"

"Uh-huh," Taffy said, not without foreboding. "And this means, what, exactly? Sir?"

Cal gave a sour smile. "It means a tiger cruise, only instead of family riding along we get the press and a bunch of NASA honchos. Also Kenai Munro's parents. It means a couple of receptions on shore when we get there, and it means—"

"Dress uniforms," the XO said with a groan.

"There might also," Cal said painfully, "have been mention made of a band."

"Oh, Christ no," the XO said.

"I'm afraid so," Cal said.

"Allah be merciful," Taffy said.

"God could help out a little, too," Cal said.

"If we got the two of them working together, maybe they could scrub the launch," the XO said hopefully.

"Jesus wept, don't even say that," Cal said, blanching at the thought of Kenai's reaction to the suggestion.

He and Taffy adjourned to a great little Thai restaurant they knew from previous inports. Command had selfishly not shared that information with the rest of the crew, so they saw no one they knew. Cal had a beer, Taffy had tea, and they both ordered entrees with four peppers next to them on the menu. "What are we going to do about Riley?"

"Let him go," Taffy said. "OSC told him not to make any decisions based on his domestic affairs, but his wife won't go back to Alaska, and he won't leave her."

"She's not kicking him out?"

"He says not."

"What about Reese?"

"What about her? The investigators say there is no case. Her story lacks credibility, and to be fair, though an acknowledged weasel, no complaints have been made against Riley of a sexual harassment nature until Reese."

"How is she taking it?"

"Philosophically. I don't get the sense that there's a lot of repressed anger there."

"Does she want to come back to the ship?"

"She says yes."

"What does EMO say about her job performance?"

Taffy shrugged, spearing a shrimp. "It's better than what OSC says about Riley's. Says his work product never was that good, and lately it's fallen off in a major way. He's counseled him numerous times, he says, but it looks like the only thing that might get the kid's attention is a bad set of marks."

"So we're looking for another OS," Cal said, sighing. "Been a run on Combat positions this tour." He took a bite of panang gai and made an approving sound. Thai food didn't count unless it made his nose run. "They're probably bored."

"So am I, but it's the job, Captain," Taffy said, draining his tea and signaling for another. "It's what we're tasked with, it's what we're paid for. If you don't like it, you can always resign."

"That does seem to be the currently popular option," Cal said.

The waitress brought the XO more tea, lingering a little for him to try it, evidently to be the recipient of a grateful smile. Cal didn't think he even registered on her peripheral vision. "Taffy?"

"Captain?"

Cal nodded at the tea. "You ever take a drink?"

"Against my religion, sir," Taffy said.

"The Muslim religion," Cal said.

"That's right." The XO bent his head over his plate again. He was a southpaw, and the gold wedding ring gleamed on his hand.

Taffy didn't talk about his private life, and he didn't socialize a great deal. "Were you raised Muslim?"

The XO nodded. "Both parents."

Cal took a bite of spring roll. "I'm curious, and if I step in it let me apologize in advance."

The XO grinned. Across the room the waitress sighed. "Go for it."

"Does your mom wear a veil?"

The XO laughed out loud. "Not hardly. She's an EMT. A veil might get in the way."

"So they're pretty modern."

The XO shrugged. "They're Americans. Their religion is important to them—it is to me, too—but they're acculturated. Just not secularized."

"Oh." Cal drank beer. "Wasn't time to ask in New Orleans, but . . ." He hesitated.

"What?"

Cal gestured at the XO's wedding band. "What happened to your wife? Wait, let me back up a little. For starters, what was her name?"

The XO's face softened. "Nur. Means 'light.' "

"How'd you meet?"

"At a college mixer for Muslim-American students. I was at the Academy, she was at Harvard."

"Harvard. No kidding. Got my first master's at Harvard."

"I know. She was probably about four years behind you, give or take. We got married the week after my graduation. She got her teacher's certificate and since I'd scored a 110 out of Chesapeake, she went to work for the Arlington School District, teaching civics and government at Patrick Henry High."

Cal winced. "Teenagers. Yikes. A brave woman."

The XO laughed again. "Yeah. You should have heard some of her stories. But she loved it, and from what I could see, shuttling back and forth between duty stations, they loved her." The XO paused, mashing rice with the tines of his fork.

Cal waited.

Taffy looked up, not bothering to hide the pain. "She'd never made a secret of her heritage. She used it in some of her classes, even. But then, 9/11 happened."

Cal was suddenly very sorry he'd asked.

"She was leading a small field trip to the Pentagon that day. She got the kids out, and then the building fell on her."

"Jesus," Cal said, putting down his beer. "I'm sorry, Taffy."

"Me, too," the XO said.

"No kids?"

The XO's smile was more a grimace. "We were waiting. Saving up, gonna buy a house, get more settled, a little more secure. You know."

They finished eating in silence.

"Seven years ago this September," Cal said.

"Yeah."

"Nobody else come along in that time?"

The XO shook his head. "She was one of a kind." He shrugged. "You never know, but I'm not looking for lightning to strike me twice."

Back on board that evening, Cal thought about the XO's tragic marriage. One of a kind, he'd called his wife.

Cal liked his life. He saw no reason to change how he lived it, in spite of his parents' infrequent pleas. If anything, his father's wishes in the matter moved Cal in the opposite direction. He supposed it was juvenile of him, but there it was. At least he knew what motivated him, and right at the top of the list was a disinclination to serve as a working trophy for his father.

One of a kind.

Kenai was one of a kind.

They'd been seeing a lot of each other over the past eighteen months, or as much as either of their jobs would permit. So far they'd managed to keep it quiet, from their families as well as from the media. Cal harbored no illusions about his own intrinsic worth to what Harlan Ellison had so aptly named the glass teat, but the press was always on the lookout for a juicy astronaut story, and if and when his father found out about them he'd want to use Kenai on campaign tours.

His mother, on the other hand, would be terrified that marriage and—horrors!—grandchildren might be in the offing. So long as Cal didn't reproduce, Vera Beauchamp Schuyler could go on pretending she was on the right side of forty.

He wondered about Kenai's parents, what they were like. She had spoken warmly of both of them, although her father seemed to predominate over any such conversation. An ex–Alaskan Bush pilot, he sounded like a hell of a guy.

Now it was no longer a matter of when he would meet them, or if. They would be watching the launch from the *Munro*.

He'd shied away from meeting the families of any of his other girlfriends. It had been more than once the rock upon which the relationship had foundered, and frequently in such instances he was accused of being afraid of commitment. In vain did he protest that it was a simple matter of him liking his life as it was and that he saw no need to change it. He didn't convince any of them, but then he didn't try that hard.

The truth was he hadn't cared enough to put in the extra effort. That made him an asshole of the first water, no doubt, but it also made him a free asshole, and in the years following his escape from the mansion on Louisburg Square his freedom had been his most precious possession, the one thing he was determined never to yield, no matter how many broad hints his father gave about founding the greatest political dynasty in Massachusetts since the Kennedys.

So far, Kenai had not offered to introduce him to her parents, nor had she asked to meet his. It worried him sometimes, how easy their relationship had been so far. After a year and a half he remained interested in her, too, which also worried him. He had made an effort, met with varying degrees of success, not to think about what any of that might mean.

He called her that night in Houston. "How's the Arabian Knight?"

"Status quo," she said. "It's his friggin' satellite that's giving us fits now."

"What's wrong?"

"One of the gyroscopes keeps throwing off weird readings during testing."

"A vital piece of the package?"

"Not once it gets into the correct orbit, no. It's supposed to help get it into that orbit, though."

"I thought you just opened the payload bay doors and released it."

"Mostly, yeah, but this is, in fact, rocket science we're talking about here."

He grinned at her mock sarcasm. "I stand corrected."

"Anyway, we fixed it." She yawned. "Man, I'm beat."

"I'll let you go," he said, "but one question."

"What?"

"Do I get to see you before you depart this sphere?" The Munros were coming aboard early and sailing up the coast of Florida with them. When she got back from orbit, Kenai would make a flying trip to Miami to have a Munro family photo taken on the foredeck of *Munro*, the Medal of Honor banner on the lookout station in the background. Two genuine American heroes, one past, one present, one standing on the deck of a ship named for the one who died in duty above and beyond the call, and a Coastie, no less. It was hard to tell who was closer to orgasm over this PR opportunity,

NASA or the U.S. Coast Guard. It was going to be hard to get around the ship without tripping over an admiral in any direction. He said, very casually, "How are we handling that, by the way?"

When she answered, she was no less casual. "We could pretend to be just acquaintances, I suppose."

"I suppose," he said without enthusiasm. "So, any chance for some alone time before this circus puts up its big top?"

"I might be able to sneak off for a couple of hours. Maybe. Possibly. If you can get up to the Cape before we go into crew quarters."

"What are crew quarters?"

"A bunch of trailers. We move in a week before launch date. It's essentially medical quarantine, so the crew doesn't catch anything from a family member or a friend and get sick during the flight. The only people we can see after that is someone checked out by the NASA flight surgeon."

"Oh." Getting checked out by the flight surgeon increased their chances of getting found out by the press.

She yawned again. "Anyway, I'm going to hit the rack." He heard the smile in her voice. "Exercise that paranormal Schuyler ability to find a really nice hotel as close as possible to KSC."

"Aye aye, ma'am," he said, and hung up with a reluctance that would have frightened the living hell out of him, if he'd noticed.

Kenai had noticed, but she refused to be distracted by it. The Arabian Knight had, among many innate talents ready-made to annoy the astronaut corps, the ability to generate news coverage. A lot of this was driven by the administration, determined to make a show of hands across the sea in spite of thousands of Iraqi and Afghani dead and further in spite of the current saber rattle toward Iran. When asked, given the less than congenial state of affairs that existed between the United States and the world's Muslim nations, if he had any qualms about sending a Qatari national into space, director Milton "Alfred E." Neuman raised surprised eyebrows and said blandly, "Why, no. Should I have?"

The astronauts had some, not least of which was the Arabian Knight's propensity for the spotlight. He was a media magnet. According to the next morning's newspapers, while they were frantically working to recover the ARABSAT-8A's gyro, he was cruising Houston's hot spots with one of the Disney blondes on his arm. "I can live with a jetsetting playboy," Rick told Kenai. "What I won't live with is someone who won't do their homework. I'm not taking anyone into orbit who doesn't know how to flush the fucking toilet."

Rick Robertson rarely swore, in public or in private. "Yes, sir," Kenai said, and departed at speed. She hunted down the Arabian Knight, who was chatting on his cell phone. She removed it from his hand, ended his call, and tossed it in a nearby trash can, where it landed with a promising thud.

The Arabian Knight erupted, in Arabic.

"Shut up," Kenai said.

He kept talking.

Kenai stepped up and got right into his face. "Shut up," she said, and this time he did. "I'm going to show you how to flush the toilet on the shuttle," she said, "and this time you're going to have the procedure down before you leave, I don't care if we're here all night."

She towed him behind her like a mother towing a recalcitrant child. His face was congested with fury and he spit what sounded like serious insults at her all the way there. They passed many NASA employees who had never seen quite that expression on Kenai's face before but were quick in clearing a path for it, especially when they saw who she had in tow. The Arabian Knight was no longer a shared joke, he was a potential hazard to the successful completion of the mission. In two years they would be retiring the shuttle, they'd already lost two, and no one wanted to lose a third between now and then, especially not due to some arrogant little prick of a part-timer who had been granted a ride-along because his daddy would sign the check to launch the satellite in the cargo bay.

There were over a thousand switches, buttons, and circuit breakers in the shuttle's cockpit, but Kenai often thought it was easier to put the shuttle on orbit than it was to flush its toilet. You had to strap yourself in with thigh clamps to what was essentially a vacuum cleaner and for number two use a sight with crosshairs to zero in on the appropriate orifice. She had planned for a male colleague waiting in the wings to handle this portion of the Arabian Knight's indoctrination into waste management training but she waited until her charge had run through his vocabulary of what she was sure was first-class Arabic invective before calling him in. She had to wear a diaper on orbit herself, so her sympathy was less than sincere, but she stepped out, and then waited for a while before going back in without knocking. More swearing, and the Arabian Knight zipped up with shaking hands and fought his way out of the thigh clamps before storming off.

Kenai raised an eyebrow. "So?"

"He got it. More or less."

"He'd better have, or the first time the Arabian Knight turns a turd loose on the flight deck in zero gee Robertson will put him and the turd into orbit without benefit of spacesuit."

"Any chance you can flush him out with the rest of the urine?"

"I wish."

There was a far more serious problem the next day, in the form of an anonymous threat from some skinhead hate group none of them had ever heard of before, claiming it was a crime against the Almighty to transport a device owned and to be operated by the heathen, and that God's Army stood ready to attack.

"For Christ's sake," Rick said.

"Exactly," Mike said.

"Just tell me we're not letting this force us into a hold," Kenai said, her jaw very tight.

"No hold," Joel said. "The FBI doesn't regard the, uh, Smoky Mountain Whites as a credible threat."

" 'Smoky Mountain Whites'?"

"That's what they're calling themselves. Evidently they're from Kentucky."

"Whatever," Kenai said, and she and Laurel left to run yet another simulation of the Eratosthenes deployment. Eratosthenes, designed to take up where the Hubble Space Telescope left off, purred through it like a kitten. "If ever mankind built a perfect machine," Laurel said, "Eratosthenes is it."

"Shh," Kenai said, "it'll hear you."

Laura gave the shiny foil exterior of the telescope a fond pat. "She already knows."

WASHINGTON, D.C.

In spite of Yaqub's complete and total meltdown in the interrogation room at Gitmo and his subsequent fervent desire to omit no detail of his work with Isa, no matter how small, he could tell them very little that was useful. Back in his Washington office, Patrick found this frustrating in the extreme.

"He knows Isa only by the alias he used in Germany, Dandin Gandhi, and by another alias in England,

Tabari Yabrud," Bob said. "The first names are common first names, and the second are names of Asian and Middle Eastern martyrs, major and minor."

"At this point," Patrick said, cradling the phone between his shoulder and his ear so he could type the names into his Isa database, "kinda not giving a shit what he called himself then. Kinda wanting to know what name he's using now and, oh yeah, where he is now, and what he's doing next."

"Isa told them that the plan was to take out Seatac, San Francisco International, and LAX."

"How?"

"He would furnish them with credentials and they would get jobs as baggage handlers. Some of the cell are engineers, big surprise, and two are chemists. He had plans for homemade bombs made out of—"

"Let me guess. Diesel fuel and fertilizer."

"Some of them, yeah," Bob said. He sounded tired. "Isa had plans for a lot of different devices, most of them to be assembled by the cell members when they arrived on scene."

"What was the play-by-play?"

"For them to fly to Canada, which they did separately. Isa transferred enough funds into everyone's bank accounts to make this possible. We've got people checking on that, but Isa's some kind of Internet wizard, you know that. We'll never be able to trace any of those funds back."

"But we'll try," Patrick said, sitting back from the computer to page through an intelligence report. Three

American Muslims had been arrested for praying on an airplane about to back away from a gate in Minneapolis. He couldn't find a great deal to get excited about there, every time he got on a plane anymore he prayed he'd be able to walk again after hours spent in what had to be the most uncomfortable seats ever designed for the human body. He turned the page.

"Yes, we'll try," Bob said. "When they arrived in Vancouver, they were instructed to proceed by public transportation to Lytton, a small town in the mountains north of Vancouver. There, they were to be picked up and taken to a camp even further in country, Sadiq says he doesn't know where."

"Do you believe him?"

"I actually kinda do. He really is a sad sack of a terrorist, Patrick. Isa must really be desperate." The two of them contemplated the thought of a desperate Isa in silence for a moment, and then Bob added, "You might want to alert our friends north of the border."

Patrick had already sent off an email. "Will do. Did you tell Sadiq we found Isa's email instructions in Brittany's jewelry box?"

"Yeah. He was astonished, he thought he'd hidden them so well. Now he thinks we're some kinda psychic."

"Good." There hadn't been much of use to them in the little slip of paper, but if it made Yaqub fear them, that worked for Patrick. "Why was he getting on a plane for Mexico City?"

"He says Isa emailed him that the LAX plan had

been aborted due to some security breach and to get on a plane for Mexico City."

The next report in the intelligence folder was of a young woman found in the back of a Ford sedan with her neck broken, in the parking garage at Miami International Airport. Other than that the young woman was a Muslim American, it seemed unfortunate but unrelated to any of his concerns. "Last-minute orders and absolute obedience to same," he said to Bob. "That sounds a lot more like him than that whole planning session in York."

He could almost hear Bob shrug. Bob's job was to interrogate, not to interpret. "I don't think Yaqub's even close to a true believer. He thought about Isa's email for a while before he complied."

"What pushed him over?"

"He says that even if Isa couldn't find him he could probably find Yussuf, since Yussuf is apparently more of a true believer than Yaqub. He was Yussuf's friend, he said. He couldn't let him down."

"Honor among terrorists. Who'd a thunk it?" Patrick turned to the next report, and then he turned back to the one on the murder in the airport garage.

The body showed signs of recent and consensual sex. The ME thought she had been a virgin. She'd had no identification, but her mother had been making increasingly frantic calls to the hospitals and the police from the first morning of her disappearance, and had identified the body within hours of its discovery. Her mother had—

Patrick sat up, his attention caught. Her mother, a Mrs. Haddad Mansour, had said that she suspected her lodger, a Mr. Daoud Sadat, of the crime. Mr. Sadat, she said, had been renting their spare room for six months, and she feared that he and her daughter had grown quite close.

Even more interesting, her description of him, precisely detailed, was very similar to the doctored photo on Adam Bayzani's passport.

A man, a Muslim terrorist who called himself Isa, or Jesus, a way of mocking the nations pursuing him.

He'd assumed the name Gandhi in Germany. After Mahatma Gandhi, perhaps? It seemed likely, even probable, especially if he then took as an alias the name of another good man, a man whose inspired leadership and vision for peace in the Middle East was a legend among all peoples, if anathema to some. "I will go to Jerusalem," Anwar Sadat had famously said. He had, and Muslim extremists had assassinated him for his vision.

"The fucker's giving us the finger again," he said, marveling, almost admiring.

"Which fucker?" Bob said.

Patrick got to his feet. "Bob, I'm sorry, I've got to go." He hung up the phone. "Melanie!"

18

The anonymous little village was built on pilings perched on a narrow strip of tropical coastline at most a hundred feet in width between the almost vertical forest and the cerulean blue sea. It consisted in the main of a waterlogged marina with a dock ending in a ramp leading down to two wooden slips. The slips looked as if they were on the verge of going under for the third time. To the north and south of the marina were a few related businesses that looked even more tatterdemalion, and some one-room, thatched-roof homes clinging to the sides of the steep coastline that were almost tree houses. At the southern end of the village sat a shabby hotel, a one-story structure whose largest room was the bar, and a half-dozen bungalows with ancient thatched roofs teeming with insect life.

Up the coast from Port-au-Prince, it was so small it didn't even have a name, which might have explained why it was on no map. Although Akil thought that absence more probably had to do with the reason for its existence, its primary industry, which encouraged a wholesale discretion on the part of its residents, always providing they wanted to live to see tomorrow. It was probably the same reason that the encroaching vegetation had been encouraged to overhang the shoreline, all the buildings, and as much of the marina as possible.

That much harder to spot, from the sea or the air.

There were a few open skiffs tied up to the marina, one painted a deep blue with a broad stern to accommodate the line of six large outboard motors bolted to it. Akil, inexperienced in the ways of boats, thought they looked very powerful.

He had been here for three days as the rest of the cell trickled in in ones and twos, some flying in on a seaplane held together quite literally with duct tape. Others came by ferry, a self-propelled scow whose arrivals and departures were as erratic as her drunken captain, a squat, scrofulous man with an almost incapacitating limp, very bad teeth, and one eye. Akil had arrived by car, although he'd had to hire a driver to find the road and then to get the car down the almost indecipherable switchback through the jungle, alive with bird calls. He imagined that he could hear the slither of snakes, too, and his driver, a gaunt, morose young man with the scarred knuckles of a fighter, enlivened the journey with a description of the various indigenous species. None of them were poisonous, the driver assured him, but Akil didn't like snakes, and this made the pit stops on the twelve-hour, twenty-two-mile journey interesting. If Akil had been in a less apathetic mood, he might have been more appreciative.

He didn't know quite what he was doing here. Yussuf, good soldier that he was, had arrived before him and had begun to gather in Yaqub's cell members as well as his own, settling them into the tiny cabana he had rented at the very edge of town. He brought them food—if all went according to plan they wouldn't be there that long but there was no point in giving away information about themselves to the investigators who would swarm about the place later—and he found women for those who wanted them. He led them in prayer, stiffening more than one spine, and when the Koran couldn't do the job, engaged the nervous in long discussions of what waited for them in paradise, with emphasis on the honey and the virgins.

During the last three days Yussuf couldn't be faulted. After the initial greeting, Yussuf had said only, "Yaqub?"

"He didn't make it," Akil said.

Yussuf muttered a prayer for his boyhood friend's soul and asked no more questions.

By comparison to Yussuf, Yaqub would have been at best only a decent aide de camp. Akil himself was superfluous.

He didn't need to be there. Moreover, he shouldn't be there. He'd known that before he'd arrived, before he'd left Miami, even. It was the first time he'd ever exposed himself to the risk of operations. For that matter the operation itself was at risk because of his actions. Sooner or later Zahirah's body would be found, and when they questioned Mrs. Mansour she would have too much of value to tell them. He cursed himself again for not returning to the house and disposing of her. He didn't make mistakes like that. It was why he was still alive, and still a threat.

He himself had flown on pre-existing reservations

from Miami to Lima, from Lima to Mexico City, and from Mexico City to Port-au-Prince, a different pass-port for the last flight. The last two men had arrived this morning.

The transportation he had arranged for six months ago was due in late this evening. He would see off the faithful, entrust Yussuf with the completion of the operation, make the hazardous drive through the jungle back to Port-au-Prince, and fly to Paris, where he already had a reservation in a hotel where all the rooms had satellite television and he could watch the results of his plan play out on CNN and the BBC, and espe-cially on Al Jazeera. It would be the glorious culmina-tion of a long and inventive career, and a fitting coda to the life of his master, the man who had taught him everything. He knew Zarqawi would approve and rejoice at this astounding blow to the fabric and pride of the infidel.

The thought steadied him, and he returned to his room to sleep away the afternoon.

She was there the moment he closed his eyes. He knew it was a dream and he struggled to wake, but she wouldn't let him.

"Adara," he said.

"Akil," she said.

"Adara," he said.

"Stay with me," she whispered, her voice husky in his ears. "Daoud," she said. "Stay." Her hands ran shyly over his body.

"Zahirah," he said.

"Yes, my love, it's me. Stay with me, oh my best beloved."

He rolled her gently to her back and slid between her legs with a feeling like coming home, a feeling he had not known since he left his village for the last time. "Zahirah," he said, her name almost a prayer. "Zahirah."

"Daoud," she said, and he looked up to see dead eyes in a dead face, her neck bent in an unnatural angle, the dark marks of his fingers around the tender skin of her neck. Her body was cold, unmoving around him.

He woke violently, covered with sweat, and rolled off the bed to the floor. He scrabbled toward the bathroom on all fours, barely making it to the toilet in time. He vomited until his stomach heaved up nothing but a clear fluid, vomited until his esophagus and his sinuses burned like fire, vomited until he was too exhausted to do anything but lie on the bathroom floor in a puddle of his own sweat. He started to doze and jerked himself awake just in time. There would be no more sleep for him today.

He became aware of a persistent knocking. "Dandin?" Yussuf's anxious voice said. "Dandin, are you there?"

"A moment," he said. He rinsed out his mouth and sluiced off his face and reached for a towel. In the mirror he saw a reflection that shocked him, a gaunt and haggard face with haunted eyes.

When had he become so old? He was only thirty-seven.

THEIR TRANSPORT DRIFTED INTO THE MARINA LIKE A ghost at half past two the next morning. An eighty-foot sailboat with a hull painted black or a very dark blue and two dark red, lateen-rigged sails, or so Yussuf told him. He knew nothing of sailboats, or boats of any kind. The younger man could barely contain his excitement.

The master of the vessel knew what he was doing; he had the boat warped in to the slip and lines around the cleats in moments. There was a mutter of exhaust from the rudimentary main street of the village, and a large, enclosed truck backed down the dock, shaking the pilings beneath it. The passenger-side door banged and footsteps went to the back of the truck. They heard the click of a lock and the sound of a sliding door rolling up. There was a bewildered murmur of voices, cut short by a vicious, low-voiced curse. When the voices quieted the first voice snapped out an order, and many people began to come down the ramp.

"You have the money," the boat's master said.

Akil handed it over. The master tossed it through the open door of the boat's cabin. "Don't you want to count it?"

The master's teeth flashed white. "If it's short, your people are going to have to walk to the U.S. from the middle of the Caribbean. And unless they're related to Jesus Christ . . ." He chuckled. "Quickly, now, before the rest get here."

He showed them to a stateroom in the bow. It had

four sets of bunk beds and its own bathroom. It was very crowded with the ten of them, but except for the weapons they were traveling very light and had no belongings to find a place for.

Yussuf was left standing in the center of the room, looking very solemn. The boat continually dipped beneath their feet as more people boarded from the slip. Muted voices could be heard speaking in Haitian through the bulkheads. A small child whimpered, quickly hushed.

They looked at him expectantly. This was the moment where he gave (to paraphrase something he'd once seen an FBI agent say on television) the "come to Allah" speech, when he spoke the words that made them truly feel that they were on a mission graced and blessed by God himself, a God who held them in his hands and would welcome them to paradise when their task was done. This was the last time he had to make them feel that their task was worthy of their deaths, for surely they would all die. "You are about to embark on a sacred quest," he said. "You will strike a blow at the very heart of the Far Enemy, this godless infidel and friend to the Jews, whose abhorrent secularism has led to abominations like homosexuality, feminism, drinking, gambling."

They looked at him, waiting confidently. There was more. There had to be more.

There was. "I am coming with you," he told Yussuf, and beneath that young man's astonished gaze went to a corner and sat down with his back to the wall, crossing his legs and closing his eyes.

Outside, he heard light footsteps pad down the deck as the lines were loosed, and canvas flapped as the sails were pulled up. Under sail power alone, they slid slowly and silently away from the dock and out to sea.

MIAMI

Doreen and Nicholas Munro came aboard the day before *Munro* left the dock. Cal had intended to hand them over to the XO after the initial greeting and dinner in his cabin, but somehow it didn't turn out that way.

He liked them, for one thing. Mrs. Munro was a short, round figure with thick glasses that gave her the look of a blue-eyed owl. Her hair was completely white and had a tendency to stand on end, and she wore polyester plaid bagged out at the seat and knees with an air of insouciance. "I'm a housewife, wife and mother, plain and simple," she said breezily, "so don't ask me what I do for a living, thanks."

Mr. Munro was a tall man with amused brown eyes and hair even thicker and whiter than his wife's. He wore a gray sport coat over an open-collared shirt and jeans worn white at the seams. He was an aviator and as Cal had learned the main influence in his daughter's life. He was very affable—"It's Nick, Captain." "It's Cal, Nick."—and Cal offered him a ride in the helo when they got out to sea, warmly seconded by Lieutenant Noyes.

He gave them the dollar-and-a-quarter tour, after trying to fob them off on the nickel tour didn't work. They were insatiably and flatteringly curious about life and work on board *Munro*, and on instantly easy terms with every crew member they met, from FS2 Steele in the galley to MPA Molnar in Main Control to MK3 Fisher doing fuel soundings on the main deck. "We have two diesel engines and two gas turbine engines. The diesels are locomotive engines, the turbines are Pratt & Whitney's, essentially the same thing they built for the Boeing 707s."

"Really," Kenai's father said. "I'd like to hear a little more about them."

"When you get settled in, I'll have MPA come get you and give you a more detailed tour. He can print out some specs for you, too, if you'd like." Cal closed his mind to what MPA's probably profane reaction would be to that much time pulled away from his precious engine room and said, "If we're using only the bow prop we can still make five knots. We can go twenty-nine if we're up on both turbines."

Grinning, Mr. Munro said, "She throw up a rooster tail when you're going that fast?"

"No, sir," Cal said, grinning back, "but she'll put up a pretty impressive wake. Until Deepwater, which is the program building the new 410s, the Hamilton class 378s were the largest cutters built for the Coast Guard. When they were built, back in the sixties and seventies, they were all about speed and endurance, which meant they sacrificed a lot of utility and ease of access. We've got twenty-two different fuel tanks, and it is a genuine exercise in Newtonian physics to get her fueled properly."

"How far can you go on a full tank? Or tanks?"

"Fourteen thousand nautical miles," Cal said, and added, "at twelve knots, that is, on one diesel."

"More than halfway around the world without stopping for gas," Mr. Munro said.

"How many crew members on board?" Mrs. Munro said.

"A hundred and fifty-one." Normally. While many of the crew members were excited about watching the shuttle launch from offshore, many others had opted for leave during what they considered to be at best a public-relations exercise. *Munro* was running north with a crew of sixty-five, well under strength. Fortunately, all the chiefs except for GMC had elected to forgo liberty until their return. He could run the ship with the chiefs alone if need be, long enough to get her into port, if need be.

He wound up taking the Munros through virtually every compartment from the bow prop room to aft steering, and he was absurdly gratified when they understood the tac number system identifying each individual compartment the first time he explained it to them. "Excellent," he said. "If you understand this system you'll never be lost."

"Good luck," Mr. Munro said.

They all enjoyed a good laugh at that.

Kenai's father had a near miss with the Darwin sorter

on the boat davit, and Cal got another big laugh when he described the little PA so blinded by love for Kenai that he'd run right into it. Mrs. Munro—"Call me Doreen."—demanded more news of Kenai's visit.

"What's involved in offshore security for a shuttle launch?" Nick said.

"Now, there's a question," Cal said. They were on the bridge. "Let's go down to the wardroom and get some coffee, and I'll walk you through it."

They disposed themselves around the wardroom table and Seaman Trimble was sent down to the mess deck for some of FS2's baked goodies while Cal made them both americanos. "You have an espresso machine on *Munro*?" Nick said.

"Well, of course," Cal said with a poker face. "It's probably one of the more important contributors to crew morale."

"It's the single most important contributor to your morale, sir," Seaman Trimble said.

The Munros laughed. "You're on report for insubordination, Trimble," Cal said. "Dismissed."

Trimble grinned and saluted. "Aye aye, sir," he said, and departed.

The baked goodies were found to be snickerdoodles, which Doreen pronounced divine.

"Okay," Cal said, "security on a shuttle mission. To begin with, there's an eight-mile security zone around the launch pad. Nobody unauthorized in or out for the duration."

"That's boats," Nick said. "What about aircraft?"

"There is a no-low-fly zone of twenty nautical miles. Believe it or not there are some private pilots out there who think they can do a flyby of a shuttle launch."

"Oh, I believe it," Nick said. "So, is the *Munro* the only sea-based security presence during the launch?"

"God, no," Cal said. "There are four small boats, two twenty-five-footers, and two shallow water boats. They're working from the shoreline to two nautical miles out. Then there are two forty-seven-foot MLBs—motor life boats—working two to six nautical miles out. A CPB—a coastal patrol boat, an eighty-seven-footer—usually acts as OSC, or on-scene commander, of all the Coast Guard assets working the mission. They're usually the offshore enforcement and response vessel."

"Usually?"

"Usually," Cal said. "Theoretically, an MEC or medium endurance cutter is the OSC, but in practice D7, the operational district responsible for this area, never has any available MECs. Not enough assets, and of course they never know how long those assets will be tied up."

"Because of launch delays," Nick said. "Kenai warned us. What's the forecast?"

"Weather's not looking like a problem," Cal said. "But it's July. Hurricane season. You never know. At any rate, *Munro* is OSC for this launch."

Nick smiled at his wife. "Because Kenai's on board the shuttle."

"Yes."

"And because she's related to Douglas Munro."

"Yes."

"Our tax dollars at work," Doreen said.

Cal laughed. "That's right."

"I like boat rides," Doreen said, twinkling at Cal.

"Me, too," Cal said, grinning at her.

"What else?" Nick said.

"We've also got a HU-25 Falcon patrolling a one-hundred-fifty-nautical-mile safety zone."

"Medium-range fan jet," Nick said. "Fast, too, got a cruising speed of over four hundred knots."

Cal shrugged. "If you say so, Nick. I don't do airplanes. The Falcon will make sure there are no vessels in the way of falling boosters."

Or shuttle parts, they all thought.

"Recently, we've added an MH-90 HITRON—an armed helicopter—as an air intercept asset. If necessary, it will enforce the no-low-fly zone."

"Impressive," Nick said.

"Reassuring," Doreen said tartly.

Nick grinned. "Do you report directly to Mission Control, or what?"

"Or what," Cal said. "We report to the Range Operations Center. The ROC reports to the Forty-fifth Space Wing of the U.S. Air Force."

"I didn't even know the Air Force had a space wing," Doreen said. She looked at her husband. "It sounds so, I don't know, what am I trying to say?"

"Thrilling?" Nick said.

"I was going to say Heinleinian," she said.

"Fictional?" Nick said.

"No. More like we've already got such a permanent presence in space that we've got a whole arm of the U.S. Air Force supporting our presence there."

"We do," Cal said.

"I guess so," she said. "I wonder if Kenai knows."

"I bet she does," Nick said, quirking an eyebrow at Cal, who smothered a grin. "What happens on *Munro* during the launch?"

"*Munro* will run security from Combat," Cal said, "you remember, from the operations center three decks down?"

"Are there often a lot of offshore security problems during launches?" Nick said.

Cal smiled at his deceptively mild tone, and shook his head. "No," he said. "Not unless you count the charter skippers whose clients sign up for a shot at a game fish and, what the hell, since we're in the area, how about a front-row seat to the launch, too, or the drunk driving the Liberty Bayliner who can't resist coming in for a closer look." He reflected. "I'm told there's the occasional poacher, hunting alligator. The place is virtually a game preserve, no hunting, trapping, and especially no shooting. But that's about it. Most people are sensible, they know enough to stay out of the area during a launch, or if they want to watch to go to one of the official viewing areas."

"Have you ever seen a launch, Cal?"

"No, I'm ashamed to say I haven't, Doreen, except on television," Cal said. "I'm looking forward to it."

"How close will we be?"

"How close? Well," Cal said, sitting back and steepling his fingers in an exaggeratedly pontifical gesture, "we are going to have media on board for this launch and, I'm told, at least one admiral. And then there's you. The Coast Guard is, shall we say, very excited about the public relations opportunity inherent in having you on board a Coast Guard cutter to watch your daughter go into space, all three of you descendants of the only Coastie to have been awarded the Medal of Honor."

"Relatives, not descendants," Nick said.

"Whatever," Cal said. He dropped the steeple and grinned. "All this together means we get to go in a lot closer than the OSC ordinarily does."

"Which means?" Doreen said.

"I aim to take us in as close as we can get without running aground. You'll have a front-row seat. Our BMC—bosun's mate chief, basically our chief navigator—is looking at the charts right now."

"When we said we'd do this, the man at NASA told us it wouldn't be as exciting as being on the grandstand."

"Distances over water are very deceiving," Cal said. "It will feel much closer than that. The sound of it will get to us a few moments after the fact, but that's true onshore as well."

"How many reporters will be on board?" Doreen said. "I do hate it when they shove microphones in my face and ask me how I feel about my only child being an astronaut."

"There were plenty of times when you wanted to launch her into orbit yourself," Nick said.

"Back when she was a teenager," Doreen said indignantly, over their laughter, "and every mother wants to launch her daughter into orbit at some point during adolescence." She reflected. "She was very stubborn."

"She still is," Nick said. "How else could she put up with the Arabian Knight?"

"The Arabian Knight?" the XO said, who had just joined them.

"The part-timer," Cal said without thinking. "The playboy sheik from Qatar who gets a ride-along on this shuttle courtesy of the satellite NASA is launching for his family business, otherwise known as Al Jazeera. The mission commander has landed Kenai with the job of babysitting him."

There was a startled silence, and he looked up from his mug to find them all staring at him. His words, he realized too late, had just outed their relationship. "Or so I read in the newspaper," he said weakly.

"Are there any of those gorgeous snickerdoodles left?" Doreen said, leaning forward and smiling at the XO.

Into this awkward silence Lieutenant Noyes opened the door of the wardroom. He looked around until he found Nick. Target acquired, he smiled. He was a friendly soul, well-liked by the crew, something that could be said of only a very few aviators. The aviator-sailor relationship was competitive and all too often antagonistic, but Noyes was one of the good guys.

"Mr. Munro," Noyes said now, "would you like a walk-around of the helo before you turn in? Give you an advance look at what you're letting yourself in for when you go flying with us." He grinned. "Might want to back out after. We're just a bunch of knuckle-draggers down in the AvDet."

"Love to, Lieutenant, but please, call me Nick."

The lieutenant smiled at Doreen. "It's a nice night, Mrs. Munro, beautiful view of the Miami skyline."

Not wholly impervious to his charm, Doreen shook her head. "Thank you, Lieutenant, but it was a long flight. I'm going to turn in."

Later, when the wardroom's other mess cook, one Seaman Crane, had been summoned to escort Doreen to the junior officers' stateroom that had been vacated for the Munros, the XO looked at Cal.

"Don't," Cal said.

"You're dating an astronaut?"

"Shut up," Cal said.

"You're dating an astronaut."

"I mean it, XO, put a lid on it, right now."

"I've always dreamed I could fly," the XO said, hand pressed to his heart.

"Good night, XO."

"Good night, Captain, and very sweet dreams."

Cal flipped him off over his shoulder, and heard Taffy laugh as he headed up to his stateroom.

19

Mrs. Mansour's face was drawn with grief, but her voice was steady and she spoke with clarity and determination. She identified Adam Bayzani's doctored passport photo as that of Daoud Sadat, the man who had rented her spare room for the last six months, although she didn't think much of the likeness, saying the individual features seemed exaggerated.

"Exaggerated how?" Patrick said. "It would help if you could be a bit more specific. Take your time."

She did, studying the likeness of a man who she believed had murdered her only child. After a bit she said, "His forehead might be a little too broad in the photograph. His was more narrow, I think. The ears and nose are too long, too, and the mouth a little too wide. It's almost—"

"What?" Patrick said when she hesitated. "Almost what?"

"It's as if someone smeared the photograph when it was still wet." She raised a hand in a helpless gesture. "That's all."

"It's a lot, Mrs. Mansour, believe me."

"Will it help you find him?"

"Yes, Mrs. Mansour," he said. "It will help us find him."

"And he will be punished?"

He held her fierce gaze, his own steady and unflinching, even though he knew he was making promises he might very well be unable to keep. "He will. I give you my word."

She detailed as much of Sadat's activities as she knew, sitting at the utilitarian metal table in one of two metal folding chairs, in the bare, grubby little room with the single overhead light, loaned to Patrick for the occasion by the Miami Dade Police Department. Sadat, she said, left the house for work every morning Monday through Friday, and returned each evening just after six. Work where? Lockheed, he had told her.

Patrick dispatched a team to Lockheed.

It was odd, she said, that all of Sadat's clothes had been new when he arrived at her house.

"How could you tell?" Patrick said.

She looked at him. "I work at a dry cleaner's," she said. "They were new."

"All right," he said.

"It seemed odd," she said again, "but it wasn't until later that I realized it might be because he was putting on a new identity with the new clothes."

Sadat, she said, appeared to have little or no social life. Outside of work hours, he spent little time out, at least at first—her lips tightened—and no friends had visited him at her home. He declared the intention of visiting various local sights: the Everglades, Miami Beach, a carnival, the zoo. He had invited the two of them to accompany him to some of these, as a way, he said, of repaying them for their kindness.

She couldn't be sure then, but now she was certain that Zahirah had begun meeting Sadat outside the home. Mrs. Mansour didn't drive so she hadn't been able to follow him anywhere even if she'd wanted to, although she had become increasingly uneasy when she saw how close her daughter and Mr. Sadat were getting.

"Was it," Patrick said delicately, not wanting to offend her, "a romantic relationship?"

For the first time her eyes teared up. "I believe my daughter thought it was."

"And Mr. Sadat?"

She had to think about that for a while, so long that Patrick had to give her a nudge. "Mrs. Mansour?"

She came back from wherever she'd gone and refocused on his face. "I think," she said very carefully indeed, "that Mr. Sadat cared more than he knew."

"Why would you say that?"

"Because he killed her," she said, her voice hard. "He could have just left her, walked away and never contacted her again. Instead, he killed her."

There was a brief, fraught silence. "I'm sorry," Patrick said in a gentle voice, "I don't quite—"

"He killed her so that there would be no temptation for him to return," she said, still in that hard voice, her eyes bright but not with tears. "I'm not a fool, Mr. Chisum. You are a federal agent. You would not be here if you did not have good cause to suspect Mr. Sadat of wrongdoing. And when you arrive with as much help as I saw in the lobby, I don't imagine you're looking for him because he's been forging checks or bilking widows out of their pensions."

She raised an eyebrow.

"No," he said.

"No," she said, agreeing with him. "You suspect him of being a terrorist. He must be very good at what he does or you would have apprehended him by now."

"Yes," Patrick said. At this point he saw no reason to lie to her.

"If he cared for my daughter, it would be a great temptation to him to return here for her after he accomplishes whatever horror he is planning. If he has succeeded in escaping your notice for this long, then he had to have known that returning here would have been a fatal mistake. Therefore, he removed that temptation."

He looked at her with respect. She'd have made a good profiler. "Tell me, Mrs. Mansour, how did you know he wasn't Egyptian?"

"His accent was Paki," she said. "He insisted on speaking English, he said the better for all of us to practice so we fit in to our new country. I think it was so he wouldn't give his true nationality away while speaking in Arabic. But he did slip on occasion. We all do. He was Pakistani, not Egyptian. I'm sure of it."

LATER, IN HIS HOTEL ROOM, PATRICK SHOWERED AND wrapped himself in the terry-cloth robe he found hanging in the closet. He turned on the television and flicked through the channels. More bombings and kidnappings in Iraq. Gaza had changed hands, again. Yet another helicopter had been shot down in Afghanistan, and in Islamabad there were demonstrations against Musharraf. Gutsy of them, although ever since Musharraf had taken to wearing business suits instead of an army uniform, and had had his photograph taken in one standing next to George Bush, he'd been a little less inclined to stomp on the opposition with tanks.

In Paris there had been a race riot involving Muslim expatriates; in Kuwait, Iran, and Qatar there were demonstrations for women's suffrage; and in Indonesia a plane had crashed into the Indian Ocean, killing all 102 people on board.

He clicked around a while longer, stopping at something called NTV. It took him a few moments to realize that this stood for NASA TV, replaying direct feeds from the space station and rerunning videos from shuttle launches going back a dozen years. Only in Florida. The channel came to rest on a long shot of the shuttle standing at the gantry, brave and white against the dark night sky. He muted the sound, pulled a chair up so he could prop his feet on the bed, and pulled his notes up on his laptop.

His phone rang. It was Melanie. "What are you doing still at work, Melanie?" he said, checking the clock. "You should have gone home hours ago."

"I thought I should wait until I heard from you," she said, her low contralto a pleasant sound. "In case you needed something."

"Thank you, Melanie," he said, a little touched. "No, there's nothing. Except—"

"Yes, Mr. Chisum?"

"What time is it in London?" He checked the clock again.

"It's five A.M. in London, Mr. Chisum."

"Okay," he said. "Do me a favor, call the Knightsbridge Institute and leave a message for Hugh Rincon when he comes in, will you? Ask him to call my cell phone number."

"As good as done. Anything else?"

"Has the director asked for me today?"

"No, sir. We haven't heard from the director since he went on vacation last Friday."

"Good," Patrick said with satisfaction. "Okay, thanks, Melanie. You can wrap it up now and head for home." He hesitated. "I wish I could tell you to take the morning off, but chances are I'm going to need you at your desk tomorrow. I'm sorry."

"It's quite all right, Mr. Chisum," she said, and he could have sworn he heard a smile in her voice. "This is important stuff. I'm happy to help out."

The warmth in her voice was unmistakable. He stammered some reply and fumbled the phone into its cradle, and sat staring at it for several minutes afterward. It had been so long since he'd experienced even a mild flirtation that he was uncertain as to what was going on here. Rumor had it she was sleeping with Kallendorf. If rumor was correct, she might be coming on to him at Kallendorf's suggestion.

If rumor was incorrect, she might be coming on to him for herself.

He shook himself like a dog coming out of the water. An improbable assumption. Just look at him, the budding potbelly, the dying hairline. It was written down somewhere that you never slept with anyone prettier than you. But he couldn't help feeling wistful. If only it were true.

His evil twin whispered, Even if it isn't true, how far would Melanie be prepared to go to get information out of you?

He immediately condemned his evil twin to silence and returned resolutely to his laptop, stubbornly determined to resolve the mystery that was Isa, and do it before Isa struck again, this time, Patrick was convinced, entirely too close to home.

Isa, who had apprenticed with Zarqawi.

Isa, who blew up a busload of people in Baghdad as a means of presenting a calling card to the Far Enemy.

Isa, who recruited acolytes in Germany and England and moved them across oceans like chess pieces.

Isa, who used the Internet as his front office while totally frustrating the best geeks, nerds, and techies the CIA had in house to trace him.

Isa, who it was reputed never bowed five times a day toward Mecca.

Isa, who seduced young men away from their families and their societies to become suicide bombers and mass murderers in the name of Allah.

Isa, who had almost certainly killed Adam Bayzani and Zahirah Mansour.

Isa, who wasn't Jordanian or Egyptian, but who might be Afghani, or even Pakistani.

Isa. Where was he, and what was he up to?

20

CAPE CANAVERAL

"How's the weather look?"

They all waited tensely for the answer. The NASA meteorologist, aware that this was his moment in the sun, paged through a sheaf of papers and took his time answering, probably partly because his answer was so prosaic. It wasn't anything they couldn't all have looked up on www.weather.com five minutes before, anyway, and he knew it. "Forecast for midnight is for clear skies and calm winds, continuing through morning. Winds will pick up a little around eleven, but you'll be long gone by then, so no worries."

There was an audible exhalation around the room. "Excellent," Rick said. He looked around at the rest of the crew. "Any concerns? Anyone?" He carefully avoided looking at the Arabian Knight, who put his hand up anyway. "Mike?"

Mike shrugged, the epitome of the cool jet jockey. "Let's light this candle." He spoiled the effect with an enormous grin.

Bill shook his head.

"Laurel?"

Laurel's brow was creased but then Laurel's brow was always creased. "Eratosthenes and ARABSAT-8A good to go." No one saw her crossing her fingers behind her back but during launch crossed fingers were a given. "We should be good to go when we get on orbit."

"Kenai?"

"All systems go. Robot arm go." Kenai heard the words coming out of her mouth but they echoed strangely in her ears. This time tomorrow she'd be on orbit. This time tomorrow she'd look out of the flight deck windows and see the Big Blue Marble. This time tomorrow, she would have the right to change the silver shuttle on her collar for gold. "We're ready to rock and roll."

This time tomorrow she would be a bona fide astronaut.

The Arabian Knight still had his hand up. Rick sighed heavily. "Yes, Jilal?"

"Yes, Commander." The Arabian Knight never addressed them by their names. He had not been invited to. "I had a few more questions about the food. I want be certain that everything is halal—"

Kenai tuned out of the conversation. That evening, she got a phone call from Cal. "I thought you were at sea."

"We're only five miles offshore. I figured I'd see if my cell phone was working. I dialed the number you gave me, and whiz bang, some guy answered and handed me off to you." There was a faint question at the end of his sentence.

"Yeah, that was Mike. Mike Smith. One of the other crew members. We're in crew quarters. You remember, in medical quarantine until we go out to the pad."

"Yeah."

After a moment she said, "So did you call just to hear me breathe?"

He surprised them both when he said, "Yeah. I think I did."

Neither one of them knew what to do with that, so she said, "You've met the parents?"

"They're great people, Kenai."

She smiled. "I know. They seem equally impressed with you. I talked to them before you left the dock." She yawned. "Dad wants to know if I'm sleeping with you."

"Oh," he said uncomfortably. "Yeah. I kinda blew it."

"He told me."

"Sorry," he said.

"I'm not," she said. "Are you?"

For the life of him, he couldn't come up with a respectable answer, probably because he didn't know what it was.

"Never mind," she said. "Let's not go there, at least not now. I've got other things to worry about."

"How's the Arabian Knight?"

"Right now, he's vetting the menu. Making sure everything's halal."

"What's halal?"

"It's Arabic for kosher, I think. Whatever. It keeps him out of our hair. Now if we could just gag him for the rest of the trip when we strap in."

"There have been protests about him."

"Yeah, they told us. Bunch of right-wing Muslims protesting a devout's close contact with secular infidels?"

"Pretty much."

"Do we got trouble in River City?"

"Nah. For one thing, the launch is miles away from anything that looks like access. I suppose they could barricade the gates or something, but what would be the point?"

"And that's not what they want, anyway," she said cynically. "What they want is film at eleven."

"Speaking of which—"

"Oh yeah," she said, and laughed. "I forgot. How many television cameras you got on board?"

"Only one, fortunately, and even that feels like one too many. They restricted it to three pool reporters, one from the *Miami Herald*, one from NPR, and one from CNN. And they all want to talk to Nick and Doreen."

"How they holding up?"

"Pretty well. That little prep course NASA runs the friends and relatives through must be pretty effective. They both smile right into the camera like it's their new best friend, and they'll talk the ear off of any reporter about how their little girl started reading Robert Heinlein by the time she was in the second grade. Oh, and I didn't know you did beadwork?"

"I do what?"

"Make bead jewelry."

"I do?"

"Yeah. Doreen seemed to feel it necessary to establish your feminine side."

Kenai snorted. "I cook. Isn't that enough?"

"You cook?"

"I make one hell of a spaghetti sauce, smartass."

"I'll let you try it out on me when you get back."

Another silence fell. "I'm not loving this," he said.

She didn't pretend to misunderstand him. "Don't worry. We'll all come back alive."

He thought of the virtual bomb she would be riding into orbit that evening, and said, "Bet your ass. Hey."

"Hey, what?"

"What if I love you?"

"What if I love you back?"

They considered this in startled silence for a moment. "Probably just the situation," she said finally. "You've never had a girlfriend before who rides rockets. I've never had a boyfriend who didn't come unglued at the thought."

"Yeah," he said, "you're probably right. Take care up there."

"I will."

"We've got a date the instant you're out of debrief and *Munro*'s in dry dock."

"You going to kill me if I say I'm not anxious for my first time on orbit to be over?"

He laughed. "No. I think the right thing for me to say right now is, have fun."

"It'll do. See you in a week."

"See you," he said, but she had already hung up.

There was a hatch that led up to the bow of the sailboat, and before their first dawn Akil had it propped open so they could get some fresh air. They took turns sitting beneath it, letting the elusive breeze tease their faces. By afternoon the sun turned the cabin into an oven, and the combination of the heat and the oily swell passing beneath the hull that pushed the sailboat into a long, continuous roll put half of them on their knees in front of the toilet in the tiny bathroom. The smell of vomit spread the malady to all of them.

The moaning of the migrants was another constant irritant and through the walls they could hear others vomiting, sounds of protest ruthlessly subdued by crew members. Screams were quickly muffled during what sounded like an attempted rape, cut short by a meaty thud of wood on skull, a subsequent dip of the sailboat to port, and a heavy splash. After that, the moans and cries of the other passengers died to the occasional whimper.

"Why do they want to go to America so badly?" Yussuf said in wonder.

"Because they believe the lies," Akil said. "America,

330

the promised land, where all your dreams come true." He looked around the room, meeting everyone's eyes in turn, willing them to believe. "They don't understand that America is a nation of unbelievers, crusaders who are determined to destroy Islam so they can remake the world in their own image. They will wipe us out, if we don't wipe them out first."

"What we are doing won't stop them."

"No," Akil said, surprising the engineer who had spoken words he thought wouldn't carry, "it won't. Not alone. But we are not alone. We are many, and our numbers are growing. They make the West fear us. Look how we have disrupted their lives. They fear to board an airplane. They fear what their own ships may be bringing into their own seaports. They can't defend themselves from us, and they know it. Each and every day, one of their newspapers has a story about how we could poison their water supply or explode a nuclear weapon in the center of one of their cities. They fear us, because they don't know where we will strike next." He paused for effect. "After tonight, they will fear us more."

"I still don't understand how we are to do this thing," the engineer said, apologetically but nevertheless insisting on an answer. "We have had training with the small arms, yes, but none of us knows how to fire the big gun."

Akil refrained from damning the engineer with a glare. This was how these things started, one man voicing doubts. It was good that he had come. He kept his tone instructive, almost pedantic. "Did I not say that Allah would provide? Trust in him, Hatim." He smiled. "And in me."

They needed more, though, he could tell from their bent heads and sidelong looks. He shrugged mentally. There were none coming back from this mission, and no opportunity for them to betray it, not with him at hand. "I have a confession to make, my brothers. I have been guilty of practicing a deception."

Their heads came up at that. "You knew you had become a part of al Qaeda."

There were nods all around.

"And you are all familiar with that martyr to our glorious cause, al-Zarqawi, most foully murdered by the infidel in a cowardly attack from the air."

More nods.

"Have you heard of Isa?" They exchanged wondering glances. "Isa sat at the right hand of Zarqawi. Trained by Zarqawi, he set up al Qaeda's online communications and banking systems so that the agents of the West would never be able to track them. He—"

"You are Isa," Yussuf said.

Akil, put off his stride, took a moment to regroup. "I am."

Most of them knew the name, and expressions varied from awe to fright to exhilaration, but Yussuf's face seemed lit from within. "Then we are truly members of the glorious al Qaeda."

Akil knew a momentary annoyance. Had he but known it, Akil's feelings exactly mirrored Ansar's when the old man told him to find Isa. "We always have been."

Yussuf was apologetic. "Forgive me, Ta—Isa. It is not that I doubted, and I understand that the utmost security is called for so that we may accomplish our mission in this great cause."

In a hushed voice Jabir said, "Are we under the hand of bin Laden himself?"

Akil gritted his teeth. "We are," he said. "He wishes me to tell you that Allah blesses our purpose."

The doubter who had spoken first said, still apologetically, "I still don't completely understand, Tabari—Isa. There are only ten of us. How are ten, against so many, able to accomplish our mission?"

"There is someone on board the ship who will help us," he said.

"A believer among the infidels?"

"Yes," Akil said. As well as someone who would be well paid. Or thought he would be. "I must speak to the captain," he said, and escaped the stateroom.

He stepped over and around numerous bodies down the passageway and up the stairs to the deck before he found the captain at the wheel in the tiny pilothouse. It was perched on top of the cabin, and was the one place on the whole of, to Akil's mind, this nauseatingly odiferous, dangerously overloaded craft where there was a semblance of order and solitude.

The captain raised an eyebrow at him and drew on his cigar. The smell hit Akil's nostrils and his sinuses ached in immediate response. He coughed, cupping his mouth and nose in his hand, trying in vain to block the smell. The captain took another drag and expelled another cloud of smoke. It drifted across the pilot-house, lit by the eerie green glow of various instrumentation screens. "I thought you didn't want anyone else to know you were on board."

"I didn't," Akil said.

"Then you shouldn't have come out of your cabin until I told you to." The captain blew a smoke ring, waited, and then blew a second inside the first.

Coughing again, Akil said, "Why is this trip taking so long?"

The captain raised his eyebrow again. "It took forty hours to get to Caicos Passage, and another fifty to get here."

"Where is here?" Akil said, mostly because the captain seemed to expect it.

The other man stepped back from the wheel, and smiled when he saw Akil's expression. "Don't worry, I've got her on the iron mike. The autopilot," he added, when he saw that Akil still didn't understand. He turned to a slanted table mounted against the rear wall and tapped the chart with the two fingers holding his cigar, now burned down to a squat, glowing stub. "Look here. We came through Caicos Passage fifty hours ago. There's no wind to speak of, and no seas, so I'm estimating that we'll be south of Abaco a couple of hours after dawn. Then we go up the inside, south of Grand Bahama—"

"I don't understand," Akil said, eyes watering from

the cigar smoke as he tried to follow the captain's explanation. "Why don't we just stay outside the islands? Surely all this maneuvering will slow us down."

The captain regarded Akil with a quizzical expression. "For one thing," he said levelly, "we'll pick up the Gulf Stream if we go inside, which is good for another two or three knots of speed. For another, we can lose ourselves in the traffic."

"Traffic?"

"Yes, traffic, other ships, as in cruise liners, fishing boats, pleasure boats, sailboats, freighters, tankers. There is a great deal of traffic up and down the Straits of Florida, Mr. Mallah. We will hardly be noticed."

"How can you be sure of that?" Akil said, studying the map through streaming eyes. "Wouldn't it be safer to go up the outside of all these islands and then move in closer to the coast?"

"This ain't my first rodeo, Mr. Mallah," the captain said. His tone was placid but nonetheless conveyed a distinct warning.

Akil changed the subject. "Where do you plan to let us off?" He didn't ask because he wanted to know, he asked because the captain would think it odd if he didn't. Akil already knew where they were getting off.

The glowing tip of the cigar moved north. "I have a few favorite spots here, in the barrier islands off Georgia and North Carolina." He smiled, the gold-capped molar flashing. "Don't worry, Mr. Mallah. America will swallow you whole where I put you ashore. No one will be able to find you." Another draw, another exhalation of smoke. "Unless of course you wish to be found."

Akil's hand closed over the comforting shape of the little GPS unit in his pocket. "No," he said. "We only want to begin a new life in America."

He left the pilothouse, and the captain returned to the wheel.

He didn't know what the group of men in the forward cabin were up to, but the price of their passage doubled the total amount all the other migrants on board had paid. He was in the transportation business, his job was to get his paying passengers where they were going, nothing more, and nothing less. His curiosity extended to the color of their money, and stopped after they had counted it into his hand.

He took another long, satisfying draft of his cigar, and placidly blew another cloud of smoke.

MIAMI

"Patrick?"

"Hugh, thanks for calling. What if I told you that Isa was Pakistani?"

"How would you know?"

"Somebody ID'd his accent." Patrick wanted to cut to the chase. "Never mind that. What does that knowledge do for us?"

Hugh was silent for a moment. "I'm not sure," he said slowly.

"Can you backtrack, run the profile through your database and see if any matches pop up out of Pakistan?"

"Can't hurt," Hugh said. "But it's a long shot, Patrick. We've already been through the database a hundred times looking for Isa before he was Isa."

"Ever go looking for him in Pakistan?"

"When he got to be big news, we looked for him everywhere. Especially when he surfaced in al Qaeda, with Zarqawi. Back then, though, you'll remember that al Qaeda leadership was all Saudi and Egyptian."

"So?" Patrick was impatient. "Nowadays it's increasingly Libyan, or at least North African. He hated Zarqawi, that is well known, but bin Laden's never been shy about rewarding initiative, wherever it comes from."

"And bin Laden's looking for Isa, too."

"Yeah, I remember. Hugh, Isa's a Pakistani. I'm sure of it. I've already talked to the ops guys in Islamabad. Get the word out to your people. This guy just spent six months in Miami, living like a monk—well, mostly—in somebody's spare room. Then he left for Mexico City, where we lost his trail. He's up to something, and he's not a small player like—oh, like the Salafist Group for Preaching and Combat, or the Libyan Islamic Fighting Group. He's the real deal. He'll be the guy to dream up another 9/11. I want to get to him before he does."

"So do I, Patrick," Hugh said, although he sounded much more placid in talking about Isa than he did when he'd found out about Sara and Isa in the elevator in Istanbul. It helped when someone you thought might quite like to kill your wife removed himself to another hemisphere. "I just don't think going back to Pakistan gets the job done."

"Humor me. It's my dime."

"It's the American taxpayer's dime. How long do you think Kallendorf is going to let you get away with this?"

"As long as I continue to produce results."

Patrick hung up and stared at the television, still set to NTV, which was running an old interview of Sally Ride and her husband and fellow astronaut Steve Hawley by Jane Pauley. Jane wanted to know if they planned on having children, and Sally told Jane it was none of her business. A charm school dropout, Sally Ride. He thought of his own close encounters of the media kind and wished she worked for him.

The phone rang. It was Bob. "Yaqub says he thinks Isa is in America."

"Not news. Anything else?"

"Well . . . He told Mary that he thinks Isa is a virgin."

"Really."

"Really. He waited until I was out of the room to tell her, and he whispered it like he didn't want Isa to hear."

"Why? Isa taken a vow of celibacy to the cause?"

"He doesn't know why, but he says Isa—who he knew as Dandin Gandhi, by the way—never went any-where near women while he knew him."

Patrick thought of Zahirah's body, skirt rearranged carefully over her recently deflowered body. "So he thinks Isa hated women?"

"You'd expect that from an avowed Islamist, wouldn't you? No, Yaqub says in fact the opposite. He was very critical of Yaqub's womanizing, thought it was demeaning to both Yaqub and the women. He used to quote at him from the Koran, something about if you be kind toward women and fear to wrong them, Allah smiles on you."

"Really," Patrick said again. "Interesting."

As soon as he hung up the phone rang again. It was the agent in Mexico City. They'd finally caught a break. Isa had been spotted boarding a flight for Haiti. Not without difficulty, Patrick managed to restrain himself until he hung up and then he leapt to his feet, pumped his fist once, and shouted, "Awright!"

He got immediately back on the phone to call his office. "Melanie? I need a seat on the next plane to Port-au-Prince."

There was a brief, startled silence. Miami was one thing. Haiti, especially given the current political climate there, was quite another. He was a bureau chief, not a field agent. "Are you quite sure about this, Mr. Chisum?" Melanie said.

"I'm sure, Melanie," Patrick said firmly. "And don't you think it's time you started calling me Patrick?"

"We'll be hanging offshore about two miles out," Cal told the Munros. "But it'll feel like you've got a front-row seat. The best place to watch will be from the bridge. I'll put us port side to, and I'll have some chairs brought up for you if you'd like."

"Oh please," Doreen said, "you don't have to go to all that trouble."

"It's no trouble, Doreen."

Nick cocked an eyebrow. "You'll be providing seating for all your guests, Cal?"

Cal grinned. "The admirals and the press can stand."

They were in Cal's stateroom, with the table set for dinner for six. There was a knock at the door and the two aforesaid admirals entered. One was of medium height with a barrel chest, the left half of which was covered clavicle to sternum with service ribbons. He had stern gray eyes and a thick, bristly flattop to match. "Admiral Matson," Cal said.

The second admiral was so tall he had to duck coming through the door, with a haircut so short he looked like he was wearing a silver skullcap. Admiral Barkley had an intelligent eye, a charming smile, and an easy manner, and he was a veteran of multiple patrols in the Caribbean, EPAC, and the Bering Sea, so he knew his way around operations and had an instant frame of reference with the skipper of a 378. He at once endeared himself to Nick by casting aspersions on aviators of every stripe. There followed a spirited debate on the relative merits of sea and air, which was accompanied by a lot of laughter and ended in an amicable draw.

In the meantime, Doreen tried to draw out Admiral Matson, who was determined not to be drawn, and other than asking Cal—twice—if the CNN reporter had made it on board, addressed himself exclusively to his prime rib. It was excellent, Cal was relieved to note, as the admiral was a noted trencherman. In Admiral Matson's defense, it had to be said that he spent all his time wrangling money out of Congress for the Coast Guard. If he regarded *Munro* working launch security with a Munro a member of the shuttle's crew solely as a heaven-sent opportunity to remind Congress of the Coast Guard's worthiness come appropriations time, there was some validity in that viewpoint. After a few minutes, Doreen, with an air of having done her best, handed Matson off to Taffy, who was seated at the foot of the table with his best attentive and respectful expression fastened firmly on his face.

The phone rang. "Excuse me," Cal said, and took the receiver from Seaman Roberts, who was doing her best not to hurry dinner along even though she wanted to take a nap when she got off duty so she'd be bright-eyed and bushy-tailed for the launch. Cal hoped fervently that no fires or other emergencies broke out at T minus ten, because most of his already skeleton crew would be on deck at that time, cameras at the ready, to watch the shuttle hurl itself skyward. "Captain," he said into the phone.

"Captain, this is the OOD. We've got a request to launch our helo to go pick up someone at the Cape."

"What?" Cal said. "Is there an emergency?" He sat up, napkin sliding from his lap. "Morgan, is this a SAR?"

The OOD, a sanguine and capable woman five years out of the Academy, said cheerfully, "No, Captain. Someone just wants a ride."

Cal laughed. "What did the XO promise you this time?"

"This isn't a joke, sir," Barbieri said reprovingly.

"I beg your pardon," Cal said meekly.

"Quite all right, sir."

"So what's going on?"

"Evidently there's a VIP at the Cape and he wants to come out and watch the launch from *Munro*."

Cal knew a sudden foreboding. "Who is this alleged VIP?"

"Senator Schuyler, sir."

THEY LAUNCHED THE HELO WITH MINIMUM FUSS, although Lieutenant Noyes did make a joke about being demoted to a taxi service. They were back in forty-five minutes, entirely too soon, roaring down the length of *Munro* at 140 knots, fifty feet off the water, a flyby for which they had not asked nor been given permission to do.

His stateroom full of strangers, two of them his

superior officers, Cal had no recourse but to greet his father in public. "Dad," he said.

Senator Schuyler swept Cal into a manly embrace, including several thumps on the back for good measure. "Your mother sends her love, as always, son."

Cal was certain as he stood there that if Vera had given any thought to her son and only offspring in the last month it was to wonder yet again if he'd finally decided to leave the disreputable life of a sailor behind for one more befitting his mother's station in life.

The honorable senator beamed impartially at the assembled company. "And who are all these good people?"

As if the senator didn't already have the 411 on every person in the room, Cal thought, and performed the introductions, if not with grace then with utility.

The senator shook hands with Matson, saying cordially, "Of course, Admiral. You've testified before the Senate Appropriations Committee on several occasions, haven't you?"

Admiral Matson, whose lugubrious countenance had brightened considerably at the news of Senator Schuyler's coming, was almost voluble in reply. The senator listened with an indulgent smile for a few moments, murmured an appropriate comment, and with a diplomatic adroitness Cal could only admire cut Matson loose to exchange greetings with Admiral Barkley, and moved on to the Munros. "I've been seeing your daughter in the news a lot lately," he said. "A beautiful girl—"

"A woman," Cal said under his breath. "She's a grown woman." He tried and failed to catch the XO's eye.

"—and smart, too. One of our best and brightest, as the phrase goes."

Nick and Doreen said something polite and avoided looking at Cal. His opinion of them, already high, rose higher.

The senator was late for dinner but not too late for dessert. Cal fiddled with his silverware, turning the dessert spoon at the top of the plate from bowl up to bowl down. Seaman Roberts set out another gold-rimmed china dessert plate with the Schuyler coat of arms on it in front of the senator (the full set of china had been a gift from his mother, commemorating his first command, and didn't he hear about that from his friends for years afterward), and quietly left the room.

A few minutes later the phone rang. Cal was on his feet, answering it well before it rang a second time. "Captain."

"Seaman Roberts, Captain."

"Yes, OOD, what is it?"

"There was a young man from Austin," Seaman Roberts said.

"I see."

"Who bought himself a new Austin."

"Yes, I can see where that might be a problem."

"There was room for his ass, and a gallon of gas."

"Certainly."

"But the rest hung out and he lost 'em."

Sternly repressing a grin, Cal said, "Tell MPA I'll be right down."

"Yes, sir." Seaman Roberts hung up.

Cal put the phone down. "I'm sorry," he said gravely. "A little problem in Main Control. No, no, nothing serious, but my presence is required."

Halfway out of his chair, Taffy said, "Is it something I can handle, Captain?"

"No, no," Cal said. "Please, sit, enjoy yourselves as long as you like. I believe dessert this evening is apple pie à la mode, and you haven't eaten apple pie until you've eaten FS2 Steele's apple pie. I'll be back as soon as I can. In the meantime"—he grinned cheerfully at Taffy—"XO has the con."

He snagged his cap and headed for the door.

On his way out, Admiral Barkley caught his eye and winked at him.

21

TEN MILES EAST OF MELBOURNE, FLORIDA, ON BOARD FREIGHTER *MOKAME*

Akil watched the tiny screen on the handheld GPS until the last digit on the coordinates changed. "All right, it's time," he said. "Everyone ready?"

It was a rhetorical question. They'd been ready for an hour and a half, since he'd brought the GPS out and left it out.

There had been very little discussion of their plan or its objective. "It really is quite simple," one of the engineers had said, sounding almost disappointed.

"Occam's razor," another said. "The simplest explanation is usually the correct one." He dared a shy smile. "Nine-eleven was a simple plan, too."

Akil smiled back. "Yes. It was. Inshallah."

"Inshallah."

At present several of them were on their knees praying toward Mecca. When they were done, they checked their weapons.

These were the smallest of small arms, the Ruger Mark II .22 semiautomatic pistol, with nine-round magazines. Each man had two pistols and a dozen magazines, all bought online through a variety of different Internet stores in different states with different identification papers and forwarded through several mail drops and a discreet, expensive customs clearinghouse to another mail drop in Port-au-Prince, where Yussuf had collected them upon arrival.

Akil's reasoning was that they were going to have to move fast and he didn't want the men to be burdened with a lot of heavy weaponry. Further, heavy weaponry would not be necessary if all went according to plan. He had ensured that his men would be trained on small arms. The Rugers were well made and reliable, and there was plenty of ammunition to accomplish the task at hand. Indeed, it was very probable they could take the ship without firing a shot. From Bayzani, he knew that at the time the ship in question was to be boarded, the crew would be unarmed, would be taken by surprise, and should be sufficiently cowed into obedience by a weapon of any size.

Lastly, and this was the most significant reason, in spite of the intensive training they had all received over some part of the past six months, these men were amateurs. They'd never seen combat. They'd never been under fire, if you didn't count the riot in Düsseldorf, and Akil didn't. Akil's plan depended on secrecy and stealth. The last thing they needed was for an inexperienced soldier of God to let loose with an AK-47 in the act of piracy on the high seas. Especially when Akil was absolutely certain none of them could hit what they were aiming at with a rifle of that size.

"Ready?" he said.

They nodded. They were wearing dark clothes and dark-colored, rubber-soled shoes. Their pistols were in doubled shoulder rigs, with the extra magazines in belt holsters. With jackets on, they looked a little bulky but that was all.

"Very well," Akil said. "Wait for my signal."

He slipped out of the door and down the passage, remembering the way from his earlier sortie even in the dark and even with all the bodies crammed into it. He tripped over some, he kicked others, but no one made a fuss. They were either too seasick to protest or too afraid of drawing attention to themselves to speak up, for fear they'd be put over the side before they reached the promised land. The first lesson had been ably demonstrated, and well learned.

When he got to the pilothouse, the captain was still there, perched on the high wooden chair in front of the wheel as if he hadn't left it in the five days they'd been at sea. "Ah," the captain said, "Mr. Mallah."

Akil had had so many different pseudonyms over the past year that for a surreal moment he wanted to look around to see who the captain was speaking to. Instead, he locked the door to the pilothouse behind him and pulled his pistol. "Captain, I'm afraid I'm taking command of your boat."

"Are you, now," the captain said, unsurprised. He took a leisurely puff on his cigar, and held it out to blow smoke on the lit end. Instead, he flicked the cigar straight at Akil, and rocketed out of his chair after it.

Akil instinctively dodged the cigar and twisted to one side to avoid being tackled. He hit the captain on the head with his pistol butt as he passed by, a glancing blow, not hard enough to knock him out but enough to get his attention. The captain hit the bulkhead hard and tumbled into a clumsy pile. He groaned.

"Shut up," Akil said, and hauled the captain to his feet and heaved him back into his chair. "Alter course to 240, due west."

Either still recovering from the blow to his head or faking it, the captain didn't immediately move. Akil took his left hand—the captain had been smoking with his right, and Akil needed him functional, at least up to a point—and flattened it against the bulkhead. He tossed his pistol up and caught it by the barrel and brought the butt down as hard as he could on the captain's little finger.

The captain screamed, a hoarse, shocked sound muffled by the engines. In Akil's experience, hands were very sensitive appendages for even the strongest of men. He'd met many a man who could barely tolerate a paper cut. "Don't hesitate when I give you an order. Alter course to due west."

"There is land due west," the captain said, cradling his wounded hand in his lap and rocking back and forth.

"I know that," Akil said. "Alter course, due west. If I have to ask you again I'll cut off your hand."

The captain believed him.

CAPE CANAVERAL, ON BOARD
SHUTTLE *ENDEAVOUR*

She had to pee.

She was lying on her back in her seat on the flight deck below the cockpit. The Arabian Knight was on her left. He looked pasty and scared, every drop of arrogance leeched out of him. It must finally have sunk in, what four million pounds of propellant could do if there was a problem during launch. He'd seen the fire trucks, and the ambulances, on their drive to the pad that evening.

It was T minus ninety, ninety minutes to launch, barring problems.

Her diaper rustled every time she moved. She could

pee if she had to, but she didn't trust the diaper. What if it leaked? She thought she'd squeezed out every last drop of liquid in her body in the pad toilet, and at this point she was more furious at this betrayal of her body than she was terrified of blowing up.

Because she was terrified, of that there was no doubt. However stoic an appearance she presented to the world, the look on the Arabian Knight's face only mirrored what she felt inside.

In preparation for this day, she had worked and trained as hard as she ever had in her life. School, soloing, getting her commercial license, flying Otters full of tourists to go look at grizzly bears, these were as nothing by comparison. She'd flown formation in the T-38s in everything up to and including IFR approaches into the middle of storms that made her understand why the Greeks had made their head god one of thunder. She had rappelled down the side of the orbiter mock-up practicing emergency egress. She'd killed and eaten a rattlesnake during survival training. She practiced on the robot arm simulator until her own arms burned from sheer tension, and in the pool at Houston she'd practiced EVA maneuvers in the three-hundred-pound spacesuit until she thought she would grow gills. She had learned the function of every single one of the switches and knobs and levers and gauges and digital readouts in the cockpit. In a pinch, if Rick and Mike were both somehow incapacitated, she could land the orbiter at KSC or at Dakar International Airport or in Cold Bay, Alaska, or at any one of the designated shuttle emergency landing sites worldwide.

She was ready. She was ready for launch. She was ready for orbit. She was ready to carry out her mission. But she was also very aware of something the men who had flown the planes into the towers and the Pentagon and that field in Pennsylvania had intuited early on.

Aircraft were nothing more and nothing less than a thin, fragile skin barely containing thousands of pounds of extremely combustible fuel. She was on the inside with the fuel. If there was any kind of a problem, she was going to burn up with it.

And she would kill anyone, including Cal, her friends, her parents, and Joel Almighty God Minster, if they tried to take her off this flying bomb.

"T minus eighty-nine." Mission Control's voice was calm, almost laconic. The beat of her heart, loud and rapid in her ears, almost drowned it out.

No. She wasn't going to blow up. She wasn't going to screw up. At fifty miles high her silver astronaut pin would turn to gold and every dream she had ever had about space flight since she was nine years old and had read Michael Collins's *Carrying the Fire* for the first time would come true.

But she still had to pee.

"T minus eighty-eight."

The shuttle stood on its tail, mated to the solid rocket boosters and the massive external fuel tank, a valiant white spear against the night sky. A brilliant cacophony of stars glittered behind it, shouting the man-made lights onshore into a pale echo. A murmur of appreciation rolled down the deck of *Munro* and up over the bridge.

"My, isn't she pretty," Senator Schuyler said.

Cal agreed with him, but he agreed with him silently. It was a matter of personal policy never to agree out loud with anything his father said.

He was well aware of how childish that was. He didn't care. Agreeing with his father was always a slippery slope, at the bottom of which the senator lurked, waiting.

They were running darkened ship, so no one's night vision would be obstructed for the launch. The Munros were seated on canvas folding chairs on the port bridge wing, with the senator leaning against the railing, Admiral Matson at his side as if he'd been superglued in place, but nevertheless casting longing glances at the CNN crew on the foredeck.

"Great view," Admiral Barkley said from Cal's other side. "Ever seen one of these before?"

"No, sir, I haven't."

"Me, either." Barkley's teeth showed in a smile. "I

was in Admiral Matson's office when he invited himself along, and I figured it'd be my only chance, so I invited myself along with him."

The CNN reporter, her impeccably coiffed hair beginning to frizz under the influence of so much salt air, was on the main deck below, working her way toward the bow, doing man-on-the-deck interviews, all of it framed by the digital video camera perched on the shoulder of her cameraman. Cal had gone below to introduce himself and welcome them to the ship, introduced them to the XO, suffered through his own interview, and handed them off gladly to Ensign Schrader, the lowest-ranking officer on board and therefore the de facto last stop for all the jobs no one else on *Munro* wanted.

"It's great being the captain," the XO had said in a low voice as they watched Schrader herd his charges safely past the Darwin sorter. "Although you might have missed an opportunity there with Ms. Teeth."

Cal controlled a quivering lip. "Ms. Trenwith, I believe she said her name was, XO."

"Well, sir, I just wanted you to know you had an in there." The XO's teeth flashed in the dark. "You know, when the astronaut begins to pall."

"Stuff it, XO."

"Certainly, sir," Taffy said, and snapped off a salute.

Munro was idling directly abeam of the shuttle. In spite of it being July and no winds, it was night and cool on the water, and the crew was bundled into fleece jackets. He looked at them crowded up against the railing and the safety lines along the 378 feet of the ship and wondered who was driving.

"Captain?"

It was BMC Gilmartin, who had relieved Lieutenant Barbieri for the watch at 2000 hours. "The Falcon is reporting a freighter in the closed area."

"What?" Cal followed Gilmartin into the bridge. "Have we got it on the radar?"

They went to look at the surface radar, a monitor mounted in a freestanding console with a constant sweep revealing surface contacts in their area, radiating from *Munro*'s position in the center. "What's the range?"

"Three miles, sir."

"So five miles from shore."

"Yes, sir."

"That's three miles inside the security zone."

"Yes, sir."

"Why the hell'd it take so long for the Falcon to notice them?"

"They didn't say, sir."

They both watched the tiny blip move slowly and unmistakably inshore.

Tramp freighters were as common as seagulls in this area, some full of legitimate cargo like bananas or coffee or molasses headed north to waiting wholesalers, some full of stolen bicycles or cars, headed south to a less legitimate market in the Caribbean or South America. Some, as he well knew, were full of migrants looking for a quick and dirty way into America.

This ship could be any one of those and probably was.

Still, they were in the middle of a countdown for the launch of a U.S. space shuttle. A shuttle, moreover, that Kenai was on. Something that might later be termed overreaction did not necessarily seem uncalled for at this moment. "BMC, what's her speed?" Cal said.

"About ten knots, Captain. I'm thinking two or three of that is the Gulf Stream."

"And our nearest assets?"

Gilmartin raised Combat, and OS2 Riley's thin voice blared out of the speaker. "We're spread out pretty thin on the coast, Captain. Because of the threatened protest, the four small boats are all working close in, making sure nobody gets ashore. One of the MLBs is responding to a SAR south of here—nothing to worry about, they lost their engine and they need someone to make sure they don't run aground while they're waiting for the tow boat to show—and the other MLB is too far north. It's us, I guess, Captain."

Cal nodded. "Here's hoping the crew doesn't mutiny when I tell them they have to interrupt their launch viewing opportunity to do some actual work. Set starboard side boat launch detail, BMC."

"Aye aye, Captain. Set starboard side boat launch detail, BM2."

"Combat, captain."

Riley's voice came back at him, the speaker distorting it to make it sound tinny and almost afraid. "Captain?"

"Why'd it take so long for the Falcon to spot the freighter?"

"Uh, I don't know, Captain. I passed on the message as soon as I got it."

"All right, Combat, captain out."

"Combat out."

Myers's voice echoed over the ship. "Set starboard side boat launch detail, set starboard side boat launch detail."

There was a wave of protest from the deck. "What?" "What'd they say?" "Are they kidding?" "Is this a joke?"

The XO had followed Cal inside. "I've got this, Captain."

"Nonsense, XO, I'll take it. You go keep our guests happy."

Good thing it was dark on the bridge so Cal couldn't see Taffy's expression.

Not that Boat Deck Captain Smith needed any help from Cal to get *Mun 1* launched. He did not turn on the spotlight mounted on the edge of the starboard wing because it would have ruined everyone's night vision. Smith and Seaman Orozco had the davit engaged and the orange, rigid-hulled inflatable out of the cradle and snugged up against the boat deck a couple of minutes later. They were manned and ready to go in five minutes. Cal's radio crackled into life. "Captain, boat deck."

"Boat deck, captain, go ahead."

"Permission to launch the starboard side boat, Captain?"

"Stand by one. Coxswain, captain."

"Captain, coxswain."

Two decks below the coxswain looked up but in the dark Cal couldn't see who it was. "Who's talking?"

"BM2 Hendricks, sir."

"Did you run a GAR?" This was an assessment by which crew readiness was calculated, run prior to an operation, especially one this unexpected.

"We're in the green, sir, total fourteen. High in crew fitness because we're all in tourist mode instead of being focused on the job, and another high in environment because we're fumbling around in the dark. The rest are all twos and threes. We know how to do this. We're ready."

"Who's on the crew?"

"Myself, Garon, Velásquez, Garza, and Clark."

Velásquez was one of their Spanish-speaking interpreters, breaking in Garza on the job. Good move, there was a strong chance that whatever this boat was, it would have no English speakers on board. "Thanks, Coxswain. Boat deck, Captain."

"Captain, boat deck."

"Permission to load, lower, and launch the starboard side boat, aye."

"Aye aye. Load, lower, and launch!" Smith's bellow was audible to everyone on the starboard bridge wing. "Boat moving!"

"Where are they going?"

Cal looked around to see the Munros leaning over the rail next to him to peer interestedly into the dark.

"We have a contact on the radar where it shouldn't be, inside the area closed during launch."

"My goodness," Doreen said. They heard the smack of the small boat's hull on the water. "Who is it?"

"We don't know yet. Probably the usual idiot joyrider." He bent his head back. "Lookout?"

A head poked over the side of the deck over the bridge. "Yes, Captain?"

"Do you have a pair of those night-vision binoculars?"

"Sure thing, Captain." The head vanished and Cal went over the ladder up to the lookout. A moment later Seaman Critchfield handed the binoculars down to him.

"Thanks, Seaman."

"You're welcome, Captain. Uh, what's going on?"

"There's a contact bearing 090 relative, and heading west."

"That would be into the area closed during launch, sir?"

"It would. Keep an eye out."

"Keeping an eye out, aye sir."

22

"I can hear their engine," Yussuf said.

"Yes," Akil said. "Captain?"

The blood had flowed freely from the scalp wound where Akil had struck him, and it had dried to his face in a half-mask that made him look like the Phantom of the Opera. The little finger on his left hand stuck out at an unnatural angle, and he was careful to hold it out of the way. He sounded resigned. "I say nothing. I do not respond to calls. I do not slow down."

"Correct," Akil said. "Yussuf, get our men up on deck."

"Yes, Isa," Yussuf said, and left. Shortly they heard footsteps coming aft and climbing the stairs to the deck.

The migrants said and did nothing, watching them pass with fear or apathy on their faces. Most of them spoke little English, and they'd probably spent everything they had on passage to the United States. They would do nothing, take no action that might delay or deny that goal.

The engine of the small boat neared. Akil could barely discern the outline of the hull against the sea. It was so dark he couldn't see where the sea ended and the sky began, but for the stars, which were many and beautiful. He thought of Adara. He thought of Zahirah.

The small boat hailed them on the marine band. "Unknown freight, unknown freighter, this is the United States Coast Guard. You are inside a closed area, I say again you are inside a closed area. You must turn around, I say again you must turn around immediately. Please respond."

"Don't answer," Akil said.

He remembered very clearly the story Adam Bayzani had told him about what it was like on a small boat at night. They were in constant communication with their ship, both the bridge and the combat center, and they were equipped with their own surface radar unit. The ship had infrared radar that Bayzani had spoken of admiringly, but not on the small boat. The cutter had night-vision goggles, which the small boat might or might not have on board as well.

These last two items of information were why Akil's men had jackets on over their weapons. If the Coast Guard did manage to get a close look at who was on deck of the little Haitian freighter in the dark, he didn't want his people to stand out any more than absolutely necessary. Or not immediately. It was also why he had instructed Yussuf and Yaqub to select recruits who looked more African than Asian. They would appear like every other Haitian migrant on board, at least at first.

The small boat came nearer and nearer. When Akil judged it near enough, he said, "Cut off the engines."

"They'll know we—"

Akil shot the captain in the back of the head. He had a silencer fitted to the muzzle of his pistol and the shot made a muted burping sound. The captain's forehead burst and splattered blood and brains all over the steering wheel and the control console. Akil wiped away some of the mess to take the boat out of gear. He had watched the captain very carefully for the last part of the journey.

He left the engine idling and went to join his men on deck. "Did you immobilize the rest of the crew?"

"Yes," Yussuf said. "They're tied up in our stateroom. There are only six of them, and I think four of them were only guards. None of them protested when they saw the guns." A trace of self-satisfaction colored the words. Yussuf was discovering the power that came with a weapon.

Akil nodded. "Good work." He was watching the shadow that was the small boat. It made a wide circle around the *Mokame* and took up position off their port side. A powerful spotlight came on and flooded the stern of the freighter with light. Akil's men put on a good show, putting up their hands to shade their faces and blinking in the bright light. They were lost in the sea of migrants surrounding them, all doing the same thing as they muttered incomprehensibly among themselves.

The loud hail came a moment later. "Unknown freighter, unknown freighter, this is the United States Coast Guard. You are inside a security zone closed to all unauthorized vessel traffic, I say again, you are inside a security zone closed to all unauthorized vessel traffic. You must depart this area at once. Please reply."

"Remember," Akil said, "we need the uniforms."

HAITI

They had crawled slowly and painstakingly through every waterfront dive and backwoods bar in the greater Port-au-Prince area. In the past week Patrick had drunk more alcohol—most of it, he was certain, distilled in someone's backyard from whatever fruit they had hanging from the handiest trees—than during the rest of his life combined. His liver was protesting, he was experiencing shortness of breath, and he fancied that his heart had picked up an irregular beat somewhere between the harbor saloon where a massive black man had offered him his sister and he had been almost too terrified to refuse, and the one-room juke joint where a three-piece band was sawing away at some of the best blues he'd ever heard in his life.

A week. Seven days. If it came down to that, 168 hours. He looked down at his suit, spattered with the remnants of seven days' worth of meals featuring fresh conch, fried plantains, and sweet potato cake. No, he was no field agent, he thought sadly.

At seven days, even Patrick, who had pursued every lead Akil had left him with bulldog persistence, was ready to throw in the towel.

And then, a miracle occurred.

One of the men working with him found an informant, a man who ran a ferry out of Port-au-Prince. He had lately taken on board five men, passengers who didn't strike him as tourists, and let them off at a marina some miles down the coast. How many? He scratched his scrofulous chin and couldn't say. Patrick's man held up a twenty-dollar bill and asked if that would improve his memory. It would, and it did.

So Patrick and the dozen other agents who had flooded into Haiti clandestinely boarded the little ferry, after the unloveliest captain Patrick had ever seen held each of them up for the twenty-dollar fare, informed them it only paid one way, and cast off.

The little ferry couldn't have been forty feet long and her unprepossessing exterior did not lend Patrick any confidence that she wouldn't sink before she got off the dock. But she did chug determinedly out of the harbor and down the coast, which cast off civilization far too rapidly for Patrick's tastes, shedding houses for jungle as if someone had thrown a switch. He felt like Lord Jim going up into the heart of darkness.

He repeated this to one of the agents. "I think that was Kurtz in *Heart of Darkness*, sir," this young man said, an ardent Conrad fan. "*Lord Jim* is another novel entirely."

"Whatever," Patrick said.

They arrived at the marina shortly thereafter. They went ashore and split up, half knocking on doors in one direction and half in the other. They met back at the marina two hours later. "If Isa was here, nobody's talking," one agent said. It was hot and they were to a man sweating profusely. Patrick actually had his suit jacket off and was fanning himself vigorously with a large leaf he hoped wasn't poisonous to the touch.

Discouraged, he said what they were all thinking. "Well, it was a long shot. We should probably pack it in and head for the barn."

Just then the young agent with the Conrad fetish showed up. He had a child in tow who looked about ten, with bright dark eyes, skin the color of a raven's wing, and a close-cropped cap of tight black curls. His blue-checked short-sleeved shirt and khaki shorts were shabby but clean and neat. He wasn't shy, looking them over with the eye of an expert who makes his living by judging a likely mark.

"He says he knows of the men we're looking for," the agent said.

Patrick looked at the kid, who met his gaze fearlessly. "Does he speak English?"

"Yes, he speaks English," the kid shot back. He had a thick accent but he was perfectly understandable.

"You got a name?"

"They call me Ti-Malice." Pleasantries concluded, Ti-Malice came right to the point. "You want to know about the strangers who were here."

"Yes. Ivar gave you a description."

"Yes."

"And they looked like that?"

"Yes, they looked like that," the kid said, aping his deliberate speech. "How much you gonna pay me to tell you where they went?"

"How much you gonna want for the information?" Patrick said.

They haggled back and forth for a few minutes before settling on twenty American dollars, which seemed to be the going rate for anything that could be bought. Patrick hoped the bean counters never questioned this particular informant fee on his expense sheet.

"Some they come by the ferry, which you know," Ti-Malice said. "Some they come by seaplane, which you don't. One, he come by car, through the jungle. He the leader."

"How do you know that?"

Ti-Malice looked at him with contempt. "They come to him with questions, he give them answers. When they leave, he get on the boat first. He the leader."

"How many of them were there?"

"Ten."

"When did they leave?"

Ti-Malice shrugged. "Six days ago, maybe?"

"What kind of a boat did they leave on?"

"Sailboat." But Ti-Malice's eyes slid away from Patrick's.

It was too blatant to be anything but intentional. Patrick sighed and got out another twenty-dollar bill. He held it out of the kid's reach. "Okay, Ti-Malice, what's the rest of it?"

"They not the only people on board this sailboat," Ti-Malice said.

• • •

"ISA'S ON A BOAT SMUGGLING MIGRANTS INTO THE U.S.?" the agent with the Conrad fetish said over the roar of the seaplane's engine as they took off from the tiny harbor. "What's that about?"

Patrick frowned through the windshield. There was something he was missing, some link in Isa's recent series of activities that he couldn't quite put his finger on.

Why would Isa go to all the trouble of infiltrating a boatload of Haitian migrants inbound for America? Look at how he had waltzed in and out of New York and Florida. He'd been in Florida for six months without anyone spotting him. Why go to all the trouble and expense and endure the discomfort of a smelly cruise on what sounded like a marginally seaworthy vessel?

He worried at the problem all the way back to Miami, in the throes of July Fourth celebrations that in Miami seemed to require much shooting off of guns into the sky. Traffic was slow coming in from the airport, and it was nine o'clock before the taxi dropped him off at his hotel.

He was still worrying when he unlocked the door to his hotel room.

Melanie was waiting for him.

His mouth dropped. "Melanie?"

"Hello, Patrick," she said. She walked toward him in the pencil skirt and slender heels she always wore, today topped by a thin, powder blue sweater with a scoop neck that hinted at cleavage. She was suddenly closer to him than she'd ever been before, and this time there was no desk between them. He backed up, only to hit the door. He dropped his bag. "What are you doing here?" he said weakly.

"I thought I could help," she said. "Here, let me get your coat."

Firm hands turned him around and lifted his coat from his shoulders. "My, you need a shower," she said. "Or do you prefer a bath?"

His tongue tied itself in knots for a moment. "Sh-sh-shower," he managed to say.

She gave him a sweet smile. "I showered when I got here—I hope you don't mind—but there are clean towels left."

"I, uh, okay," Patrick said, and fled.

When he came out, slightly pink from the scrubbing he had given himself, and the belt of the terry-cloth robe knotted very tightly around his waist, she was sitting next to a table set with Caesar salad, a crusty loaf of bread, and a bottle of chardonnay, which she'd already poured into two glasses.

He sat down in the chair opposite her with a thump, his legs oddly incapable of holding him up any longer. He stared at her. "Melanie, what are you doing here?"

She waved her hand at a briefcase sitting on the desk across the room. "There was some paperwork I thought I'd better deliver in person." She dimpled delightfully. "And I've never been to Miami."

He knew he was being seduced, probably at Kallendorf's instigation, and he couldn't do a thing to stop it. When they finished eating and she took his hand and led him to the bed, he did not resist.

"That was wonderful, Melanie," he said later, and kissed her in gratitude. "Thank you."

She smiled and held her hand to his cheek. "You're very sweet, Patrick. I've wanted this for a long time."

He couldn't tell if it was a lie or the truth, but he didn't really care. He sighed and reached for the robe discarded on the floor. "I'd better take a look at what you brought."

"It's a report from Mr. Rincon. He faxed it to the office this morning."

He forgot the robe and trotted over to the briefcase naked, riffling through the paperwork to find the report with the institute's deliberately vague logo, a quill pen crossed with a broadsword and the words LITTERA SCRIPTA MANET written beneath in a discreet little font. It was only when you looked more closely that you saw that the pen was larger than the broadsword and in a fair way to eclipsing it altogether.

"Mrs. Mansour was right, he is Pakistani," he said, reading rapidly. "Akil Vihari, brother of—holy shit."

"It's an awful story, isn't it," she said gravely. "Yes, I read it when it came in. I know I wasn't supposed to, Patrick, but I couldn't resist."

"I remember reading about this," Patrick said, unheeding. "It was something of a cause celebre, especially when her brother disappeared and Amnesty International and the rest of them figured he'd gone for revenge against the tribesmen and they'd killed him. It was in *Time*, it was on the *Nightly News* and BBC."

There was a picture of Adara, the one taken for her identity card. It was blurry but it looked familiar. It took him a minute before he made the connection.

"She looks like Zahirah Mansour." He thought of what they had found in the backseat of that car and felt a little sick.

She dozed off while he skimmed through the rest of the report. No wonder, he thought, looking at her slumbering form, lovingly outlined by the sheet. It was after eleven. She must be exhausted.

He'd be happy to crawl in beside her but he felt restless. The television was on. He skimmed the news channels. Nothing new; a bombing in Baghdad and another on the West Bank, a small plane crash in Alaska that everyone had walked away from, a mudslide in California and a tornado in Kansas. NASA was about to launch another space shuttle, and among the crew there was a relative of a World War II hero after whom someone had named a ship, a U.S. Coast Guard cutter. There was a clip of her parents on the cutter, standing next to the captain, a fit, handsome man in his midforties who looked as if he wished he were anywhere else but there. Patrick wished he looked like him. Then maybe Melanie would have slept with him because she wanted to, not because Kallendorf did.

He clicked over to NTV for a little mindless entertainment, and watched as time-lapse photography darkened the sky over the agglomeration of ship and fuel tanks waiting next to the great steel Tinkertoy that held it upright until ignition. They were set to launch at midnight.

The scene switched to the standard NASA-issue press conference, the six astronauts dressed in the now-familiar blue flight suits with the mission patch on the breast sitting at a long table, facing a room full of reporters with notepads and microphones and cameras. It was the second mission for the commander and one of the mission specialists, the first for the pilot and the other two mission specialists. The sixth was a Qatari who worked hard at giving the impression that his job was to single-handedly launch the ARABSAT-8A, the communications satellite for the Al Jazeera news network.

The camera flashed on the mission commander, who for a moment looked like he'd been stuffed. One of the mission specialists, a woman from Alaska, diverted attention with a laughing complaint about the reporters' lack of interest in Eratosthenes, the orbiting observatory named for the ancient Greek scientist who had only been off three thousand miles when he estimated the circumference of the earth three hundred years before Christ.

That persistent little voice at the back of his mind telling him he was missing something became a full-fledged nag.

Zarqawi betrayed and killed.

Isa, Zarqawi's devotee, on his own after Zarqawi's death, breaking with bin Laden to form his own group.

Isa, recruiting Yussuf and Yaqub in Germany, and more in England.

Yaqub in Toronto, waiting for the go signal.

Mexico City, Haiti, a boatload of illegal immigrants.

Patrick paused with the glass of water halfway to his mouth.

Isa was Zarqawi's apprentice. Osama bin Laden hated and distrusted Zarqawi, and because of that Isa would never be regarded as a true member of al Qaeda.

But Isa was ambitious, and al Qaeda set the gold standard for terrorism with 9/11. Isa wanted to surpass it, and to do so he would use bin Laden's name.

One of the reasons Isa could be operating independently of al Qaeda was because he saw bin Laden's tactics change from attacking the Far Enemy on their own ground to engaging them in battle closer to home.

What was it that loser, Karim, had quoted Isa as saying? *He said that Bush said that it was better to fight us on our ground than for the Americans to fight us on theirs. And then he said he thought Bush was right.*

Instead of hitting the Far Enemy in Iraq, where the Far Enemy could hit them back, Isa was looking to bring the jihad back to the Far Enemy's backyard, where he believed it had belonged in the first place.

And the first thing he would look for was a target of opportunity, something universally recognized as a symbol of American might and power, something that symbolized everything the Far Enemy stood for that the true believers hated. Their technology. Their secularism. Their greed.

And their open, unabashed determination to corrupt the faithful.

He stared at the television, at the shuttle, white against the enormous fuel tank, flanked by the slender rocket boosters, steam curling up from the tail to make it look like the whole assembly was floating on air.

In the orbiter at this moment were five astronauts, two of them women, one of them black. One was a Protestant, one was Catholic, one was Bahai, and two were undeclared.

And then there was the sixth person on board.

One of the faithful.

One of the faithful, yes, Patrick thought, but from Isa's viewpoint also a Qatari, a citizen of a nation whose women would have the right to vote in the next election. A bona fide Muslim, scion of a powerful and influential Muslim family, a family that owned a controlling interest in a global media organization whose twenty-four-hour news feed could be found on every television in every coffeehouse in every souk in the near and far East.

An organization rich enough to launch its own satellite, which satellite was at this very moment tucked into the cargo bay of the shuttle he was staring at now.

Suddenly Patrick knew why Isa had boarded a boat in Haiti that was headed north.

"Fuck me," he said, and lunged for his cell phone.

23

"Now?" Yussuf's whisper was agonized.

"Wait," Akil said, his voice a mere thread of sound. "Wait."

The migrants' attention was fixed fearfully on the Coast Guard small boat. They barely registered Akil and his men's presence. With every part and fiber of their being they wanted to be safely ashore in America.

The small boat came closer in an ever-narrowing circle. Once again the hail, "Attention, unknown freighter, this is the U.S. Coast Guard. This area is closed to all traffic, I say again this area is closed to all traffic. You must turn your vessel around immediately and leave this area."

The small boat's orange hull was twenty-five feet away from the *Mokame*'s stern, then twenty, then fifteen. "Safeties off," Akil said softly, "and remember, head shots. We need the uniforms."

He waited until the small boat had closed to within five feet of the *Mokame*, when he could see beyond the brightness of the spotlight to the members of the small boat's crew. He raised his gun and shot the coxswain between the eyes.

"The coxswain sits in front on the left," Bayzani had said, illustrating with the salt and pepper shakers, so eager to instruct, so eager to please. "He's the captain of the small boat, so to speak. The man on his right maintains communications with the ship."

Without pausing Akil shot the man sitting next to the coxswain, and one of his men, Mahmoud he thought, reached over the side with a boat hook and snagged the bow of the inflatable.

"What the fuck?" the man in the bow said, staring open-mouthed. Yussuf shot him. The bullet hit his shoulder, high and to the left, and Akil was irritated. "We need the uniforms!" he repeated.

He had to raise his voice over the increasing cries of the migrants, who after the first shock were scrambling, clawing, fighting to get away from the guns. One man, braver than the rest and more stupid because of it, made a clumsy attempt to tackle Yussuf. Akil's bullet caught him in the stomach and he skidded backwards, to sit down hard on the deck. He looked with surprise at the rapidly growing stain on the front of his shirt.

Those migrants below had panicked at the sound of the gunshots, pouring out on deck, with screams and cries and pleas to their gods, only to fall back in fear when they saw the guns.

One of the two men left alive in the inflatable was trying to pull the coxswain's body free of his seat. Akil shot twice and missed twice when the man ducked, but by then his men had found their range and the next time his head popped up three bullets hit it more or less simultaneously. Miraculously, they had managed not to hit the boat.

The fifth man stood up in the back of the inflatable, hands raised in the air, his face a white blur in the night. The flap on his sidearm had been unfastened but his hands were empty.

At least five guns spoke at once, and the man tumbled backwards over the edge of the small boat and hit the water with a splash. There were other splashes as some of the migrants went in, some voluntarily, others falling. By now the *Mokame* was listing heavily to starboard because all the migrants were crowding the starboard side gunnel, trying to crouch as far away from the armed men as they could get.

Akil cursed with a fluency that momentarily stopped them all in their tracks. "Secure the boat!" he said.

Mahmoud knotted the end of the small boat's bow line around one of the cleats on the *Mokame*. Five of his men half jumped, half fell into the small boat and began stripping the bodies.

ON BOARD THE SHUTTLE *ENDEAVOUR*

"T minus sixty."

The urge to urinate was by now all Kenai could think about. She still didn't trust the diaper, but her tonsils were floating. She ran a swift calculation. An hour to go till launch. From launch, it took ten minutes to get into orbit, when she could change into dry clothes. She would spend seventy minutes lying in her own pee if the diaper didn't work.

She decided to risk it. It took a few moments to convince her urethra that this was okay, prone on one's back not the most conducive environment for urination.

Her urethra got the message, and her bladder emptied out in a warm rush. The relief was immense, and she sighed. She sent out feelers for diaper failure, but her back was still dry, so far as she could tell.

All righty then. "Bring it on," she said.

"What's that, Kenai?" Rick said, his voice raspy over her headset.

"Nothing, sorry, Rick. Just hurrying up the count."

"Hear, hear," Laurel said.

"T minus fifty-five," said Mission Control.

ON BOARD USCG CUTTER *MUNRO*

"Less than an hour to go," Cal said to the Munros.

They smiled, their eyes glued to the binoculars. They didn't look or act apprehensive, but like any parent of any astronaut, they had to be thinking of *Challenger*, and *Columbia*.

He was.

When he wasn't monitoring boat ops on the bridge, that was. He went back inside. "BMC?"

"Yes, Captain," Gilmartin said. "We haven't heard from *Mun 1* since they sent their last ops normal call."

"When was that?"

"Five minutes ago."

They weren't overdue, and Garon's last communication had been to inform them that the contact appeared

376

to be a sail-rigged coastal freighter loaded with migrants. "The message sounded kind of garbled, like their radio was failing," BMC said apologetically. "OS2 Riley says the same."

"Oh, great," the XO said.

ET3 Lang, on watch during boat ops, said in a puzzled voice, "I don't know what can be wrong with the boat's radio, sir. I ran the morning check and it was fine."

They became aware of the presence of Admiral Matson standing in the doorway. "What's going on?"

Heads swiveled toward Cal. "We have a freighter that is refusing to identify itself inside the security zone, sir." He saw Barkley's head peering over Matson's shoulder. "We've launched the small boat to go over and take a look. The small boat's been out of touch for a little longer than we'd like, but that may be due to radio problems."

"Nothing interferes with *Munro* standing by this launch, Captain," Matson said, and returned to the port bridge wing.

There was a short, uncomfortable silence.

"One thing at a time," Cal said to his crew. "The BT will start the checklist, get the boat and crew information, if they're talking. In the meantime, we'll get this bird in the air. Then, if they haven't returned and we still haven't heard from them, we'll go over and take a look for ourselves."

"Works for me," the XO said more cheerfully.

Akil, Yussuf, Mahmoud, and two of the others had donned the uniform shirts and life vests stripped from the dead boat crew. Mahmoud, the only experienced boatman among them, was in the coxswain's chair. He took a moment to familiarize himself with the controls before starting the engine.

Akil, sitting next to him, donned the headset and keyed the mike. He spoke tentatively, not entirely certain that the script he had put together from information received from Adam Bayzani and the traitor on board *Munro* was accurate enough to pass muster. "*Munro, Mun 1.*"

The answer was prompt and sounded relieved. "*Mun 1, Munro.*"

"The captain and crew are Haitian," Akil said. Unchallenged, he gained confidence. "The captain says his home port is Port-au-Prince." He dropped his voice as he said the last words.

"*Mun 1, Munro*, say again?"

Akil did so, again mumbling the words and keying the mike and throwing in the odd whistle and growl.

"*Mun 1, Munro*, you're breaking up."

"All right?" Akil said to Mahmoud.

"Yes, Isa," Mahmoud said.

"Then take us to the ship."

"Yes, Isa," Mahmoud said.

"*Munro*, *Mun 1*, the radio is breaking up. *Mun 1* returning to base."

The tedious months of waiting, the interminable hours on the freighter, now it was all finally culminating in glorious action, action that would make them household names around the world, feared by their enemies and canonized by their friends. Mahmoud was a true believer, and if Akil could not easily make out his face in the darkness, he could plainly hear the joy in the other man's voice.

"Allahu Akbar!" Mahmoud said.

Eight of them responded, if not as joyously then with as much manufactured enthusiasm as they could bring to bear, knowing that they were going almost certainly to their deaths. Even the most fanatic among them suffered at least a pang of uncertainty when faced with the near future.

And then they looked to Akil sitting on the side of the small boat, at the calm certainty on his face, and were reassured. This was Isa, after all, Zarqawi's right-hand man, the author of too many successful actions taken against the infidel to count.

They could not fail.

Exalted they might be, careless they were not. They approached the cutter on the starboard side. A shout from the bridge.

"Radio's down!" Akil shouted back.

They waited a few moments, and then another shout from a man in a white hard hat two decks down. That would be the boat deck captain. "Captain says he'd like to leave the lights off until after the shuttle launch so we don't screw with everyone's night vision. You okay with that?"

In a passable American accent, Akil said, "No problem!" From Adam Bayzani and the traitor, he knew the boat crews practiced boat ops in the dark all the time. In this case the dark was a friend to him. Five of his men were lying flat on the bottom of the small boat, hidden by the men in the stolen uniforms.

The tension on the small boat was palpable as they heard the whine of the boat davit and the clink of the shackles as they were lowered. The man in the bow grappled for his shackle, missed, grabbed again, and this time caught it. In spite of the calm seas the small boat did move up and down and he fumbled with the clasp. When he got it on he threw himself backwards.

"Bow on?" The boat deck captain sounded testy.

"Bow on!" Akil said.

The stern shackle was even more recalcitrant, but it was finally fastened to the small boat and this time Akil's man bellowed, "Stern on!" without prompting.

There was a clank and a whine and a moment later the boat began to rise in the air.

"Cut the engine!" came the irate yell from the boat deck. Further comments were clearly audible, and probably meant to be. "Crissake, one shuttle launch and suddenly the boat crew doesn't remember how to run a boat."

Hastily Mahmoud cut the engine.

Akil wondered if the boat deck captain was annoyed

at the possibility of his missing the shuttle launch himself. He didn't know it yet, but he was about to witness something far more spectacular and significant.

Something truly historic.

"Stand by, we're putting you in the cradle, we don't have any crew on the main deck," the white hat said. The whine of the davit increased. They ascended past the main deck and were swung aboard with neatness and dispatch, the hull settling into the cradle with a small jolt.

"You guys are supposed to report to the captain, as in pronto. Come on, Orozco." A door clanged open, and shut again.

"Quickly, now," Akil whispered, "and silently."

His men, galvanized, slid over the small boat's gunnel to the deck of the cutter. As Akil had hoped, the starboard side of the main deck was deserted. All of the cutter's crew was on the port side watching the shuttle.

"You have your radios?" Akil said in a low voice.

Yussuf held his up and clicked it twice. The click was repeated in the radios held by Akil and Mahmoud.

"You remember the plan?"

"I remember, Isa," Yussuf said, and surprised him with a fierce embrace. Five shadows went up the flight of stairs forward of the boat.

"Go," Akil said to Mahmoud. Mahmoud opened a door to the main deck and went inside. Akil and the rest followed.

Inside, the ship was dimly lit by red lights. Akil paused at the top of a flight of stairs and watched

Mahmoud walk down the passageway toward the door leading into the engine room. He waited long enough to see Mahmoud open the door. Mahmoud and four men entered. The door closed firmly behind them, and Akil waited until he saw the levers lower and lock. He turned then and went down two flights of stairs, ending up in a tiny alcove between two heavy steel doors.

He straightened the life vest and the uniform shirt beneath it, and pulled on the bill of his cap. It was too large, and stiff with the coxswain's blood and brains.

He didn't look up at the closed-circuit television camera mounted above the door. *It doesn't work,* the traitor had told him. *It's supposed to but we don't have the money for it.*

He pressed the buzzer beside the door on the left.

They're not expecting someone with a gun.

He waited. A trickle of sweat snaked down his spine.

They'll open the door to anyone, especially if they're in uniform.

There was an answering buzz, and the sound of a bolt going back. The door cracked open and he stared at it in momentary disbelief.

The door didn't open any further. He realized that whoever had opened it had walked away, leaving him to enter on his own. He pulled the door open and walked in.

It was a large, cool, dark room, with many banks of screen displays, radios, and control consoles. There were four people looking up at a square screen. One of them looked over his shoulder. "Hey, Hendricks, come on—wait a minute, who are—"

Akil shot him. The woman next to him screamed, and he shot her, too. The third man put his hands out and backed up. "No," he said pleadingly, "no—"

He was the third to die in that room.

But not the last.

The fourth man sat where he was, a rictus of a smile on his face, his eyes wide behind round, silver-rimmed glasses. "You did it," he said.

Akil ejected the magazine and slapped in another.

"I didn't think you'd do it," the man said. He couldn't stop grinning.

"You were wrong."

"I intercepted the Falcon's transmissions about the freighter. I jammed the small boat's radio calls. I still didn't think you'd actually do it."

"We don't have much time," Akil said.

Riley quoted the words he had spoken in that hotel room in Istanbul. " 'Nothing will look out of the ordinary until the very last moment, and by then it will be too late.' I didn't think you could do it."

"We haven't done it yet, Riley." Akil holstered the pistol. "What about communications?"

Riley reached up to flip a switch. "I slaved all communications to a single switch," he said, as if he were expecting applause.

"Telephones? Internet access?"

"All," Riley said. "No one can call in or out."

"Cell phones?"

"I don't have any control over those."

"All right. Show me the controls for the 76mm."

Riley folded his arms across his chest. "Show me the money first."

Akil stared at him.

"I want my money before we go any further with this," Riley said. "I'm about to be a very wanted man. Maybe even one of the ten most. Maybe I'll even be on *America's Most Wanted*."

The idiot sounded proud of it.

"I'll never be able to show my face in America again," Riley said. "It'll be expensive, staying in hiding. Show me the money. Isa."

He gave a crow of laughter at Isa's look. "Did you think I didn't know? Did you think I couldn't figure it out? Of course you are Isa. Zarqawi's right-hand man. Why do you think my price was so high?"

"If you knew who I was, you could have turned me in for about the same price as what I'm paying you," Isa said. "Why didn't you?"

Riley, still with that rictus of a smile on his face, said, "I figured this would be more fun."

ON BOARD SHUTTLE *ENDEAVOUR*

"T minus twenty-two. *Endeavour*," MCC said, "we're going on hold here."

Curses echoed over everyone's headsets. "What's the matter?" the Arabian Knight said. "What's wrong?"

"Relax," Kenai said to him, "there's no problem,

everything's fine." She switched channels. "Rick, what's the problem?"

"Ah, something's going on with the GLS. Sit tight, they'll fix it."

Kenai mentally condemned the ground launch sequencer to the city dump.

At least her bladder was empty.

ON BOARD USCG CUTTER *MUNRO*

Cal wondered if he was imagining the list to port. Half his remaining crew was on the hangar deck, sitting around the helo in lawn chairs, cameras at the ready. The other half were lined up along the port side. "I sure hope somebody's minding the store," he said. As he said the words, he heard a noise.

"What the hell's that?" he said, in a low voice so as not to alarm the Munros, although he saw Admiral Barkley's head turn. The senator had gone down to the hangar deck to work the crowd, and Admiral Matson had gone with him.

The XO cocked his head. "It sounds like the 76mm."

"That's what I thought."

They looked at each other. "XO, I don't think even the gunnies would think shooting off the 76mm during a space shuttle launch was a good thing."

"No," the XO said decidedly.

"Not to mention which, GMC and almost all of the gunnies are on liberty."

"There's that, too," the XO said.

They both drifted back inside the bridge. "OOD, did you hear that?"

Gilmartin was on the phone. "Yes, Captain, I'm calling CIC to find out what's going on but I'm getting no answer."

"Call the armory."

"I did, sir. No answer there, either."

"Get the BMOW down on the gun deck right now and find out what the hell is going on."

"Yes, sir." Gilmartin jerked his chin at Myers, who reached for the 1MC.

He didn't live to make the pipe. The silenced bullet took him in the back and he fell forward with barely a cry.

They all stared at the body on the deck, the red stain spreading beneath him, uncomprehending.

"If everyone will please remain calm until we are through, we will leave and no one else will have to be hurt."

A man in casual clothes stepped into the bridge. He was holding a small automatic pistol in each hand, and at first Cal thought stupidly of John Wayne. It was so dark on the bridge Cal couldn't make out the man's features. His voice was young, with an edge of excitement for all his apparent composure.

He stood aside and a second man shepherded the Munros into the bridge at gunpoint. In the dim light Cal could see that Doreen was white and shaking. Nick looked angry. He thought he caught a glimpse of a body sprawled on the bridge wing. Admiral Barkley. Christ.

On the bridge were Gilmartin, the XO, and himself, along with the Munros. He couldn't tell how many pirates there were, if indeed these were pirates. Somehow he didn't think so.

He himself was standing a little in back of the XO. It was dark on the bridge. He might be out of range of the glow from the radar screens. He put his hand in the small of the XO's back and pressed.

After a moment of hesitation, the XO took a step forward. "What the hell's going on here?"

"Who are you?"

"Captain Schuyler, I'm in command here," Taffy said. "And you are?"

Instead of answering the first pirate took a step forward to peer into Taffy's face. "You look like a Muslim, friend."

"And you look like a pirate, asshole. What's going on?" The XO took another step forward. "What do you want with my ship?"

"Yeah." Gilmartin had somehow intuited what Cal wanted, attention diverted from whatever it was he was going to do. He rose to his feet from where he'd been trying unsuccessfully to revive Myers. "Good question, sir. Just what the hell is going on?"

As BMC and the XO stepped forward Cal took a step back, until he could feel the air coming through the starboard side door.

"Stay back!" the pirate said. As small as the pistol

was, he'd already killed Myers with it. They froze. "All of you, back behind navigation." He snapped a phrase in what Cal thought must be Arabic, and the second·man herded the Munros, Gilmartin, and the XO behind the nav table. No one betrayed his presence by so much as a glance and Cal took advantage of it to duck down on all fours and peer out the door.

He couldn't hear anything, and he couldn't see anything. He slipped outside, duckwalked aft, and pulled himself hand over hand headfirst down the flight of stairs to the small deck that gave off his quarters. He got the door open and ran for the phone.

He cursed and slammed the receiver down. "Dead." He keyed his radio. Dead. He went for the computer. Access denied.

Hijacked two miles off the coast of goddamn Florida. What the hell did they want? What justified this big an operation?

He felt a sudden chill. The space shuttle.

The 76mm. They were going to use it to bring down the shuttle.

They must have been on board that freighter. They took the small boat when *Mun 1* did the ROA. He spared an agonized thought for the boat crew, but he knew there was nothing he could do for them right now. The pirates, no, these weren't pirates, they were terrorists. Call the sons of bitches what they were. The terrorists had pretended the radio went bust and brought the small boat back to the cutter.

"Son of a bitch," he said out loud. "We actually brought them on board."

They had the bridge, CIC, and the 76mm for sure. Probably Main Control. They had to have Main Control if they wanted to maneuver the ship. They'd want control of the ship so he couldn't take it back and screw with their aim.

The gun locker. Forward of the hangar deck, just off the boat deck. One deck down from his cabin.

He cracked open his door and listened. The interior of the ship was as quiet as he'd ever heard it, the online diesel muted. He slipped into the passageway and moved quickly into Chief's Country. He opened every door he came to. No one was home, they were all out on deck watching the launch, on duty, or on liberty.

He kept moving.

CIC

"How far offshore are we?"

"Two miles."

"Range is what, six miles?"

"About."

"Good."

OS2 Riley's hands worked the controls nimbly, although they were shaking. "There. Target is acquired, and the automatic tracking is engaged."

When Akil didn't reply, Riley said more insistently, "We're done here. So long as your guys got the ammunition in the right holes, it's all up to the machines."

"Yes," Akil said, "it is. Stand away from the controls, please."

Riley rose to his feet, a sickly expression on his face. "I've done everything you want, everything you asked me to do."

"And you were well paid for your efforts," Akil said. "At least your family will suffer no needless privation from your death," and he shot him, once. A third eye appeared between Riley's eyebrows. He fell back without another sound, eyes wide open and staring at the bulkhead above.

"I'm sorry, but I never trust a traitor," Akil told him, and left CIC without haste, disabling the lock before he pulled the door shut behind him.

MIAMI

Patrick was almost weeping. "Sir, I am telling you. Isa is at this moment attempting to hijack a United States Coast Guard cutter off the coast of Florida."

It had taken an interminable half an hour to track down Kallendorf's location, and another ten minutes to pry the phone number out of directory assistance. For a spy agency, Patrick thought bitterly, we're just not very damn good, are we?

Melanie was a warm presence against his side, her hand cupping the back of his neck, her eyes loving and concerned. While he'd been waiting on Kallendorf, he'd used the hotel phone to call the local authorities. The problem was he didn't have a working relationship with anyone in Miami, except for a bored third-class detective down at Metro Dade who had long since packed it in for the night. He'd called the Pentagon. They'd promised to call him back right away. He was still waiting.

He'd woken Melanie in the mad scrabble for his cell phone. He couldn't use the hotel phone, not for something like this, it wasn't secure. He'd finally found his cell behind the nightstand when he called the number on the hotel phone and it went off. He must have kicked it there when he and Melanie—

"Patrick, what have you been smoking? I haven't heard of anything like this in the wind, and you just admitted, neither have you. Do you really think even your pet terrorist could pull something like this off without leaking a whisper of it to someone?"

"If anyone could, Isa could, sir."

"Patrick, look, I think maybe you've been working a little too hard. Why don't you take some time, catch some sun and sand and—"

"Goddammit!" Patrick said, surging to his feet.

Melanie flinched away from the bellow, crouched on the bed, staring up at him in alarm and not a little wonder.

"Why, Patrick," Kallendorf said, "I didn't know you had it in you."

"Sir, this is no time for your adolescent jokes. If you don't call the Coast Guard right now, I swear to God I'm calling the White House! I'll go over your head, sir, I sure as hell will! I'm telling you Isa is hijacking a

Coast Guard cutter even as we speak, so he can use one of its weapons to take down the space shuttle! They're minutes away from launching, sir, minutes! Do you really want to go down in history as the CIA director who fiddled while the enemy blew up the most iconic symbol of American might and power ever? Do you?"

24

ON BOARD SHUTTLE *ENDEAVOUR*

"T minus ten."

Ten minutes to launch. Still wearing dry pants. Still with her heart beating faster than any human heart ever had.

In twenty minutes she could be in space.

Correction.

In twenty minutes she would be in space.

ON BOARD USCG CUTTER *MUNRO*

There couldn't be that many of them if they'd all fit into *Mun 1* on the way over. He could raise a hue and cry and alert his crew.

But none of his crew were at present armed. He thought of Myers. The terrorists were.

He looked at his watch. Ten minutes to launch. Nine.

He swung around the foot of the stairs and diverted momentarily to put his head into the chief's mess. No one there, either. He wanted GMC and he wanted him now, but GMC was on liberty. He stepped back and turned to head for the door to the main deck and crashed into someone coming from the opposite direction.

There was a clang of metal dropped on metal followed by a curse not spoken in English. Going on instinct Cal hit out blindly, his right hand connecting with someone's belly. He shoved him out of the way and went scrabbling about the floor looking for what the man had dropped. A foot connected solidly with his side and he grunted. His hand touched the butt of a pistol and he snatched it up and brought it to bear. His finger was squeezing the trigger when the same foot came out of nowhere and kicked it out of his hand.

His hand went instantly numb. He dropped the weapon.

The pistol clanged off down the passageway. The other man went after it. Cal went for the door, got it open in record time, and tumbled out on the main deck. He hotfooted it to the forward stairs and pelted up to the boat deck. Behind him he heard running footsteps. They hit the stairs. He ran aft, making sure his own footsteps hit the deck loudly enough to be heard, ducking out of the way of the Darwin sorter.

As he had hoped, his pursuer was not so lucky. He hit the Darwin sorter at full throttle and from the sound of it laid himself flat out on the deck. Cal didn't stop to check, didn't try to find the pistol in the dark, he kept going until he got to the forward door of the hangar, worked the lever, and got inside, pulling it shut behind him.

"Captain?"

He jumped about a foot. "Jesus!" he said, peering through the dark. "Who's that?"

"Noyes."

The aviator. "What are you doing here?"

"I was in the av shack, getting another pair of binoculars. I heard some funny noises and I came to check. What's going on?"

"We got some bad guys on board, trying to shoot down the space shuttle, I think."

There was a startled silence.

"No, I'm not kidding," Cal said fiercely, "and this is not a drill."

Recovering, Noyes said, "How the hell did they get on board?"

"There was a freighter—never mind that now. I don't know how many of them there are, ten or twelve, I think, but they've got the bridge and CIC and I'd guess Main Control, too. All our communications are out, I can't yell for help."

He spun around and felt for the door to the gun locker. "Is there anyone else in the av shack?"

"No. Captain, why don't we just stick our heads out the door and yell for the crew?"

"Because the crew can't shoot back. Yet." Cal's fingers felt for the lock.

"Do you want me to turn on a light, Captain?"

"No! No." He found the lock and delved in his

pocket for the massive ring of keys he always carried.

It wasn't there.

He felt the other pocket.

The key ring wasn't there, either. "Goddamn son of a bitch." They must have fallen out of his pocket during the fight.

"Captain, hold up a minute. We've got the radios in the helo."

Cal's hands stilled. He hadn't even thought of the helo's radios.

AKIL GAINED THE BRIDGE TO FIND ALL QUIET UNDER THE watchful eye of Yussuf, who greeted him with a triumphant smile. On the gun deck forward, the barrel of the 76mm had been trained on the sky over the shuttle.

They could have destroyed it on the ground, but Akil wanted to hit it in flight. According to Bayzani and to Riley, with the automated tracking gear installed during the ship's last refit, it shouldn't be a problem.

The shuttle's destruction would produce the maximum amount of shock and horror in the viewers. Millions would be watching; online, on television, later on the news channels over and over and over again.

When they were done they would know two things they hadn't known before.

One, that no one was safe from him and his forces. No one was beyond his reach.

And two, that henceforward Isa and Abdullah were names of respect, of awe and admiration, names to be taken seriously by every Western nation in the world.

NO ONE ON THE HANGAR DECK WAS AWARE ANYTHING untoward was happening elsewhere on the cutter because no one on the hangar deck could hear anything over the multiple boom boxes playing everything from Dave Matthews to the White Stripes. The 76mm was forward, that was where the attention of the terrorists would be concentrated. The hangar deck and his people were aft. For the moment, Cal wanted it kept that way. He didn't think his crew would panic but he didn't want to test the thesis, either.

He and Noyes walked to the helo at a casual pace, Cal unable to refrain from taking a look over the port side at the shuttle gleaming white and brave under the lights.

Noyes opened the door of the helo and slid inside. "Shit," he said a few minutes later. "The radios are dead. They've already been here. Somebody had some good intel, Captain."

"Yes, they did," Cal said. He scanned the crowd, a few of whom were giving them curious looks.

He looked at his watch.

"There can't be that many of them, Captain," Noyes said urgently. "We can rush them."

"They've got hostages," Cal said, "the Munros, BMC, the XO on the bridge. The watch standers in Main Control and CIC. They've killed Myers and I think everyone on the boat crew and they're not out of ammunition."

"They'd rush the bridge."

"I know they would. I don't want them to."

"How about rushing the 76mm?"

"They've got people on the doors leading to the gun deck."

"But we can't let them take out the shuttle."

"Did they just take out communications, or can you still get this bird in the air?" Cal scanned the crowd and didn't see the other aviator. "And can you do it alone?"

Noyes flicked a few switches. His frown cleared. "I think she'll fly, sir." He looked at Cal. "But sir, there isn't enough time to fly to shore and get help. The shuttle launches any second now."

"I know."

Noyes looked confused at first, and then he understood. His face changed in the reflected glow of the lights on land. "Oh. Shit. You want me to be a hero."

"If I knew how to fly it, I'd fly it," Cal said.

Noyes, amazingly, grinned. "Can you shoot the M-240?"

"Will it do enough damage to get the job done?"

"You said you think they're not going to start shooting until after the shuttle launches. Do you know what spiking a gun means?"

"Yes," Cal said, and realized what Noyes meant. "Yes!" There was another way, a better way, and maybe no one else would die.

They conferred hurriedly and came up with a plan.

"There's only—"

"What?"

"They could shoot us down."

"I haven't seen anything bigger than a .22 pistol. They're traveling light. If you can stay out of range until the last minute, and if you're willing to take the risk—"

"Let's do it," Noyes said.

Cal looked at the crowd, and then at his watch. Six minutes. "We have to clear the hangar deck. Oh, Jesus. And we have to get rid of them."

"Them" was the CNN crew, now snaking its way through the crowd on a dead reckoning for the helo. "Start the engine, that'll get all the bright ones moving," Cal said, and slammed the door shut. He grabbed the first crewman he saw, which turned out to be FS2 Mellot. "FS2."

Startled, she said, "Captain?"

He looked past her. "SKC? YNC? Come here a minute." He led the food service officer and the two chiefs away from the helo, along the way collecting MK3 Ochiai and DC2 Milton, all reliably levelheaded crew members. "We need to launch the helo. Never mind why, it's an emergency, just help me clear the hangar deck. And folks? We have armed hostiles on board. Let's not attract any attention. As quietly as possible, please, get everyone down on the fantail. Now!"

ON BOARD SHUTTLE *ENDEAVOUR*

"T minus thirty-one seconds. Go for auto-sequence start."

Her mouth was dry and her heart was racing. Cal, Mom, Dad, she thought, watch me fly.

The rotors were beginning to turn and the noise of the engines increased. The hangar deck was deserted. Cal's picked band of crew members had shoved, muscled, and strong-armed everyone down onto the fantail or into the hangar, the CNN crew protesting all the way.

He fought with an intransigent buckle on one of the tiedowns and swore out loud. The buckle came free and he threw the tiedown over the side to follow the first three. The last thing they needed was some piece of debris getting caught up in the rotors' backwash and he didn't have time to run anything back to the hangar.

Onshore, clouds of steam were beginning to boil up from beneath the shuttle's tail. Kenai, he thought, it'll be all right, I promise, go, go, go!

Camera lights went off like popcorn all along the main deck. He risked a look around the corner of the hangar. Was that a dark figure he saw slipping from shadow to shadow? They couldn't all hit the Darwin sorter, worse luck.

He duckwalked beneath the rotors and climbed in the back of the helo. Noyes was taking off as Cal's foot left the deck.

Munro fell away beneath him.

ON BOARD SHUTTLE *ENDEAVOUR*

"T minus ten seconds. Go for main engine start."

"Five . . . four . . . three . . . two . . . one . . ."

The hold-down bolts blew and they were hit with seven million pounds of thrust from two solid rocket boosters and three main engines.

The noise was deafening, the vibration threatened to shake her hair loose from her head, and the G-force flattened her against her chair like a steamroller.

Her teeth were rattling so loudly in her head that she almost couldn't understand Rick when he said, "What the hell was that?"

ON BOARD USCG CUTTER *MUNRO*

The boom of the 76mm firing was loud even over the noise of the engine. Cal yelled something, he didn't know what, and looked over his shoulder to see the shuttle was off its pad, rising slowly into the air, straining bravely for the stars. He knew a wave of relief so strong it was dizzying.

"Get ready!" Noyes yelled, and the sound of his voice steadied Cal. The aviator had already unlimbered and loaded the M-240. Its barrel pointed out of the left side of the helo and Cal's hands were tight on the grip. Noyes maneuvered the aircraft until it faced *Munro* port side to port side.

Cal's finger tightened on the trigger and the M-240

chattered, spraying the hatchway leading to the gun deck where he was certain one of the terrorists was on guard. It's where he'd have stationed a man if he'd been running this op, it was a chokepoint in case anyone decided to rush the 76mm. He couldn't get a direct shot but with all the metal the ricochet was bound to hit something. He prayed it wouldn't be a member of the crew.

"All right!" he yelled, and Noyes crabwalked the helo in closer, so close it seemed to Cal as if the rotors were going to slice into the bridge. "Jesus, Noyes, be careful!" he yelled. He wondered for a wild moment if Noyes could even hear him over the engines. They hadn't had time to don helmets. He crouched next to the M-240 in the door of the helo.

There was a muzzle flash from the bridge, and the helo jolted hard.

"Fuck that," Noyes roared, "jump, goddammit, jump!"

Cal jumped, pushing against the doorframe of the helo with his feet, launching himself in a shallow dive for the gun deck. Behind him he heard the helo roar off, and more gunfire, and more impacts.

It was the longest two seconds of his life.

He hit hard, just forward of the gun deck port hatch. He actually remembered to tuck and roll, and by a miracle came up on his feet.

Nobody shot him. That was a good thing because for just one moment he was frozen in disbelief that it had been that easy.

In the next he broke and ran for the side of the house. His right foot stepped in something slippery and he went down to one knee. He was up again almost immediately. The slippery something was blood. Yes, man down, one of them, groaning, pistol on the deck just beyond his outstretched hand. Cal scooped it up and ran back out onto the gun deck, for the exterior of the 76mm. He paused for one moment to try the hatch in the deck aft of the gun, just on the off-chance the men inside had forgotten to lock it. No, locked, and then someone shot at him from the starboard side of the gun deck, the shot clanging into the deck two feet away and whining off to port.

He shot back with the terrorist's pistol and they ducked back out of sight. Someone shot at him from the bridge wing. He ran around to the front of the 76mm.

The casing of the big gun was a smooth, slippery white surface. He stuck the pistol in the back of his pants and climbed on the railing in front of it. He put both hands on the casing and jumped up, grabbing, clutching, clinging to the casing, pulling himself up, his muscles straining, his teeth bared in a snarl of determination.

He heard excited voices coming from the gun room below the deck, voices speaking what he supposed was Arabic. The big gun moved on its mounting, tracking the shuttle as it rose into the sky. "No," he said through his teeth, "no, goddammit, not on my watch you don't!"

He pulled himself from the casing to the barrel, a snout longer than he was and a mouth large enough for the job. Clinging to the barrel like a leech, by an act of will not sliding off, he freed one hand, reached around for the pistol, and dropped it into the open muzzle of the gun.

He let go and fell to the deck, falling awkwardly this time. He limped around to the back of the gun. A bullet whined off the deck next to his left foot, spurring him into a shambling run.

He'd just reached the hatch behind the wounded terrorist when the 76mm fired for the second time. The round hit the pistol, lodged halfway down the barrel.

The barrel of the 76mm exploded, shredding into threads of twisted metal, some of it severed into shrapnel. Most of it went overboard. Some of it hit the forward part of the bow and the front of the house.

A dark, hot force caught Cal in the small of the back in mid-stride and lifted him up. He literally flew down the deck and hit the bow of *Mun 2*, sitting in its cradle.

He hung there for a painful second, watching the shuttle climbing slowly, steadily, and most beautifully higher and higher into the sky.

He slid to the deck and knew no more.

WHEN THE 76MM BLEW, THE NOISE AND THE SHRAPNEL blinded and frightened everyone. All the windows on the bridge shattered. A moment later, the man Akil thought was the captain went for Yussuf, slamming him into the bulkhead and sending his guns skittering across the floor. Two others went scrambling after them. The woman must have ducked down behind one of the consoles because she was suddenly nowhere to be seen, or acquired for use as a hostage.

For a frozen moment Akil, ears ringing, was aware only of the bent and broken fragments of his dream, buried beneath alarms and smoke and flying metal. There were screams of fear and bellowed orders. On his left the space shuttle climbed into the sky on a column of molten gold.

The wreckage of the big gun caught fire, first a flicker, then a glow. An instant later a siren went off, almost painfully loud, impossible to ignore. Crew members began pouring up into the bridge. The man he thought of as captain began shouting orders.

He walked to the door with no outward sense of haste. On the bridge wing, he tossed his gun into the water and climbed over the railing. He kicked away from the side of the ship, falling feetfirst into the water, and struck out for shore.

25

WASHINGTON, D.C., AUGUST 2008

"Isa got clean away?" Kallendorf was not pleased.

Neither was Patrick. "Unfortunately, sir, yes."

"Very unsatisfactory."

Patrick tidied his file together. "Not entirely, sir," he

said mildly. "The attack was foiled. The shuttle and its crew made it safely into orbit, and they are now safely back. I understand the first round fired from the cutter's cannon got close enough for them to see. It gave them a few bad moments, but all in all, a happy ending, I would think.

"The helicopter, though damaged in the firefight, landed safely onshore at the Cape, although I understand the pilot was taken into custody by NASA security for a few hours until everything was sorted out. The cutter suffered severe damage when the gun exploded, but the hull remained intact and the cutter made it into port."

"How did they get control of the engine room?" Kallendorf asked idly. He wasn't all that interested.

Patrick allowed himself a prim smile. "Akil's people didn't know much about ships, sir. All the compartments are watertight, but there are many different entrances. The executive officer and the, what I believe is called the health services chief, or corpsman, colluded on a gas of some kind to introduce into the engine room. I believe the chief component was ammonia. When the terrorists became incapacitated, a welder cut through one of the doors and the terrorists were, uh, overpowered by the crew."

"Knacky people, those Coasties," Kallendorf said.

"Yes, sir. Always prepared is, I believe, their motto."

"Still. Isa escaped." Kallendorf sighed. "Not good, Patrick, not good."

"We now know who Isa is, sir, and where he comes

from. This will, I believe, be a great help in predicting his future actions.

"And lastly, this attack underlined something the agency has been trying to get across to Congress for years."

"Oh? What's that?"

"That our nation is immensely vulnerable to attack by sea. This time it was a hijacked Haitian freighter. Next time? It might be a hijacked oil tanker, mined to explode as it runs aground . . ." Patrick shrugged. "Well. Pick a target, sir. Maybe, just maybe because of this action, Congress will listen the next time." He stood up. "Anything else, sir?"

Kallendorf looked at him broodingly. "You swore at me, Patrick."

"Yes, sir, I did." Patrick made a superhuman effort and didn't apologize.

Kallendorf grinned. "Get out of here."

"Certainly, sir."

Patrick went on his way rejoicing. When he reached his office, he paused with his hand on the door for a moment, and then went in. "Hello, Melanie."

"Hello, sir." There was a smile in her eyes.

"Any messages?"

"Just one." She handed him a slip of paper.

"Ah. Get Mr. Rincon on the phone for me, will you?"

THE CURRENT CARRIED AKIL SOME MILES NORTH OF CAPE Canaveral, where he managed to thrash his way to shore on a sandy beach that lined the edge of a swamp.

He slogged through the swamp to a road, which he followed until he came to a town. On a clothesline in someone's backyard he found dry pants and a shirt. He walked to the next town where he caught a bus to Jacksonville. The woman across the aisle was reading the *Miami Herald*, which had a large, grainy picture of Adam Bayzani's doctored passport photo on the front page, but she never looked at him twice.

Talk on the bus was all about the attempt to bring down the space shuttle. "We ought to just nuke the whole Middle East and be done with it," one old man said, and there were nods all around.

The story was running on all the televisions in the Jacksonville airport. He looked at the flight board, identified several possibilities, got cash from an ATM, and took a cab to a local mall, where he bought a new wardrobe and a carry-on suitcase to put it in. He found a small motel nearby and checked in. He used the motel's business center to buy his tickets.

That night he dreamt again of Zahirah, and woke in a sweat-soaked panic.

Once, all his dreams had been of Adara.

The next morning he showered, packed, and went to the airport. The passport he had with him was in the name of Suud Bathinda, an Indian national, a computer programmer from Mumbai. He offered the TSA official grave apologies on behalf of all Asians for this latest attempt on America's might and substance. He had no trouble getting through security.

In Atlanta he boarded a flight for Paris, in Paris

another for Barcelona, not going to the Hotel Arc de Triomphe as he had planned.

He'd always liked Barcelona. The second day he even went back to the Maritime Museum, and stood in long contemplation of the Royal Galley that had fought at the Battle of Lepanto.

He never once thought of Adam Bayzani.

That evening he strolled down to the waterfront and dined well on fresh seafood at an open-air café. On the way back to his hotel, he became aware that he was being followed. He took no notice, continuing his placid pace.

When he opened the door to his room, Ansar was sitting in a chair, watching *Baywatch* on television. "Ah, Isa, I was wondering what was keeping you." He smiled. "The old man wants to talk to you."

Akil knew a sudden and a great weariness. "Certainly," he said. "I am at his disposal."

"YOU'RE SURE?" PATRICK SAID.

"He was seen, and identified. Besides, it's all over the net. Irhabi's blog has the story, almost the real one. I think someone in the al Qaeda organization doesn't like our Isa."

"Will bin Laden have him killed, do you think?"

"I don't know," Hugh said thoughtfully. "We've been talking that over ourselves. The whole attack on the space shuttle was pretty gutsy. A lot like 9/11, it was simple, and pretty cheap. His guys talking yet?"

"Some of them are. The ones who still can talk after

the Coasties got done with them. They were pretty pissed."

"Really?" Patrick could hear the smile in Hugh's voice. "May I tell Sara?"

"Sure. Anyway, Isa's bunch don't know much."

"I suppose bin Laden could be upset that this was going on in his own backyard without him knowing it."

"If he didn't know it," Patrick said. "Ah, the hell with it. I'm going on vacation, Hugh. I'll be gone for two weeks."

"Alone?" Hugh said. "Or in company?"

Hugh really was very good at what he did. "None of your business," Patrick said primly. "Leave a message if anything else crops up, will you? And, hey, thanks. We did some good work here."

THEY WERE SITTING ON A STUMP OVERLOOKING Kachemak Bay in Alaska. The view, both near and far, was breathtaking.

Kenai was more relaxed than he'd ever seen her, the tension that had kept her at peak performance expended now in a job well done. "Eratosthenes is in orbit and working, just a flawless deployment," she said. "Laurel is ecstatic, and so are all the astronomers. The Al Jazeera satellite deployment went without a hitch, too, so all the Arab nations could watch their guys take a shot at us. Sons of bitches."

"Did you see them shooting?"

"No, but Rick and Bill did. Like a big tracer across

the nose. Way too close for comfort. Said it cleared up their sinuses."

"I'll bet," Cal said.

"Other than almost getting shot out of the sky, it was a great mission. Even the Arabian Knight managed to behave." She reflected. "Probably had something to do with the fact that his people had very nearly shot up his own sweet ass. Rick told him straight out that if he even so much as sneezed in the direction of anything even remotely resembling a control switch Rick would duct-tape him to a bulkhead and leave him there for the duration of the mission. The Arabian Knight believed him."

"Wise of him."

"Very. Rick was thinking of doing it anyway, just on general principles, and he didn't decide otherwise because any of us talked him out of it, believe me."

"What it's like?" Cal said. "The view from orbit?"

Kenai leaned back in the deck chair and contemplated the dark blue bay and the mountain peaks cutting white wedges into the darker blue sky. "I don't know what I can say that will do it justice, Cal," she said finally. "It's beautiful. It's terrible. It's glorious." She turned her head to meet his eyes and smiled, but her eyes were sober. "Earth is such a small place. So far, we're all there is. If we don't make it, if humanity doesn't make it, we've had it. We have got to figure out a way to get along with each other, or we have just flat had it."

They sat in silence for a few moments. "And you?" she said. "How are you?"

He shifted in his chair, wincing a little. "Mostly I'm just sore from all the bruises I got falling all over my ship. Taffy says for a Coast Guard captain I sure am a honking big klutz."

"Your father okay?"

Cal's grin was wry. "What, you haven't seen him on CNN, describing his escape from death by inches, all due to this heroic son?"

She sat up and reached for his hand. She opened it and kissed his palm, her lips warm against his skin. She cradled it against her cheek. "You saved my life. You saved all our lives."

Acutely uncomfortable, Cal shifted in his chair again. "Yeah, well, don't let it get around."

She held his hand between her own. "No, Cal. Tell me. Say the words."

He thought about it first. He wanted to say this right.

"I've never been the most dedicated soldier," Cal said. "I've never wanted to die for my country. Staying alive and living the best life you can has always made a hell of a lot more sense to me."

He smiled at her. "But guess what?"

"What?"

"Turns out I'm willing to die for you."

Her eyes brightened with a sheen of tears. With some difficulty she said, "I'm glad you didn't."

He laughed. "Me, too."

They went inside, and closed the door of the cabin firmly behind them.

• • •

Kenai Munro flew once more on the space shuttle before it was retired in 2010. She is currently employed by NASA as a manager in the development of the next manned space flight program.

Captain Callan T. Schuyler, decorated for his actions during the attack on *Munro*, was later promoted to admiral. He retired from the USCG the next day to go to work for George Soros's Drug Policy Alliance as an expert advisor in support of the effort to end the war on drugs.

The bodies of Yussuf al-Dagma and three of the other terrorists who attempted to shoot down the space shuttle *Endeavour* were cremated. The other terrorists apprehended at the scene were tried and convicted of piracy on the high seas and sentenced to life without parole. They are currently serving out their sentences in a federal maximum-security prison.

Karim Talib and Yaqub Sadiq were imprisoned without trial, first in Guantánamo Bay, Cuba, and after that facility was closed down in a series of facilities in foreign nations friendly to the United States. Their current whereabouts are unknown.

The new administration in Washington, D.C., discovered to its great and well-publicized dismay that there had been a consistent culture of blackballing of whistle-blowers and dissident government employees by the previous administration. An internal review was conducted in the full light of the media. One of the results was that Sara Lange was promoted to captain, and offered command of a 210 in Kodiak, Alaska.

Lieutenant Commander Mustafa Azizi was promoted to full commander and in June 2009 took command of a 210 out of Alameda, California.

Hugh Rincon now works part time from Kodiak, Alaska, as a data analyst for the Knightsbridge Institute.

Mrs. Haddad Mansour buried her daughter, sold her house in Miami, and moved to Houston, Texas, where in an odd twist of fate she wound up cleaning house for the Robertsons, the family of Kenai's first mission commander.

Arlene Harte continues to travel and make friends wherever she goes.

Akil Vihari, alias Isa, remains at large.

ACKNOWLEDGMENTS

My eternal gratitude goes to U.S. Coast Guard Captain Bark Lloyd and the crew of *Munro* during my two-month ride-along in the eastern Pacific Ocean on patrol doing narcotics interdiction and immigrant interdiction in the spring of 2007. XO CDR Steve Rothchild and OSC Luke Cutburth helped solve important plot points, weapons officer LTJG Kevin Beaudoin and GMC Greg Colvin helped with armaments, and blame the mole on BM3 Tim Stamm, BM3 Gary Susalis, and BM2 Tim Myers, who were united in their desire for the bad guy to be some snotty little OS.

My thanks also to USCG Captain James Monaghan for his very timely information in regard to Coast Guard operations during a shuttle launch.

How do I know what I know about terrorism today? I listen to NPR, I read *The New York Times*, and I subscribe to *Atlantic Monthly.* For general background on modern-day terrorism, there was *Know Thy Enemy: Profiles of Adversary Leaders and Their Strategic Cultures*, edited by Barry R. Schneider and Jerrold M. Post, and Jean-Charles Brisard's *Zarqawi: The New Face of al-Qaeda*, both very helpful.

Michael Collins's *Carrying the Fire* and Mike Mullane's *Riding Rockets* are the two best written, most informative, and certainly the most entertaining astronaut autobiographies published to date.

As always, I am my father's daughter, I never let the truth get in the way of a good story, so when I alter facts to suit my fiction, don't blame any of these good people.

Thanks are also due to research librarian Nancy Clark, who in spite of a husband, two kids in preschool, a new job, and helping put on an international crime fiction convention never fails to dig up what information I need when I need it, no matter how esoteric.

My thanks also to Der Plotmeister, whose heroic efforts to keep my plots grounded in reality shall not go unrewarded, and in whose eyrie this novel was completed the week the Dave and Dan Show came to install my office shelves.

Center Point Publishing
600 Brooks Road ● PO Box 1
Thorndike ME 04986-0001 USA

(207) 568-3717

US & Canada:
1 800 929-9108
www.centerpointlargeprint.com